Seven
Brothers

Cover design by Martin Best of My6Productions
from painting by Erkki Tantto.

Seven Brothers

A novel by

Aleksis Kivi

Translated by

Richard A. Impola

Aspasia Books, Inc.
Beaverton, Ontario, Canada

Aspasia Classics in Finnish Literature

Seven Brothers
ISBN 0-9737165-2-5
ISSN 1498-8348

Published in 2005 and 2010 by Aspasia Books, Inc.
25040 Maple Beach Road,
Beaverton, ON L0K 1A0, Canada
aspasia@aspasiabooks.com
www.aspasiabooks.com

Translated from the original Finnish *Seitsemän veljestä*
First published in Finnish 1870. First published in English in 1991
by Finnish American Translators Association

© 1991 Translation Richard A. Impola
© 2005 Aspasia Books, Inc., English language edition

Cover design by Martin Best based on a painting by Erkki Tanttu.

Introduction by Börje Vähämäki

Translator's Foreword by Richard Impola

Aspasia Classics in Finnish Literature Series editor Börje Vähämäki

Printed in China 2010

****

Library and Archives Canada Cataloguing in Publication

Kivi, Aleksis, 1834-1872.

   Seven Brothers / Aleksis Kivi ; translated by Richard Impola

(Aspasia classics in Finnish literature 1498-8348)
Translated from the Finnish.
ISBN 0-9737165-2-5

   I. Impola, Richard, 1923- II. Title. III. Series.

Aleksis Kivi:

Seven Brothers

Aleksis Kivi (1834-1872)

INTRODUCTION

Aleksis Kivi's novel *Seven Brothers* is the classic *par excellence* among the classics in Finnish Literature. Published in 1870 by the Finnish Literary Society, it was the first novel of note written in the Finnish language. Most agree that it is also the most significant and masterful novel in the history of Finland's literature, paralleled in significance only by Väinö Linna's trilogy *Under the North Star*, which, by the way, is also available in English translation in the Aspasia Classics in Finnish Literature series.

Aleksis Kivi (1834–1872) is often referred to as "the father of Finnish literature." This epithet reflects the extraordinary number of "firsts" associated with his name: as playwright he wrote the first full-fledged five-act tragedy in Finnish, the Kalevala inspired *Kullervo*, and the first, yet enduring, comedy *The Village Shoemakers*, a.k.a. *Cobblers on the Heath*. As novelist he penned the first novel *Seven Brothers* and as a poet he stands high above of his contemporaries, particularly with his collection *Kanervala*.

The reception of *Seven Brothers*, however, was harsh and condemning. The novel was, to put it mildly, "controversial". The leading literary scholars *cum* critics saw little or no merits in it. Especially devastating was the criticism levied by the influential critic of the time, professor of Finnish language at the University of Helsinki, August Ahlqvist, who was also an accomplished poet under the pseudonym of A. Oksanen.

In order to understand the reasons for the negative reviews, it is helpful to remember that the decade of the 1860s represented the tail end of the Romantic period, a time not yet ready to embrace realism. *Seven Brothers* distanced itself from Romanticism in fundamental ways. It exudes humor, which was alien to romantics, abounds in scenes and situations that present the brothers engaged in rough, "primitive" behavior. *Seven Brothers* depicts characters that were profoundly and truly human, but at the time considered "not fit to be role models". The language of the novel, particularly in the abundant dialogues, was criticized for crudeness and improper language.

The weight of Ahlqvist's venomous criticism, which in part went beyond the literary, has been considered a contributing factor to Kivi's mental breakdown in 1870 from which he never recovered. He died on newyear's eve 1872. While the murderous reviews were devastatingly disappointing to Kivi, it is more likely that he fell ill from mental exhaustion, having rewritten the manuscript multiple times and having reportedly worked with feverish intensity for a lengthy period of time.

Writing *Seven Brothers* exhausted Aleksis Kivi's creativity and mental powers, which is not surprising when one considers the deep-probing power, originality, and genius of the novel. It is a book of multiple dimensions: it displays an exceptionally versatile use of the Finnish language, serious and deep as well as unbridled humor, an exceptional understanding of culture, society, and psychology. The novel insightfully employs Finnish local folklore and mythology as well as a wealth of allusions to the Bible and Biblical folkbeliefs.

Aleksis Kivi wrote his masterpiece in veritable social and intellectual isolation and without the benefit of an existing literary tradition in the Finnish language. Yet, it is fair to say that he did have literary models. He was quite familiar with ancient classical Greek plays, with Shakespeare and Cervantes; in fact, it has been established that he was versed in a significant number of classics of world literature available at the time.

The 1860s was a momentous decade in Finland's history. The Finnish Literary Society, which had been established in 1831, was actively committed to the Finnish Nation Building agenda. The nation building was boosted by the publication of the "Finnish national epic", the *Kalevala* in 1835. *The Kalevala*, a compilation of old Finnish-Karelian epic narrative poems, patently satisfied the national romantic objectives of the time. However, the construction of a Finnish-language nation required a fully developed Finnish language and a viable literature in that language. This was the Finnish Literary Society's highest priority.

The Society's eyes were set early on the genius of Aleksis Kivi, who participated in and won several literary competitions in the late 1850s and in the 1860s. Aleksis Kivi quite obviously responded to the call for high quality Finnish language literature in various genres. He exceeded all expectations, repeatedly. In the mid-1860s, maybe even earlier, he conceived of a plan to write a major novel about seven brothers. He worked on it for many years. He is reported to have said, in anticipation of possible criticism, "I will never abandon my Brothers." Richard Impola, the translator of this novel is exactly right when he points out in his foreword that Kivi was guided by three great loves: love for his land, love for his people, and love for his language.

Without embarking on attempts to interpret the novel, it is clear that *literacy* is an important theme in *Seven Brothers*. The Finnish society and the Lutheran church had long required that its members pass *lukukinkerit* 'a reading test' to become full members of society and the church and so to receive the right, for example, to get married. This has often, misleadingly, been taken as proof that Finns were literate for centuries. In actual fact, what was required was the ability "to recite the Cathechism." The 19th century is when the Finns really learned to read as a result of the creation of a school system as well as the emeregence of newspapers and of a literature in Finnish.

Learning to read is a particular challenge for the brothers in the novel. Literacy, therefore, is clearly given a prominent role in the novel. Literacy is, however, also what separates an illiterate worldview from a literate one. The country underwent a transition from virtual illiteracy and a preliterate worldview early in the 19th century to near full literacy by its end. Kivi's novel captures that transition in progress, with all its dynamics and implications. The old traditional society held age-old cultural values: primogenity, folkbeliefs and superstitions, a mixture of mythology and Christianity, justice by strength, vengeance and retaliation, all perpetuated in the oral tradition. With literacy, enlightenment and modern "civilization" arrived. Kivi's *Seven Brothers* reflects brilliantly this process of transition in

Finnish culture and society, in the brothers' lives, experiences, joys and sorrows. In *Seven Brothers,* as in all great art, the universal and the particular are one.

Ultimately, however, the novel describes the brothers as delightful human beings, full of imagination, initiative, humor, and *joie de vivre*. They love freedom and live freedom and in so doing they learn the joys and hazards of unbridled freedom, and the importance of keeping their temperaments in check. Their sense of responsibility gradually emerges from within. *Seven Brothers* is a timeless novel and a fantastic read.

Börje Vähämäki

TRANSLATOR'S FOREWORD

Next to the *Kalevala,* Aleksis Kivi's *Seven Brothers* is the best-known and most revered work of Finnish literature. It is a threefold labor of love on Kivi's part: love of his land, love of his people, and love of his language.

Kivi's love of the Finnish countryside permeates the entire novel. It is epitomized in the last chapter where Eero's feelings toward his country are described:

> To him, his native land was no longer an indefinite part of a vague world, its kind and location completely unknown. He knew where it lay, that dear corner of the world where the people of Finland lived and built and struggled, in whose bosom lie our forefathers' bones. He knew its boundaries, its seas, its quietly smiling lakes, and the woody picket fences of its piney ridges. The complete picture of our homeland with its kind, motherly face was forever imprinted deep in his heart.

Kivi's affection for his characters is obvious. They are hardly idealized, yet they are as appealing a group of rowdies as any in literature. In the beginning, they are at home only in the wilderness, to which they must flee for refuge. They have good intentions, usually thwarted either by their own failings or by dogmatic authorities, but they finally bungle and struggle their way through to a place in society.

With regard to language, Kivi, like European writers some centuries earlier in the Renaissance, was faced with a choice. In that day, authors could write either in their own native tongue, or in Latin, the international and academic language of the time. In Kivi's day, Swedish was still the language of education and officialdom in Finland. Kivi chose to write in Finnish, the first professional author to do so.

Many a writer in the Renaissance was concerned with enriching and polishing his own language to make it a fit vehicle for works that could rival the great literary monuments of classical antiquity. Kivi, who was well read in those writers, also seems bent on showing what his language can do. In *Seven Brothers,* the often rhythmic and patterned prose, the use of epic similes to heighten the action, the set pieces of narration in the work, and the joyous virtuoso passages such as Lauri's exuberant mock sermon on the Rock of Hiisi all demonstrate his delight in the richness of the Finnish language and his desire to put it through its paces.

A comparison of *Seven Brothers* to the masterpiece of the American writer Mark Twain is a revealing one. *Seven Brothers* was published in 1870, fourteen years before the appearance of *Huckleberry Finn* in 1884. A basic theme in both works is the flight from civilization. In Kivi's novel, the brothers go through a long and painful process of education and finally take their places as members of an orderly society. Once they have mastered themselves, they learn that institutions are not the ugly and threatening forces they had once seemed to be. It is interesting to note that the same word "sivistys" serves for both education and civilization in Finnish.

Perhaps it is American "individualism" which prevents Huck Finn from following a similar path. To Twain's character organized society is and remains the enemy. Huck's natural moral choices are superior to those condoned by social custom: He helps the slave Jim to escape despite the fact that society condones slavery. He reacts with horror to the feud between the Grangerfords and Shepherdsons. The results of his encounters with "civilization" suggest that his instincts are superior to social codes. His last words at the end of the novel are: "But I reckon I got to light out for the territory ahead of the rest, because Aunt Sally she's going to adopt and sivilize me, and I can't stand it. I been there before." There is no resolution of the conflict between individual and society. One needs a frontier to escape to.

The two writers also provide an interesting contrast in literary technique. Both are realists. Kivi was viciously attacked in his time for what we would call his realism. But his work has another dimension made possible by the tales inserted in it. The brothers tell stories supposedly heard from others, romantic and exotic tales completely alien to the world in which they live and act. The stories are suspended in the action as set pieces of narration. They appeal to a romantic sensibility.

Twain, on the other hand, can only parody romance. Tom Sawyer introduces exasperating complications into Huck's life by trying to make it conform to the patterns of romantic fiction. The poetry of Emmeline Grangerford, who "could write about anything you choose to give her to write about just so it was sadful," is a wonderful take-off on romantic melancholy. But Kivi can tell a poignantly melancholy tale for effect. Compare the stories of the "Pale Maiden" and of the imprisoned Christian in *Seven Brothers* with the "Here a Captive Heart Busted" chapter in *Huckleberry Finn*.

Although there are times when the brothers do comment on the stories, the actions which precede and follow the romantic tales are a more effective commentary. Kivi may have learned the strategy of allowing context to serve as commentary from Shakespeare, who is a master of that technique. Twain uses the simpler method of direct parody.

A concomitant theme of the novel is that of taming the wilderness. In American literature, the frontiersman is usually idealized. The seven brothers hardly conform to the ideal. Rather, they are closer to the type which, in the opinion of some historians, inhabited the lawless outer fringe of the frontier: misfits and outcasts from society. But the seven brothers develop a rich and productive farm while redeeming themselves through work and self-education. It is a reader's good fortune that Kivi chose to treat the theme in a comic vein. The story of virtue rewarded is more palatable in comedy.

The last lines of the novel read:

But this is the end of my story. And so I have told you of seven brothers in the wilds of Finland. What more is there to tell of their days and deeds here on earth? Their life ran a peaceful course to its height at noon, and sank as peacefully down to its evening rest, during the circuit of many thousands of golden suns.

The passage rounds off the novel neatly, but as Kivi says, "What more is there to tell...?" The "happy ending" is appropriate; the episode of the Christmas reunion is an idyllic genre piece. But it is their past adventures the brothers talk over as they sit around the table at Jukola on Christmas Eve.

...days in the dark woods and the stump-strewn meadow of Impivaara under the chasmed roaring mountain. The memories of past dangers, battles, and toils blended sweetly into one, just as woods, valleys, mountains, and upland heaths merge in the blue haze of distance.

Memory is already transforming the brothers' past experiences into legends in their own minds, legends that "merge in the blue haze of the distance." But there is no blurring of the legends bequeathed to us by the creative talents of Kivi. The actions and characters of the brothers are a living and unfading literary heritage. Impulsive Juhani, who usually manages to act before he thinks, wise but preachy Aapo, mighty Tuomas, slow-witted Timo, sincere but fallible Simeoni, quiet Lauri, and mocking Eero — their trials and triumphs are as fresh and living as on the day they were first penned.

Richard A. Impola

CHAPTER I

On a rocky north slope near the village of Toukola in the southern part of the province of Häme stands the Jukola house. Below it lie fields where full heads of grain once rippled in the wind before the farm went to ruin. Further down is another field fringed with clover and crossed by a zigzag ditch, which grew hay in abundance before it became a common pasture for the village cattle. Great expanses of wilderness lands, woods, and swamps also belong to the farm. They were acquired by its founder through astute dealings at the time of the Great Land Distribution long ago. More concerned for the welfare of his posterity than for his own profit, he took as his share a tract of burned-over woods, and thus gained ownership of seven times the land of his neighbors. But the effects of the fire had long since disappeared and dense woods had grown up on the tract. This is the home of the seven brothers whose life story I am about tell.

In order of age, the brothers are Juhani, Tuomas, Aapo, Simeoni, Timo, Lauri, and Eero. Tuomas and Aapo are twins, as are Timo and Lauri. Juhani, the eldest, is twenty-five, but the youngest, Eero, has just turned eighteen. They are all sturdy and broad-shouldered, of average height except for Eero, who is still rather short. Aapo is the tallest, although not the broadest of shoulder. That honor falls to Tuomas, who is actually famous for his build. They all have a bronzed complexion and an unruly mop of hempen hair, the coarseness of Juhani's being especially striking.

Their father, an avid hunter, met sudden death in the prime of his life, battling a maddened bear. Man and animal were found lying dead, side by side on the bloody field. The man was mauled more severely, but the beast's throat and side were slashed by a knife and its breast pierced by a cruel bullet. Such was the end of a rugged man who had killed more than fifty bears. But he had neglected his farm for the hunt, and without supervision, it had gradually decayed. His sons, having inherited their father's zeal for the chase, were equally averse to plowing and planting. They set out snares, traps, loops, and grouse-coops for the slaughter of birds and rabbits, spending their boyhood years in such pursuits until they could handle guns and dared approach a bear in the wilds.

Their mother tried by means of scolding and punishment to lead them to hard work and diligence, but their stubbornness was proof against all her efforts. She was in most respects a good woman, known for her frank and forthright, if perhaps too stern nature. Her brother, the boys' uncle, was a fine man too. He had traveled distant seas as a proud young sailor, had seen many nations and cities, but had become stone-blind and was spending the dark days of his old age in the Jukola house. Often, as he whittled dippers, spoons, ax handles, pestles, and other useful household items by touch alone, he told stories to his sisters' sons, regaling them with accounts of wonderful events both at home and abroad, with Biblical tales and happenings. The boys listened devoutly and committed them all firmly to memory. But they were less pleased by their mother's bossing and scolding, turning a deaf ear to her in spite of frequent whippings. Often, when they knew a thrashing was at hand, the whole gang took flight, bringing grief to their mother, and making their own lot worse.

This is the story of one such childhood escapade. The boys knew of a hen's nest under their grain-drying barn, which belonged to an old woman called 'Granny Pine' after the grove near Jukola where her cabin stood. One day they had a yen for the taste of eggs and decided to rob the nest and run off to the woods to enjoy their loot. They did as they planned, emptying the nest, and running off as one to the forest. There were six of them; Eero was at the time an infant still clinging to his mother's skirts. When they came to a rippling brook in a dark spruce grove, they built a fire on its bank, wrapped the eggs in rags, dipped them in water, and set them sizzling to bake in the hot ashes. When the delicacies were ready, they ate a tasty meal and then set off contentedly for home. But a cyclone greeted them on arrival, for their deed had been discovered. Granny Pine raged and ranted, and their mother came rushing angrily upon them, a whistling rod in her hand. Unwilling to face the storm, the boys fled back to the shelter of the woods, ignoring their mother's shouts.

A day went by, then another, but there was no word from the fugitives. The delay made their mother distraught; her rage turned to tears of grief and pity. She went out to look for her children, searching the woods high and low without finding them. Things looked darker and darker, and finally the authorities took a hand in the matter. The bailiff was sent for; he immediately assembled everyone from Toukola and the vicinity. Under his command the entire group, young and old, men and women, strung out in a long line, went poking through the woods. The first day they searched near at hand, but without the desired result. The next day, they went further out. Climbing a high hill, they saw a blue column of smoke curling up into the air far away on the edge of a swamp. Making careful note of where the smoke was rising, they continued in that direction. When at last they drew near, they heard a voice singing:

> *Life was good in olden days*
> *Out here on this far bank.*
> *The flood brought us fuel for the blaze.*
> *For ale it was water we drank.*

The mother of Jukola was delighted by what she heard, for she recognized the voice as her son Juhani's. The frequent crack of bursting rocks assured the searchers that the runaways' camp was near. Their leader ordered them to surround the boys, to slip up on them softly, but to stop at a short distance from their lair.

The group did as they were told. Circling the brothers on all sides, they stopped when they had come to within some fifty paces, where the following sight met their eyes: A small shelter of fir boughs had been built at the base of a rock. On a mossy spot by its door lay Juhani, gazing up at the sky and singing. Some three or four yards away a cheerful fire was blazing, and Simeoni was roasting a snared grouse over the coals for dinner. Their faces blackened with soot from a game of goblins, Aapo and Timo were roasting turnips in the hot ashes. By a small puddle sat Lauri, silently shaping clay whistles in the form of cocks, bulls and proud colts. He already had a sizable row of them drying on a mossy log. Tuomas was playing "fire hammer": he would spit a foamy slug on a rock embedded in the earth, set a fiery coal on it, then hurl another rock down on the first with all his strength. An explosion as sharp as a real rifle-shot echoed around, and sooty smoke spun into the air from between the rocks.

Juhani:
> *Life was good in olden days,*
> *Out here on this far bank...*

But you can bet that the devil will get us in the end, my young bucks.

Aapo: That's what I said when we ran off. What a bunch of fools we are! Let outlaws and gypsies live under the open sky, for my part.

Timo: At least it's God's sky.

Aapo: Living out here with wolves and bears.

Tuomas: And with God.

Juhani: Right you are, Tuomas. With God and His angels. Ah, if we had the eyes of the blessed, we would plainly see a whole flock of winged guardian angels hovering around us, and good gray old God Himself sitting right in our midst like a loving father.

Simeoni: But what is our poor mother thinking?

Tuomas: That she would beat us to a pulp if she could get her hands on us.

Juhani: Oh, man, that would be a whipping.

Tuomas: A real shellacking! You know that well enough.

Aapo: We'll have to face it sooner or later.

Simeoni: Of course. That's why it would be better to get it over with now and end this fool's holiday once and for all.

Juhani: Bulls just don't go willingly to the slaughterhouse, my friend.

Aapo: What kind of nonsense is that, boy? It'll soon be winter, and you know we weren't born with a fur coat on our backs.

Simeoni: So it's just "Homeward, March!" and take our licking. And with good cause, with good cause.

Juhani: Let's spare our hides a few days longer, brothers. In the meantime, who knows what kind of trick God may cook up to save our hides. So let's muck around yet for awhile, spend the day by the fire and snore the night away side by side like a row of mama-piggy's babies in the straw. But Lauri, old buddy, down in your claypit, what do you have to say? Shall we go home and take our medicine?

Lauri: Let's stay for awhile.

Juhani: I think that's best too. Well, then! You've got a real herd of livestock there.

Tuomas: The boy has birds too.

Juhani: A huge flock. You've got the makings of a real whistle-maker.

Tuomas: A first-rate one.

Juhani: A master whistle-maker. What kind of Russian doll are you setting down now?

Lauri: It's sort of a little boy.

Juhani: Well, look at that!

Tuomas: He makes boys like a real man.

Juhani: As solid as pine stumps. And he feeds his men and livestock like a man. But hey, brothers, hurry up with that food. My belly is starting to growl. Pile on the hot ashes to bake that turnip. Whose turn is it to steal next time?

Simeoni: It's my turn to sin again.

Juhani: To stay alive, we have to pinch a little from others. If that's a sin, it's a small sin in this rotten world. And look, if I die with only that tiny blot on my record, it won't keep me out of heaven. Maybe out of the real bridal chamber, but at least I'll get some sort of doorman's job, which in itself will be a terrific joy. That's the way to look at things, so let's just stuff our bellies full once more.

Aapo: But we'd better pick out another turnip field and stop stealing from Kuokkala. If his patch keeps on shrinking, he'll put a guard on it day and night.

Bailiff: No worry on that score, my boys, none at all. Now, now, why all the panic? A flock of guardian angels has you nicely surrounded.

Terror-stricken by the words, the brothers leaped to their feet and scrambled wildly in all directions, only to find every exit barred. The bailiff went on in this vein: "You're trapped now, you scamps, neatly trapped, and you won't be freed until you lose a little hide as a reminder, a gentle reminder, of all the tramping your tricks have cost us. Bring on your birch-rod, Mother, and lay it on with a heavy hand. If they resist, there are plenty of women here to help you."

Then came a beating at their mother's hands that passed from one to another until it encompassed them all.

Loud was the wailing in the Kuokkala woods. Their mother wielded the rod with a vengeance, and yet the bailiff insisted that they had gotten off too lightly. When the mission was finally accomplished, everyone headed for home, Mother and sons with the rest. She railed at and scolded the fugitives all the way home, nor did the storm subside on their arrival. She went on scolding while she set out a meal, threatening them with another whipping. But seeing how hungrily they sank their teeth into the bread and salt fish, she turned away and wiped a furtive tear from her rough brown cheek.

So ended the youthful escapade for which I have interrupted my story. The boys' favorite pastime was a game called "batting the puck," which they continued to love even as grown men. Divided into two teams, they fought savagely to drive the puck toward an assigned goal. The running, shouting, and collisions were fierce, and sweat poured down their faces as they played. The bounding puck whistled along the road, often rocketing off a bat straight into a boy's face. When the game was over, there were likely to be huge lumps on foreheads, cheeks puffed out like sweet wheat buns. And so the days of their youth went by: summers roaming the woods or batting the puck on the main road, winters baking in the sweaty heat atop the huge stone oven at home.

But even the brothers realized that time brings changes. Events forced them to give some thought to tomorrow and mend their ways a little. — Their mother died, and one of them now had to take charge of the household to save it from utter ruin and to pay State taxes on the farm, not a large amount considering the size of the Jukola land and forest. Besides which a neglected farm demands time and effort. Worst of all, the new church provost was fearfully stern in the execution of all his duties. He was particularly merciless to slow readers and used every possible tactic against them, including punishment in the stocks, and his sharp eye had already fallen on the Jukola boys. He sent them an urgent official summons to appear in all haste before the sexton and begin their reading lessons. With this in mind, the boys gathered in the large sitting room of their home one late summer evening to hold the following discussion:

Aapo: I tell you, this wild life won't do. It'll end in rack and ruin. Brothers, let's change our ways if we hope for peace and quiet.

Juhani: You're right. I can't deny it.

Simeoni: God mend us. Our life has been wild and abandoned to this very day.

Timo: There are lives and lives and worlds and worlds. This one is good enough, even if it is a little rough.

Juhani: You can't deny that we've lived too wildly, or rather carelessly, but remember: 'The young are foolish but the old are wise.'

Aapo: And it's time to be wise, to harness our whims and wishes to the yoke of reason, to do what's gainful rather than sweet. Let's set about restoring the farm to a decent state right now.

Juhani: Well said. First we'll attack the manure pile like dung beetles. Let the brush-chopping block ring round Jukola's walls from morning till night. Let our plump cows push out dung piles high enough to rival the golden walls of a king's castle. That's what we'll do. We'll start next Monday from the ground up.

Aapo: Why not tomorrow?

Juhani: Next Monday. There's no harm in letting our thoughts ripen. That's it, then. Next Monday.

Aapo: But one issue must be settled right now. If we expect to have method and order in our farming, then one man has to lead and command. We know that right and duty belongs to Juhani, both as first-born and by Mother's decree.

Juhani: Exactly so. The right, the power, and the authority belong to me.

Aapo: But see that you use it wisely and for the benefit of all.

Juhani: I'll do my best. If only you'll obey without the use of force or the whip. But I'll do my best.

Aapo: The whip?

Juhani: If it's necessary, you'll see.

Tuomas: Talk of whipping to your dog.

Timo: You'll never tan my hide, not ever. If my back ever itches for a whipping, then law and justice can take care of it.

Juhani: Why latch on to a loose word? Things can go well for us if good will prevails and everyone pulls in his horns.

Eero: How we are to treat each other must be carefully spelled out.

Aapo: And every voice must be heard.

Juhani: What does tight-lipped Lauri have to say?

Lauri: I have a plan. Let's head for the woods. To hell with this jangling world.

Juhani: What?

Aapo: The man is raving.

Juhani: Head for the woods? That's crazy.

Aapo: Pay no attention to him. Look, this is what I think. Juhani, you have the right to be head of this house, if you choose.

Juhani: I do choose.

Aapo: Then as long as we others don't marry, we'll stay on in our dear home and work the farm in exchange for food and clothing. Every first Monday of the month, we'll have a day off, but we'll be fed then too. Every year, each man will get a half-barrel of oats to sow, and we will all have the right to slash-and-burn three acres for use as a common field. So much for our bachelor home. I know that none of us wants to leave our beloved Jukola, and there's no lack of space to force us to it. There is land enough here for seven brothers. If in time one of us wants to start a home and family, but doesn't want the farm split up by legal process and survey, won't he be content with this? Let him have a piece of acreage to build a home and clear fields around it. Let him have some meadowland for hay, and the right to clear more hayfields from the woods, enough to feed a team of horses and four or five cows. And without any taxes or other obligations, let him till his fields and enjoy their fruits, he and his children, living in peace on his own land. That's what I think. What do you say?

Juhani: Good thinking. Let's consider these proposals.

Lauri: But I have a different and better idea. Let's go deep into the woods. We'll sell this worthless Jukola, or lease it to Rajaportti the tanner. He's told us he'd like a deal to have the farm for at least ten years. Let's do as I say and move with horse, dogs, and guns to the foot of steep Impivaara. We'll build a nice little cabin in a bright meadow sloping east, and there we'll live by trapping wild animals, far from the ways of the world and its ill-tempered people. That's been my plan for many years.

Juhani: Has the devil addled your brains, boy?

Eero: Or a wood nymph, if not the devil.

Lauri: I've thought about it, and some day I'll do it. There we'll live like kings, snaring birds, squirrels, rabbits, foxes, wolves, badgers, and shaggy bears.

Juhani: What the devil! Let's bring on the whole of Noah's ark, from Mouse to Moose.

Eero: Now that's great advice. Kiss our salt and bread good-bye and go to suck blood and to mince meat, like mosquitoes and Lapland witches. And are we to eat foxes and wolves there too, like hairy mountain trolls out in the nooks and crannies of Impivaara?

Lauri: We'll get pelts from foxes and wolves, money for the pelts, and salt and bread for the money.

Eero: We can dress ourselves in the pelts, but let meat, bloody, steaming meat be our only food. Apes and baboons don't need salt or bread in the woods.

Lauri: I've thought about it, and some day I'll do it.

Timo: Let's figure this out from A to Z. Why shouldn't there be salt and bread to eat in the woods? Why not? Eero is a scoffer, always in our way like a high stump in a hayfield. What's to keep a woodsman from going to town now and then when he has to? Or would you take a club to me, Eero?

Eero: No, Brother, and I'd even "trade you salt for your berries." Go ahead and move, boys. I won't stop you. I'll even give you a swift ride from home.

Juhani: Wood demons will give them as swift a ride back, I'll vouch for that.

Lauri: "Once out the door, return no more." I know the refrain, so don't expect me to come knocking again once I've left. I'm moving on May Day.

Timo: Maybe I'll go with you.

Lauri: I'm not telling you to go or to stay. Do what your heart thinks best. I'm leaving for Impivaara Meadow on May Day. At first, until my own snug little cabin is ready, I'll live in Grandpa's mossy charcoal-burner's hut. There, when the day's work is done, I'll lie in my den of peace, listening to the bear whistling in the woods and to the call of the grouse out in Sompio.

Timo: I'm going along too, Lauri, I've made up my mind.

Tuomas: If things don't get better here, I'll go along too.

Juhani: You too, Tuomas. You'd go along too?

Tuomas: If things don't get better here.

Lauri: I'm leaving on May Day even if we're feasting on cake at Jukola.

Timo: You and I will move to Sompio Swamp like the cranes in the spring when the whole sky is singing.

Juhani: Oh man, I have to admit that Lauri's plan has a sneaky appeal. The woods are so tempting. The devil if I don't see the beautiful blue stretch of sky beyond them right now.

Aapo: You fools, what are you thinking of? Move into the woods! Why? We have a house and farm, a precious roof over our heads.

Juhani: It's true we have a farm, and will cling to it tooth and nail so long as it yields us a crumb. But look, if hard luck ever thwarts our best plans, let's have the woods as a reserve, a place we can fly to when the last kernels of grain grind in the mill. So then, we'll take care of the farm work like that, rip through it at top speed. But to get back to the real issue at hand. In my thick-skulled opinion, Aapo has weighed matters wisely and all will go well if everyone strives for peace and harmony. But if we look for a fight, there will always be a reason for neck-hairs to bristle.

Simeoni: There will always be a reason while the Old Adam prickles and stings in our bodies.

Timo: I've always pictured Old Adam as a sober old grand-dad in a felt hat, a black frock-coat, knee breeches, and a red vest reaching below the navel, plodding along deep in thought behind a team of oxen.

Simeoni: By 'Old Adam' I mean original sin, the root of all evil.

Timo: I know he's the emblem and image of original sin, the horned devil from hell, but yet I picture him as an old geezer driving his oxen. I can't help it.

Juhani: Let's forget the Bible and stick to the subject. Aapo, what are your plans for our two *torppas,* Vuohenkalma and Kekkuri?

Aapo: We must remember that both their tenants have wrested their fields from the raw and desolate forest, and should not be driven from their land. That would be wrong, so long as they have the strength to till it. And the law decrees that it provide for them in their old age. So much for what is right in their case. But let's consider a fact which, I think, has us in a quandary. It's a most important step, one that can turn heads prematurely gray or bring us fair skies and end our days in a sunset glow. And it concerns you first, Juhani. Listen to what I have to say. A man without a wife is lame and incomplete: a house without a woman on the granary path...

Timo: Is like a den without a she-wolf or a boot without a mate. It would really go limping, as Aapo said.

Aapo: A house without a wife on the granary path is like a cloudy day: loneliness sits at the family table like a pining autumn eve. But a good wife is bright sunshine in a house, giving light and warmth. You see her rising first in the morning. She mixes the dough, sets breakfast on the table for the men, packs their lunches for the woods, and then goes pail in hand to milk the spotted cows. Now she is kneading the dough, hurrying and scurrying, now at the table, skipping to the back bench, a loaf in one hand, now blowing up the fire which pours smoke and flame from its glowing jaws. Then at last, while the bread rises, with her child at her breast, she snatches a bite of breakfast, a piece of bread with fried herring, sips soured milk from a mug. Nor does she forget the faithful watchdog on the steps or the cat that peers sleepily from atop the stone oven. Again she scurries about, tripping and turning, mixes another batch of dough to rise in the trough, baking and cooking, sweat streaming down her brow. But see, come twilight the bread all hangs from the ceiling, pole upon pole, breathing out fresh life. And when the men come home, a scrubbed table set with a steaming dinner is waiting for them. But where is the wife? Out in the yard milking her crooked-horned cows, the fresh foaming milk hissing and swirling in the pail. Thus she scurries about, tripping and turning, and only when everyone else is asleep and snoring does she kneel in prayer by her bed. But her chores and duties are not over. Without complaint, she stays awake at night by the minute or hour to quiet her child when it cries in the cradle. That, my brothers, is a true mistress of a house.

Juhani: Well said, Aapo, and I see what you're driving at. You're trying to get me to marry. Well, I understand. A wife, you say, is a necessary part of a household. That's true. But don't worry. I think your hopes will soon be fulfilled. So then. I admit that I've fallen head over heels for a girl who will be my wife, and a good one, if the old signs hold true. So, my brothers, other days and other ways will soon be upon us, and my stewardship weighs heavily on me. The head of a household must carry an awful load and has much to answer for on Judgment Day. I am now responsible for every last one of you. Keep that in mind.

Tuomas: You are responsible? How so?

Juhani: I am your master. Some day my palms will bleed for your sake.

Tuomas: I'll answer for myself, both body and soul.

Timo: And I for my own self too, hah!

Aapo: Brother Juhani, such words give rise to bad blood.

Juhani: Bad blood, bad flesh! I meant nothing of the kind. But every loose, empty word sticks to you like tar, or burrs on a hot summer day, even though you know me to the bottom of my heart. I'm sick and tired of it.

Aapo: Forget it. Tell us now what girl your heart is set on.

Juhani: I'll tell you right out. The girl I love so desperately is Granny Pine's Venla.

Aapo: Hmmm.

Juhani: What?

Aapo: I only said, "Hmmm."

Tuomas: It's a ticklish question.

Simeoni: Venla. Well, well. Let's leave it in God's hands.

Aapo: Hmmm. So it's Venla.

Juhani: What are you mumbling about? Oh, oh — I have a sneaking suspicion — God help us. What is it? Spit it out!

Aapo: Listen: I've worshipped the girl for years.

Simeoni: If God grants her to me, I won't complain.

Eero: Not at all. He may grant her to you, but I'll take her for myself.

Juhani: What do you say, Tuomas?

Tuomas: It's a ticklish question. I admit I like her a lot.

Juhani: Is that so? Well! And what about you, Timo?

Timo: I admit it too.

Juhani: Holy Jesus and Jumping Jacks! But what about Eero?

Eero: The same frank confession, the same frank confession.

Juhani: Better and better. Ha, ha! And Timo, even Timo.

Timo: I love the girl deeply. It's true she thrashed me once, dusted me soundly when I was a kid, so that I still remember the beating. And so...

Juhani: Quiet. The question is: "Do you love her?"

Timo: Yaah, yaah, I do, and deeply. That is, if she loves me too.

Juhani: So you're in my way too.

Timo: Not at all, not at all, unless you can control your tongue and your temper. Yet I love the wench a lot, and will do my best to win her as a wife.

Juhani: Good! Good! But what does Lauri have to say?

Lauri: What do I have to do with the girl?

Juhani: Whose side are you on?

Lauri: I won't get involved on one side or the other.

Juhani: This is going to be a real stew.

Lauri: I'll keep my spoon out of it.

Juhani: All of you then, except for Lauri. Boys, boys! The Jukola brotherhood, my many kin. It's time for blows. Let earth and heaven tremble! Now, my dear brothers. It's knife, ax, or club, one against all and all against one, like seven mad bulls. So let it be! My weapon is a club. I pick this one with the cross-grained handle. Whoever finds a splinter from it in his skull has only himself to blame. Take up your clubs, boys, and step up if you dare face a man.

Eero: Here I stand in arms, although a little short of the others.

Juhani: You little pipsqueak. I see that sly, mocking, hang-dog grin on your face. You're making fun of the whole thing, but I'm going to teach you a lesson.

Eero: Never mind my joking, as long as my club is in earnest.

Juhani: You'll soon find out what's what. Grab your clubs, boys, grab your clubs.

Tuomas: Here I stand with my club, if it has to be this way. I don't like anger and fighting, but if it has to be...

Juhani: Tuomas, your club!

Tuomas: To hell with your clubs, you blockhead.

Juhani: Well, I'll be damned!

Simeoni: This is a monstrous quarrel, fit only for pagans and Turks. I withdraw from the game and leave the marriage to heaven.

Lauri: Count me out too.

Juhani: Then step aside, out from under our feet. Take up your club, Aapo, and let the walls of Jukola echo the sound of skulls cracking. Fire and brimstone!

Aapo: What a wretch man is! You're a horrible sight to behold, Juhani, with your eyes rolling madly and your hair standing on end like bunch grass.

Juhani: Let it stand, let it stand. It's a plain and proper man's head of hair.

Eero: I mean to dust it a little.

Juhani: You Tom Thumb, you. You'd better stay put in your corner. Get out of here, I feel sorry for you.

Eero: Stick that awful jaw of yours in the corner. That's what I feel sorry for. It's starting to quiver and shake like a palsied beggar.

Juhani: So is this club. Just look at it.

Aapo: Juhani!

Eero: Go ahead and hit me. You'll get back a hailstorm, and every stone the size of a club. Hit me!

Juhani: I will!

Aapo: You will not, Juhani.

Juhani: To the dunghill with you. Either take up a club and defend yourself or I'll soften your skull a little. Take up a club!

Aapo: Juhani, where are your brains?

Juhani: In this cross-grained club of mine. Hear it whispering to you.

Aapo: Wait, brother, wait until I pick up my weapon. — Well, now, here I stand gripping my solid club. But first a word or two, my Christian band of Jukola brothers, before we fall to fighting like mad wolves. An angry man is not a man, but a bloodthirsty beast of prey. He is blind to all that is right and reasonable, totally unfit to sort out affairs of the heart in his rage. But let us try to use our intelligence on the question that is bringing brothers to blows. Now this is my plan. The girl is hardly likely to be in love with all of us. She will take only one, if any, as the man of her choosing, to lead her hand in hand over the thorny hill of life. It's best, then, that we all go to her, and soberly state our case, asking her with true heart and tongue, if she will give her heart to one of us. If she agrees, the man who draws the hoped-for lot can thank his lucky stars, but he who is left out in the cold must accept his fate without grumbling. He must swallow his grief in the hope of some day finding his destined darling here. If we do this, we are acting like men and true brothers. If we do this, the bright spirits of our mother and father will step through the radiant gates of heaven to stand on the brink of a shining cloud and shout loudly: "So Juhani, so Tuomas and Aapo, so Simeoni, Timo, and Lauri, just so, my little Eero! Now are you sons dear to our hearts!"

Juhani: Man, you talk like an angel from heaven. A little more and you'd have me in tears.

Simeoni: We thank you, Aapo.

Juhani: I thank you too, and throw away my club.

Timo: And so do I. This fight has ended as I hoped from the start that it would.

Simeoni: Aapo holds up a mirror to us and we should thank him for it.

Eero: Let's all thank him properly and sing Simeoni's "Hymn of Thanks."

Simeoni: Mockery, mockery, sneers and mockery again.

Timo: Don't poke fun at God's word, Eero, at Simeoni's "Hymn of Thanks."

Aapo: So young and so hardened.

Simeoni: So young and so hardened. Eero, Eero, I say no more, but I sigh for you.

Juhani: I predict, Eero, that some day we'll be forced to let you feel a father's heavy hand.

Simeoni: He must be disciplined while his heart is still young and impressionable but let's do it with a loving, not an angry hand. Wrathful punishment drives the devil in, not out.

Eero: Well, take that! From a very loving hand.

Simeoni: Why, the little devil hit me?

Eero: And right in the snout. Men have lost their temper for less.

Juhani: Come over here, boy. Timo, get that stick from the corner.

Simeoni: And now, Juhani, just hold him nice and snug on your knees while I drop his pants.

Eero: The hell you will?

Juhani: No use to squirm, you squirt.

Simeoni: Don't let go of him.

Juhani: Look at the eel wiggle. But he can't get loose.

Eero: Hit me, you devils, and I'll set the house on fire. I'll send the whole thing up in smoke, just see if I don't.

Juhani: What a temper! So you'll set the house on fire? What a temper!

Simeoni: God save us. What a temper?

Juhani: Bring the stick here, Timo.

Timo: I can't find it.

Juhani: Are you blind? Can't you see it there in the corner?

Timo: You mean this one? The birch?

Juhani: That's just the one. Bring it here.

Simeoni: Hit him, but do it carefully, and not with all your strength.

Juhani: I know, I know.

Lauri: Not one lick, I say.

Tuomas: Leave the boy alone.

Juhani: His tail needs a little dusting.

Lauri: Don't lay a finger on him.

Tuomas: Let the boy go? This minute?

Timo: Let Eero-Boy be forgiven, at least this one time.

Simeoni: Forgive and forgive, until weeds and thorns crowd out the wheat.

Lauri: Don't touch him.

Aapo: Let's forgive him. It will be like heaping hot coals on his head.

Juhani: Go, and thank your lucky stars.

Simeoni: And pray God to grant you a new heart, mind, and tongue.

Timo: But I'm going to bed.

Aapo: Let's consider one more proposal.

Timo: I'm going to bed. Come along, Eero, and forget this piss-ant world that reeks and fumes in the rain.

Juhani: But what proposal did you want to decide?

Aapo: God mend us! The fact is that we don't even know the first letter of the alphabet, and that knowing how to read is the first duty of every Christian citizen. The power of the law, of church law, may force us to it. And you know what kind of contraption the State has watching, eager to snap us up in its jaws if we don't obediently learn to read. The stocks are waiting for us, my brothers, the black stocks, their cruel jaws gaping wide like those of a black bear. The provost has threatened us with those hellish pincers, and he is bound to carry out his threat unless he sees us eagerly studying every day.

Juhani: Learning to read is impossible.

Aapo: People have done it before.

Tuomas: It's enough to make a man sweat bullets.

Juhani: And huff and puff too. I have such a thick skull.

Aapo: But where there's a will, there's a way. Let's buckle down, get ourselves primers from Hämeenlinna, and go to school under the sexton, just as the provost bids us. Let's do it before we're compelled by the Crown.

Juhani: I'm afraid we must. God have mercy on us. But let it go until tomorrow. Let's go to bed.

CHAPTER II

It is a calm September morning. Dew shines on the fields; a mist lingers at the tips of leaves turning yellow on the trees before it finally evaporates into the air. The brothers have risen early, brushed their hair, and put on their Sunday best. They are surly and silent, for today they have decided to go to the sexton's school.

They are eating breakfast at Jukola's long pine-plank table. The meal of brown peas seems appetizing enough, but there is little joy in their demeanor. On the contrary, a sour look of mortification hangs on their brows, for soon they must begin the journey to school. Having eaten, they delay their departure to sit and rest for awhile. In silence, one stares dejectedly at the floor, while another glances through his red-bound ABC Book, turning over its thick pages. Juhani sits at the south window of the house, gazing up the rocky slope at the thick grove of pines where he can see Granny Pine's cabin with its door framed in red.

Juhani: There's Venla tripping along the trail. She's so light on her feet.

Aapo: I thought the girl and her mother were supposed to go to Tikkala yesterday to top turnips and pick cowberries. And stay till late autumn.

Juhani: Stay till late autumn? Now that's a bad sign. They'll probably go, and the hired hand at Tikkala is a handsome scoundrel, and there go all my hopes. I think it's time for the big event, time to pop the question, the question of questions. So let's go and ask the girl: will she give in, will her heart catch fire?

Tuomas: I think so too.

Timo: Me too.

Juhani: So then, there's nothing to do but go courting one and all like young sparks. God help us, there's nothing else but to go courting, to go courting. We're dressed in our best, we're washed and combed; we look just like Christians — neat and new-born. I'm getting nervous, but on to Venla. The time is ripe.

Eero: And may this be a happy day.

Juhani: Whose happy day? Whose? Hah! What do you mean, boy?

Eero: Maybe all of ours.

Juhani: In other words, she'll marry all of us?

Eero: Whatever you say.

Juhani: Stop it!

Simeoni: How in God's name would that be possible?

Eero: In God's name, anything is possible. Let's all believe, hope, and love as one.

Juhani: Be quiet, Eero. We're going courting now, and afterwards it's off to school with packs on our backs.

Aapo: But let's do it right. Let one of us act as spokesman at the cottage.

Juhani: A crucial point. But you, Aapo, are the man for the job. You have the gift to stir fire and flame in anyone's heart with your words. It's true. You were born to preach.

Aapo: What do I know? And why talk of gifts? Out here in the woods they're lost in a fog of ignorance, they disappear like rippling brooks in the sand.

Juhani: Hard luck kept you from school.

Aapo: Where would the money for me to study have come from on our farm? It takes years of trudging back and forth to school before a man can climb into a pulpit. But let's get back to the subject. Have it your way. I'll speak for all of us and try to sound wise.

Juhani: Then let's get on with it. Oh Lord Jesus! But it can't be helped. Full steam ahead. We'll leave our packs outside the cottage, and Lauri, who has no irons in the fire, guard them from the pigs. Let's go now. We'll march into the bridal chamber with our ABC Books in hand. It'll make us look more dignified.

Eero: Especially if we leave the rooster page in sight.

Juhani: So you're at it again. The rooster reminds me, though, of an awful dream I had last night.

Simeoni: Tell me about it. Maybe it's an omen for us.

Juhani: I dreamed there was a hen's nest on the fireplace with seven eggs in it.

Simeoni: Jukola's seven sons!

Juhani: But one of them was ridiculously tiny.

Simeoni: That was Eero!

Juhani: The rooster died.

Simeoni: That was Father!

Juhani: The hen died.

Simeoni: That was Mother!

Juhani: Then a horde of mice, rats, and weasels attacked the nest. What do those animals mean?

Simeoni: Sins and lusts and worldly desires.

Juhani: That could be. On came the weasels, rats, and mice, and they turned and rolled and bumped and banged the eggs until they were all broken. The little egg gave off an awful stink.

Simeoni: Pay close attention, Eero.

Juhani: When the eggs were all broken, a horrible voice, like the roar of a thousand rapids, thundered in my ears from the fireplace: "All is broken and the ruin is great." That's what the voice said. But anyway, we began to gather up the mess and make a sort of omelet of it. And then we feasted on it and even gave some to our neighbors.

Eero: That was a fine dream.

Juhani: It was a foul dream, a foul dream. You stank like the devil. It was a foul dream about you, my boy.

Eero: But I had a very sweet dream about you. I saw the ABC rooster lay a huge pile of candy and sugar lumps as a reward for your wisdom and industry. You were delighted and sucked away on your sweets, even giving me some.

Juhani: So I even gave you some. Now that was well done.

Eero: A gift is always welcome.

Juhani: Always, and especially if I were to let you have a little of this stick.

Eero: Why just a little?

Juhani: Shut your mouth, you calf.

Tuomas: Both of you shut up and let's get going.

Aapo: Everyone pick up his pack and ABC Book.

So off they went to court the neighbor's daughter. Silent, in single file they marched over the potato cellar and up the rocky slope till at length they stood outside the door of Granny Pine's shanty.

Juhani: Well, here we are. Let's drop our packs here and Lauri will guard them well until we get back from the betrothal room.

Lauri: Will you be long?

Juhani: That depends on how things go. Does anyone have a ring?

Eero: We don't need one.

Juhani: Does anyone have a ring in his pocket?

Timo: Not me. No one else does either, as far as I know. What rotten luck! Looks like a young man should always carry a shiny ring in his pocket.

Juhani: The devil! Here we are now, and only yesterday the pack peddler Isaac visited us and we could have bought both ring and kerchief from him. But like a stupid ass, I didn't think of it.

Aapo: We can buy all that later. It's best to make sure which one of us, if any, will get to make the happy purchase.

Juhani: Who is opening the door? Is it Venla?

Timo: It's the old crone with her witch's chin.

Juhani: Venla's spinning wheel is humming like a happy dung-beetle on a summer evening, forecasting sunny weather. Let's go now. Where is my ABC Book

Aapo: In your hand, brother. Your head seems in a whirl, my God's creature.

Juhani: Don't worry, brother. But my face isn't dirty, is it?

Eero: Not at all. It's as clean and warm as a fresh-laid egg.

Juhani: Let's go!

Eero: Just a minute. As the youngest, I should open the door and enter last. Just step inside now.

The brothers stepped into the low-ceilinged cottage with Juhani in the lead and the others following on his heels. Juhani's eyes were wide open and his hair stood on end like the quills of a porcupine. So stepped they in, and Eero slammed the door shut behind them, but he himself stayed outside and sat down on the grass, a sly grin on his face.

The woman in whose home the brothers stood as suitors was a sharp and spry old soul who earned her living by keeping poultry and picking berries. Summer and fall, she and her daughter Venla scurried and sweated, scouring stumpy clearings and hillocks where strawberries and cow-berries grew. The girl was considered pretty. Her hair was auburn, her eyes were sharp and roguish, and her mouth was soft but perhaps a little too wide. She was short in stature, but broad of shoulder and was also said to be strong. Such was the brothers' love bird in her nest among the pines.

But soon the door creaked on its hinges and Juhani came storming out, crying angrily to those still inside: "Come on out, boys!" At length they all emerged with glum faces and started off toward the church village. When they were some fifty paces from the house, Juhani snatched up a fist-sized rock and hurled it at the door with an angry grunt. The hut trembled, and the old woman inside shrieked and opened the door. She stood there railing and cursing and shaking her fist at the retreating brothers. ABC-Books in their hands and packs on their shoulders, they marched single file along the road to the church without saying a word. Anger speeded their steps; the sand hissed underfoot and their packs jounced nor did they notice how fast they were walking.

Eero: How did it go?

Juhani: Uh-huh! How do you think? Did you come in with us, you magpie, you crow-chick — you didn't dare, you just didn't dare. What can one expect of a crow-chick? Venla could hide you under her hood. And look at all the dreams I've had about you. Come to think of it, I had another one last night. It's strange. There you and Venla sat all loveydovey among the pine trees and I sneaked up on you. And you know what Venla did when the two of you saw me? Damned if she didn't hide you under her skirts! "What have you got wrapped up in your skirts?" I asked her. "Just a little crow-chick," the flirt answered. Haa, haa, haa! And this wasn't really a dream, darned if it was. I made it up all by myself from my own head. Uh-huh! I'm not as dumb as you think.

Eero: It really is strange the way we keep having dreams about each other. This is one I had about you. You and Venla were also standing in the pine grove, loving and cuddling and mooning up at the stars. You were looking to heaven for a sign that your love was favored. The sky and the woods were listening and even the little birds were hushed as the two of you waited in deepest silence for what was to come. Finally an old crow came flapping through the still air and glared down at you for a minute. Then he looked away, spread his legs, and let fall a white blob that splattered on the forehead of boy and girl, completely smearing their faces. But don't be angry about this, because I dreamed it all and didn't make it up in my own head.

Juhani: You devil, I'll...

Furiously he rushed at Eero, who fled quickly from his enraged brother. Off the road ran Eero, flashing like a rabbit over the fields, with Juhani charging after him like a maddened bear. Their packs jounced and the dry ground thundered beneath their feet. The remaining brothers shouted after them, urging restraint and harmony. Eero ran back to the road, and his brothers rushed to save him from the claws of the rampaging Juhani, who was right on his heels.

Tuomas: Calm down, Juhani.

Juhani: I'll tear his hair out.

Tuomas: Take it easy, boy.

Juhani: Damn him!

Aapo: He was only paying you back.

Juhani: Damn his tongue and damn this day. This day, as God knows, Venla turned us down. Horned trolls and all the armies of Heaven! I can't see a yard ahead of me; earth and sky are as black as my heart. Damn her!

Simeoni: Don't curse, man.

Juhani: I'll curse till the world spins and shatters like a flimsy sled under a falling mast-pole.

Simeoni: What are we to do?

Juhani: Do? If this book wasn't God's word, God's very own book, we would smash it to smithereens, to tiny smithereens right this minute. But watch this. I'm going to mash my food pack into the ground. Do you want to see me do it?

Simeoni: For God's sake, don't destroy what is given by God. Remember the maid of Paimio.

Juhani: In my heart's misery!

Simeoni: "Misery on earth brings manna in heaven."

Juhani: What do I care for the manna of heaven if I can't have Venla? Oh, my many brothers. If you knew how foolishly my thoughts have revolved around the hussy for almost ten years, then you would understand. But my hopes are gone like ashes in the wind.

Timo: We were given the gate today.

Juhani: Every last one of us.

Timo: No mercy for anyone, not a bit of it. We all got the gate.

Juhani: Every last one of us. But better this than for one of us to have her for his wife. Devil take me if I wouldn't flatten the one who got her.

Tuomas: We really had no hope. You could tell that by the girl's mocking grin when Aapo stated our case.

Juhani: She deserves a whipping, the hussy, making fun of us! Just you watch out, you hussy! And there's no denying that Aapo did his best, but even an angel's tongue would have been no help in this case.

Timo: But if we had marched up to her in a black broadcloth coat with a watch bulging in a vest pocket like a fat field turnip, a key clinking on its chain, a silver-trimmed pipe belching out smoke in our teeth, then hang it all, we would have come through with flying colors, I'll be damned if we wouldn't.

Juhani: Both women and magpies have a yen for shiny things. But Aapo is as still as a frozen lake.

Aapo: Voices don't carry in a storm. Is the tempest in your breasts beginning to die down?

Juhani: The wild waves are still lashing my heart. But go ahead and talk. What is the word?

Aapo: I have several, so listen now. Take your heart in your hand and whisper to it with the voice of reason: Venla won't have you because she doesn't love you, so why be angry with her for turning you down? It is Heaven that kindles the spark of love and not the mind of man. A beggar girl falls for a king: a princess dotes madly on a chimney sweep. The breeze of love blows hither and yon, but nobody knows its source.

Timo: The breath of love blows where it will. You can hear it sigh, but you don't know where it comes from and where it is going, as the old beggar woman used to say. Though I think she was talking about God's love.

Aapo: Tell your heart to stop whining now, Juhani. Venla was right to turn you down. Marrying without love is asking for failure; everything goes wrong and life is all torture, as we see and hear every day to our sorrow. So my brothers, let Venla take her destined one, and let us do the same.

Timo: Some day I'll find the girl who was made from my rib, let the devil scream as he will. And I know something else: a man's heart rests on the left and a woman's on the right of her breast.

Juhani: But my heart won't rest: it rages and seethes like a pagan. Oh you flibbertigibbet, you gypsy hussy, why did you spurn a farmer like me, a real clay farmer and the first-born son of the house?

Aapo: There's no need to wonder. Our farm is a complete ruin, and the girl hopes, in vain I think, to become the lady of a much finer house. I've heard that the prettyboy Juhani Sorvari is cozying up to her.

Juhani: That needle-chin. If I had my mitts on him now, I'd mop the floor with him. Lead on a girl and shame her forever!

Aapo: Indeed, it's a mad and deceitful world we live in. Venla has looks and Juhani his hooks and crooks. Sorvari is a farm with a good name and it acts as a bait to lure her, while Jukola, this pauper's nest, is a total ruin and we, its seven heirs, are even more wretched in the eyes of the world. When people remember the lazy and often wild days of our youth, they no longer expect anything decent of us. Ten years of proper and completely respectable behavior will hardly serve to restore us to full human esteem in the eyes of our countrymen. It's so hard to clean off the mud of a bad name once it sticks to a man. But better to rise at last than to sink forever in Satan's filth. So let us strive for a conversion, for a conversion, with all our might.

Juhani: We've already made a start. But this disastrous courting trip gave my heart such a deep wound that it will suffer for days, no for weeks.

Aapo: A deep wound, but I know that time will form a scar and film of forgetfulness over it. Who is that on the road?

Timo: A happy gang from Toukola.

Juhani: The good-for-nothings. Roaring drunk and loafing away a Monday.

Timo: And they're urging us to join them.

Juhani: Here comes temptation.

Timo: They're having so much fun.

Juhani: And us? What's in store for us? One thousand horned devils! Having our hair yanked till our scalps burn, that's what is!

Eero: What a difference — yammering out our ABC's in the sexton's corner or spending a free and happy Monday in good company.

Juhani: It's a big difference, like that between being down in a well or up as high as heaven. Which do we choose, brothers?

Eero: Let's take heaven.

Aapo: The well, the well, to drink deep of the waters of life. To steep ourselves in knowledge, art, and wisdom.

Tuomas: On to the sexton! On to the sexton!

Juhani: Well, let's start trudging then.

Eero: Listen to Aapeli Kissala's clarinet.

Juhani: It sounds beautiful.

Timo: It sounds like the archangel's bassoon.

Juhani: Played while the heavenly armies drill and march till the dust flies. How beautiful!

Timo: They're urging us to join them.

Juhani: That's plain to see. Here comes temptation. This is it now. As the brothers were talking, the men from Toukola drew near, but their approach was not as courteous and amiable as the men of Jukola had anticipated. Well on the way to drunkenness and in a mocking mood, they serenaded the brothers with a newly composed ditty called, "The Strength of Seven Men." Up they marched to the scholars, singing to the tootling of Aapeli Kissala's clarinet:

> *Let us strain our throats in song,*
> *Singing as we march along*
> *The strength of seven brothers.*
>
> *Seven stars in the Great Bear*
> *Seven sons at Jukola there,*
> *Lazy, hulking loafers.*
>
> *Juha roars till the rafters ring*

Rules his roost just like a king
A hard man is our Jussi.

Like an oak tree Tuomas stands
As Aapo preaches reprimands
That Solomon of Juko.

Scroggly-bearded Simeoni
Wails his lamentations phony
Over 'wretched, sinful man.'

As Simeoni cooks the peas,
Timo mixes in the grease
And spits in the boiling pot.

Lauri-Boy pokes through the woods
Searching out his 'artsy' goods
Snooping like a badger.

Bringing up the very rear
Is slippery little Eero here
Juko's snappish puppy.

There you have the roster full
As noble as a herd of bulls
The seven strapping brothers.

The brothers listened to the song in silence though they were gritting their teeth. But when their tormentors continued to mock and shower them with gibes, especially about the eggs the ABC rooster would be laying, their spleen began to rise and their eyes to glow and contract to the size of a mink's as he looks out at the light of day from under a stump in the dark woods. Then one of the scamps from Toukola, passing by Juhani, suddenly snatched the ABC Book from his hand and ran off at top speed, with the outraged Juhani thundering at his heels. At the same moment, the remaining brothers rushed hotly upon their tormentors and a general battle raged. First the combatants whacked each other's ears, then they went for the throat, and finally they began —

blindly panting — to rend, tear, and to flail away with their fists. The men of Toukola fought back fiercely but the sons of Jukola were more savage. Like clubs of iron the brothers' fists rained blows upon the heads of their enemies. The battlers threshed about in the dust and dirt that rose in clouds from the dry road; sand and gravel rustled the leaves of the nearby trees. The noisy onset had not lasted long before the brothers, who had the upper hand, began shouting, "Do you beg for mercy?" and the echo from the clouds answered, "Mercy!" But the men of Toukola resisted for a long time until at last they fell helpless to the ground. There they lay, their coats in shreds and their faces swollen, gulping fresh air into their hot, panting innards. The brothers stood victorious, but their figures revealed that they too had had their fill of fighting and were pleased with the respite.

Eero had fared especially ill in the melee; his short stature gave his opponents a great advantage. Often during the fight, he was to be seen tumbling like a little dachshund at the feet of larger males, and only timely aid from his brothers had saved him from total destruction. His hair awry, he sat on the edge of a ditch, panting heavily and gathering new strength.

Just as the others stopped fighting, Juhani came up with his man, dragging him by the collar and choking him from time to time. The face of the oldest Jukola brother was a dreadful sight to behold. Rage burned in his rather small eyes, which were bloodshot and rolling wildly in his head. Salt sweat steamed from his face and he was huffing and puffing like a warhorse.

Juhani: Go and get my ABC, my alphabet book, this minute. Look, either you get it or I choke you till you burst a gut. For Christ's sake, get my red-bound ABC Book, you ape, or I'll let you have it like this.

Man from Toukola: Don't hit me!

Juhani: My ABC Book!

Man from Toukola: I threw it in the brush there.

Juhani: Get it and give it to me ever so nicely, you ape. Do you think this is some kind of dance we're doing? Are you going to get me that red-bound ABC Book?

Man from Toukola: You're crushing my throat — my throat?

Juhani: The ABC Book, God help us? The ABC Book?

Man from Toukola: Here, you monster.

Juhani: Give it a little kiss. Come now, kiss it nicely.

Man from Toukola: What? Kiss it?

Juhani: Kiss it oh so nicely. Do it, in God's name. If you can feel an itch, if life is dear to you, then do it, do it. Do it or your blood will call out for vengeance on me this very minute, as Abel's once did. You can see my face is as black with rage as a sauna troll's. So kiss the ABC Book and I'll pray for you for both our sakes. Now that's the way.

Man from Toukola: Are you satisfied?

Juhani: Very satisfied. Now go and thank the Lord you got off so easily. And if you should see any marks like those from the jaws of a vice on that piece of body between your head and shoulders, or if you feel anything like the mumps there, don't be too surprised. So go now. But a word, one more word, my friend. Who made up that song we had to listen to so attentively just now?

Man from Toukola: I don't know.

Juhani: Spit it out.

Man from Toukola: I don't know.

Juhani: Well, I can always find out. But give my regards to Aapeli Kissala and tell him that if we ever meet, his throat will sing a lot more shrilly than his clarinet just did. Go now, my company isn't exactly good for your health and don't start to mutter anything about getting even. Just be careful I don't take a notion to come after you and give you a little more for good measure.

Tuomas: Leave the poor thing alone now.

Juhani: He got what he had coming, I'll vouch for that. But let's get away from this torn and trampled patch of road. It's not safe here now;

the law takes a dim view of fighting on the highway. It can get a man into real trouble.

Aapo: Let's go. But what a lambasting that was. I would have been soundly dusted off if it hadn't been for Simeoni. He pulled a whole gang of them off me.

Simeoni: Oh, why did we lay hands on them? But man is weak and cannot master his rage or hold out against the power of sin. Alas, when I saw Tuomas laying men low with his fists, I thought it would come to murder.

Tuomas: Well, maybe I was a little careless, but blows have been struck for less. Let's hurry; it's getting late. They hurried off, but resentment and chagrin still showed on their faces and their hearts rankled sorely as they recalled the lampooning verses of the Toukola boys. Anger spurring his pace, a silent Juhani strode in the lead, shaking his head and spitting from time to time. Finally he turned to the others and spoke:

Juhani: Who in the devil made up that song?

Eero: Aapeli Kissala.

Aapo: That would be my guess too. He has a biting wit. He wrote the nasty lampoon about the old curate who, God help him, got ink smeared on his nose at the yearly reading test.

Timo: For a pint of liquor and a whispered word in the ear of Ananias Nikula, I'd soon have reams of verse to show the world what kind of man this Aapeli is. A worthless hobo wandering from place to place with his clarinet, knocking up maids and living off his old mother. He's a rat through and through.

Juhani: Listen, if that nonsense jingle they call "The Strength of Seven Men" is from his skull then the first time I see him, even if it's in the churchyard, I'll tear off a strip of his scalp from neck to eyebrows. But can't we have the law on him?

Aapo: The law won't convict a man without reliable witnesses.

Juhani: Then let him swear an oath of innocence. I think he'll think a little before casting his soul into the pit of hell. And if he does commit that wretched act, then good night neighbor and rest in peace as far as I'm concerned.

Aapo: I don't think the law permits a defendant in a case like this to take an oath.

Juhani: Then let him have a taste of my fists. They have the same healthy sting as the salt of the law and the courts.

Simeoni: Let's forget this song and this wild brawl on the road for the time being. There's the pine stump where I once fell asleep while tending the cattle and where I dreamed a wonderful dream. Although my belly was growling with hunger, I thought I was in heaven, sitting on a soft and yielding sofa. Before me was a table piled high with steaming foods — they were delicious, absolutely delicious, and so juicy. I ate and drank, and little cherubs waited on me as if I were a prince. Everything was beautiful and festive beyond compare. The music of an angelic choir rang out in a golden room next door; I could hear them singing the new and glorious song. That was my dream, and it kindled a spark in my breast which I hope will never die.

Juhani: It was the partner you had then, that old bookworm cowherd, that red-eyed, thin-whiskered Tuomas Tervakoski who addled your brains a bit — that was the spark.

Simeoni: Well, we shall see on Judgment Day.

Tuomas: There's the spruce tree where Father once shot a lynx — it was his last.

Timo: That's true. He never again came home on his feet but was dragged from the woods a dead man.

Juhani: He was a good man, a first-rate man, but as hard and unyielding as a rock with his sons. He was rarely seen in the yard at Jukola, but lived in the woods while the mice grew fat at home.

Aapo: It's true he neglected his home because of that cursed hunting fever, but he was a good father and he died an honorable death. May he rest in peace.

Timo: And that goes double for our mother.

Juhani: She was a virtuous and pious woman even if she couldn't read.

Simeoni: But she prayed on her knees morning and evening.

Juhani: So she did. She was a matchless mother and housekeeper. I'll always remember the way she marched between the plow handles as sturdy as a giantess.

Eero: She was a good mother, but why weren't we obedient children, toiling in the fields like seven bears? Jukola would be a different place now if we had. But how was I to know that when I was just a little brat in shirt-tails?

Juhani: Shut your mouth. I still remember the nasty, peevish way you treated poor Mother. But she always forgave you the way a father and mother usually do with their youngest. It's the oldest boy who always gets his hair pulled. How well I know it. The devil knows I've been whipped like a dog in my day. But I hope that with God's help it will all work out for the best.

Simeoni: Punishment really does good if you bless the rod and punish in God's name.

Eero: Especially if you warm up the rod first.

Simeoni: I won't listen to your infernal mockery, you blind, spoiled brat.

Timo: They say a good child punishes himself but that's a trick I'd like to see.

Simeoni: Here we are at the Sonnimäki crossroads. It was from the graveyard to this point that the dead man's ghost always followed the blasphemous glass-cutter of Kiikala, the one who uttered an awful, godless oath as he went by the church one night. Let this be a warning to you to shun the sin of cursing.

Juhani: We're on the crest of Sonnimäki Hill now and we can see the church. There gleams the sexton's red lodge like a flaming nest of devils. There all is hellish authority, frightful wisdom, and dread honor. Now my limbs grow numb; my legs refuse to obey me. Oh, what shall I, your miserable oldest brother, do in this hellish moment?

Eero: As our oldest brother, set us a good example and turn back from this road to hell. I'll be right behind you.

Tuomas: Quiet, Eero! Not one step backward.

Juhani: Oh horned devils! The sexton's door looks like death's gate.

Aapo: It's the door to respect and honor.

Juhani: A scalding honor, a scalding honor! Woe is me! There lies the sexton's pomp, the parsonage in all its glory, and my nature rebels — God help me — it rebels. What do you say, Timo?

Timo: It's not easy.

Aapo: No it certainly isn't, but then life isn't always a bed of roses.

Juhani: A bed of roses! When has it ever been a bed of roses?

Aapo: Life often gives us bitter pills to swallow, my brother.

Juhani: Bitter pills! Haven't we had enough bitter pills to swallow? Oh, my poor Aapo. We've been boiled in many a stew and our hair has been blown by many a storm. And all for what? What have we gained from it? This world is one big pile of manure, that's what it is. To hell with sextons and priests and reading-days and books and officials with their stacks of paper. They are our tormentors, every last one of them. But of course, when I said "books," I didn't mean the Bible, the Hymnal, the Catechism, and the ABC's, and not that horrifying book about the voice crying in the wilderness — I really didn't mean them. But why was I ever born?

Simeoni: Don't ever curse your days of grace.

Juhani: Why, oh why was I ever born?

Timo: I too was born to be a miserable wanderer here. Why couldn't I have seen the light of day as a hare-lipped bunny under that spruce tree over there?

Juhani: Or I as that squirrel on a pine limb, chattering away with his tail in the air? The cones are his carefree bread and the lichen his blanket in his mossy hut.

Timo: And he doesn't have to read either.

Aapo: Everyone has his assigned lot which is always made to fit the man. It does no good to whine and complain; the only remedy is work and toil. So onward now, my brothers.

Timo: Onward to the sexton's though it be through the roaring sea.

Juhani: What are you thinking of, Eero my boy?

Eero: I'm thinking of going to school.

Juhani: Well, let's go then. Let's get moving. Oh dear Lord. Sing brother Timo, sing.

Timo: I'll sing of the squirrel in his mossy bed.

Juhani: Sing, sing.

> *Sweetly sleeps the cheerful squirrel*
> *In his cabin built of moss.*
> *Never has the biting frost*
> *Or the huntsman with his snare*
> *Penetrated there.*
>
> *From his little room on high*
> *He can view the world around.*
> *Battles rage upon the ground.*
> *Overhead the peaceful banner*
> *Of a fir-bough flutters.*
>
> *Happy is the life he leads*
> *Rocking in his castle-cradle*
> *Lulled on the beloved breast*
> *Of his mother-spruce*
> *By a woodland harp.*
>
> *There the flutter-tail sits dozing*
> *At his tiny little window.*
> *Birds that sing beneath the sky*
> *Are his escort every eve*
> *To the golden land of dreams.*

CHAPTER III

Two days have passed. At a table in the main room of the sexton's house sit the brothers, mouthing the alphabet as it is repeated for them by the sexton or his little eight-year-old daughter. Open ABC books in their hands, sweat standing out on their brows, they pore over their lessons. But only five of the Jukola brothers are to be seen on the bench by the table. Where are Juhani and Timo? There they stand in the corner of shame near the door, their hair still tousled from the grasp of the sexton's strong hand.

The brothers have proven to be terribly slow learners and their teacher's frightful strictness is no help in their progress. Quite the contrary, it has further dulled their incentive and numbed their minds. Juhani and Timo have barely learned the letter "A"; the others have advanced a few more steps in learning their letters. Eero is the shining exception: he has gone beyond the alphabet and is deftly working at spelling out words.

Evening is drawing near, but the brothers have not had a crumb to eat all day. The sexton has confiscated their food to try the effect of hunger pangs as an incentive to learning. Hunger pinching his stomach, Juhani stands in the corner, spitting and shaking his head, and glowering at the sexton like a mad bull. Timo stands nodding by his side, indifferent to the affairs of this world.

Finally the sexton stops reading and says: "Stop now and eat, you woodenheads, go and chew your cud like goats in a pen. But remember that after this meal, not a crumb will pass your lips until you know the alphabet, you block-headed bulls. I'll give you an hour to eat, but you are not to step outside this door. In my opinion, it is good, very very good for you to be kept in until evening. But open your maws now; you'll soon have your paws on your feed bags." So saying, he left the room and sent the brothers' lunch to them by way of a maid servant. But when she left, the door was securely locked behind her.

Timo: Where's my bag?

Lauri: There's yours and here's mine. I'm so hungry I could eat rocks.

Juhani: We're not going to eat a crumb.

Lauri: What? We're not eating?

Juhani: Not a crumb.

Lauri: You'll sooner dam the ocean with your bare hands than stop me.

Juhani: Leave the bags nicely alone.

Aapo: What's the meaning of this?

Juhani: It's to spite the sexton. We won't eat until tomorrow. My blood is boiling, boys, and my head is spinning like Kerttula's windmill, but we'll give him tit for tat.

Aapo: That kind of spite will make the sexton split his sides laughing.

Juhani: Let him laugh. I won't eat. So Eero can spell already — well and good, but I won't eat.

Tuomas: Neither will I, not here anyway. But on Sonnimäki Heath, I will. I'll soon be sitting on a cushion of ferns there.

Juhani: That's it. Soon we'll all plump down there.

Eero: Count me in, boys.

Aapo: What madness are you up to now?

Juhani: Out of this prison.

Aapo: Listen to reason!

Juhani: Listen to the pines of Sonnimäki!

Eero: Right on. And hurrah to that, says reason.

Juhani: Spoken like a man.

Aapo: Simeoni, do your best.

Simeoni: Settle down now, brothers. But we're really not cut out for reading, so goodbye to all this hassle. Yet we'll lead a decent, upright life. As long as we believe, we can live as good Christians even if we don't know how to read.

Aapo: You're tearing down instead of building up, you wretch.

Juhani: Simeoni is only speaking right and reason. Let's go brothers. My nature can't take this any longer.

Tuomas: It burned my heart to see Juhani so badly roughed up. Let's get out of here.

Juhani: It's settled then. But don't feel sorry for me, Tuomas. Revenge is in my grasp. It's true I've been thumped and torn like crab bait, but I've got in my pocket a handful of flax plucked from my scalp by the sexton, and if I don't stuff it down his throat some day, it'll be because I'll have a thing made of it. The sexton has a neck, yes indeed, he has a neck — I say no more.

Eero: I have a better idea. Let's use the bunch of hair in your pocket to spin a fishing line and give it to the sexton as a gift to pay him for his good teaching. But why am I urging you to sin, since I know and we all agree how unspeakably much good punishment does, as we were saying in such a brotherly way on the road.

Juhani: Eero knows how to spell already. So just be a nice boy.

Eero: It's really a disgrace to study spelling when one is so old.

Juhani: So old? What about us?

Simeoni: He's needling you.

Juhani: So you're needling me again, you thorn in our wheat field, you sour lump in the Christian, brotherly bread-dough of Jukola, you porcupine, you prickly piglet, you frog.

Simeoni: Shh! The sexton will hear you.

Juhani: Out of this prison as one man. Anyone who objects gets his hide tanned.

Tuomas: Let' high-tail it, every last man.

Aapo: Timo, my gutsy brother, what do you say?

Timo: That you "can't make a silk purse out of a sow's ear" or "teach an old dog new tricks." So let's pack our bags and hit the road, all of one mind. And I'll clinch the case with one last proverb: "Sharpen both sides of a double ax."

Aapo: Lauri, what will you do?

Lauri: I'm for Sonnimäki.

Aapo: The very dead will cry out from their graves. "You stubborn mules, you madmen!"

Juhani: That won't help. It's "Forward March!" boys. Are you coming? If not, you'll be roasted and basted. Are you coming?

Aapo: I'm coming. But let me say one word more.

Tuomas: Even a thousand won't help.

Juhani: Not if every word were a thousand swords.

Eero: And every sword had a thousand blades.

Juhani: A thousand blades flashing fire. Let's leave this Marstrand, this Siberia, this wilderness, like seven shot from a canon. Here are the canon and the shot, a loaded cannon getting hotter and hotter, now it's red-hot and ready to explode. Oh my dear blood brothers, carried by the same mother, you saw how he wound my forelock around his index finger, then grabbed with his whole hand and shook like this until my teeth rattled. Hah!

Tuomas: I saw it and my cheeks puffed out with rage.

Eero: I heard Juhani's teeth rattle and saw Tuomas's cheeks puff out with rage and it shocked me, but I thanked God on your behalf, remembering how much good punishment does.

Juhani: Don't do it, my dear brother, don't touch a spark to the powder pan, to my two ears, that is. Don't do it!

Tuomas: Why make him angry, Eero?

Juhani: Eero is the sexton's pet. Well, that's good too, very good. But what wrong have I done to make the sexton torment me like this? Is it a crime to have a thick skull? I could almost cry.

Timo: What have I done to get my hair yanked so damnably? Is it because I have the brains that God in His wisdom gave me?

Lauri: I've had my hair pulled three times too.

Juhani: We all have sweet memories of this place. Open the door!

Aapo: But you can see that we're locked in.

Timo: There's a strong prop against the door.

Juhani: We'll snap it like a straw. But look, there's a window too. One swing of my bag and you'll hear a sweet clinking and tinkling sound.

Aapo: Your brains are really scrambled.

Juhani: From two days of beating, brother, two days of beating.

Simeoni: But let's not break the window. Let's talk things over calmly with the sexton.

Juhani: Go to hell and talk things over with the devil! Let's smash the window and get out of this jail. "Battalion, Fall Out!" as the captain shouted when he lost his temper.

Tuomas: Fasten the hook on the door, Eero.

Eero: That's the way. Lock the front gate while the battalion marches out the rear. There now, the hook is fast.

Aapo: I warn you!

Juhani: What's done is done. Watch this!

Aapo: You holy, godless terror.

Simeoni: Well then, it's done. There goes the window.

Juhani: The window smashed and the sky flashed with one swing of Jussi's bag. That was a knockout blow.

Simeoni: Woe is us!

Juhani: The way is open. Are you coming?

Simeoni: I'll follow you, dear brother.

Juhani: The way is open, Aapo. Are you coming?

Aapo: Drop your fists, you fool, I'm coming, I'm coming. What else is there to do once the fat is in the fire?

Juhani: Nothing but sit and burn.

Tuomas: Packs on backs and out the window. There's a banging out on the porch.

Juhani: Is it the sexton? I'll let him have one.

Tuomas: Come on.

Juhani: It is the sexton. I'll let him have just a little one.

Tuomas: Let's go, I tell you.

Juhani: Don't stand in my way. I love you, brother Tuomas, but...

Tuomas: I won't let you do such an awful thing. Just jump through the window with me now. The others are already running across the field. Come on!

Juhani: Let go of me. What awful thing are you afraid of? I'll just lift up his long coat tails and give him a whack with my bare hand, my good right hand. Let go of me, dear brother, or my heart will burst like Korkki's bagpipes. Let go! You see how my head is shaking.

Tuomas: We'll be enemies for life if you don't listen to me now. Listen to me!

Juhani: Well let's go then. But I wouldn't agree to this if I didn't love you dearly.

They stopped talking, leaped through the window into the yard, and dashed across the sexton's potato field. Gravel crunched underfoot and clods of earth flew through the air. Soon the two disappeared into a thick grove of alders after the rest. The sexton, in a frightful rage, charged into the room brandishing a thick rattan cane. He shouted after the fugitives in a loud, shrill voice, but all in vain. Out of the alder grove dashed the brothers, and went bounding over a stretch of rocks and crags, through a dense tract of yew, across the parsonage's wide Neulaniemi meadow with its reedy shore, and lastly over a flat, echoing wilderness clearing. Finally they stood on the sandy road beneath the slope of Sonnimäki. Up the rock-strewn rise they climbed, and having reached its crest, decided to pitch camp there on the heath under the pines. Soon the smoke of their campfire rose to the treetops.

The boys were lodged on high ground. From it they could see the curb roof of the parsonage beyond a hill. At the crest of the hill were the red-painted sexton's house, the church village, and there in its shelter of trees, the austerely handsome church. They could see the isle-studded lake, ruffled by a northeasterly breeze blowing softly and gently under the bright sky, over the lake and fields and forests, over the pine woods of Sonnimäki where the brothers rested and roasted their turnips at a blazing campfire.

Juhani: Now we'll have a royal feast.

Timo: A really high-class meal.

Juhani: Beef from our bags and roast turnip from the ashes. They'll be done in a second.

> *Light breezes rock the treetops above.*
> *Far away sounds the voice of my love.*

What pigheaded stupidity it was for us to sit for two whole damned days on the sexton's bench with our ABC books in our hands.

Eero: But to stand in the corner, that was something else.

Juhani: Good little Eero, wise little Eero, you Tom Thumb, you shrimp. In the sexton's corner, is that it? I'm going to teach you a lesson, you imp!

Aapo: Stop it, you heathens!

Tuomas: Calm down, Juhani. Pay no attention to what he says.

Juhani: Take off your hat when you eat, you turd.

Tuomas: That's what I say. Take it off.

Juhani: No two ways about it. You have to listen to us.

Simeoni: Always wrangling, forever wrangling. May God bring light to your minds and souls some day.

Juhani: He's always teasing me.

Eero: You keep calling me a grain of sand, a Tom Thumb, a little button. But that's why I'm so tough.

Juhani: You're a snappish little cur, as they say in the song, "The Strength of Seven Men."

Eero: I have sharp teeth and I bite back.

Juhani: You're full of spite.

Aapo: Let me get in a word. Maybe there's a kernel of truth in what Eero says. Maybe we have brewed the spite that he takes out on us now and then. Just remember, we're all the same Maker's handiwork.

Timo: Absolutely. And if I have two noses, one the size of a last and the other of half a loaf, is it anyone's business but my own? They're my noses. But let's forget all about noses and poses and makers and takers. Here Juhani, is a turnip as soft as a puffball. Sink your teeth into it and forget that brat's talk. He's young and stupid. Eat, brother.

Juhani: That I will.

Timo: Life is like a wedding celebration here on this high echoing hill.

Juhani: Like a wedding in heaven. But we were miserably treated Just now in that hell down below.

Timo: This world has its ups and downs.

Juhani: So it does. What does brother Aapo have to say now?

Aapo: I did my best, but it was no use. I'm not angry now, and for once I'm going to let fate decide things. Here I sit.

Juhani: Here we all sit with the world at our feet. Over there the sexton's house glows like a red rooster, and there the tower of the Lord's temple rises toward Heaven.

Aapo: Some day we'll sit at the foot of that tower in the black stocks of shame, heads bowed like seven young crows on a fence and hear people say as they point us out: "There sit the seven lazy brothers of Jukola."

Juhani: The day will never come that the boys of Jukola will sit in the black stocks of shame, heads bowed like seven young crows on a fence, and hear people say "There sit the seven lazy brothers of Jukola." That day will never come because I'll be hanged first or march with the Heinola Battalion carrying a rifle to the end of the world. For "why should I worry, a young rogue like me?" Now that we've eaten, my brothers, let's sing loud enough to shake the earth.

Simeoni: Let's ask a blessing and sleep.

Juhani: First we'll sing "Why should I worry." Clear your throat, Timo.

Timo: I'm ready.

Juhani: How about you, Eero-boy? Are we friends again?

Eero: Friends and brothers.

Juhani: All is well then. But crank up your throat.

Eero: It's in tune already.

Juhani: Good. The others can listen while the pine trees ring. Now, boys, let's hear it.

> *Why should I worry, a young rogue like me,*
> *Chest like a hillside, sturdy and free?*
> *Tralala tralala tralalala*
>
> *To find me some girls I'll fly this old coop*
> *And join the proud boys of Heinola's troop.*
> *Tralala tralala tralalala*
>
> *A uniformed hero I won't care the least*
> *For any old scarecrow like parson and priest*
> *Tralala tralala tralalala*
>
> *Trot along, Rusko, turning the wheels.*
> *The Czar's own hardtack will do for my meals.*
> *Tralala tralala tralalala*
>
> *So why should I worry, a young rogue like me,*
> *Chest like a hillside, sturdy and free.*
> *Tralala tralala tralalala*

Juhani: That's how it's done. Boy, this is the good life.

Simeoni: Less noise, less noise! You make a racket like a herd of trolls. Quiet, quiet! There are people coming.

Juhani: People? Look closer, and you'll see it's a band of gypsies. It's Rajamäki's Regiment.

The approaching procession was a roving family whose home was a small hut in the wilderness meadow of Rajamäki, on account of which everyone called them Rajamäki's Regiment. Their lord and master is the well-known Mikko, a short but agile man wearing a black felt hat. He peddles pitch on his rounds and deftly wields a sharp gelding knife. He also plies the fiddler's trade, making shrill music with his maroon-colored instrument of joy at dances and working-bee celebrations, stopping to drink whatever is offered.

His wife, a sharp-tongued woman with a snuff-stained face, is a skilled cupper. Rarely does she come to a sauna without its being set smoking in preparation for bleeding the neighborhood women. Then her blade dances, she smacks her lips to start the flow, and she sweats horribly, but her purse swells with her profits. They have a brood of children who follow them on their rounds from village to village and farm to farm. Two of them can travel on their own, skipping merrily down the road, now ahead of and now behind their parents, but the three youngest make up their parents' wagon load. Kaisa always pulls in the shafts while Mikko pushes from behind with a staff. The noise is deafening wherever they go, and a sarcastic wit had composed a long and mocking lampoon named for them. This was the rollicking troupe traveling the road below Sonnimäki Heath toward the church village as the brothers enjoyed their freedom like happy goats on the high ridge.

Juhani: Hey, hello! Hello, you regiment, hello!

Timo: "Who stole the till?" said the Swede.

Eero: "Cop oo see why?" said the Russian.

Kaisa: What do you want up there?

Eero: We want the woman to come up and suck a really sharp horn from my brother Juhani's brown butt.

Juhani: Mamma taps and sucks while the old man plays the fiddle — now aren't they a perfect match?

Mikko: Go to the devil, you Jukola raiders.

Eero: The old man won't play, so let's sing a rousing march.

Juhani: A rousing march, as we pass by the Rajamäki Regiment. Hit it, Timo and Eero.

> *Get ready now to hit the road,*
> *Take the hills without a hitch,*
> *Geld the stock and bleed the folk*
> *And sell the sacks of pitch.*
>
> *Snuff-faced Kaisa in the shafts*
> *Loves to pull the cart.*
> *Mikko chomping on his quid*
> *Pushes for his part.*

Juhani: That's the way. Now that's a rollicking song.

Kaisa: Now listen you devils, we're respectable people, but you roam the woods like thieves and wild animals. I bleed people and make them healthy, while Mikko gelds and makes fat pigs and stout steers and handsome geldings fit for kings of kings to ride. Hear that, you devils.

Juhani: A verse or two to top that sermon, boys. Timo and Eero, my lively lads, all together now.

> *On her cupping tool*
> *Kaisa smacks her lip.*
> *Greta talks through gritted teeth,*
> *Squirming in her grip.*
>
> *But what's that other racket*
> *Out there in the yard?*
> *Sows and boars are wailing,*
> *Piglets squeal so hard.*
>
> *Why are the sows all shrieking*
> *And teeth of piglets gnashing?*
> *Look, beneath the pigpen door*
> *Mikko's knife is flashing.*

Juhani: A really rollicking song, you can't deny that, Mikko.

Mikko: Keep your bread-trap shut, and know that I am Master Mikko, who snipped the governor's stallion above a clean sheet without spilling a drop of blood, and as a reward, got a license that the Roman Emperor himself couldn't revoke. That's the kind of Mikko I am.

Eero: Oh you double-died gelder Mikko with your witch-wife to boot.

Kaisa: Watch out or I'll bewitch you into a pack of wolves the way the old man did the wedding party.

Juhani: Here I stand in my very own pants still the same Juhani Jukola as ever, and hope to stand so from now on, with God's help. You poor old woman, no more will come of your witchcraft than did last year when you predicted the end of the world. All that did was cause a lot of women to ask their husbands to forgive them for being mean, and all for nothing.

Kaisa: Listen to my prophecy.

Eero: Go ahead and wish us a hot sauna and you to cup our necks.

Juhani: Now that's a stupid wish. I do mean to heat the sauna and take a nice bath, but I don't mean to get the slightest nick in the Adam's pelt on my neck.

Kaisa: Listen, just listen now. Your sauna will burn and your house will burn and you yourself will set out in a miserable state to wander the woods, bogs, and swamps seeking shelter for your freezing bodies. Ah, bloodily will you fight with men and wild beasts and lay your cursed head on a bush, gasping like a dying rabbit. Hear this and remember it.

Juhani: Go to hell...

Tuomas: Shut up, now, shut up!

Simeoni: You godless wild woman.

Juhani: Go to a fiery red hell. Go to the sexton and curse his throat with an everlasting case of the mumps.

Eero: And let him squeal and bellow like an old tusked boar in Mikko's hands.

Juhani: Yes, and as for the church provost, that rich, gilded, phony-pious, grease-and-sausage provost, what shall we serve up for him? Tell us, Eero.

Eero: Let his dinner roast turn out like the publican's at the gates of Oulu. Let him wind up with a cat-pie in his sack.

Juhani: Right, a Paltamo fish-pie with a hairy cat all ground up in it.

Eero: And let him preach a hellfire and brimstone sermon next Sunday, so fierce and violent that he busts his fat gut, busts it wide open.

Juhani: Yes, and then let the devil take him, grab him by the neck and fly off with him the way devils do with priests.

Eero: Let him carry off the high-and-mighty provost to keep the rich man company in hell.

Juhani: These are the greetings we want you to carry nicely to the sexton and the provost. And if you do all this, you can go ahead and charm me into a wolf the way you threatened to do.

Eero: Such a greedy wolf that he'll swallow up the Rajamäki Regiment in one gulp.

Juhani: Yes, and a sack of cupping horns to boot.

Eero: And the pitch sack for dessert.

Juhani: Right on the nail, you hammerhead.

Kaisa: Good. So we're to carry greetings to the sexton and provost from you. You'll drink of the same cup yourselves one day, damn you. Send them a stone as a goodbye gift, Mikko, one big enough to split a skull.

Mikko: Here's a good-sized stone, just made to order. Take that, you billygoats. Let's go, Kaisa. "Forward, March."

Juhani: The devil! He threw a rock and almost hit my forehead.

Eero: Let's send the ball back.

Juhani: Aim it so that it flattens the old man's hat.

Tuomas: Don't throw it, boy, if you want to stay in one piece.

Aapo: Don't you see the children there, you wretches.

Juhani: Don't throw. They're running so hard the ground is thumping.

Simeoni: Oh, you devils, you Mongolian mongrels, you dog-faced dingoes. A peaceful peddler can't even go by without being insulted. Oh, you villains.

Juhani: Me? I wouldn't touch a hair on their heads. But you know how it is when a man is all worked up and fits of rage run right through him... well, you know how it is. This man was locked up for two whole days. But I sent that sexton a fine greeting to let off steam.

Aapo: And an even more stupid one to the provost. We'll live to regret it some day.

Juhani: But why should I worry, a young rogue like me. A young man's life is like this roaring, echoing heath. There to the northeast rises the rough bulk of Impivaara and to the southwest shines the lake near the church village and other lakes gleam far off on the horizon. I can see the three lakes of Kolistin there.

> There is no help,
> there is no aid,
> I must into the lake.
> My sweetheart is so *angry,*
> She hisses like a snake.

Our old sexton often sits out on that lake with a fishing pole in his hand. Oh, if he were only sitting there now and I was a heavy gust of wind, a sudden sharp squall from the southwest, I would know where to come rushing in to turn his boat over.

Simeoni: What a sinful wish!

Juhani: I would do it. I would toss the boat and him along with it into a whole lake boiling like a stew.

Timo: And turn the man into a dish for the wolves.

Juhani: I'd throw him into a wolf pit and celebrate by dancing around it.

Aapo: Once the bear's enemy, the fox, lured him into a pit. He laughed and laughed as he circled the pit taunting the bear. Then he climbed on the back of a lynx which carried him to the top of a tall spruce tree nearby. The fox began to sing happily, calling the winds from all four quarters to sound like a harp in the spruce to accompany his song. Soon the winds came — east, west, and south — and the spruce tree roared and tossed. Then came a strong north wind, rushing through the mossy wilderness, roaring and crashing. The spruce tree howled, shook, and bowed deeply and finally cracked and fell toward the pit, tossing the fox from its top into the arms of the bear in the deep pit.

Timo: Well, damn it. What happened then?

Juhani: You can guess what happened. The bear took a good grip on the fox's body and shook it till its teeth rattled, the way the sexton shook me. But I see Aapo's point. He wants to remind me that the man who digs a pit for another may fall into it himself. That may be true, but I still want the sexton to fall into a wolf pit.

Timo: I wouldn't mind seeing him there either. But I wouldn't torture the old rag of a man in such a damp hole for long. Only for a couple of hours, that's all, and then let him live in peace, not even wishing him to fall into the bitter pit of my heart. But I'm amazed at one thing: How can you believe such blather as the story about a fox and a bear? Oh, my brothers, a fox isn't likely to talk such nonsense, much less call the winds of the world to help him. You may believe it, but I think it's nothing but a lie.

Juhani: Everyone knows that Timo's head isn't the world's best.

Timo: Maybe not. But I get along in this world as well as you or any other man or woman.

Aapo: Timo doesn't understand fables.

Juhani: Not at all, the poor boy. But look, Timo, I'll explain things to you. The tale of the bear and the fox must come from a time when all things in nature, even the trees, could talk. The Old Testament says so, and I've heard our dead blind uncle say so too.

Aapo: You don't understand the story or its meaning either.

Timo: And yet "the pot will call the kettle black," when one is as black as the other.

Juhani: Are you getting smart now? Believe me, I thank God I'm not as dumb as you are, my poor Timmy.

Timo: Maybe not, but it doesn't bother me.

Eero: Do what the publican once did, Timo. Just beat your breast and see who comes off the better man.

Juhani: So that little publican Eero is putting his two cents in.

Eero: That was a smart slap you just dealt little Zaccheus, the chief publican himself.

Juhani: I'm not interested in your Zaccheuses and your sweet slaps, but I'm going to lie down now for a sweet sleep like an ant hill under the snow. But God help us, because we've picked an awful place to stop.

Aapo: What do you mean?

Juhani: It is that strange and frightening stone that gives such a sad echo to the sound of the church bells. And look at the eyes that keep staring out at us. I'm scared. In God's name, let's get out of here.

Tuomas: Let's just sit here calmly.

Juhani: But there is a stern and angry forest-spirit here.

Aapo: Only for those who swear and act in ungodly ways. So don't you do it. But the story of the pictures on that stone is an old one.

Lauri: Won't you tell it to us?

Aapo: First look more closely at the stone. You can see four radiant golden spots on it. They are the melting eyes of two lovers, a pretty maiden and a proud young lad. You can see the outline of their images in the rock. Squint a little as you look. There they sit, joined in the sweetest of embraces, and at their feet crouches an old man pierced by a sword.

Timo: It's just as you say.

Lauri: I think I see something like that. But tell us the story.

And this is the tale that Aapo told:

A beautiful castle once stood near this spot, and its lord was rich and powerful. He had a motherless stepdaughter, as sweet and lovely as the dawn. A young man loved the girl, but the lord of the castle hated them both, for there was no room for love in his heart. The girl loved the proud youth too, and they often met on the echoing heath. The base of this very rock was their trysting place. But the girl's father learned of the alliance and swore a terrible oath to her: "My daughter," he said "don't ever let me find you in one another's arms in the woods at night. If I do, my sword will join you as one in a bloody death. This is my vow and my sacred oath." Thus he spoke, and the maiden was horror-stricken at the oath. But she did not forget the lord of her heart, and her love burned more hotly than ever.

It was a calm summer night. The maiden sensed in her heart that the youth was roaming the heath in search of his love. Finally, when she supposed everyone in the castle to be sound asleep, she started out on her love-journey wrapped in a thin, lacy shawl. Creeping out like a shadow, she disappeared into a dewy thicket with a flash of her blue shawl and was soon lost to sight deep in the woods. But not everyone in the castle was asleep. The lord himself stood by the window watching the maiden move off like a ghost in the night. He buckled on his sword, snatched up a spear, and disappeared into the woods on her trail, a beast of prey hunting a soft-eyed lamb.

The girl hurried panting over the heath and met her lover at the foot of the gray stone. There they sat in a blissful trance, arms around one another, whispering words of love. They were no longer of this world; their souls were wandering the flowery fields of Heaven. A few moments passed, and then the horrible lord of the castle rushed forward, driving his sharp spear with such force into the left side of the maiden that it passed through both of them, the point emerging from the right side of the youth. Thus did he join them in death. They sank down against the stone, and their blood flowed in a single stream, dyeing the blossoms of heather red. There, joined by the blade, they sat on their seat of stone, speechless but forever locked in a dying embrace.

And like four golden stars, their eyes shone upon the lord of the castle, who was struck with wonder at their unbelievable composure in the jaws of death. Suddenly a thunderstorm came up. The sky flashed and rumbled, and in the bluish glare of the lightning, the eyes of the young couple shone with blessed joy, like four candles in the holy air of a heavenly chamber. The murderer gazed at the sight while the wrath of heaven raged around and above him. The dimming beauty in the eyes of the young, the torrent of blood, the thunder in the heavens spoke strongly to his soul. For the first time, he was moved: cold, black remorse stirred in his heart as he gazed at the wondrous eyes of the dying pair, which continued to shine happily upon him. His heart trembled with dread as heaven thundered and lightning flashed and spirits of horror assailed him on all sides. A boundless rage gripped his soul.

He looked once more at the young pair, but their eyes still shone smiling upon him, although now they were dimmer. Then he folded his arms and turned a frozen stare toward the east. For a long time he stood there in the gloom of night. But at last he threw back his head and loosed a long scream, a long, frightful scream that resounded through the region. Again he stood silent for a time, listening long and intently until his cry had died out in the remotest distance. When that happened, still looking east, he once more screamed horribly. For a long time the cry echoed through the area, while he listened intently as it rebounded from crag to crag. But finally the trembling voice died away in the distance, the lightning ceased, and the glow was gone from the eyes of the young: only a heavy rain sighed in the woods. Suddenly, as if awakened from a dream, the lord snatched his sword from its scabbard, plunged it into his breast, and fell at the feet of the young. The sky flashed once more, flashed and thundered, but soon silence reigned over all.

Morning came and the dead were found at the foot of the stone on the heath. They were carried away, and laid side by side in a grave. But since that time, their images can be seen in the stone: two young people in each other's arms, with a stern, bearded man on his knees below them. And four wondrous orbs, like four golden stars, shine day and night from one side of the stone, recalling the beautiful, fading eyes of the lovers. A long bolt of lightning, so the story says, etched these images in the stone with its flame. And just as they are in the picture, the young man and the maiden sit happily enthroned on high, and the lord of the castle, like the man there, grovels on his bed of punishment. And whenever the bells in the belfry ring, he strains his ears to hear the echo from the rock, but the tolling is always a dismal sound. But some day, a marvelously gentle and happy note will sound from the rock, and that will be the moment of atonement and salvation for the man, but it will also mean that the world's last moment is at hand. Therefore people always listen uneasily to the echo from the rock whenever the bells are ringing. They would gladly accept the man's atonement, but they are terrified when they think of the day of judgment.

Such was the story Aapo told his brothers on Sonnimäki Heath.

Timo: But what a long time the old man has to sweat it out! Until judgment day! Oh my!

Simeoni: You dumbbell. Watch out that the trumpet of doom doesn't sound right this minute.

Eero: There's no need to fear the end of the world as long as there are heathens left on earth. And, God mend us, here are seven wild pagans in the very heart of Christendom. But nothing is so bad that some good can't be found in it. We're pillars of the world, we are.

Juhani: You a pillar of the world, you six-incher?

Simeoni: You laugh now Eero, but you'll shiver and shake when the last day arrives.

Timo: No he won't, I guarantee you. But oh, what chaos and confusion there will be on that day. Two upheavals have already taken place; the third is yet to come. Then the sign of great bliss will appear. Then the earth will turn to dust and ashes like a dry birch-bark shoe. Then the cattle in the pastures will bawl and the pigs in the lane will squeal, that is, if destruction comes in the summer, but if it should come in the winter, the cattle will rear and bellow in the barn and the poor pigs will scream in the straw of their pens. Then there will be a huge commotion. There have already been two upheavals; the third is yet to come, as our blind uncle used to say.

Simeoni: Yes, let us remember that day.

Juhani: Silence, brothers. God keep us, but you make a man's heart do flip-flops with that kind of talk. Go to sleep, just go to sleep.

So did they speak, but at last the conversation flagged and one by one they dropped off to sleep. The last one awake was Simeoni, who sat in deep meditation on these last days of the world and that great Day of Judgment. His eyes burned with a moist red fire and the bronze flush on his coarse cheeks shone from afar. Finally he too slept, and they all lay in sweet dreams by the fire, which glowed for awhile but gradually faded and died.

Twilight fell and thickened into night. The air was soft and warm. Now and then a flash lit up the sky to the northeast, for a violent thunderstorm was brewing. It approached the church village with the speed of an eagle, hurled fire from its womb, and touched into flame the parsonage grain-drying barn, which was full of dry straw and soon flared up like a huge torch. The bells in the village began to ring and the village to stir; people rushed in from every direction, a flood of men and women, but all to no avail. The barn burned frightfully, and the arch of the sky turned blood red. Now the wind gusted toward Sonnimäki, where the brothers lay in a deep sleep, the heath resounding to their snores. But they will soon awaken to a dreadful peal of thunder and get the worst scare of their lives. Horror will seize their sleep-befuddled senses, for the first thing to come to mind will be the sad story they have heard, and images of the world's end, as nature rages around them in the dismal night. Whatever light there is will come from the flashes of lightning and the strange glow from the billowing flames in the village.

A flash of lightning ensued, followed instantly by an enormous peal of thunder that awakened the brothers immediately. With shrill screams, they leaped to their feet as one man. Tousled hair standing on end like reeds, eyes wide as saucers, they stared at each other for a few moments.

Simeoni: Judgment Day!

Juhani: Where are we? Where are we?

Simeoni: Is this the end?

Juhani: Help us, have mercy!

Aapo: How terrible! How terrible!

Tuomas: It's more than terrible!

Timo: Heaven protect us poor boys!

Simeoni: The bells are already ringing.

Juhani: The rock is jingling and dancing. Aaai-eee!

Simeoni: "The bells of heaven are ringing."

Juhani: "And the powers of earth are failing."

Simeoni: Is this the way it will end?

Juhani: Help us, mildness and mercy.

Aapo: How terrible!

Juhani: Tuomas, Tuomas, grab my coat tails. Aaai-eee!

Simeoni: Aaai-eee! We're going, we're going!

Juhani: Tuomas, my brother in Christ!

Tuomas: Here I am. What do you want?

Juhani: Pray!

Tuomas: Yes, let's pray now.

Juhani: Timo, pray if you can.

Timo: I'll try.

Juhani: Right now.

Timo: Oh God of great sorrow and Bethlehem, seat of mercy!

Juhani: What does Lauri have to say?

Lauri: I don't know what to say amid all this misery.

Juhani: Misery, endless misery. But I don't think this is the end quite yet.

Simeoni: Oh, if we only had one day of grace.

Juhani: Or a week. One precious week! But what are we to make of that awful light and the wild jangling of bells.

Aapo: There is a fire in the village, good people.

Juhani: That's right, Aapo, and the alarm bell is clanging.

Eero: The parsonage grain barn is on fire.

Juhani: Let a thousand grain barns burn, as long as this worm-eaten world and its seven sinful children survive. God help us. My whole body is swimming in a cold sweat.

Timo: My very breeches are shaking.

Juhani: What a time!

Simeoni: This is God's punishment for our sins.

Juhani: That's true. Why did we have to sing that nasty song about Rajamäki's Regiment?

Simeoni: There was no sense of shame in the way you made fun of Mikko and Kaisa.

Juhani: That's true. But God bless them and God bless us all. God bless every one and the sexton too.

Simeoni: That prayer will be welcome in Heaven.

Juhani: Let's leave this awful place. From here the flames look like the fiery furnace of destruction, and those eyes glow so sadly from the side of the rock. You know it was Aapo's story about those cat's eyes that first sent the shivers down our spines. But let's get going, and don't any of you forget his bag and ABC book. Let's go, brothers. Let's go to see Kyösti at Tammisto Farm, with God's help, and then go on home tomorrow if we're still alive. Let's go now.

Lauri: But we'll soon be caught in a heavy rain. It'll soak us like rats.

Juhani: Let it soak, let it soak. We have been granted mercy. Let's go now!

They charged off, hot-footing it one after the other, and soon reached the sandy road along which they headed toward Tammisto Farm. Lightning flashed and thunder roared over the length and breadth of the sky, but they kept on walking until a heavy rain began to pour down on them. Then they broke into a run till they reached the "Ku-lomäki Spruce," a tree famed for its height and density. It stood just off the road and had afforded shelter from the rain to many a traveler. At its foot sat the brothers, while the storm raged and the huge spruce moaned in the wind, but when the weather lifted, they went on their way. Nature grew calm: the wind died down, the clouds disappeared, and a yellow moon rose above the treetops. Easy and carefree, the brothers strode along the splashy road.

Tuomas: I've often wondered what thunder is and where it comes from — all that flashing and roaring.

Aapo: Our blind uncle said that the uproar in the sky is caused when dry sand carried upward by the wind gets in between chunks of clouds.

Tuomas: Maybe that's it.

Juhani: But a child's mind can imagine anything. Do you know what I thought about thunder when I was a shirt-tailed kid? I thought that God, you see, was driving around Heaven, and the iron-rimmed wheels of his wagon were striking sparks from the rocky roads. Ha, ha, ha! Kids have such childish minds.

Timo: What about me? I used to think something like this when I was just a little squirt trotting down the lane in shirt tails. God is harrowing the fields up there, I thought, He's harrowing the fields and sharply cracking His bull-pizzle whip, and when a blow lands on the fat rump of His gelding, it gives off sparks, like the haunch of a well-fed horse when you rub it. That's what I used to think.

Simeoni: When I was a child, I used to think — and I still do — that this flashing and roaring is a sign of God's anger at sinners on earth, for great are man's sins and numberless as sands in the sea.

Juhani: Sinners there are here, one can't deny it, but they are salted and peppered and parboiled here too. Think of our trip to school, my boy, and what we suffered while it lasted. The sexton clawed and dusted us like a hawk. I can still feel it, and it makes me grit my teeth, my boy.

But their night-time journey came to its end with their arrival at the Tammisto house. They entered soberly and Kyösti made up comfortable beds for them. This Kyösti was as stout as an oak and was the only son of the house, but had no desire to take it over. He preferred to live as he pleased and to be left alone. At one time he had roamed about the village like one possessed, preaching and shouting at people. It was said that brooding on religious matters had brought him to this state. When he became lucid again, he was the same as before, but he never ever laughed. Another peculiar thing happened. From then on, he considered the Jukola brothers his best friends, although he had scarcely known them earlier. This was the man with whom the brothers found lodging for the night.

CHAPTER IV

Next day the Jukola brothers once again were seen approaching their home, walking single file. But they were in a wretched state, their clothing in shreds and their faces mottled with cuts and bruises. Juhani, their leader, sported a left eye that was swollen nearly shut, Aapo's lips were puffed up hugely, an enormous lump jutted out from Timo's forehead, and Simeoni hobbled along in their wake. All their heads had been badly pummeled; one had an empty lunch bag wrapped around his, while another had torn strips of cloth from his jacket to bind his wounds. Such was their appearance on their return from their scholarly sojourn. Their dogs Killi and Kiiski rushed forward to fawn happily upon them, but the brothers were unable to return the caresses of their faithful watchdogs.

But who had treated them so badly? Who had humbled the sturdy Jukola brothers? An act of revenge it was, wrought by the men of Toukola. Learning that the Jukolas were at Tammisto, they had joined forces twenty strong and hidden in thickets by the roadside to await their enemies. For a long time they dozed and kept watch, stout weapons in hand. When the scholars finally approached, they charged out upon them with fiery speed, attacking from both sides of the road. A dreadful play of clubs ensued, in which the brothers were badly beaten. But the men of Toukola did not emerge unscathed from the fray. Many of them felt the dizzying effects of the brothers' fists. Two of their number, Eenokki Kuninkala and Aapeli Kissala, were carried home unconscious. A strip of Aapeli's skull was laid bare from neck to forehead and shone like a pewter pot. It was Juhani's hand that wrought this rough job of defoliation.

At length the completely exhausted brothers sat in the spacious main room of their home.

Juhani: Whose turn is it to heat the sauna?

Timo: It's mine.

Juhani: Heat it till the stones crack.

Timo: I'll do my best.

Juhani: Do it right because we badly need the steam for our wounds. And Eero, you go to Routio for a quart of liquor. I'll pick the best tree in our woods as payment. A quart of liquor.

Simeoni: Maybe that's too much.

Juhani: It's hardly enough to make up a salve for seven men. God knows we have as many wounds as there are stars in the sky. This eye of mine stings and throbs badly enough, but the heart and gall inside me are even worse. But all is well, all is well. Jussi Jukola is still alive and kicking.

Evening fell, a melancholy September evening. Eero returned from Routio with the liquor and Timo brought word that the sauna was ready. Their surly mood softening a bit, the brothers went to bathe. Timo threw on the water, the blackened stones of the fireplace cracked, and clouds of hot steam floated about the sauna. Each man now swung a lovely sap-soft bath whisk with all his might. They bathed and steeped their wounds and the brisk slapping of the bath whisks could be heard far away from the sauna.

Juhani: The whisks are dancing a real Turkish polska on our wounds. Sauna steam is the best cure on earth for a sick body and soul. But my eye stings like the devil! Well, let it sting and smart away, I'll pour on the heat all the more. How is your snout, Aapo?

Aapo: It's softening up little by little.

Juhani: Slap away and beat it like a Russian his nag, and that will soften it. Throw on more steam, Timo, since it's your turn to wait on us tonight. That's the way, my boy, just let it come. It's really hot, really hot in here. That's the way, my slippery brother.

Lauri: It burns my fingernails.

Juhani: Let them take a beating too.

Aapo: Stop throwing on water now, boy — we'll all be driven out.

Eero: Praise him a little more and we'll all be burned to a crisp.

Juhani: That'll do, Timo, don't throw any more. Damn it, don't throw any more! Are you going down, Simeoni?

Simeoni: I'm going down, all right, poor me. Oh, if only you knew why.

Juhani: Tell us.

Simeoni: Remember the furnace of the damned, man, and pray day and night.

Juhani: What rot! Let's take care of our bodies. The hotter the steam, the better and stronger the cure. You know that very well.

Simeoni: Whose warm water is this in the bucket near the fireplace?

Juhani: It's mine, as the smith said of his home. Don't touch it.

Simeoni: I'll just take a little splash of it.

Juhani: Don't do it, dear brother, or there will be trouble. Why didn't you heat your own?

Tuomas: Why squabble about nothing? Take some of mine, Simeoni.

Timo: Or some of mine under the benches there.

Juhani: Take some of mine, then, but leave at least half.

Lauri: Eero, you devil, watch out or I'll throw you down from the benches.

Aapo: What tricks are you two up to there in the corner?

Juhani: What are you squabbling about, hey?

Lauri: Blowing on a man's back.

Aapo: Behave yourself, Eero.

Juhani: Hey, you pest!

Simeoni: Eero, Eero, doesn't even the broiling heat of the sauna remind you of hellfire? Remember Juha Hemmola, remember Juha Hemmola.

Juhani: On his sickbed, he saw the fiery lake from which he was saved one more time because, as they told him, the sauna benches always reminded him of hell. But is that daylight shining through the corner?

Lauri: Bright daylight.

Juhani: Oh damn it, this sauna is on its last legs. So let my first job as master of the house be a new sauna.

Aapo: We need a new one, all right.

Juhani: A new one, a new one, that can't be denied. A house without a sauna is bad both for bathing and birthing the children of wives and servants. Yes, a smoking sauna, a barking dog, a crowing cock, and a mewing cat — these are the signs of a good house. Yes, the man who takes over this farm will have his hands full. We need a little more steam again, Timo.

Timo: You've got it.

Simeoni: But remember that it's Saturday night.

Juhani: And let's see to it that our skins don't wind up hanging on the rafters the way that servant girl's once did.

Simeoni: The girl never bathed with the others, but kept dawdling in the sauna after they were already asleep. And one Saturday night, she stayed there later than usual. They went to look for her then, but what did they find? Nothing but her skin hanging on the rafters. It had been stripped by a master hand, for her hair, eyes, ears, lips, and even her nails were still attached to it.

Juhani: Let this story be a — Ow, ow, how the steam stings my back. It feels as if it hadn't tasted a switch since New Year's.

Lauri: But who skinned her?

Timo: Who? Who? You should ask? Who else but...

Juhani: Old Nick himself.

Timo: Right. The one who roams around like a roaring lion. What an awful story!

Juhani: Hand me my shirt from the rafters, Timo-boy.

Timo: This one?

Juhani: Hmmh! He offers Eero's patch of a shirt to a grown man. Darn you, the one in the middle.

Timo: This one?

Juhani: Now that's a grown man's shirt. Thanks. That was an awful thing — what we were just talking about. But let it remind us that "the evening crowns the feast." Let's wash ourselves as clean as a baby from a midwife's quick hands and then into the house with shirts under our arms to take the cool air on our burning bodies — I think this eye of mine feels a little better now.

Simeoni: But my leg doesn't. It hurts and stings like burning ashes. What's to become of me with it, poor thing that I am.

Eero: Go nicely to bed when you get in and pray salve onto your leg and thank your Creator who watched over you today to "keep you from bruising your foot on a stone" as our evening prayer says.

Simeoni: I don't hear you, I don't hear you.

Eero: Then pray for an ear-salve too. But get moving or you'll be left as prey for the devil.

Simeoni: My ears are closed to you, closed in a spiritual sense. Do you understand, man?

Eero: Come on now, or your skin will soon be hanging on the rafters in a real and bodily sense.

Naked and steaming, they entered the house, bodies aglow like the sun-baked bark of a cherry birch. Once inside, streaming with sweat, they sat down to rest awhile and then gradually dressed themselves. Now Juhani began to cook up a salve for the wounded brotherhood. He set an old metal pan without a handle on the fire, poured the quart of liquor into it, then stirred in two cups of gunpowder, a cup of sulphur, and an equal amount of salt. When it had boiled for an hour, he set the concoction to cool, and the salve, a kind of pitch-black gruel, was ready. They rubbed it onto their wounds, especially those about their heads, and spread fresh, yellowish-brown pine tar over it. They gritted their teeth and wore black looks on their faces, so fiercely did the bitter medicine sting in their wounds. Then Simeoni set out their supper: seven ring-loaves of rye, a round of dried beef, and a heaping bowl of baked turnips. But they had little taste for food that night and soon left the table, stripped off their clothing, and lay down on their beds.

It was a dark night, and stillness reigned over all. But a sudden glow lighted up the area around the Jukola house — the sauna had caught fire. Timo had heated the gray stone fireplace so hot that it caused the wall to smolder and finally burst into flame. And so the building burned to the ground in perfect peace, unseen by a single eye. When morning dawned, only a few smoldering embers and the glowing ruin of the fireplace were left of the Jukola sauna. Finally, around noon, the brothers awakened and rose somewhat refreshed from the previous night. They dressed and began to eat the food which now seemed to taste better. For a long time they ate in silence, but at last they began to discuss the violent incident on the road between Tammisto and Toukola.

Juhani: We took a real beating, but they jumped us like bandits with their staves and poles. If only we'd had weapons and been on the lookout for danger. They would be sawing coffin boards now, and the gravedigger would be busy in Toukola today. Anyway, I gave Aapeli Kissala what he had coming.

Tuomas: There's a white hairless streak from his forehead to his neck, like the Milky Way in an autumn sky.

Juhani: You saw it?

Tuomas: I saw it.

Juhani: He got his. But the others, the others, Lord Jesus.

Eero: They'll feel our revenge in their bones yet.

Juhani: Let's put our heads together and come up with a revenge that no one can match.

Aapo: Why bring on unending destruction? Let's resort to law and justice and not to our fists.

Juhani: The first man from Toukola I can dig my claws into, I'm going to eat alive, every hide and hair of him, and there's your law and justice.

Simeoni: My poor brother, do you ever hope to inherit the kingdom of heaven?

Juhani: What do I care about heaven as long as I get to see Matti Tukkala's blood and guts.

Simeoni: You monster, you monster, you make me weep.

Juhani: Go weep for a dead cat and not for me. Hah, I'll grind them into sausage.

Tuomas: I'll get even for this beating some day, I promise. I swear I will. Only a wolf treats a man like that.

Juhani: A savage wolf. I swear to do the same.

Aapo: Revenge will only rebound on our own necks, but the law's decree will punish them and reward us.

Juhani: But the law won't make them feel the wounds that sting us.

Aapo: So much the worse for their wallets and their honor.

Simeoni: Let's forget about revenge, bloody revenge, and put our trust in the law. That's what I'm for, although I'm scared to death of the noise and bustle in court.

Juhani: Well, if it comes to that, here's a boy who can hold his own even in court. It's true my heart was pounding a bit when we first stood at the bar, but a real man soon recovers. I still remember the time I was a witness for poor Kaisa Koivula when she was asking for child support. I remember how the bailiff yelled out, "Juhani, the son of Juhani Jukola from Toukola!"

Timo: "And his younger brother Timotheus!" I was there too, and Kaisa got a father for her child just like that. I was a witness there too, Juhani.

Juhani: So you were, so you were. But what a crowd there was in the hall, on the stairs, and out in the yard. I sat in the hall talking to

Kyösti Tammisto about what a man should say in court and how he should say it. I was all wrapped up talking to him just then, and he was picking at his coat buttons like this, when that wolf-caller, the bailiff, shouted so loud that everyone pricked up his ears and stared pop-eyed: "Juhani, the son of Juhani Jukola of Toukola!"

Timo: "And his younger brother Timotheus!" And doggone if Kaisa didn't get a father for her child.

Juhani: She sure did.

Timo: Even though we weren't put under oath.

Juhani: It's true we weren't, but our plain, honest testimony made a big impact.

Timo: Hey, and our names were written down on records and petitions that went all the way to the Czar.

Juhani: That's a well-known fact. So the bailiff shouted and this boy's heart skipped a beat, but he soon got used to things and spoke the rock-solid truth like the apostle himself, without a thought to the crowd's giggling and laughing.

Timo: That's how things are in court when all goes well, but there's many a snare set and many a quick foot out to trip you up there.

Juhani: That's right, but truth and justice win out in the end, even with all their tricks.

Timo: That's true, even with all their tricks and dodges. Unless there is the very devil of a lawyer who can turn night into day and day into night and black tar into buttermilk. But why two when one will do? Why didn't God put court verdicts on a firmer footing here, a foolproof foundation? Why have witnesses, long-drawn out inquiries, and lawyers' tricks? This is what I think would be the quickest way to truth and justice when a case is unclear and can't be sifted out. Have the whole court, with the judge in the lead, step out into the yard and have the bailiff blow a great big birchbark horn, to be called the court horn; he would tootle a few blasts with the horn pointing up at the sky. Then the sky would open up and the angel of justice would appear to all the people, asking in a loud voice, "What does the bailiff want?"

The bailiff would answer in a loud shout, "Is the accused innocent or guilty?" Now the bright angel would give an answer which would leave nothing to doubt and accordingly the man would either have to be left to God's care or be given a sound whipping. In that way everything would go well, I think.

Juhani: Why all the orders and rigamarole. This is how I have the thing doped out. The Creator might have set things up like this: Let the accused confirm his words with an oath, a sacred oath, and if he swears the truth, let him march off home a free man, but if he's a liar, let the wormy earth open up under his feet and swallow him down into hell. That would be the shortest way to the truth.

Aapo: That might work out, but maybe everything is for the best just as the Father of Wisdom first set it up.

Juhani: For the best? Here we sit torn and bruised and half-blind, like tomcats in March. Is this right? The devil it is! The world is the craziest thing to be found under the sun.

Simeoni: The Lord has made it so to test the strength of people's faith.

Juhani: The strength of faith? He tries and tests men, but that testing sends souls swarming thick as mosquitoes to the everlasting sauna, to a place where I wouldn't even send a snake, sinner that I am.

Tuomas: Life on this earth is a hard game. There's small hope for a man when only Joshua and Caleb were chosen from among six hundred thousand.

Juhani: Right. What is this life? The doorway to hell.

Simeoni: Juhani, curb your thoughts and your tongue.

Juhani: In my darker moods, I see life as hell itself, where I'm a soul in torment and the men of Toukola are pitchfork-wielding devils. And people behave like evil spirits to us.

Aapo: Let's look into our own hearts a little. Maybe we've kindled and kept their hate alive ourselves. Remember how we romped through their turnip fields and pea patches, tramped down their riverside hayfields on our fishing trips, shot the bears they had cornered, and pulled many other such tricks, deaf to the law and the voice of conscience.

Simeoni: We've made heaven and earth angry. Often when I go to bed and remember the wicked deeds of our youth, the fiery sword of conscience painfully pierces my breast and I seem to hear a strange rustling like a far-off sigh of rain, and a sad voice seems to whisper in my ear, "God and man sigh for the seven sons of Jukola." Ruin threatens us, my brothers, and our lucky star won't shine until we are reconciled to people. Why shouldn't we first ask forgiveness and then promise to change our ways from now on?

Eero: I'd weep if I could. Simeoni, Simeoni, "It wouldn't take much..." Yeah, it wouldn't take much. "But go your way now."

Simeoni: Well, we'll see what's what on Judgment Day.

Timo: Will I change my ways and ask forgiveness? I don't think so.

Tuomas: Not till the raven turns white.

Eero: Which will happen when we "come to judgment." Then the raven will be as white as snow, in the words of the boy and the song of his loving granny. As for me, I'll gladly wait till the last second before I start to pray.

Juhani: Believe me, Simeoni, it's not healthy to be forever checking the state of our souls, to be forever remembering the fires of hell, or the devil and his imps. Such thoughts either muddle a man's head or make him put a rope around his neck. We should think of those crazy old stunts of ours as wild oats and not as sins in the strictest sense of the word. And besides, I've come to believe that sometimes a person has to shut his eyes and pretend not to see what he sees and know what he knows. That's what a man has to do if he wants to get through life's rock-crusher with a whole skin. Stop gaping at me like that; there's no reason to. I'm talking about those little sins toward God, not toward our neighbors. Neighbors and kin are proud and touchy and have to protect their own interests just like me, but God is a far-seeing and merciful man and always forgives in the end if we pray with a sincere heart. Yes indeed, I mean, it's not healthy to be always and forever splitting hairs and putting our actions and those little misdeeds of ours directly into the scale with God's word and commandments. It's better to back off halfway: we should avoid foul sins in every way, I say, and pray for salve for our eyes, but as for those smaller sins — toward God, I mean — let's not always be hanging them to weigh on the hooks of our conscience, but back off halfway, back off halfway.

Simeoni: Good God! That's the kind of thing Satan whispers into people's ears.

Timo: The way old lady Olli eggs on Mäkelä's wife when she needs a drink.

Aapo: I'm surprised and angry at these words of Juhani's. Brother, is that what God's commandments teach us? Is that what Mother taught us? Not by any means. In God's eyes, one is as a thousand and a thousand is as one. Why are you babbling about lesser sins then, about backing off halfway? You are advocating the service of two masters. Tell me Juhani, what is sin?

Juhani: What is truth, you Solomon of Jukola, Lord Big-Mouth, and Pope of Savo? "What is sin?" What a wise question, how wonder-fully wise! "A good head that boy of ours has," it's true he has. So why say any more? "What is sin?" Aha! What is truth? I ask you.

Tuomas: Why twist and turn, boy? Admit that you're teaching devil's doctrine.

Juhani: I'll give you a strong living example to back my belief. Remember the church-village tanner. The man started to get strange notions about his soul, and about sin and worldly riches, and began to change his former ways completely. He suddenly stopped dealing in hides on Sundays and holidays, not caring how important it was for farmers to take care of two matters on one trip to town. When his friends saw his work shrinking from day to day while that of his brother tanner next door grew and grew, they tried in vain to warn him. But the fool would always answer: "God will ever bless the work of my hands, though there be less of it, but he who thinks to snatch the bread from my mouth, he will in the end reap curses from the sweat of his brow, for he has not honored the Lord's Sabbath." Thus he spoke, and on Sundays he went gawking around, hymnal in hand, goggle-eyed and hair standing on end like Pete the Bomber's. But what happened to him in the end? That we know. He soon had a heavy rod to carry, a beggar's staff, and the open road for his path. Now he wanders from village to village tipping a glass whenever he can. I met him once beside the road on Kanamäki Ridge. He was sitting on the edge of his sled, very drunk, the poor man. "How are things, tanner?" I asked. "Things are as they are," he answered with a cold glare. But again I asked how the master was doing. "I do as I do," he answered once more and set off, pushing his sled before him and yodeling some crazy kind of song. That was the end of him. And what about the other tanner? He got very rich, and died a rich and happy man.

Aapo: A narrow creed and spiritual pride ruined the tanner and the same thing happens to all of his kind. No matter what you say, you are still teaching wrong doctrine and belief.

Simeoni: False prophets and the end of the world.

Timo: He's trying to tempt us to the Turk's belief. But you can't sway me. I'm sure and strong, as sure and strong as the eye of an ax.

Juhani: Hand me that half a loaf from the end of the table, Tuomas. "False prophets"? I'm tempting no one to sin and wrong. I wouldn't steal an awl from a cobbler or the eye of a needle from a tailor. But my heart burns when what I say is always twisted to the worst meaning, made pitch-black when dark-brown would do.

Aapo: You spoke so plainly and reasoned things out so clearly from point to point that there was no mistaking your meaning.

Timo: I'll bet my hat that he was trying to convert us to the Turkish faith.

Simeoni: God have mercy on him!

Juhani: Shut your trap right now! Praying to God for my sake and scolding me like a weak-eyed preacher. It won't work. I have just the right amount of brains, even if I'm not pure wisdom like our Aapo, for example.

Aapo: God mend us! Even he isn't wise enough.

Juhani: Pure wisdom, pure wisdom! And keep your bread-trap shut or you'll get this shin-bone across your snout a little worse than yesterday. That's what I have to say. And I'm going to stop eating now, because my belly is full.

Timo: We're all as full as sucking horse-flies, I'll swear to that.

Eero: But why don't I see the sauna?

Juhani: What could a sawed-off shrimp like you see? But — the sauna is gone to hell!

Eero: No, but to heaven in a fiery chariot.

Juhani: Could it have burned?

Eero: How do I know and what business is it of mine? It belongs to the master of Jukola, not to me.

Juhani: Eero steamed his carcass there yesterday evening too, if I remember rightly. Oh well, the master's to blame for everything that I know. But let's go and see. Where's my cap? Let's go and see, brothers. I know our sauna is ashes.

They went to see what the sauna was like. All that was left of it were the blackened fireplace and smoking rubble. The brothers gazed at the scene of destruction for some time with troubled minds and finally returned to the house. Juhani brought up the rear carrying two iron hinges, which he angrily tossed onto the table.

Juhani: So. Jukola Farm is without a sauna now.

Eero: "And a house without a sauna won't do," says Juhani.

Juhani: Timo heated the dear old fireplace too hot, and the sooty walls and rafters we loved, which sheltered us when we were born, are burned to ashes. Timo heated the fireplace too hot, I say.

Timo: At your command, at your command, you know that very well.

Juhani: To the devil with my command. We're men without a sauna, and that's a problem. Putting up a building doesn't bring in any bread.

Aapo: It's a problem, but the sauna was old anyway and its corners full of holes. And you yourself decided yesterday to build a new one.

Juhani: Well it was old and its timbers were steamed to the core, but we still could have eked out a year or two from it. The farm can't spare the manpower to build a sauna; it's the fields, the fields we have to work on first.

Tuomas: Your fields are going to be left just like our fine Plains Meadow last summer, where the rich hay was left to rot without a stroke of the scythe. But it was your will. Every time I reminded you about cutting it, you answered, "Not just yet; the hay is growing so fast you can hear it crackling."

Juhani: That's in the past, and it does no good to beat your gums about it. The hay will grow so much the better there next summer. But who is that coming through the field toward our house?

Timo: It's Mäkelä the juror. What does he want?

Juhani: Now there's the devil to pay. He's come in the name of the law, because of that damned fight with the Toukola men.

Aapo: We had the law on our side in the last fight, but we have to watch out for our interests in the earlier one. Let me explain the matter to him.

Juhani: But as the oldest brother, I want the floor too, since it's our common good that's at stake.

Aapo: Be careful not to talk us into a corner if we have to be a little devious.

Juhani: I know how to act.

Mäkelä, an eminent juror, well-disposed toward them, entered the room. But he came on another errand than they had assumed.

Mäkelä: Good day?

Brothers: Good day?

Mäkelä: What a terrible sight! What happened to you boys? All cut, bruised, and scabbed, and your heads wrapped in rags! You poor devils!

Juhani: "A dog will lick his own wounds," but let the wolf care for himself. Is that why you're here now?

Mäkelä: How could I know about this? But did brothers beat one another up like this! Shame on you!

Juhani: You're mistaken, Mäkelä. These brothers have treated one another like angels. This was the work of neighbors.

Mäkelä: Who did it then?

Juhani: Good neighbors. But can I ask why you've come to visit us?

Mäkelä: For no good reason. Boys, boys, the day of ruin is upon you.

Juhani: What kind of day is that?

Mäkelä: The day of shame.

Juhani: When will it dawn?

Mäkelä: I've received a stern order from the provost to bring you to church next Sunday.

Juhani: Why does he want us in church?

Mäkelä: In plain words, to put you in the stocks.

Juhani: For what reason?

Mäkelä: He has many reasons. You mad fools! You broke the sexton's window and ran off from him like wolves.

Juhani: The sexton acted like a wild wolf with us.

Mäkelä: But what has the provost done to you?

Juhani: Nothing at all to hurt us.

Mäkelä: And yet you mocked and shamed him by way of that vile, loud-mouthed Cupper-Kaisa. You sent a most filthy, most villainous greeting to the noble shepherd of our parish by that terrible Rajamäki Regiment. Such an act can't be matched for bare-faced gall.

Juhani: "That's true enough but prove it," said Jaakko Kakkinen. But I didn't say that.

Mäkelä: And now, I tell you, the provost's direst revenge is upon you. He will show no mercy.

Aapo: Sit down, Mäkelä, and let's discuss the matter more fully and deeply. Look at it this way: would the provost be likely to clamp us into the stocks just because of Kaisa Rajamäki's lies? No way! There would have to be legal witness to what we said and how we insulted him.

Juhani: "Investigate, then castigate." It's an old refrain.

Mäkelä: But there's still another matter, your reading. Church law gives him some power there, which he is sure to use against you in his anger.

Juhani: In all this fuss about reading, God's law and edict are for us and against them. Look, God gave us such hard heads in our mother's womb that we can't learn to read. What's to be done, Mäkelä? Brains are very unevenly distributed here.

Mäkelä: The hardness of your heads is purely imaginary. Patience and daily practice conquer all obstacles in the end. Your father was one of the best of readers.

Aapo: But our mother didn't know one single letter, and yet she was a true Christian.

Juhani: And she raised and ruled her sons in the fear of God. God bless the old woman.

Mäkelä: Did she try to get others to help you?

Juhani: She did her best. She even hired Granny Pine, but that hot-tempered old woman soon started beating our backsides and her house became the worst of goblins' dens to us. In the end, we refused to step inside it even if they thrashed us like burn-beaters.

Mäkelä: You had no understanding then, but now you stand here like men, and a sensible, healthy man can do anything he wants to do. So show the provost and the whole world what a man can do. Aapo, you have such a sharp mind; you know so much, and you remember everything you see and hear. I have to wonder why you haven't acted differently.

Aapo: It's little enough that I know. Oh well, I do know a bit of this, that, and the other. Our dead uncle told us many things about the

Bible and his sea voyages and what the world was like, and we listened carefully.

Juhani: We listened with our ears pricked up like rabbits because our uncle told us about Moses and the children of Israel and about what happened in the Book of Kings and the wonders of Revelation. "...and the sound of their wings was as the sound of chariots of many horses for they were running to battle." Lord Jesus! We know many wonders and things and we're not just the wild pagans people think we are.

Mäkelä: But you have to start with the ABC book in order to become proper members of a Christian congregation.

Aapo: You see those seven ABC books there on the shelf that we bought at Hämeenlinna? Let them be proof that we are trying to learn. Let the provost show us a little more patience, and something may be born, bred, and grow from this matter.

Juhani: Let him show patience. I'll pay him double tithes, and he'll always have young game birds on his table in season.

Mäkelä: I don't think prayers and promises will do you any good when I consider his just and burning anger toward you.

Juhani: Just what does he want from us then, and what do you want? Even if you came after us with seventy men, blood would flow.

Mäkelä: But tell me how you plan to go about learning the alphabet and the Small Catechism, which is the most important order of the provost?

Juhani: We'll try Granny Pine or her daughter Venla's teaching here at home. Both women are good readers.

Mäkelä: I'll tell the provost of your plans, but for your own peace of mind, you should go and ask him to forgive your shameless behavior.

Juhani: We need to consider that point.

Mäkelä: Do as I say. I know that if he doesn't see you hard at work in serious study, one of these Sundays you'll be perched neatly in the stocks, yes indeed, in the stocks by the church basement.

Juhani: Goodbye, goodbye.

Tuomas: Did you really mean what you said about Granny Pine and her daughter? Did you really mean your promise to go crawling to the provost?

Juhani: Not at all. There wasn't an ounce of truth in it. I told him that nonsense just to gain time. Granny Pine or Venla holding the pointer for us! Every pig in Toukola would be laughing at that. You heard him threaten us with the stocks, with certain shame. One thousand fiery devils! Can't a man live by himself in peace and freedom if he meddles with no one, hurts no one's rights? Who can argue with that? I'll say it again: preachers and officials with their books and papers are the evil spirits of mankind. Oh you black pig! Oh this cursed day! We are so battered by fate and abused by people that I'm ready to run my head against a wall. Oh you black bull! Venla gave us the gate, they wrote a poisonous ballad about us, the sexton abused us like the devil, the men of Toukola hacked us like clods of earth, we were flayed like Christmas porkers, and now we stand here, heads wrapped in rags like one-eyed goblins, like real Christmas elves. And besides, our home lacks the poor man's only pleasure, the hissing steam from a sauna stove. The ruins of our dear sauna lie smoldering there and the most devilish thing is still to come. Agh! The stocks across from the church porch leer at us with their ten mouths. Balls of Fire! If a pack of troubles like this won't make a man put a razor to his throat, what will! Oh you horned bulls!

Eero: Your memory is a little off. There aren't ten holes in the stocks.

Juhani: How many are there then?

Eero: How many stars in the Big Dipper? How many sons at Jukola?

Juhani: There are seven of us. Seven holes for seven brothers. So much the worse. Seven holes. Worse and worse. How the whole world and grim fate have plotted against us. Seven holes like the eye of a millstone. What a mean trick of fate. But let them shoot all their arrows of hate at us, we'll harden our much-abused hearts like flashing steel. Let them spit poison at us from all sides like snakes, let heaven pour down pure gall on our heads, yet with eyes closed and teeth gritted, bellowing like wild bulls, we'll fight them, and if at last the power of the Crown drags us to those foot-clamps, then I will sit in the stocks in perfect joy.

Aapo: Why in joy?

Juhani: My brother, you don't understand the condemning strength of anger. The thought of revenge makes a man forget all shame, and it's our shame they aim at. The thought of bloodying our master provost is like the taste of honey to my angry mind. I wouldn't use a knife or gun, like the man of Karja once did, but I would be at his throat with tooth and claw like a wolf-lynx. I would tear the man to pieces, into a thousand pieces, so that I could smack my lips over the sweet tidbits of revenge. That's what I would do. If I had ten souls, and every one were to be tortured in a spiked barrel for ten years, that would be nothing compared to the joy of revenge.

Aapo: You're stirring up the very depths of your soul. Pour the cooling waters of patience, that wander gently through the meadow, over the scalding kettle of your heart.

Simeoni: Your face is black as pitch and your eyes roll piercing and bloody. Have pity on yourself.

Tuomas: Of course we would take revenge if we were set in the seat of shame, but let our hearts rest in peace until it happens. All hope is not lost yet.

Juhani: The dawn of peace still shines for us from one corner of the world. Lake Ilves beside Impivaara is our harbor to ride out the storm. My mind is made up.

Lauri: Mine was made up already last year.

Eero: I'll follow you into the deepest cave of Impivaara where they say the old man of the mountain boils pitch with a helmet made of a hundred sheepskins on his head.

Tuomas: We'll all go there.

Juhani: We'll go there and build a new world.

Aapo: Won't the long arm of the law reach us there too?

Juhani: The forest shelters her cubs. It's the only place we can be at home. Like squint-eyed moles, we'll dig ourselves down to the earth's core. And if they want to hound us there, they'll find out what it's like to disturb the peace of seven bears in their den. Let's go to the tanner and draw up a lease. Let someone else have the farm for ten years.

Simeoni: I too long for a haven of peace. Brothers, we'll make a new home and a new heart for ourselves in the lap of the woods.

Juhani: All of us together!

Aapo: What do you say, Timo?

Timo: "Birds of a feather..." as the saying goes.

Aapo: If you go, should I stay behind like a lone pine in the Jukola barnyard? All of me, root and branch, is bound up in your circle. It's settled then, and we'll hope for the best from our journey. I'm with you.

Juhani: Great! Now to the tanners to draw up the legal papers. All of us together?

They went in a body to draw up the papers leasing the farm to the tanner for ten years, with the following provisos in writing. The tanner would run the farm for ten years, the first three rent-free, after which he would pay the brothers seven barrels of rye per year, and he would also build a new sauna before expiration of the lease. The brothers could hunt freely anywhere in the Jukola woods all the kinds of animals permitted by law. They could have the northern part of the farm around Impivaara at their disposal, to do as they pleased in field and forest. The tanner was to take over the house on All-Saints' Day, but the brothers could, if they wished, take shelter in the home of their birth for the coming winter. These were the main articles of the lease.

Come November, the tanner arrived in the Jukola yard with his load and took over the farm for the allotted time. To avoid the provost and his subordinates, the brothers spent most of the winter skiing and hunting in the woods, living in the charcoal-burner's hut in the meadow at

Impivaara. They did not, however, complete the move with their horse and other equipment. That had been set for the coming of spring. Nevertheless, they made provision for a future home, cutting logs to dry for the spring and rolling stones for the foundation to the stump-filled clearing at the foot of the steep hill.

So the winter passed, during which the brothers received no summons or reminders from the provost. Was he merely biding his time, or had he left them to their fate?

CHAPTER V

Spring had come. The snow had melted, a gentle wind was blowing, the earth was turning green, and the birch trees were leafing out. Guns on their shoulders and birchbark packs full of powder and shot on their backs, the brothers were traveling the rocky, winding road through the woods from Jukola to Impivaara. Juhani was in the lead, flanked by Killi and Kiiski, Jukola's two large and pugnacious dogs. Behind them came Timo, driving old Valko, the brothers' one-eyed horse, who was pulling the hay wagon. The others followed the loaded wagon with pack and gun, lending a hand to help Valko through the worst places on the road. Eero brought up the rear, cradling Jukola's proud rooster in his arms. Unwilling to leave him, the brothers were taking him with them to announce the arrival of dawn in the wilds of Impivaara. On the wagon were a trunk, some traps for wolves and foxes, and a huge pot containing two oaken bowls, a dipper, seven spoons, and other cookware. On the pot was a coarse sack filled with peas, and on top of everything was a small sack in which Jukola's old cat squirmed and mewed. In this fashion did the brothers leave their old home; sadly and silently they traveled the rough and rocky woods road. The sky was bright, the air was still, and the wheel of the sun was already rolling downhill in the west.

Juhani: Man is just a sailor on the stormy seas of life. And so we sail our land schooner from the dear nook where we were born through woods that lead men astray to the steep isle of Impivaara. Ah me!

Timo: I could almost cry, toad that I am.

Juhani: That doesn't surprise me, when I look into my own heart at this sad moment. But crying does no good in this world. Harden your heart like a rock. Man was born a wanderer; he has no lasting rest here.

Timo: He wanders, he is tossed to and fro a little while, and in the end, he sags and sinks down like a rat at the foot of a wall.

Juhani: Well said, wisely put.

Simeoni: And if only that were the end of it, but then...

Juhani: Then comes the accounting, you mean to say. That's true!

Timo: Then one must speak plainly and openly, "Here I am Lord, and here is my accounting."

Simeoni: A man should always consider his end, but his heart is hard.

Juhani: Hard, hard indeed, I can't deny that. But the same is true of everyone under the sun. Yet from now on we'll try to live as righteously as men should, now that we've come to this warm and peaceful refuge. Let's make a firm resolve to cast off all sinful behavior, all hatred, strife, and enmity in this nest of ours. Away with anger, wrath, and pride.

Eero: And putting on airs.

Juhani: Right!

Eero: And showy, sinful dress.

Juhani: Right!

Eero: And soft-springed church buggies and all that fancy folderol.

Juhani: What? What did you say?

Simeoni: He's teasing again.

Juhani: I can see that. Watch out or I'll wring your neck. That is, I would if that idiotic babble bothered me. It doesn't matter to a real man like me. How are you carrying that rooster, you damned calf? Why is the poor bird squawking like that?

Eero: I was just fixing his wing. It was hanging down.

Juhani: I'll fix you pretty soon. Be careful I don't wring your neck. You know that's the best rooster in the county when it comes to doing his job, so dependable and always on time. He crows first at two o'clock and then again at four, which is the best time for getting up. We'll have much joy from that rooster out here in the woods. And that cat up on the load. Oh you Matti-boy. There you go bouncing and jouncing along, peeking out through a hole in the sack and mewing so pitifully. "Poor old jock, you old sock." You don't have many days left to pad around in this world; your eyes are growing dim and your voice is getting hoarse. But maybe you'll perk up again when you get your claws on those fat woods mice. I hope so. But you, Killi and Kiiski, I feel the most sorry for you. Like us, you were begotten, born and bred at Jukola, you've grown up like brothers to us. Oh, how your eyes burn into mine! So Killi, so Kiiski, my boys, so! Wagging your tails so gladly. Well, you don't even know that we're leaving our beautiful home. Oh, you poor things! It makes me want to cry, makes me want to cry.

Timo: Remember what you told us just now. Harden your heart, harden your heart.

Juhani: I can't, I can't, when we're leaving our dear home.

Tuomas: This is a heavy day for us, but soon we'll have another home, maybe just as dear to us.

Juhani: What are you saying, brother? No place on earth is as dear as the home where we were born and grew up, where we tumbled around in the fields as little, milk-bearded kids.

Aapo: It's really heart-breaking to leave; even a rabbit loves his home thicket.

Juhani: What was it the mother rabbit once said when more little bunnies were on the way and she told her little son to leave and make room for them?

Timo: Go your way, my little son, and always remember what I say: "There's a trap on every trail and a snare at every step."

Juhani: That's what she said to her son, and the boy went scooting off, sneaking and skulking across a field and over a heath. And that's how he left home, split lip spread in a grin in the sad glow of evening.

Eero: That was Jussi-Rabbit.

Juhani: I'll ignore that. So he left his home, and so we leave ours. Goodbye home. I could kiss your porch and your manure pile now.

Aapo: Well, brother. Let's try to shake off our sadness. Soon we'll be moiling and toiling, soon trees will fall crashing, axes will ring, and a towering house will rise up in Impivaara Meadow with the wild woods all around. Look, we're already going through a rugged forest of sighing spruce.

So they talked on as they traveled through the gloomy woods. But soon they were traversing higher terrain where the road wound through a stretch of wooded land known as Teerimäki. Here and there were mossy outcroppings of rock, like massive burial mounds, surrounded by stout, stubby growths of murmuring pines. The rocky ground jolted the wagon wheels and jarred Valko's shoulder blades. In places, the eye could barely make out the course of the old road. It kept to the spine of a ridge, with bottomless marshes spread out on either side. The brothers did their best to lighten the load for their old, one-eyed horse. At last they reached the high point of the ridge and paused for Valko to catch his breath while they gazed at the flatland below. Far off, their eyes could see clusters of houses, meadows, blue lakes, and the high church tower on the wooded fringe to the west. On sloping ground to the east, Jukola Farm glowed like a lost paradise, filling the brothers' breasts with yearning. But at length they turned their eyes to the north, where they could see the steep heights of Impivaara with its dark crannies, its slopes decked with storm-torn mossy spruce. At its foot lay a pleasant, stump-strewn meadow, their future dwelling place, around it a wilderness that would yield them stout timber for building a house. All this they saw, and the waters of Lake Ilves sparkled through the pines and a golden sunset glowed on the northwestern slope of the mountain; and the sweet light of hope gleamed in their eyes and made them square their shoulders.

Off they went again, now hurrying boldly, faster and faster, toward their new home. Descending the hill, they came to a heath pillared with pine trees, where alternating patches of heather, cowberry, and withered grass covered the echoing earth. Next came a sandy, man-made road leading from Viertola Manor to the church; this they crossed, following their own forest trail over the crown of the heath.

Aapo: This is the heath which, old folks say, was once the court of the snakes. The king snake was their judge, the white one so rarely seen, who wears a crown of matchless beauty on his head. But a bold horseman stole this crown from them, as the story goes.

And Aapo told them the following tale as they descended the heath toward barren Sompio Swamp.

A man came riding on the heath and saw the king snake with a glittering crown on his head. He rode up to him and snatched off the crown with the tip of his sword. Spurring his horse, he flew away like wind and cloud with his treasure. The snakes did not tarry, but set off at once in angry pursuit of the bold robber. Curled up in a ring, they sped forward hissing, a thousand hoops spinning on the riders' heels like disks spun down a road by boys at play. They soon caught up with the rider, swarmed at the horse's feet and slithered up its sides. Great was the man's danger. In a panic, he threw down his hat as a sop; at once they tore it to pieces and swallowed it down in their rage. But the ruse did not help the rider for long. Soon the snakes were rushing at his heels again, and the sand swirled high above the road. Even more hotly the hero spurred his panting horse; blood ran in streams from the gashed flanks of the proud stallion and frothy spume spattered from his mouth. The rider fled into a woods, but the woods did not stay his foes' course. He came to a stream, and rising in the saddle, rode into the current, and the horse bore him swiftly across. The snakes too came to the stream, and with the roar of a thousand rapids, they hurled themselves into its surging bosom. They crossed with the speed of a tempest, and the foam rose high in the air. The man rode on with the enraged army of snakes close on his heels. He saw a raging brush fire in the distance and spurred his horse into it. Wrapping himself in his cloak, which was soaking wet from the stream, he plunged into the sheet of flame, but the snakes delayed not a second in following him. As a hero on his way to heaven glides through the clouds, he rode; again he dug his spurs into the sides of the stallion and once more he surged ahead, but then the gasping stallion fell, forever oblivious to the feverish game of life. But the man now stood in open air, safe from the flames and his hideous enemies; the fire had burned the innumerable horde of snakes. There stood the hero, a look of exultation in his eyes and a wonderful treasure in his hand.

Aapo: That is the story of the white snake's crown here on Teerimäki Heath.

Juhani: A great story and an even greater man, to snatch a crown from a snake's head and win it for himself in the end. What a man!

Timo: That snake is seldom seen here, but anyone who sees it becomes most wise, so the old folks say.

Juhani: They say too that whoever catches this snake in early spring before the cuckoo calls, then cooks and eats it, will understand the raven's speech and know what the future will bring.

Eero: And another thing they say is: whoever does all this after the cuckoo calls in the spring will understand the raven's speech and will know what has happened in the past.

Juhani: Oh, my brother, what a stupid thing to say. Don't all men already know the past without eating so much as a speck of snake meat? Eero has just shown what a real numbskull he is. "...know what has happened in the past." How could a man even think such a thing? Oh, you poor boy!

Aapo: Easy now, Juho. Whether Eero was being stupid or was only up to his old tricks again, he has given us real food for thought. Consider what he said and I think we can squeeze some wisdom from it. Knowing what has happened is very wise, from one point of view. If you consider which past deeds have yielded good fruit and which have yielded bad, and then live accordingly, you are a wise man. If our own eyes had been open wider, I don't think we would be dragging our-selves off into exile like this.

Juhani: Under the open sky, like wolf-cubs. But what's done is done.

Tuomas: What we've lost in Jukola, we'll make up for at Im-pivaara. Come lend a hand, all of you, and help Valko through this bog. Come here, all of you. The wagon wheels are already sinking a span deep into the mud.

While they talked, they had descended the heath, crossed Matti Se-unala's broad meadow, passed through a thick fir woods, and now stood on the edge of Sompio Swamp. A dismal marsh, its surface var-ied from wet and muddy open spaces, to mossy hillocks, to cranberry bogs, with here and there a short, withered birch tree sadly nodding its head in the evening breeze. The swamp was narrowest down the cen-ter, the ground more compact and firm there than elsewhere. Here grew short, moss-covered pine trees and dark-green, highly-scented bog-billberry bushes. An arduous trail ran over this stretch to the other shore of the swamp, where the dark forest began again. Along this trail, the brothers were now crossing the swamp. Some tugged at the shafts alongside Valko, the others pushed the wagon forward. Finally, though it was hard work, they reached the border of the swamp and traveled some five hundred paces on dry ground along a forest path laced with roots. But at last, the stump-dotted meadow gleamed before them, and they stood in the appointed place under the crannied hill.

There once the brothers' grandfather, a hard worker, had cultivated the burned-over clearings and kept his huge charcoal pits fuming. Many a grove had he felled and burned around this hill; many a black-ened field had he sown and dragged with a stick harrow, finally bring-ing in the rich sheaves of grain to the drying barn. A ruin to one side of the meadow still showed where the drying barn had stood; from it he had brought home the finished grain, leaving the straw and chaff to wait for winter sledding. A short distance from the ruins of the drying barn, on the boundary between woods and meadow, was an enormous black pit where he had burned the logs from his clearings to clinking charcoal. Here had this proud former owner of Jukola hustled and bustled under many a burning sun, often pausing to wipe the beads of sweat from his brow. At night he had rested in a sod-roofed hut guarding his charcoal pit, the same hut the brothers had settled on as their temporary dwelling.

The stump-strewn meadow is broad, but you cannot see beyond its boundaries, for your view is cut off to the east, south, and west by forests, and to the north by the high mountain. But if you climb to the top of the ridge, which is crowned with scattered spruce trees, you can see far in every direction. Down below your feet to the south, you see first the gently sloping meadow already mentioned, further on is the gloomy forest with Sompio Swamp beyond it, and there on the horizon stands the pale blue shape of Teerimäki. To the north, the mountain slope is gradual; it was once burned over for tilling and is now covered with a thick grove of young birch trees, along whose grassless paths heath grouse skip and partridge sound their melancholy whistle. To the east is a level, piney heath; to the west, clusters of mossy crags here and there, with a low but strong and dense growth of pines on their crowns. Beyond these pines, about a thousand paces from the meadow, gleam the clear waters of Lake Ilves, teeming with fish. You will scarcely find more to see, though you look long and hard; the dark sea of the wilderness looms all around. You may catch a dim glimpse of Viertola Manor to the northeast and the gray tower of the church on the northwestern horizon. Such was the spot the Jukolas had chosen as their dwelling, and its surroundings.

This evening the brothers had settled down near the hut, freed the tired Valko from the shafts, put him out to pasture with a bell on his neck, and started a cheerful fire of stumps and sticks in the meadow. There Simeoni was grilling herring and roasting turnips and beef for their common supper, while the others bustled about unloading the wagon and carrying every tool and utensil to its proper place. When this was done and the food was ready, they sat down to supper in the meadow. The sun had already set beyond the mountain.

Simeoni: So this is our first meal in our new home. May it bring good luck and God's peace to all our meals here.

Juhani: May good luck, the greatest good luck, be with us in all our works and doings here.

Aapo: I would like to say something important.

Juhani: Well, spit it out.

Aapo: A headless body is no good, I say.

Juhani: It runs into walls like a headless chicken.

Timo: Even with a head, a chicken will fly around here, there, and everywhere when the spell is on. Granny Pine's chickens often did, and then the old woman would say that witches' arrows were flying through the air.

Juhani: But spit it out, brother Aapo.

Aapo: This is what I think. If we want to start things out right here, one of us should always be the head man, the one to lead discussions and settle disputes. In a word, for the sake of order, let one man be our leader.

Juhani: I'm the oldest here.

Aapo: You are the first-born of Jukola, so the right should be yours.

Juhani: I rank first here, and I know how to demand obedience. If the rest of you would only follow orders.

Aapo: That is right and reasonable. But every man's voice should be heard on matters that concern us all.

Juhani: I'll always listen gladly to your advice. But I'm the first.

Aapo: Of course! But what kind of punishment shall we set for anyone who is stubborn and rebellious?

Juhani: I'll shut him up in that mountain cave and block its mouth with 200 pound stones. He can sit there for a day or two depending on the case and what it involves. Yes indeed. He can sit there sucking his thumb and think about making his peace.

Lauri: I won't agree to that.

Tuomas: Me neither.

Timo: Am I some stripy-nosed badger to live in a stinking mountain cave? Forget it!

Juhani: You're starting to rebel.

Tuomas: That punishment rule is no good.

Timo: "It won't cut the mustard," as the saying goes. I'm no badger either, not me.

Juhani: Then always be nice and peaceful so you'll escape the awful punishment of my anger.

Timo: But I'm no badger nor wolf, nor bear nor rat either. So just watch your step a little. "Watch your step, said Willie Pep." Hahaha!

Aapo: Could I have the floor?

Juhani: Gladly. What's on your mind?

Aapo: I don't approve the proviso for punishment that you want to set up for us either. I think it's too harsh and brutal to apply among brothers.

Juhani: So you don't approve? You don't approve? You really don't approve? Tell us a wiser one then, since I never know right from wrong.

Aapo: I won't.

Juhani: Tell us the wise proviso to approve, you wise man of Jukola.

Aapo: I fall far short of wisdom. But this...

Juhani: The proviso, the proviso!

Aapo: This is really...

Juhani: The proviso! The proviso! Tell us the wise proviso!

Aapo: Are you crazy? You're yelling as if your pants were on fire. Why are you screaming and shaking your head like a screech owl?

Juhani: The proviso, that's what I'm screaming about! The brand-new, age-old wise proviso! Tell it to us, and I'll listen as still as a fish when a frog is croaking.

Aapo: Here is my thought on the subject. Anyone who ignores advice and warnings, who acts up all the time and sows discord among us, will be expelled from our league and banished far away.

Tuomas: Let that be law.

Lauri: I agree.

Timo: Me too.

Simeoni: We all agree to it.

Juhani: Well then, let it be so. And remember, anyone who feels like acting up gets his walking papers and a kick in the butt to send him on his way. Well, what job do we take up tomorrow, you sluggards? I'm going to teach you, all right.

Aapo: You sound a little miffed, but we won't let that muddy our calm, clear waters this evening.

Juhani: What shall we start working on tomorrow?

Aapo: Building a house comes first, naturally.

Juhani: That's true. Early in the morning, four men ax in hand will take their places at the corners: I myself, Tuomas, Simeoni, and Aapo. The others will hue the logs and roll them up to us. And when the house and a small storage hut are ready, then we're off on hunting and fishing trips to lay in food. Remember that?

At length they finished their meal and went to bed in the charcoal hut. The May night fell calm and dark. Hoot owls sounded their hoarse call in the wilderness, ducks quacked on Lake Ilves, and now and then the sharp whistle of a bear could be heard. Otherwise, peace and deep silence prevailed in the world of nature. But downy-winged sleep did not come to the brothers in their sod-roofed hut. In silence, but tossing and turning, they pondered over the way of the world and the instability of life.

Aapo: I don't think anyone has closed an eye yet.

Juhani: Timo is sound asleep, but the rest of us are tossing and turning like wieners in a boiling kettle. Why are we so wide awake?

Aapo: Our life took a rough turn today.

Juhani: It makes me restless, very restless.

Simeoni: My heart is heavy. What am I? Just a prodigal son.

Juhani: Mm. A sheep lost in the wilderness.

Simeoni: We have cast off our neighbors and Christian kin.

Tuomas: Here we are and here we stay, as long as fresh meat is to be found in the woods.

Aapo: All will be well if we always use our heads.

Simeoni: The hoot owl is calling in the woods, and his cry is never a good omen. He foretells fire, bloody battles, and murder, as old folks say.

Tuomas: It's his business to hoot out in the woods and it doesn't mean a darned thing.

Eero: This is our whole world now, this sod-roofed house at Impivaara.

Simeoni: But now the prophet has shifted his perch and is calling from the crest of the mountain. The "Pale Maiden" once prayed there for her sins to be forgiven, all night long she prayed, both winter and summer.

Juhani: That's where the mountain got its name of Impivaara ('Maidenmount'). I heard the story once as a child, but I've forgotten most of it. Brother Aapo, tell it so as to while away this tiresome night.

Aapo: Timo is snoring away like a real man, but let him sleep in peace. I'll gladly tell you the story.

This is the tale of the pale maiden that Aapo told his brothers.

Long ago there lived in this mountain cave a horrible monster, who terrorized and murdered people. He longed for and lusted after two things in life: to gaze upon and fondle the treasure hidden deep in his cave and to drink human blood, for which he had a burning thirst. But his power to do violence was good only within eight paces of the mountain, and so he had to use cunning on his forays. He could take on whatever shape he pleased; sometimes he might be seen roaming about as a handsome youth, sometimes as a beautiful maiden, according to whether he thirsted for a man's or a woman's blood. Many were overcome by the hellish beauty of his gaze, and many lost their lives in the dreadful den of the monster. This was how the ghoul drew his luckless victims to him.

It was a mild summer night. A young man sat on the green grass holding his beloved, a young maiden, who rested on his breast like a glowing rose. It was their farewell embrace, for the boy had to go off and leave his heart's companion for a time. "My love," he said, "now I must leave you, but scarcely a hundred suns shall rise and set before I see you again." The girl answered: "The setting sun does not bestow so loving a farewell glance on its world as I do on my departing lover, nor does the flame of heaven shine so beautifully in rising as will my eyes when I see you again. And all the bright, live-long days you are gone, my soul will have room only for thoughts of you, and in the dim world of my dreams, I will be with you always." So spoke the girl, and the youth answered: "Your words are beautiful, but why does my soul forebode evil? My dear, let us now swear eternal faith to each other under the eye of heaven." And they swore a sacred oath, made a vow before God and heaven, while woods and mountains listened breathless to their words. And finally, as dawn was breaking, they embraced for the last time and parted. The youth hurried off, but for a long time the maiden wandered the dim woods alone, thinking of her handsome sweetheart.

As she roams the depths of the dense pine woods, what is the wondrous shape that approaches her? She sees a young man, as noble as a prince and as beautiful as the golden dawn. In his hat a tuft of feathers glows and flickers like a tongue of flame. A sky-blue cloak hangs from his shoulders, spangled like the heavens with glittering stars. As white as snow is his tunic, and a purple sash girds his waist. He looks at the maiden, and a hot love radiates from his eyes. There is bliss in the sound of his voice as he speaks to her: "Do not fear me, sweet maiden, for I am your friend and will bring you endless good fortune if I can embrace you just once. I am a powerful man. I have treasures and precious jewels without measure, and I can buy this whole world. Come

and be my sweetheart; I will take you to a gorgeous castle and place
you on a shining throne by my side." So he spoke, in a bewitching
voice, and the maiden stood dumfounded. She remembered her recent
vow and turned away, but then leaned back toward the man, her mind
in absolute turmoil. Covering her face with her hands as if to shield it
from the burning sun, she turned to him, but again she looked away.
And yet once more she turned to gaze at the wondrous figure. Forceful
adoration beamed out at her, and suddenly the maiden sank into the
prince's arms. He rushed off with his prey, who lay in his lap as
though delirious. Over steep hills, across deep valleys they went steadily, and the forest grew ever darker around them. The maiden's heart
beat uneasily and a tortured sweat ran down her brow, for she had finally noticed something horrible and beastly in the enchanting flame
of the figure's eyes. She looked around at the gloomy spruce trees
flashing by as her bearer ran headlong. She looked at the young man's
face and shivers of dread ran through her, but yet a strange fascination
gripped her heart.

On they went through the woods and finally they saw a high mountain with its dark caves. And now, as they were only a few short paces
from the mountain, an awful thing happened. The man in the kingly
raiment changed suddenly to a horrible monster: horns jutted out from
his brow, stiff bristles rustled on his neck, and the miserable girl now
felt sharp claws digging painfully into her breast. And there the luckless girl screamed, writhed, and struggled in her agony, but in vain.
Shrieking malignantly, the monster dragged her into the depths of his
cave and sucked out her blood to the very last drop. But a miracle occurred; life did not leave the maiden's limbs; she remained a living
creature, bloodless and snow-white, a mournful specter from the land
of the dead. The monster looked in astonishment, tore at her tooth and
claw with all his might, but could not kill her. Finally he decided to
keep her with him always in the dark bowels of his cave. But what service could she do him, what advantage could she bring the monster?
He set the maiden to work cleaning his treasures and precious jewels

and heaping them up constantly before him, for he never tired of gazing on and admiring them.

For years the pale, bloodless maiden lives on, imprisoned in the bowels of the mountain. But at night she can be seen silently praying on its crest. Who grants her this freedom? Is it the power of Heaven? Every night, in rain, storm, and freezing cold, she stands on the mountain top, praying for her sins to be pardoned. Silent and motionless she stands, a pale, bloodless image, head bowed and hands on her breasts. Not once does the poor wretch dare raise her eyes to Heaven, but keeps them fixed on the church tower at the far edge of the woods. For a secret voice keeps whispering hope in her ear, hope that gleams like a tiny spark thousands of miles away. It is thus that she spends her nights on the mountain. No complaint ever passes her lips; no repining sigh ever swells her praying bosom. So passes the gloomy night, and at dawn the ruthless monster snatches her back into his den.

A scant hundred suns had lighted the earth before the youth, her beloved, returned happily from his travels. But no beautiful maiden rushed forth to welcome him. He asked where the lovely one lingered, but there was no one to tell him. He searched for her tirelessly, day and night, but in vain. Like morning dew, the maiden had vanished without a trace. In the end he abandoned hope, and forsaking all life's joys, wandered his days on earth like a silent shadow. Finally on a bright and shining day, the night of death put out the light in his eyes.

Thus horribly long years dragged on for the pale maiden: days in the monster's cave, cleaning and heaping the treasures before her cruel tormentor's eyes, nights on the crest of the mountain. Silent she stands, a bloodless, snow-white image, head bowed and hands on her breasts. She does not dare raise her eyes to heaven, but keeps them fixed on the church tower at the far edge of the woods. She does not complain; no repining sigh swells her praying bosom.

It is a clear summer night. The maiden stands again on the mountain, recalling the time she has spent in her painful captivity. A hundred years have passed since she parted from her heart's companion.

Terror overcomes her; her thoughts droop, and cold beads of sweat roll down her brow and fall to the mossy ground as she relives the slow passage of decades.

One night she dared to look up for the first time, and soon saw a marvelous light coming toward her like a shooting star. The nearer it came, the more its shape changed. It was no shooting star, but a shining youth with a flaming sword in his hand. His face was delightfully familiar to her, and her heart beat rapidly, for now she recognized her former lover. But why was he coming with a sword in his hand? She was frightened and said weakly: "Will this sword at last put an end to my grief? Here is my bosom, young hero, strike here with the sharp steel and give me the gift of death I have yearned for so long." These words she spoke on the mountain, but the young man did not bring her death. He brought instead the sweet breath of life which was already sighing around the pale maiden like a fresh morning breeze. With love in his eyes, the youth took her in his arms and kissed her. Soon the pale maiden felt a sweet rush of blood in her veins, her cheeks glowed like a cloud at dawn, and a flush of joy lighted her limpid brow. Resting her curls on her lover's arm, she looked up at the bright sky and sighed forth decades of suffering from her breast. The youth ran his fingers through her hair, which fluttered prettily in the soft breeze. Blissful was the moment and the morning when she was saved and set free. Birds twittered in the trees on the steep slope of the mountain, and the glowing rim of the sun rose in the northeast. It was the same kind of morning as when the lovers had parted on the green grass such a long time ago.

But now the vicious monster, bristling with wrath, was climbing up the mountain to snatch the maiden back into his chambers. But barely had he reached out for her with his claws when the young man's sword, quick as lightning, pierced his breast, and his black blood gushed out onto the mountain. The maiden turned her face from the sight and pressed her brow into her lover's arm as the monster, shrieking horribly, tumbled dead down the ridge. Thus was the world saved from a ghastly terror. The youth and the maiden, swathed in a silvery-bright cloud, soared upward. Smiling happily, her brow pressing into his bosom, the bride rested on her bridegroom's knee. Through space they glided, leaving woods, hills and criss-cross valleys far below, and at last everything was lost to sight as in a blue mist.

This was the tale of the pale maiden which Aapo told his brothers in the sod-roofed hut that sleepless night on Impivaara Meadow.

Juhani: But Timo is waking up now just when the story is over.

Timo: What's keeping you up, boys?

Juhani: We're all caught up in story-telling. Well, that was some story about a long-gone girl and a monster.

Simeoni: But they say the awful monster is still alive. Hunters have seen him. He has only one eye that shines in the dark like a glowing coal.

Juhani: What about the thing that happened a couple of years ago to old man Kuokkala, who's in God's hands now. He was out hunting during grouse mating-season in the spring, sitting by his fire in this meadow, waiting for midnight to pass. He saw the same gleam at the foot of the mountain and heard a voice asking over and over again: "Shall I throw it? Shall I throw it?' it kept on asking like that, many thousands of times till the old man, who was made of the old-time stuff and wasn't easy to spook, finally lost his temper and snapped out: "Throw it and be damned!"

Timo: And that's all it took.

Juhani: Well then, you tell us, Timo — what happened next?

Timo: Well then, in a second a grinning skeleton came crashing down onto the old man's fire as if ten men had heaved it there, putting it out to the very last spark. The old man snatched up his rifle and ske-daddled far away from the whole mountain, though he was, as Jussi says, made of the old-time stuff and wasn't easy to spook.

Simeoni: So we're moving into a hangout of devils and demons.

Aapo: Here we are and here we'll live unafraid. Even if the monster is still alive, he's lost all his power; we've just seen that in his treatment of old man Kuokkala. All he could do in his rage was put out the fire, and that only with the old man's permission. The youth's sacred sword destroyed his power forever.

Juhani: But I have to feel sorry for the girl in those dark caves with that bristly-necked fiend.

Simeoni: Why didn't she resist temptation?

Juhani: Oh, my boy, don't say that. For instance, what would happen if you should meet a king's daughter as pretty as a rose in some peaceful, flowery valley? If she should come mincing up to you in silks, shawls, and sweet-smelling lotions, her golden trinkets glittering like a peacock, if a hussy like that should come and want to hug and kiss you, what would happen to your poor heart? I ask you, Simeoni.

Simeoni: I would pray for my faith to be strong.

Timo: I wouldn't let her hug me, much less smack me with noisy kisses. Stay away from me, I would say, keep your distance, you slut or else I'll get a stick from that bush and give you such a walloping that by tomorrow your back will turn the colors of a ladybug's wings. That's what I'd do. I'd show no mercy, and that would be the end of it.

Juhani: Oh, little brother! You would sing another song if you'd seen a little more of the world — if you had been to Turku, for example. I was there once driving oxen from Viertola Manor. It made me wonder to see how show and display can turn a man's head. Oh roaring town! Oh dizzy life! Coaches rumbling here, there, and everywhere. Sitting in them are clowns with mustaches, girls like china dolls filling the air with the smell of costly lotions. But look over there! Jesus save me! There's a real temptress, a mam'selle or miss or whatever, comes tripping up all decked out in gold feathers. Look at her neck! It's as white as milk. Her cheeks are fever-red, her eyes blaze like a daytime bonfire. And toward her comes a poor excuse for a man wearing a top hat and a shiny black tailcoat, and squinting — the devil take him — squinting through a square piece of glass that gleams on the scalawag's left eye. And look at them now, the two of them wigwagging at one another, she puckers up her mouth like a

strawberry and twitters like a swallow on a roof by day, and the hum-
bug of a man before her tosses his tail with one hand, waves his hat
with the other, and scrapes sparks from the paving stones with his feet.
"Oh you popinjays!" I thought as I stood there on the street corner, just
a kid with a bundle of fresh oxhides on my shoulder, grinning at this
mating dance.

Tuomas: Gentlemen are really clowns.

Timo: As childish as milk-bearded brats. And the way they eat, too,
with rags over their chests. And — doggone it — they can't even lick
their spoons clean when they leave the table. I've seen it with my own
eyes, and I was really amazed.

Simeoni: But when it comes to cheating and ripping off a farmer —
they're mighty good at that.

Juhani: Well, there's a lot that's silly and sissified about gentlemen,
I could see that on my trip to Turku. But if a tempting slut like that
should come up to one of us, frills all fluttering and smelling of lotions, wouldn't it shake up a man's heart? Uh-huh, my boys! Earthly
desires are strong temptations. I could see that on my trip to Turku.
But I say again that my heart aches for that girl on the mountain. It
was about time for her to be saved from that hell and to sail away with
her lover to a peaceful harbor, to which God help us all in the end. In
that hope, let's try to sleep now. But Simeoni, you go and bank the
coals with ash so I won't have to waste time striking sparks in straw
tomorrow and can start right in notching logs like a red-headed woodpecker. Go on now.

Simeoni went out to do Juhani's bidding, but was back instantly, hair
standing on end and eyes popping, bleating out something about a
ghost and a burning eye out near the wagon. The others leaped up,
blessed themselves body and soul, and stepped out of the hut in a
body, their hair looking like witches' brooms in a birch tree. They
stood as mute and motionless as pillars, looking in the direction
pointed out by Simeoni's finger. Staring fixedly, they could clearly see
a strange glow behind the wagon, which disappeared from time to time

but soon glowed visibly again. They would probably have taken it for the one eye of Valko, their horse, but nothing white could be seen, and there was no clank of a bell. The brothers stood in amazement, not moving a muscle. Finally Tuomas spoke in a harsh voice:

Tuomas: What do you want?

Juhani: For God's sake, don't talk so sharply to it. It's *him!* What'll we do, brothers? It's *him!* What should we say?

Aapo: I just don't know.

Timo: Now the verse of a hymn would be the thing.

Juhani: Doesn't any of us know a single prayer by heart? Speak up, my brothers, in God's name, come out with anything you remember, whatever pops into your head, without bothering about chapter or verse. Something, dear brothers, even if it's from the home baptismal.

Timo: I might have known a verse or two from the hymnal once, but now I seem to have an awful block in my brain.

Simeoni: The devil won't let you speak any more than he will me.

Timo: He won't let us.

Juhani: This is awful!

Aapo: Awful!

Timo: Really awful!

Juhani: What shall we do?

Tuomas: I think it's best to stand up to him. Let's ask who he is and what he wants.

Juhani: Let me ask. Who are you? Who are you? Who are you and what do you want from us? Not a word in answer.

Lauri: We'll pick up firebrands.

Juhani: We'll pick up firebrands and pelt you till you roast if you don't tell us your name, family, and what you're doing here.

Lauri: No, I mean we should grab firebrands right now.

Juhani: If we dared.

Tuomas: We owe God a death.

Juhani: Yes, we owe God a death. Grab the firebrands, boys.

Soon they stood in a row, holding flaming brands as their weapons. Juhani was first, his eyes as round as a hoot-owl's, staring at the eye in back of the wagon, which looked back at him with a strange gleam. So stood the brothers on the dark meadow, their weapons shedding sparks, while a hoot-owl shrieked from a fir tree on the mountain, the gloomy woods behind them sighed heavily, and dark clouds covered the sky.

Juhani: When I say, "Now, boys!" let's throw our firebrands at the devil's neck.

Simeoni: First, let's try to conjure him away.

Juhani: Good thinking! Conjure a little first. But what should I say to him? 'Whisper it to me, for now I'm struck dumb. Whisper the words to me and I'll throw them in his face so loudly that they'll echo.

Simeoni: Listen to what I say. Here we stand.

Juhani: Here we stand!

Simeoni: Heroes of faith, fiery swords in hand.

Juhani: Heroes of faith, fiery swords in hand!

Simeoni: Go your way.

Juhani: Go to hell!

Simeoni: We are baptized Christians, soldiers of God.

Juhani: We are baptized Christians, warriors of Christ!

Simeoni: Even if we cannot read.

Juhani: Even if we cannot read!

Simeoni: Yet we believe.

Juhani: Yet we believe and trust firmly in faith!

Simeoni: Go now.

Juhani: Go now!

Simeoni: Soon the cock will crow.

Juhani: Soon the cock will crow!

Simeoni: And the Lord's Day will dawn.

Juhani: And the Lord Zebaoth's day will dawn!

Simeoni: But he's paying no attention.

Juhani: But he's paying no... No, he doesn't care even if I scream angelic words at him. God bless us, brothers, there's nothing to do but — now boys!

They all hurled their firebrands at the ghost, which shot off with the speed of an arrow, its four hoofs thundering and the glowing coals flashing on its back for some time. Thus it fled from the fiery melee, and when it reached the edge of the clearing, it found the courage to stop and give first one and then another echoing snort. The brothers' ghost, the appalling apparition, was after all only their one-eyed horse, who had temporarily lost his white color in the black mudholes of the swamp into which he had fallen. There he had wallowed for a long time until at last he made it back to dry ground again. In his thrashing, he had also torn the bell from his neck, a fact which had led the brothers far astray on this occasion. This was the eye that had gleamed in back of the wagon on this dark night, as many a creature's eyes shine in the dark. But only after a long time, and then with caution did the brothers approach Valko and recognize their error. Grim-faced, they returned to the hut, and dawn found them all sound asleep at last.

CHAPTER VI

Eventually, the brothers' house was finished. It was thirty feet long and eighteen wide, its length running east and west. When you entered the door at the east end, there was a sauna stove of stone to the right and a manger to the left, built for Valko's use in the winter. From the threshold to about the midpoint, you stood on fir branches spread over bare earth, but to the rear, a fine floor of planking had been laid down, from which rose a broad loft, for the brothers were to use the new house as both a dwelling place and sauna. Some twenty paces from the house stood a storehouse built of small, round spruce logs.

With a fitting shelter from rain, storm, and winter's cold, and with a storehouse for their foodstuffs, the brothers could devote their full attention to hunting, to fishing, and to trapping of all kinds. Now death loomed for partridge, heath and wood grouse, for rabbits, squirrels, and fierce badgers, as well as the ducks and fish of Lake Ilves. The hills and the endless spruce wilderness rang with the baying of fierce Killi and Kiiski and the banging of rifles. Now and then a shaggy bear fell to the brothers' bullets, although it was not yet the season to hunt the honey-paw.

Fall arrived with its frosty nights. Grasshoppers, lizards, and frogs died or fled deep into hiding. Now was the season to catch foxes with the gleaming jaws of the trap, an art the brothers had learned from their father. Many were the fleetfooted Reynards that had to pay with their fine pelts for a few tasty morsels. And, as is known, rabbits have a habit of beating paths in the soft snow of the woods; along these trails the brothers set brass-wire snares by the hundreds, which were the death of many a whitecoat. Over a brushy ditch at the east end of the meadow, they had also built an ingenious wolf-pen with a fence that sloped inward, and as a further trap for wolves, they had dug a very deep pit in level, sandy ground some distance from the house. Many hungry wolves were lured into the sturdy pen by a cut of meat, and when the brothers spotted their cornered prey, the dark autumn night would be shattered by the thrashing and crashing at the pen. One brother would mount the fence, gun in hand, trying to dispatch the coarse-furred brute with a bullet, while another stood by with a flaring torch of tarry pine. Sometimes one of them would help Killi and Kiiski to drive the surly, snarling brutes out of thickets, waving a pine torch here and there. Great was the bedlam of shouting men, raging dogs, and roaring rifles, and the woods and the caverned walls of Impivaara rang ceaselessly with the clamor. As they scuffled, the snow was stained an ever-deeper red and trampled in every direction until the last of the beasts lay dead in its blood. Then came the fuss and bother of skinning their prey, but it was work the brothers enjoyed to the hilt. And sometimes a slant-eyed son of the forest would fall hurtling into the pit at the west end of the place.

It happened early one morning while the others were still in bed. Timo went out to check the baited pit. Even from a distance, he could see its partially caved-in cover, which gave him good cause to hope. Reaching the edge of the pit, his joyful eyes saw a pale gray shape in its depths, a big wolf lying motionless, its muzzle pressed to the earth, its eyes looking sullenly up at the man. What did Timo decide to do then? Why, to kill off the wolf by himself and walk in on the others with the furry burden on his back, much to their joy. Setting to work, he took down the ladder from the wall of the house, lowered it carefully into the pit, and climbed down the rungs with a heavy club in his hands, planning to bash in the brute's head. For a long time, he flailed away with the club, gritting his teeth, but his blows landed on empty air. The wolf's head darted nimbly to right or left as the man hammered at it with his clumsy weapon. Finally he dropped his club and left it with the wolf unable to think up any scheme but to climb out, rush to the house, and tell his brothers.

The brothers soon left the house, equipped with clubs, ropes, and nooses to catch their prey. But when they reached the pit, it was empty. The wolf had climbed neatly up the ladder left behind by Timo and scooted away, thanking his lucky stars. Realizing at once what had happened, and cursing and gnashing their teeth, the brothers turned their enraged eyes to search for Timo. He was no longer within reach, but was already fleeing to the edge of the woods, where he soon disappeared into the sheltering pines. He understood that there was nothing to be gained by staying for further discussion. The others ran screaming after him, waving their fists and vowing to beat him to a pulp if he once dared open the door of the house again. So they threatened, left the pit irate and angry, and returned to the house. Timo wandered the woods as a fugitive, but the brothers soon regretted their treatment of him, realizing that the accident was the result of foolishness, and not of spite or malice. So before evening, Juhani climbed to the top of Impivaara and shouted loudly in all directions, calling to Timo, reassuring him and swearing that he no longer need be afraid to return. Thus he shouted, and shortly Timo did return, scowling and glowering fiercely. Without a word, he stripped off his clothing, lay down, and was soon snoring away in a sound sleep.

The best season for bear hunting had now arrived. The brothers took up their spears, loaded their rifles with heavy shot, and set off to awaken the king of the wilds, now asleep far down in his den under the snowy spruce trees. Many a massy-jawed bruin fell to their guns as he charged raging from his peaceful den. Often a fierce struggle ensued: the snow flew in all directions and was stained red with blood that flowed from wounds given and taken on both sides. So the fight would rage, until the rugged-featured bear lay at rest. But the brothers, having arrived home happy with their burden, rubbed their wounds with a medicine made of hard liquor, salt, gunpowder, and ground sulfur.

With this they salved their sores and then spread yellowish-brown pine tar over the mixture.

Thus they garnered food from woods and hilly thickets, filling their storehouse with many kinds of animals: with birds and rabbits, badgers and bear-meat. They had also seen to faithful old Valko's winter rations. On the shore of the swamp was a huge, smoothly-capped stack of hay mown by their sickles and sufficient to last out the winter. Nor had they neglected fuel to keep the house warm. A towering wood-pile stood near the storehouse, and close by the wall of the house was a soaring stack of pine stumps looking for all the world like a huge heap of Hades' elkhorns. Thus equipped, they could look frost-bearded winter in the face without flinching.

It is Christmas evening. The weather is mild: gray clouds shield the sky, and a fresh snowfall covers hill and dale. The sound of a soft rustling is heard in the woods as heath grouse sup on birch catkins, waxwing on ruddy mountain-ash berries, and the magpie, that greedy miss of the pines, carries twigs for her future nest. Peace and joy prevail in cabin and goodly manor, and also in the brothers' home on Impivaara Meadow. Outside the door you can see a load of straw drawn by Valko from Viertola Manor, to be used on the floor in honor of Christmas. Even here the brothers are unlikely to have forgotten the rustle of Christmas straw, the happiest memory from their childhood days.

From the house comes the sound of water hissing on the hot stones of the sauna stove and the slapping of bath-whisks. The brothers are taking a rigorous Christmas bath. Having finished the last torrid, burning bout with steam, they stepped down, dressed, and sat resting on the timbers along the wall that served as benches. There they sat, puffing and dripping with sweat. A flaming torch lighted the room; Valko munched on oats in his manger, his Christmas too not forgotten, the rooster sat nodding and yawning on a rafter, Killi and Kiiski lay near the stove with muzzles on their paws, and Jukola's old cat sat purring on Juhani's knees.

Eventually Timo and Simeoni began to make supper while the others carried in the sheaves. Opening the bindings, they spread the straw a half foot deep over the floor, but deeper yet on the loft, where they usually spent their evenings and nights. At last their supper was ready: on the table were seven ring loaves, two oaken bowls of steaming bear meat, and a bucket of ale. They had brewed the ale themselves, accurately recalling their mother's methods. But they had made it stronger than ordinary home brew. It foamed a dark red in the bucket, and if you drank a few mugs of it, your head would spin a little. Now all the brothers sat at the table, enjoying the meat, bread, and the foaming ale from the bucket.

Aapo: The table is heaped high with food now.

Juhani: Let's eat and drink boys, for it's Christmas now for everyone, for man as well as beast. Pour the beer over the oats in poor old Valko's manger now, Timo-brother, at least a quart. No scrimping tonight. Let everyone have his fill, horse, dog, and cat, as well as Jukola's merry brothers. Let the rooster rest in peace and inherit his share in the morning. This is for you, Killi and Kiiski, a huge haunch of bear meat, and this is for you, poor kitty. But give me your paw first, you squint-eyes. That's it! And now both paws! Look at that cat's tricks and tell me I'm not a master-teacher. He shakes hands with both forepaws and then sits back like a sober old man and sticks the both of them into my hand, the scamp. Like that!

Aapo: What foolishness!

Timo: What a man will take up in his old age.

Juhani: It took me a long time to teach him, I tell you. But I didn't let up on the lad until he thanked his teacher with both paws. Now he does it like a man, and the teacher has his pay. Now that's a cat! Look at that, now! Stick this piece of bear meat in your cheek. Now for Killi and Kiiski. That's the way! "You can hit a man, but not his dog." Right! But I'll add to that: "Hit Jussi Jukola, but not his cat."

Eero: Pass me the bucket of ale, Juhani.

Juhani: It's yours. Drink, brother, drink, you piece of God's creation, for it's Christmas and there's no shortage in the storehouse. How are we doing here? What do we care if a wave of fire burns this whole world to dust and ashes, except for Impivaara and the land around it. Here we live off the fat of the land, we live on our own without having to duck and dodge around mean-tempered men. We have it good here. The woods are our meadows and fields, our mill and our nest forever.

Timo: And our meat-house too.

Juhani: Just so. We have it good here. Thank you, Lauri, for the way you thought up to get us out of the world's rat race. Here there is peace and freedom. I ask you again: What do we care if a golden fire burns this whole world up if it spares Jukola Farm and its seven sons?

Timo: If a golden fire swept over the whole world, then Jukola Farm would be dust and ashes, and its seven sons to boot.

Juhani: I know that well enough. But look, a man can think whatever he wants; he can think himself the lord of creation or a grubbing dung beetle. He can think that God's devils, the angels and all mankind, all living things on land and sea or in the air are dead, he can think that earth, hell, and heaven have vanished like a tuft of flax in a fire, that darkness has taken over, in which no rooster will ever crane his neck to proclaim God's daylight. A man's thoughts can fly around like that, and who can set nets to catch them?

Timo: Who can understand this world? Not the son of man, who is as dumb and stupid as a bleating goat. It's best to take each day as it comes and then let it go, be it good or bad, and just go on living.

Juhani: How are we doing here? What more do we need?

Timo: "Neither God's mercy nor bird's milk." The storehouse is crammed with food, the house is warm, and we're swimming in straw.

Juhani: We're like bull-calves rolling in rustling straw. We can bathe when we please, whenever the notion strikes us, and eat when we like. But we're full now, so let's just bless our bellies and clear the table.

Simeoni: Wait until I say grace and sing one verse of a hymn.

Juhani: Let's forget it now. Why didn't you do it before we ate? Eero-Boy, since you're the youngest, go and draw some ale from the bucket.

Simeoni: And you won't let us sing a hymn in honor of Christmas?

Juhani: My dear brothers, we're no singers. Let's sing and pray in our hearts, which is the most pleasing offering to God. But there's the ale bucket again, frothing and foaming like Kyrö Rapids. Thank you, my boy, this will do the trick. Wet your whistle with this, Tuomas, in the good old way.

Tuomas: It won't take me long.

Juhani: You chug-a-lug it like a man. Gulps like that will give us throats fit for a lead singer.

> *Life was good in olden days*
> *Out here on this far bank*
> *The flood brought us fuel for the blaze.*
> *For ale it was water we drank.*

Just so. But our drink is brown barley juice, our fuel is blocks of wood and pine stumps, and the bed under us is of soft straw, a mat fit for kings and grand dukes to wrestle on. A word with you, Tuomas. Aapo once claimed that you were stronger and tougher than me, but I just don't like to believe that. What about a go at it? Let's try our strength!

Simeoni: Let's stay right here, and God spare this shiny straw at least until tomorrow.

Juhani: The fun is at its height now; "the evening crowns the feast." And the straw will wind up in the chopper some day no matter what. What do you say, Tuomas?

Tuomas: It's okay with me.

Juhani: Waistband wrestling!

Tuomas: It's okay with me.

Juhani: Let's get started, let's get started!

Aapo: Watch it, boy. Let Tuomas get a firm grip on your waistband.

Juhani: Let him, let him!

Eero: Juho, why are you rolling your eyes and gritting your teeth like a bull in a slaughterhouse? Oh, my brother, watch out that you don't bring shame on yourself.

Aapo: All set? Who gets the first turn?

Juhani: Let Tuomas have it.

Tuomas: Let the oldest be first.

Juhani: Then get set.

Tuomas: I'm trying.

Juhani: Are you all set?

Tuomas: I'm trying.

Aapo: Hip, hip, hooray, boys! That's the way, that's the way! You fight like heroes of the faith. Juho jerks and twists like old Israel, and "like an oak tree Tuomas stands."

Eero: "As Aapo preaches reprimands." But look at Juho's mouth and you'll be shocked. Why, if I put a steel blade between his teeth — Snap! — it would be bitten in two. I'm horrified, horrified!

Aapo: It's only men fighting. The floorboards are sinking and rising under us.

Eero: Like organ pedals, and Tuomas boots are turning up the straw like a plow.

Aapo: They're not exactly handling each other with kid gloves. By God, if they were wrestling on the mountain, their cleats would strike sparks from the crags.

Eero: Pretty golden sparks to fly into the woods and start a jolly forest fire. But Tuomas is still on his feet.

Tuomas: Have you had enough of tugging yet?

Juhani: It's your turn.

Tuomas: I'll try. But watch out now, the floor is spinning.

Eero: Remember, Juho, remember!

Aapo: That was a throw.

Eero: It was a thump from Samson's sledge, a blow from Vulcan's hammer.

Timo: And here like a malt sack lies Juhani.

Eero: Poor-boy Jussi!

Timo: That's what he called himself when he was little.

Aapo: But one should know how to throw a man. Remember, Tuomas, that the human body is made of flesh and bone, not iron.

Timo: Yes, even if it does wear pants.

Tuomas: Did I hurt you?

Juhani: Look out for yourself.

Tuomas: Get up.

Juhani: I will, and then I'll show you how a strong man pulls the bar. Now that's a real test of strength.

Tuomas: Eero, bring us a limb from that corner. Now sit down over there, Juhani.

Juhani: Here I am. Now toe to toe and grab the limb.

Aapo: When I say "Now," then pull, but no jerking. Put the limb above your toes, right above them, not an inch to either side. Now, boys?

Timo: Juho popped up like a jack-in-the-box.

Aapo: Even feeling sorry won't help him.

Juhani: Go and get some ale, Timo.

Timo: You're limping, brother.

Juhani: Go and get some ale, you damned calf? Did you hear me, or do you want ears boxed?

Tuomas: Did I hurt your foot?

Juhani: What do you care? Just take care of your own hoofs. What difference does it make if my boot heel broke off? It slipped off in wrestling like a slice of turnip. But watch out for yourself. You've shown you can beat me at wrestling and pulling the bar, but just come and fight me.

Aapo: This is no time to be fighting.

Juhani: It is if we want to fight.

Tuomas: I don't want to.

Juhani: You don't dare.

Aapo: You know that wrestling is only play.

Simeoni: I know it's play, but it's play of a kind that often leads to brawling and murder.

Juhani: I admit that Tuomas has won, but Juhani bows to no one else here. That I swear, and I'll prove it on every man in this whole bunch. One bout, Aapo. Will your waistband hold? Will it hold?

Aapo: You're just wild and for no reason? Hold it, hold it? We'll wrestle the proper way.

Juhani: Hellfire and damnation!

Aapo: Hold it, I said. OK. Now throw me.

Eero: Juhani is dancing the polska like a boy, even if he is limping.

Juhani: What do you have to say now, brother Aapo?

Aapo: That I'm lying under you.

Juhani: It's your turn now, Simeoni.

Simeoni: I wouldn't profane this holy day for a thousand dollars.

Juhani: We'll do honor to the Christmas holiday. A little harmless wrestling won't breach it if it's done with a cheerful mind and a pure heart. Just one try, Simeoni.

Simeoni: Why do you tempt me?

Juhani: One try.

Simeoni: You devil!

Aapo: Leave him alone, Juhani, leave him alone.

Juhani: It's okay to try. There now, just one tug at your waistband.

Simeoni: Go to hell, you evil spirit! I concede you the win.

Tuomas: I'll believe it when I see it. I don't think Simeoni's muscles are made of calf meat.

Juhani: So let him come and try. We'll see if they're of calf meat or of sinewy black bear.

Aapo: Leave him alone and let another man step up, someone who is more willing to face you. Brother Timo is always feisty.

Juhani: Does he feel like it?

Aapo: Windward ho, Timo. You've never been chickenhearted.

Tuomas: Never, but always frisky, always right at home. I'll never forget the stunt he pulled in that dandy set-to with the Toukola gang.

He got a solid clunk on the noggin when he wasn't looking, but that didn't bother him a bit — he turned around as calm as you please, took the pole from the man's hand, and hit him over the skull so hard that the pole snapped. It snapped in two, and the man flopped to the ground like an empty sack. That's what Timo Jukola did. And I know he'll stand up to any man.

Juhani: That's just what I want. But let me get a good grip on your frame too. Now we're ready.

Aapo: Let Timo have the first try.

Juhani: Let him. It'll give me time to catch my breath.

Timo: Take that now.

Juhani: No, my boy.

Tuomas: Quite a heave, Timo, my boy. Can you do better?

Juhani: It's not that easy to shake me off.

Tuomas: Can you do any better, Timo?

Timo: I should. How about this?

Juhani: "It's not that easy to shake me off," said the Hyvämäki beggar.

Aapo: Once more, Timo.

Tuomas: Can you do any better?

Timo: I should. And this?

Juhani: "It's not that easy to shake me off," said the Hyvämäki beggar.

Tuomas: But you felt that pull.

Eero: No danger. Juhani's voice shook just the least bit — no harm done.

Juhani: I'm still standing.

Tuomas: Once more, Timo.

Timo: We'll try, we'll try.

Juhani: Hey hold it! My pants are falling!

Timo: "Let 'er rip, said Kaitaranta."

Juhani: My pants are falling! Did you hear me?"

Timo: So there you are, my brother!

Aapo: Is Juhani kissing the floor again?

Eero: And snorting like a bullock. But it's good that he has "time to catch his breath."

Timo: The boy is lying under me like a wet slipper-sock.

Tuomas: But his pants played a dirty trick on him.

Aapo: Let it be said in the name of truth that Jussi's own trousers turned on their master and allied themselves with Timo.

Eero: That's a fact. So everyone take off his pants and start all over again.

Simeoni: Keep your mouth shut, you magpie, or I'll let you have one in the nose. Haven't you had enough of this hellish game?

Eero: So let's switch to a heavenly game. Take your pants and shirts off and wrestle like two angels in the fields of Paradise.

Tuomas: Why are you sitting on his neck, Timo?

Timo: If I had a stick now, I would whack him across the buttocks.

Aapo: Why? This is a wrestling match, not a fight.

Eero: Is Timo angry?

Timo: Not at all, not at all, but I tell you, if I had a stick or a rod now, I would whack him across the buttocks.

Tuomas: Let him up.

Timo: Get up, God's creature.

Juhani: I will get up, and I'm letting you know that when I get my pants closed again, it'll be your turn to fall, and not the way I did. I stumbled by accident, poor me, and you were quick to take advantage of it, you worm, you bootjack.

Aapo: Cool off now. I'm sure he hardly noticed your trouble with your pants before you were down. He did it in the heat of battle, poor boy.

Juhani: He knew it, all right, the otter-pup. But you're all on my neck, like vultures. Didn't I yell out like an umpire, "Hold it, my pants are falling?" But he paid no attention, just tore at me tooth and nail like a cat. Balls of fire! I'll teach you to take advantage of a man with his pants down in the future. I'm going to teach you good and proper.

Timo: I did it in the heat of battle, poor me.

Juhani: I'll teach you when I get my pants up and my belt as tight as a barrel hoop.

Timo: I don't give a damn about the whole wrestling match. I won so I won and there's no use to grumble. What do pants have to do with it? It's the man who wrestles, not his pants or leggings or other stuff.

Juhani: Hands to waistband and chest to chest again! Balls of fire!

Timo: Should I join him in that kids' game again?

Eero: Why ask? Go, God's creature, go while the going's good.

Simeoni: Don't go, I tell you.

Eero: Of course, if you're all scared and shaky, don't go.

Juhani: Being scared and shaky won't help you now. You have to wrestle again, this very God's minute.

Eero: Have mercy on him, Juhani. Have mercy.

Timo: Why, Eero, why? All right, then, one more bout or so. Get set!

Juhani: I'm ready.

Tuomas: Nicely, Juho, nicely!

Aapo: Nicely! They're fighting like two starving hawks.

Simeoni: Fighting, out-and-out fighting!

Aapo: Get ahold of yourself, Juhani!

Simeoni: Oh, you monsters, you monsters!

Eero: Don't cripple your brother!

Simeoni: Aha! So even Eero's turning pale. You got just what you were fishing for.

Tuomas: Juhani!

Simeoni: You're wrecking the house, you damned animals.

Juhani: "Vot, boy," said the Russian. Well now, why are you lying on your back looking up at the roof?

Timo: You whipped me now, but let time knead us for awhile, and you'll grow old and shrunken, while I'll grow bigger and stronger.

Juhani: This whole world will rot and die some day, not to mention poor, sinful man. Time wears us all down to the same level, brother, so get up and take a swig and admit you're just an ounce or two weaker than I am.

Timo: We saw that. I was on my hands and knees with you on top like a huffy bear.

Juhani: Take a swig, my drinking buddy, from this elbow-bender's mug. As far as strength goes, I'm second best of the Jukola bunch. Of course, Lauri and Eero are still untested, but they'll hear bees buzzing in their ears if they try. And Simeoni has already admitted that he's weaker than I am. But not one of the Jukola boys is a featherweight, I'll swear to that. Bring on as many as fifty Toukola men, fist to fist. I can carry the weight of five barrels on my back, and Tuomas a bit more, if there is someone to pile them on.

Tuomas: But I would really like to see Lauri and Eero wrestle.

Aapo: That would be a sight to see. One as easy-going and steady as a winter thaw, the other no bigger than a dwarf, but as quick and fiery as a flame. So windward ho, and there you have a weasel battling a jackrabbit. I'm not calling you a rabbit because you're timid, Lauri — no cause for that — or because of the way you move — you march away like Konni the smith's figure with the hoe, which has a nifty clockworks in its belly to move its feet and hoe — but because I think it would look like a fight between a weasel and a super jackrabbit.

Juhani: One bout, boys, one bout of lapel or waistband wrestling.

Lauri: What's the point of wrestling with Eero? You can never get a good hold on him. He slips through your crotch like a cat, claws and squeezes your groin so that you can hardly get your breath. That's just what he did when we wrestled in Aro Meadow last fall, and who won or lost, God only knows. Why should I mess with him again?

Eero: I wasn't a hair stronger than you are, believe it if you like.

Lauri: I believe it, since I know you're weaker.

Juhani: Let's settle it with an honest wrestling match.

Lauri: Why should I mess with him again?

Simeoni: Let's go to bed, you savages.

Juhani: There are plenty of nights in a year, but only one Christmas, so let's celebrate. Rejoice you house of Christmas, all Israel rejoice! Tonight, this very minute, a great wonder has come to pass in the city of Babylon. Rejoice! What shall we play? Will it be blind-man's buff or stick the pig or spill the straw man?

Simeoni: What next? Are we going to start jumping around like wild animals now? Go away!

Juhani: A young bachelor's life is just a dance, isn't it, Timo?

Timo: Hee-hee-hee!

Juhani: Isn't it?

Timo: That's what it is.

Eero: You're exactly right, dear Jussi.

Juhani: As the fox said to the rabbit. Right! This is the good life. We feel jolly every now and then and even kick up our heels a little. Let's do the Russian dance. I'm a real whiz at it. Watch me!

Aapo: Has our ale gone to your head?

Juhani: You toss down a few mugs and see if it doesn't strike a few sparks in your upper story. But sing, Eero, while Jussi-Boy dances. Sing out!

Eero: What kind of song do you want?

Juhani: Any kind, so long as it's loud and jumpy. Sing out, boy, shout till you raise the rafters! Sing, you otter-pup, while I dance like a billygoat and leap right up to the roof. Sing!

Eero: I'll try:

> *Joy is ours and revelry*
> *Christmas is upon us.*
> *Vats are overflowing now,*
> *Mugs and buckets brimming.*
> *Vats o'erflowing, vats o'erflowing,*
> *Mugs and buckets brimming.*
>
> *At the fair in Anja Field*
> *We swilled the beer and liquor.*
> *For the price of one black bull*
> *We bought betrothal presents.*
> *We bought them, we bought them.*
> *For the price of one black bull*
> *We bought betrothal presents.*
> *Jussi Jukola, rag-tag Jussi!*

Aapo: Shut up, Eero, don't get him mad.

Juhani: Just keep on singing. I won't get mad. More, more! I can't dance without music.

Eero: *Jussi Jukola, rag-tag Jussi!*
    Jazzy Jussi, pasty-face.
    Chopping up the pig-pen straw.

Timo: Hee-hee-hee, the crazy things you're singing.

Juhani: Keep singing, keep singing. I won't get mad.

Eero: *Jazzy Jussi, pasty face...*
I'll sing and snap my fingers too.

    Chopping up the pig-pen straw,
    Warming up the pen for piggies,
    Jussi Jukola, rag-bag Jussi!

    Down to the shore went Ida
    And wrote into the sand
    Her sweetheart's name
    Her sweetheart's name

    When I heard my lover's voice
    On the first day that we met
    I thought I was in heaven's bliss
    Mingling with the seraphim.
    I thought I was in heaven's bliss
    Mingling with the seraphim.
    Jussi Jukola, rag-tag Jussi!

    Remember Mary
    Gulping strawberries
    And making merry.
    Tra la la la la!
    Gulping strawberries
    And making merry
    Tra la la la la!
    Jussi Jukola, rag-tag Jussi!

    Poor Aato, don't you
    Scold our Jussi,
    For you know
    That he's a strong man.

Jussi's sitting in the jail
Tethered like a goat
And every last one of us
Is in the same boat.
Tra la la la la

Willie the Weeper
And Silly the Preacher
Bully-Boy Bucky
And Simpleton Ducky!
Tralalalala
Bully-Boy Bucky
And Simpleton Ducky
Tra la la la la

Oh the wild boy that I am,
Why ever did I do it!
Though I have a house and home
I sit here in my chains.
Though I have a house and home
I sit here in my chains.

Juhani: That's the way! That's the way! I've got no chains to keep me down. Keep on singing!

Eero: *Jussi Jukola, rag-tag Jussi*
Jazzy Jussi, pasty-face.
Chopping up the straw in pigpens
Warming up the pens for piggies
Jussi Jukola, rag-tag Jussi

Isn't that enough?

Juhani: More, more! We're dancing at Karja-Matti's wedding. More! More! Karja-Matti's wedding!

Simeoni: Even the rooster is squawking in fright at this godless roaring and prancing.

Juhani: Shut your beak, rooster. Stop your cackling.

Tuomas: That's enough already, Juhani.

Aapo: That Turkish dancing will kill you.

Juhani: This is Russian dancing, isn't it Eero?

Eero: It's Jussian.

Juhani: Let it be then, and let's have some twenty more leaps of this Jussi-dance.

Simeoni: You're a wild man!

Timo: Look at that, look at that! Hee hee hee! Now the devil take you!

Juhani: Out of my way, or I'll trample you the way the Cossack's horse did the drunken braggart at the fair. Hey!

Aapo: His belt is taking a beating there in back, bouncing up and down, slapping his back and then his butt. Oh my!

Juhani: Tra la la! Now that was a pounding. It's only the second time I've danced in my life. The first time was at Karja-Matti's wedding. Only three old women were there, but a whole gang of us men. And when Karja-Matti made us a cup or two of powerful coffee-punch, nothing else would do but for the men to start hammering down the floorboards so hard the sinful earth sighed underfoot. The old women blessed their escape from the pounding: we would have danced them to pieces. It was a devil of a time! But let's strip down to our shirts and go up to the loft. We won't shut our eyes just yet, but there in the torchlit warmth by the foaming bucket of ale, we'll tell happy tales and stories.

They undressed, filled the bucket with ale once more, and stepped up to the loft as one man. All in shirt tails, they sat there in the brooding warmth. The foaming bucket passed busily from man to man while the golden flame of the torch flared from a crack in the timbers. But a thought struck Juhani, which he uttered aloud, and it brought bad luck in its wake.

Juhani: Here we are, roasting ourselves like pork sausages in the oven, with the sauna's hot stones to warm us. Eero, pour a mug of ale on the stones so that we'll get a whiff of steam from the barley juice.

Tuomas: What kind of crazy trick is that?

Juhani: A great trick. Pour it on.

Eero: I must obey my master.

Juha: A couple of mugs of ale on the stones.

Tuomas: Not one drop! If I hear the slightest hiss, woe to the man that caused it.

Aapo: Let's not waste good drink.

Timo: We can't afford to live in ale steam, we just can't afford it.

Juhani: It would be a treat to get a whiff of it.

Tuomas: I say no and I mean no.

Juhani: It would be a treat to get a whiff. Tuomas is pretty cocky after winning at wrestling just now and thinks he can rule the roost as he pleases. But remember that when a man really builds up a mad, he's got the strength of seven. In any case, I don't feel like waiting on you yet.

Simeoni: The wrestling match, the wrestling match is the cause of all this!

Juhani: Splash it on, Eero. I'll answer for it and protect you.

Eero: It's my master's voice and I must obey. If I don't, I'll be driven out on Christmas night.

So Eero, teeth gritted and lips stretched in a sly smirk, quickly carried out Juhani's wishes. There was a splash on the sauna stove, followed by a loud hissing. Enraged, Tuomas leaped up and flew at Eero like an eagle, but Juhani rushed to the defence of his younger brother. A general scuffle ensued, in which the burning torch was knocked from the loft to the lower floor. Unnoticed by the brothers it soon ignited a lively fire in the straw. As a circle on the surface of the water spreads evenly in all directions from the center, so the bright ring of fire expanded steadily over the floor. Reaching higher and higher, it flared onto the floor of the loft before the house's occupants noticed the danger below them. It was too late now to save anything but their own lives and the animals in the house. All around surged the flames, and great was the panic and confusion. They all rushed toward the door, and as it opened, men, dogs, cat and rooster burst out almost simultaneously with a dreadful clamor. It looked as if the house had vomited them out from its smoking gullet onto the snowy earth, where they now stood vying with one another in coughing. The last one out was Lauri, leading Valko by the halter rope, Valko who would otherwise have been left a victim to the fire. The violent flames were already shooting out through the small windows and finally through the door and roof. The sturdy house at Impivaara blazed in one sheet of flame and its dwellers stood exposed on the snowy plain. The charcoal hut, their first shelter, had already been leveled to the ground, and the storehouse standing there was as drafty as a magpie's nest. There the brothers lingered, a tow shirt their only protection against the wind and cold. Not even a hat or birch-bark shoes for their feet had they managed to salvage from the flames. All that was left of their household goods was their guns and birch-bark packs, which had been taken to the storehouse before they bathed. The brothers stood in the snow, their backs to the roaring fire, lifting now a left and then a right foot, which, basted with snow and fire, glowed red like goose feet.

Thus the brothers enjoyed the last benefit their house could afford them, the warmth of the fire, and fiercely did it blaze. Up rose the mighty flames, the dancing light shone all around, and the mossy spruces on the ridge smiled as sweetly as they did at dawn. A thick, pitch-black pillar of smoke rose to the clouds from the heap of pine stumps and rolled along under the roof of the sky. There was light around and about the meadow; ruddy day prevailed in the depths of the dark winter night. Amazed by the strange apparition, birds stared down from snowy branches as the stoutly-built house at Impivaara turned to ash and embers. But the brothers, tearing their hair in grief and rage, stood around with their backs to the warming fire. Finally the flames died down, collapsing at last into a heap of embers, filling the night with thousands of flashing sparks. Then to their horror, the brothers noticed that the sky was beginning to clear and the wind to shift from south to north. The mild weather was turning cold.

Aapo: We're saved from the fire to become victims of the cold. Look, the sky is clearing and a cold north wind is blowing. Brothers, we're in awful danger.

Juhani: Death and damnation. Who was the cause of this?

Tuomas: Who was the cause? How can you ask, you fire-bait? By rights, I should throw you into the hot coals to roast.

Juhani: No Tuomas can ever do that by himself, not ever. But cursed be the man who brought this night of hell on us.

Tuomas: He's cursing himself.

Juhani: Cursed be the man, and his name is Tuomas Jukola.

Tuomas: Say that again.

Aapo: Tuomas!

Simeoni: Juhani!

Lauri: Quiet!

Timo: You can't come to blows now, you can't, you rough-necks. There now, calm down, and let's warm ourselves like brothers.

Simeoni: You heathens!

Aapo: Stop being angry and fighting when we're facing a miserable death.

Tuomas: Who's the guilty one, who's the guilty one?

Juhani: It's not my fault.

Tuomas: Not your fault! Bright balls of fire! I'll eat you alive!

Aapo: Calm down, calm down!

Simeoni: For God's sake, calm down!

Aapo: Let's decide the question of guilt later. Only flight can save us now. Our house is in ashes and we're standing nearly naked in the snow. What good is this rag of a tow shirt? But it's lucky that our guns and ammunition are in the storehouse because we need weapons now. I hear the wolves howling on Teerimäki.

Tuomas: What shall we do?

Aapo: The only thing I can think of is to hurry to Jukola for fear of pale death. Two of us will ride Valko at all times, and the others can run behind. That's what we'll do, take turns running and riding. With the horse we won't have to tramp through snow all the way, and with God's help, we may still be saved.

Juhani: Our feet will be mincemeat long before we stand by the warm fire at Jukola.

Simeoni: But it's our only hope. So hurry. The wind is getting sharper and the sky is clear. Hurry!

Eero: This is the end!

Juhani: The end for seven sons of Jukola.

Simeoni: Our plight is desperate, but the power of Heaven's Lord is great. Hurry!

Tuomas: Get the guns and packs from the storehouse.

Juhani: What a horrible night! Facing freezing cold on the one hand and hungry, howling wolves on the other.

Timo: We're in danger, us and Valko too.

Juhani: Ours is the greater. I've heard that in winter a naked man is a great delicacy to a wolf.

Timo: It's a known fact that a man and a pig taste the same, and a pig is the swag-tail's favorite dish in the winter. We're in for it now, chapter and verse, no doubt about it.

Juhani: What shall we do?

Aapo: Head for Jukola like witches' arrows winging through the night before the frost intensifies and turns our blood to ice with its burning cold. On to Jukola over shrieking Teerimäki. We have weapons to use against wolves, but not against the ice-bearded Frost King.

Tuomas: Here are the guns and packs. Now gun on shoulder and pack on back, each and every man. Two of you up and ride; the rest of us will trot along behind as best we can. But hurry, hurry, for the sake of our immortal souls.

Juhani: The north is clearing and the stars are bright. Hiyah! Let's go!

Aapo: Tomorrow we'll come for whatever the fire has left us and pick up the cat and rooster too. They'll be warm enough tonight beside the hot ruins. But our trusted friends Killi and Kiiski can come with us. Where are they?

Tuomas: They're nowhere to be seen. Quiet? Listen.

Eero: They're running far away from here. You can hear them barking in back of the mountain.

Tuomas: They're trailing a lynx that must have come close enough to the house for them to pick up his trail. But let them chase all they please. We have to forget about them and start off on our own rough trek.

Juhani: So be it! Life and death are going at it like two male bears.

Aapo: Let's run with all our strength?

Juhani: With all our strength of body and soul down to the very marrow.

Tuomas: Keeping in mind that we are facing a miserable death.

Juhani: Black death threatens us on both sides. Hi-yah! It's either a frozen nose or guts on the ground if this boy doesn't soon stand on slippery straw by a fire. It's going to be one or the other before the hour is up. But no use to stand dilly-dallying, no use at all. I'll just grit my teeth and go through mountains of ice, no matter how thick.

Simeoni: In God's name and with His help, we'll try.

Juhani: With His help. For what can a man born of woman do on his own? But we are well protected.

Eero: Let's go at once!

Juhani: And without fear. Let's go now!

Tuomas: We're all ready then. You get up on Valko's back, Eero and Simeoni, and ride off toward Jukola, but see to it that those of us who are trotting after you are always close on the nag's heels.

So they set out, naked but for their tow shirts, each with pack on back and gun in hand or on shoulder. So they set out along the dark, wintry road, fleeing the cold which attacked them from the swamps of Pohjola. But at least the weather did not put on its most awful face, did not get worse for the time being. True, the sky would clear occasionally, but sailing clouds would cover it again, moderating the north wind. The brothers were well acquainted with the cold, their skins toughened by many a shrieking frost. In former days, running wild as boys, they had ramped barefoot in the snow by the hour. But yet they were terri-

fied, utterly terrified, at the prospect of the journey from Impivaara to
Jukola. Onward they fled, fear in their hearts. In the lead on Valko
rode Simeoni and Eero, with the others running close on their heels
kicking up snow that swirled around them. Back at Impivaara
Meadow, the cat and the rooster sat near the glowing sauna stove staring mournfully at the dying fire.

On toward the village charged the brothers, leaving Sompio Swamp
behind and approaching Teerimäki, from which could be heard the
constant, blood-curdling howl of wolves. In a spruce woods between
the swamp and Jaakko Seunala's meadow, they switched riders: Eero
and Simeoni dismounted and two others rushed to take their place.
Without a pause, they resumed their journey, dashed along the spine of
the heath, crossed over the Viertola road, and went through the broad,
soughing pine woods. Finally they reached the crags of Teerimäki, and
suddenly the discordant cry of the wolves fell silent. They soon stood
atop the ridge, pausing to let the horse rest; two riders stepped down
and two others took their place. For a short time they stood on the
snowy crag; the north wind blew, the sky cleared momentarily, and the
position of the Big Dipper's handle showed it to be past midnight.

Having rested, they plunged on again down the smooth mountain
road, and reaching its end, they entered a dark spruce woods where
gloomy nature encompassed them round. The pale moon looked down,
and hoot owls sounded their cry. Deep in the woods were scattered
weird shapes that looked like huge forest bears — mossy roots of
fallen spruce trees reaching high into the air. Motionless as frozen
ghosts, these bear-figures stared at the strange procession racing by
them. They watched motionless, but soon frightening movement was
visible around and about them in the dismal spruce woods. Hungry
wolves circled the brothers, coming nearer and nearer. Now ahead,
now behind, now darting across the road, now among the spruces to
either side, they were seen to scurry. Raging and thirsting for blood,
they pursued the nocturnal refugees from Impivaara, and dry branches
snapped and cracked as they were broken off at the foot of spruce

trees. Trembling and snorting, the skittish Valko ran on, and the lead rider could barely control his flight. But the beasts of prey grew ever bolder. Panting with blood-lust, they would often dash close by the men, and now and then the brothers' guns would roar to the right or left as they sought to scare the animals off. But that did not drive them far.

They came to Kiljava Flats, a heath burned over by a forest fire, where here and there a dry pine trunk stood as a perch for hawks and hoot owls. The rage of the wolves was frightening now, and great was the brothers' danger. Tuomas and Timo were riding; the others who ran behind on foot suddenly turned and fired a heavy volley of shots at their pursuers, who withdrew in fright to a distance. Again the men dashed forward, but it was not long before the stalking pack of wolves was again rustling close around them, and the danger was greater than ever. Then Tuomas stopped the horse and shouted: "Anyone whose gun is empty, load it right now, and in a big hurry!" Thus he shouted and stepped down, telling Timo to keep a tight rein on Valko. The brothers stood and loaded their guns, nor did they feel the cold on their feet or limbs. The wolves too stood some fifty paces from the men, their greedy eyes fixed on them, their tails whisking excitedly. The dome of the sky shone clear now and a bright moon looked down on the heath.

Tuomas: Are your guns loaded?

Aapo: They are. What are you thinking of doing?

Juhani: All together again.

Tuomas: Not if you value your life. Someone should always have a loaded gun, remember that. Lauri, you have the steadiest hand and the sharpest eye. Step beside me here.

Lauri: Here I am. What do you want?

Tuomas: A hungry wolf will eat even his bloody brother. If we can manage this trick, it will save us. Let's try it. We'll aim at the first one on the left and shoot at the same time, but the rest of you hold your fire. Aim with an eagle-eye now, Lauri, and fire when I say, "Now."

Lauri: I'm ready.

Tuomas: Now!

They fired simultaneously and the wolves scrambled away. But one of their number was left on the field, trying unsuccessfully to crawl after the others. The men ran on full tilt once more, six of them on foot and Timo alone riding. A short time went by. Soon the wolves stopped retreating and turned back to trot swiftly after the nocturnal procession again. The snow swished and swirled around them and their paws thumped the smooth surface of Kiljava Heath as they dashed ahead in a pack. With fiery speed, they drew near their companion crawling in his own blood and passed him by, but quickly turned around when the enticing smell of blood reached their nostrils. Around they whirled, tails lashing; the snow flew up in gusts and their eyes burned in the night with greed and longing. Then snarling horribly, they fell in a pack on their wounded brother; an ear-splitting melee erupted on the heath, so horrendous it seemed heaven's pillars must be falling. The ground shook and the snow turned to a ghastly slush as his former comrades tore to shreds the son of the wilderness, whose blood had been set flowing by the accurate shots of Tuomas and Lauri. Then silence reigned over the nocturnal heath once more; the only sounds were a soft panting and a cracking of bones as the wolves, faces bloody and eyes burning, tore and ate their victim.

Far from their awful adversaries, the brothers journeyed on. The noise of the wolves' carnage on Klljava was music to their ears, a sweet and happy message of salvation. Soon they were approaching the broad meadow of Kattila, around which the road curved in a hilly by-pass. To save time, they decided to cut across the meadow. As one, they rushed upon the fence, which gave way. Valko, with two brothers on his back again, stepped over the fallen barrier and set off at a run across the level field with his riders whipping him on, followed by those whose turn it was to tramp through the snow. A winter road to the church village ran through the meadow, along which a party with three horses and sleds was just then traveling. Both men and horses were frightened when they saw the brothers approaching them from the north. They saw charging upon them a horse and seven men clad only in shirts, with guns on their shoulders, and took the group for angry goblins from the caves of Impivaara. There was a mad scramble on the meadow, with horses rushing here and there and men shouting, praying, cursing or screaming so loudly that they roused echoes. The brothers paid little heed to the frenzy, and raced across Kattila Meadow toward Jukola, churning up a spray of snow before them. They came to the opposite fence of the meadow, rushed upon it as one man, bringing it down with a crash, and soon they were back on the hilly road again.

But it had been a ghastly, horrible night for them. They were running hard, panting, their feet flying, goggle-eyed with apprehension, their wooden gaze fixed and staring always toward their former home of Jukola. Without saying a word they rushed on, never pausing, the snowy earth receding rapidly beneath them. Finally they reached the elevation of Pohjanpelto, saw Jukola house on the slope in the pale moonlight, and almost with one voice cried out: Jukola, Jukola!" Down the hill they ran, crossed Oja Meadow like winged goblins, climbed the rise again, and stood on the threshold of the house outside its bolted door. They had no time to knock and wait for admission, but lunged forward with all their strength. The stout door fell open with a clash and a clatter. Stamping and banging, they rushed from the porch into the '*tupa*' and then like a gust of wind over to the warm embers of the fireplace, which breathed a precious warmth toward them. But the tanner's sleep-befuddled family was roundly scared, thinking robbers were attacking them.

Tanner: What monster would come into an honest man's home like this on Christmas night? Answer. My gun is aimed at you.

Tuomas: Put your gun down, my good man.

Aapo: Don't shoot the people of this house.

Juhani: We've come, God help us, from Impivaara.

Timo: The seven former sons of Jukola.

Simeoni: God have mercy on us! Seven souls on the way to eternity this very moment, this awful moment. God have mercy on us!

Juhani: Fire burned our fine house in the forest and all our goods. We ran here like rabbits without a stitch to cover our poor bodies but for this rag of a shirt. It was a terrible trip.

Tanner's Wife: Lord Jesus save you!

Tanner: Oh, you poor things.

Juhani: Now does this make any sense? Here we sit like magpies crying to God for mercy. Oh, I have to cry.

Wife: You poor dear children! Hurry up, old man, and build up the fire.

Eero: Oh unlucky night. Oh unlucky us!

Aapo: Oh horrible night!

Simeoni: Oh alas!

Juhani: Don't cry, Eero, don't cry, Simeoni, don't snivel at all.

Aapo: Don't cry, don't cry, brother Eero. We're safe now. But it was a Turkish march!

Wife: Oh man-child in this world, Oh!

Juhani: Dear lady, your tears and pity make me cry again. Oh, but don't cry woman, don't cry! We've escaped from the clutches of animals and cold into the warmth of Christian kin, thank God for that.

Tuomas: Misery, total misery, is our lot. But build us a roaring fire, bring us a few sheaves of straw for a bed on the floor, and take Valko to the barn and give him some hay.

Aapo: Forgive our begging so much, for right and life's sake.

Juhani: Angels of mercy! My life was at the tip of my nose, ready to go, ready to go. If you have meat and beer in the house, then bring it on. That was a rough time, a drubbing we'll remember. Bring meat and warm beer for our dear lives' and souls' sake.

Tanner: All we can get and have time for, as soon as I get a light in the house. You poor things! Nothing but shirts on!

Juhani: Not a rag for our heads or an old shoe for our feet. Look at these goose feet, look!

Tanner: It gives me the chills. Come and see, woman.

Timo: Come and look at my legs too.

Juhani: They're nothing compared to mine. There boy, look at that. They're parboiled.

Timo: What about these?

Juhani: What are your feet to mine?

Timo: My feet? Pay no attention to him. Look here. Is this human flesh?

Tanner: Come and see, woman.

Wife: Well, goodness gracious and heavens above!

Juhani: Yes, isn't this just too much. Even Tuomas has tears in his eyes. Don't cry, Tuomas. As I said, isn't it too much?

Timo: That's how a poor man-child gets tossed around here.

Wife: How they blush and glow, blush and glow! Goodness gracious!

Timo: Like iron in a forge, like wrought iron. Hee-hee!

Wife: So red, so red. Lord Jesus protect us.

Juhani: They're just like "molten brass," as the Bible says. Heaven help us poor wretches.

Wife: Oh, you poor dear children!

Lauri: Do what we asked. You promised.

Aapo: We beg you to hurry. We'll build up the fire ourselves since there are blocks in this corner, big blocks with plenty of bark.

Juhani: So we're in old Jukola, sitting under these familiar sooty rafters once more, and we'll stay at least until May Day. Let our old "tupa" be our lodging for this winter yet.

Tuomas: But let summer come.

Juhani: Let summer come and there will be another house on Impivaara Meadow, grander than the first.

Tuomas: As soon as the snow is gone, let the woods and mountains ring with the blow of axes. Then the Jukola brothers will no longer need to beg others for shelter.

Juhani: Well said! Tuomas, let's forget the cursed prank that set our house on fire and think of the new house we'll build.

Tuomas: Let me tell you that all my anger disappeared when we started on that fearful trip. When you were running behind me gasping like a drowning stallion, it cut me to the heart.

Juhani: Then let's be glad that the journey is over and we're standing in a warm house again. They're bringing us food and drink and two huge sheaves of shining straw. Let's thank God, my dear brothers.

The open birch fire burned cheerfully and the brothers basked contentedly in its mellow warmth. After standing there awhile in a row of seven, they moved to the table to enjoy the meat, bread, sausages, and mulled ale which the tanner's wife, a compassionate woman, served up to them. The host himself took care of Valko, leading him to the stable and filling the manger with hay. At last the dogs too, following the trail of the men, returned from their gloomy journey; they arrived panting and fawning, their eyes shining with happiness. The brothers welcomed them with great joy, pitying, feeding, and coddling them in every way.

When the brothers had eaten, they sank down on their soft straw beds, and soon, wrapped up in sleep's filmy shawl, they forgot life's struggles. Sweetly they rested, and for a long time the blazing fire kept them warm until it eventually died down to embers. Then the wife closed the damper and a delicious warmth flowed from the fireplace into the room, after which she went back to bed and again there was silence everywhere in the room. But outdoors the frost skipped cracking along the fence, the north wind blew strongly beneath a sky sparkling with stars, and the pale moon looked down smiling.

CHAPTER VII

In early spring, even before the coming of the cranes, the brothers left Jukola for Impivaara Meadow, where they pitched in with might and main to build a new house for themselves. Soon a single course of stout timbers rested on corner stones, upon which walls rose tier by tier. Day after day, from dawn to dusk, the axes rang and the heavy mallet thumped. Juhani, Aapo, Tuomas, and Simeoni each sat at a corner, while the others hued the logs and rolled them up skids to the structure. Sweating, but always cheerful, they worked on; the walls rose steadily as the fresh scent of pitch drifted around. But there were days when the brothers did not swing an ax; instead they snored away sound asleep from one evening to the next, sometimes even till the morning of a third day.

But before the grain had turned yellow in the fields of the village, the house in Impivaara Meadow stood ready. It was on the same site and had the same shape and form as the original — but it was still grander. And with their sturdy house now ready, the brothers could again concentrate on their hunting and fishing trips. Equipped with both rifles and fishing gear, they set out with the dogs, whose eyes flashed fire. Tirelessly they scoured the wooded hills, swamps, and grounds; their keel plowed over the whole bright surface of Lake Ilves as they gathered provisions both for the day and for the severe winter ahead. So many a denizen of Ahti's waters and Tapio's woods met its doom.

But now I would like to tell about old Tinder-Matti, the brothers' only company out here in the woods. — There was an old man called

Tinder-Matti; he lived on a knoll thickly covered with cross-grained birch, alone he lived in a small hut a few thousand paces from Impivaara. He made the softest tinder in Häme and the toughest birch-bark shoes, trades that brought him a steady supply of daily bread. In his youth he had traveled in the North as the loyal driver to his former parish church provost, who had moved away to the very border of Lapland. There Tinder-Matti had spent the next summer, hunting bear, wolverine, and cranes in the endless swamps of the North. He had many stories to tell of his trips and an incomparably keen memory; he never forgot anything he had seen or heard. He also had great powers of observation served by a sharp eye, and wandered through the maze-like forests without ever getting lost. He believed he knew, with hair's-breadth accuracy, the direction of any place he had once visited, no matter how far off. He would point toward it with his thumb, and it was useless to argue with him, so unshakable was his opinion. If, for example, you asked, "Where is Vuokatti?" he would answer promptly by shoving a thumb toward the horizon: "There, sight along my thumb, you'd hit it if you shot there. That little knob is where Kuusamo Church is, but just a shade to the right runs a line to Vuokatti." Likewise, if you asked him, "Where is the battlefield of Porrassalmi?" he would answer at once, shoving his thumb toward the horizon, "There, sight along my thumb, you'd hit it if you shot there." The old man was that precise, and he knew the woods for scores of miles around his hut. He had criss-crossed them many times, now seeking fungi, now birch bark for shoes, now checking his snares. Sometimes he stopped on these rounds to say hello to the brothers at Impivaara. That was a jolly time for them; they listened mouths agape to the old man's stories, mouths agape and ears pricked up like a bat's. One August night, he sits in the brothers' house, telling them about his hunting trips in the North.

Juhani: Is that so? And then what happened?

Tinder-Matti: Let's see. How did it go? We came to a kind of clearing, a squooshy bog, and slithered over the quaking pit on our skis. We found lots of cranes' nests, shot many of the whooping birds, crammed our bags with eggs and feathers, and tossed a good-sized bundle of the birds over our shoulders. And then we took a drink. And then we took off again over the shaky-quaky, squishy-squooshy bog, dogs and cranes draped over our necks, and often a man was near sinking forever into the depths with a whining dog over his neck. But then we came to an echoing hill, a stretch of solid ground, and we were as wet as drowned rats. There we pitched camp for the night, lighted the flaring fire, and stripped off our sopping coats. And nothing else would do but to peel off our pants and shirts too, peel them off like eelskins. Our clothes were soon steaming on tree limbs, cranes' eggs sizzling in the hot ashes, and we ourselves swiveling and turning in the nice heat from the fire, as naked as night goblins. And then we took a drink. And how did it go then? How did the May night pass? The dogs kept sniffing around with their moist nostrils and glaring up at the treetops. In the end, we looked up too, and what do you think we saw there?

Juhani: Tell us. It must have been a squint-eyed bear cub.

Timo: Or a spook or a goblin in person.

Tinder-Matti: Neither, but a swarthy, fat lump of a wolverine sitting in the fork of a mossy dried pine. Heiskanen shot, but with no effect; Little-Jussi shot, but with no effect; finally I let fly, with the same blessed result. The wolverine twitched once and gave a ferocious growl, but stayed in his neat perch on the limb. Then Heiskanen yelled, "Witches' tricks, witches' tricks!" and took a dead man's tooth from his pocket, chomped on it a few times, and spat on the bullet that he put back into his gun. Then he sawed the air a few times with one hand, rolled his eyes fearfully and said, "Spawn of the devil!" and a few other weird and horrible things, and then he fired, and down from the tree flopped the wolverine. But the devil was still far from dead, and the fun started again. Naked as we were, we couldn't go near the thing, and the dogs didn't want to either, just skipped and yelped from a couple of yards away as the wolverine kept spitting and growling at them from the bushes. The witches' powers, you see, were still effective. But Heiskanen again started muttering awful words, flailing with his hand, and rolling his eyes horribly. And lo, one of the dogs charged on the red-mawed rascal, charged in like a flashing rocket, and then there was a dust-up. Well Lord, how that dog carried on with that wolverine — this way and that way and thus and so. The devil take it if there was ever a pasting and basting to match it, not ever.

Timo: That would have been fun.

Tinder-Matti: It was great fun and games, it was!

Timo: And did you put the wolverine in the sack?

Tinder-Matti: It was too hefty a chunk to stuff in a sack, a really fat lump. So, then we took a drink. Then we put on our coats again, dry as powder now, and went nicely to bed in the heat of that blazing fire. But we didn't get much sleep, for the witches' arrows kept sailing criss-cross through the air over our fuddled heads like fiery snakes. Often enough, Heiskanen would leap up shouting, "Out, out, you witches' arrows!" and many of them did fall whizzing into the woods or the gray swamp, but still more of them skimmed along on their smooth course, in spite of his cries. At one time a devilish mean and fierce snuffling sound could be heard streaking from north to south, followed for a long time afterwards by a faint gibbering. "What blowhard went scooting by?" I asked Heiskanen, who growled back after a minute, "That was Old Harry himself."

An hour went by, and then another as the mild, foggy air flashed fire. Suddenly a sound like the roaring of mossy spruces was heard from the eastern shore of the swamp and another sound answered it from the western shore, as gentle as the whisper of small birches. "What was that roar and rustle?" I asked, and Heiskanen finally growled, "Old Father Spruce is talking to his daughter." But at last the night ended. Dawn arrived and we went tramping off again. And look, just as we reached the edge of the woods, we saw a devil of a big gray wolf, but he took off like drying pea stalks in a whirlwind. The last thing in sight was his hind leg. I aimed my gun and shot his paw off, snapped it off like a piece of crisp bacon. I shot the poor old bugger's paw in two, yet he saved himself.

Timo: The devil you say! Snapped his paw off like an icicle, and it lay there like a pickled pig's foot?

Tinder-Matti: Well, not exactly.

Tuomas: But how did you know the foot was broken off.

Tinder-Matti: We ran after him for a long way and saw in many places how wolfie-boy's limp, dragging paw had sort of made figure tens in the sand.

Timo: Well, the devil take you. Figure tens in the sand. Hee, hee, hee!

Tinder-Matti: Clear figure tens.

Juhani: The wolf had a rough time of it.

Tinder-Matti: And the men too. But the damned dogs wouldn't go more than a couple of yards from our feet, just moped along with their tails between their legs, the same dogs that had always been so brave before this.

Aapo: What killed their spirit?

Tinder-Matti: Witches' tricks, spell-binding fumes the air was full of, like powder smoke on battlefields. Heiskanen tried his best, cursing and swearing and sawing the air, but all in vain. And that rascal, Little-Jussi, he trotted along like a dwarf, feet thumping the ground and sweating bullets. The boy's legs were only a foot and a half long at the most, but he had a real otter's back, long and tough. He was tough all over, just as damned tough and stubborn as an otter itself. For the longest time he kept barreling along with the wolf limping away ahead of him, but it did no good in the end. He had to leave the wolf to the woods. And so we took a drink. And then we marched off for home, carrying a rich haul. We tramped along, bags full of eggs, feathers and odds and ends from the woods, skis and cranes on our backs, guns in hand, with the wolverine bobbing up and down on each man's shoulders in turn. So we marched along. A squawking snipe went flying along at the edge of the clouds; I shot him and stuffed him into my bag. After we walked awhile, I saw a flying squirrel in the top of a pine and I shot the flat-bellied big-eye and put him in my bag.

At last we came to a high, spreading meadow and could see Turkkila Farm to our south, where we had started out on our tough trip. We came to a bloody place the owner of Turkkila had pointed out to us when we left on the hunt, where a bear had killed a stallion a couple of days earlier. We took a look at the brute's bloody table and saw that he had been there lately, probably the evening before, to enjoy the scraps from his feast. I guessed he would come back again that day at sundown and made up my mind to stay and wait for him, but the others were glad to go on ahead to eat supper at Turkkila. There I stood, thinking and thinking and scratching my head, wondering where I could wait for my visitor in that open meadow without a single tree to climb. But "brains are better than brawn." I finally came up with a gimmick, a really neat trick. I saw a pine stump close by, a monstrous-huge black thing heaved at least two feet up into the air by the spring frosts. With my ax I hacked off the tap root that ran straight down, pulled it out, and opened up the hole a little more. I crawled inside, stuck my gun out toward the bloody field, and waited for Brother Bruin, nicely protected by my overhead fort. He came lumbering up from the meadow, sank his teeth into the torn flank of the stallion, and I decided to carefully give him a dose of lead in the forehead. But damn it all! The brass plate on the stock of my gun made the tiniest clink against one of my coat buttons and the brute's sharp ears caught the sound right off. He charged at me in a rage, but I banged away. He paid no attention, just kept on coming, roaring ferociously. I heard a crashing overhead; roots crunched and the earth split as the many-rooted stump was lifted up from over my head. And I, poor boy, thought my last day had come and waited gun in hand for the monster's mouth to gape open before my eyes. But suddenly the noise stopped and everything was still, as still as the grave, and the hand-to-hand struggle I was expecting never did come. I waited a little longer and finally peeked out between the roots of the stump, and there was the bear stone dead, the uprooted stump in his arms, blood pouring out from his breast onto the earth. Hallelujah, I thought, a free lad once more under the open sky. The stump had been lifted as neat as can be from over my head.

Juhani: "Hell's bells, said Hesku-Jaakko!"

Timo: By all the seven smiths!

Juhani: The neatest trick ever pulled!

Tuomas: A brave trick, a manly trick, yours and the bear's.

Juhani: Oh you black bull!

Timo: Doggone it! What more can a man say? But then what happened?

Tinder-Matti: Well, you can guess, can't you? They heard the shot even at Turkkila, like a shout from the bottom of a barrel, and men were soon swarming in the meadow like mosquitoes. Now there was a real uproar as they carried the brute home on a bending, sagging pole. He was a real Grand-dad. Hanging from the cross-bar, he darkened the whole room at Turkkila, like a thick thundercloud in the sky. So that's what happened on that day and on the whole trip. And then we took a drink.

Juhani: And had a merry funeral for the bear.

Tinder-Matti: It started at Turkkila and wound up at the parsonage with gravy-stained faces and bleary eyes. That's the way it was, but those days have come and gone. Yet an old man likes to remember and talk about his stunts in better days.

Aapo: And we like to listen to them.

Juhani: Keep telling stories all night and we'll forget there's such a thing as sleep.

Tinder-Matti: It's time to amble off to my shack again, it's that time. God keep you, brothers.

Juhani: God protect you, worthy Matti.

Aapo: Stay in good health. You're always welcome in our house.

Ax on his shoulder, Matti set off for his little hut on the hill with its thick stand of birch trees. The brothers went to their night's rest, for darkness was gaining the upper hand and the fading light of evening shone but faintly through the small window-holes of their house. But for a long time, excited thoughts swarmed through their minds, expelling restful sleep. They kept thinking of Tinder-Matti's account of the northern wilderness, of the enchanted air and of witches' arrows that flew hissing helter-skelter through the dark night. Like the sparkling arrows and flaming guns, their hearts too burned with a strange zeal and desire. The thought of the crane roused their highest ardor, that bird with the shrewd, clever eyes, whose solemnly raucous cry echoes through the northern marshes; their minds glowed with the pleasant warmth of feathered nests in the skirts of bog-bilberry bushes, nests filled with gleaming eggs. To hunt the long-necks there and rob their nests, that was the brothers' lust now. Their minds were strongly drawn to the solemn gloom of the northern swamps.

But it was Juhani who lay awake the longest. He pondered over the means to carry out a hunt here in this home parish that would rival the one in the dark swamps he had just heard about. He thought of Kourusuo, which in fact had no cranes, but teemed with speckled ducks. And since the repeated drinks of the men in the north tempted him so strongly, he remembered that liquor was to be had at Viertola Manor. So he put together in his mind a version of the noble northern hunt and, having decided to put it into effect in the morning, he fell asleep at last. But in his dreams, he was romping far away on Tinder-Matti's mighty expedition. Once he sat bolt upright in his sleep, crying out wildly, "A wolverine — a wolverine! Grab the crane-neck!" Half-awakened by the shout, the others barked out peevishly from their corners but soon sank back into sleep. For a long time Juhani stared around until he realized that he was not surrounded by a gray expanse of swamps in the misty regions of Lapland, but was in the peaceful loft of his own home. Gradually, his mind cleared and he lay back and slept soundly. But when he rose in the morning, he remembered his nocturnal decision and immediately broached it to his brothers.

Juhani: Listen, brothers, and I want you to think carefully about what I have to say. I know a place that's full of game. I really wonder how we could have forgotten about Kourusuo till now, where huge flocks of waterfowl swarm among the reeds and in the clear ponds. Let's go hunting there. We'll bring back whopping big ducks by the sackful.

Tuomas: I'll go along with that.

Timo: Me too, gladly.

Eero: Me too, and when I tramp through Kourusuo, I'll pretend to be Little-Jussi in the bogs of Lapland. Let's do it!

Aapo: I have nothing against the plan. It could bring us food for many a day.

Juhani: It's settled then. But it's a long way to Kourusuo, a long, long way, and we'll be there at least overnight, so I think there's no harm in having a little drink since we're sleeping out in the open.

Tuomas: There's liquor to be had at Viertola.

Juhani: And good liquor too.

Tuomas: Seven half-pints, boys!

Juhani: Right! One for every man.

Aapo: Shouldn't we forget about the liquor. It's not exactly a habit with us yet.

Juhani: You've had a nip every now and then just like me.

Eero: Take the man's little hint, Aapo. Let us for once be able to say, "And then we took a drink," when we're graybeards and tell our war stories to the young. Let's imagine that we're really blasting wolverines in Lapland.

Juhani: What's all this nonsense? A man has to feed his body. This trip will have us tramping through marshes and spongy bogs and spending the night sopping wet on a bed of moss. A little nip from a pocket flask would do us good then, I think. Let's say it's best, then, to have a medicinal draft in our packs when we start out. We'll send Lauri to Viertola now with our best fox pelt in his pack; it's sure to pry loose the booze.

Lauri set out for Viertola for liquor to fortify them during their duck hunt at Kourusuo. This vast swamp, which is surrounded by gloomy forests, lies some five thousand paces from Impivaara on land belonging to Viertola Manor. Its surface, a favorite habitat of ducks, varies from clear ponds, to patches of tall herbage, to islet hillocks with stands of dried pines. It was there the brothers had decided to hunt the quacking ducks, hoping for a rich haul.

Lauri returned from Viertola carrying the sparkling liquor in a pewter bottle, once their father's hunting canteen. Along with the drink he brought news that further inflamed the brothers' enthusiasm. He told them that a bear had felled one of Viertola's best bullocks, and he also knew where the slaughter had taken place — On Viertola land north of Impivaara close to the boundary of Jukola. The brothers determined to pass this spot on their journey to Kourusuo and not to set out until evening was near. They were hoping perhaps to run into the bear, an animal that usually comes back at sundown to enjoy the remains of his fallen prey. After a hearty dinner, they set off in the waning afternoon with full equipment, packs on their backs and guns heavily loaded. Lauri brought up the rear, leading the dogs and carrying the liter and a half of liquor in his pack. He had been ordered to stay back with the dogs some three hundred paces away from the site of the slaughter and to unleash Killi and Kiiski when he heard shouting or the sound of gunfire. So he stood awaiting the event at the foot of a spruce tree. The others approached the place where the bullock had been killed and found the animal's haff-eaten carcass on the bloody ground in a gloomy spruce grove. They hid themselves in the cover of a short but dense clump of spruces within reasonable firing range and resolved to wait there.

Considerable time passed but eventually they heard the soft padding of feet on the ground and the rustle of twigs, and judged the guest to be approaching the feast. And so he was. Among the trees, cautious and striving for silence, a huge black bear was drawing near. But he seemed to sense danger and stopped a good distance from his victim, snuffling and turning his snout in the air. He shilly-shallied for a long time, and finally it looked as if he would go back without corning within rifle range of the men. The brothers waited in total silence among the spruces, until finally Timo, ignoring the negative gestures of the others, started sneaking in an arc toward the ferocious enemy. And now, when he thought he was near enough, he fired a shot, but only the powder in the pan flared up without igniting the charge in the barrel. The enraged bear, which looked like a huge, mossy boulder, came charging at the man, who instantly threw himself face down on the ground and lay there motionless. The beast sniffed at him and clawed and tore at his hair, grumbling and grunting viciously. Timo would probably have died then if Juhani had not rushed to his aid, taking aim at the bear's spine. But thinking of his brother who lay beneath the bear, he did not dare aim low, and the bullet did not find its mark, at least not in a vital spot, for the prince of the forest lunged at Juhani even more wildly, leaving Timo with his face in the dirt. Then Jussi, to save his own life, turned the butt of his rifle toward the beast's open maw, and a frightful struggle was imminent. But now Tuomas let fly, sending a fiery bullet into the beast's leg. To avoid hitting his brother, he too could not aim at the head or breast where a wound would be surer to cause death. The bear felt the lead in his flesh, and the blood ran down his fat, round leg. With a horrible, savage roar, he rushed at Tuomas but took such a sharp blow on his brow from the man's gun that he stopped in his tracks, shaking his head. And now the enemies stood for a second, defiantly facing each other.

Then the dogs rushed up like two swift, silent streaks, and when they reached the merciless bear, an angry melee erupted. Killi raged at the bear's face, always staying a step or two away, while Kiiski attacked him from the rear, sometimes daring to nip at the fur on his thighs, but always dodging nimbly aside whenever the honey-paw of the forest turned his bulk around between them like a great, dark-gray haystack. Finally, after a few vain rushes at his tormentors, the bear fled with the raging dogs at his heels.

All this happened quickly, before the other brothers arrived on the battlefield. Juhani and Tuomas were already reloading, hoping to catch up with the bear again. Timo rose slowly to his feet and stared around for awhile as if not knowing which way was up or where the wind was blowing from. The others scolded him angrily for his stupid rashness, which might have cost men's lives and forever ruined the hunt. Without a word, Timo sat down on a hillock and began reaming out the touch hole of his gun and sharpening his flint by tapping it with the haft of his knife. Soon they all stood ready to continue the chase.

The dogs' barking moved farther and farther away, fading almost beyond earshot, and the brothers began to doubt that they would find their quarry again. But soon the sound of Killi's and Kiiski's voices grew clearer again, coming nearer and nearer. It was plain that the bear was circling as usual and returning to his starting point. Gun in hand, the brothers stationed themselves in appropriate places to wait for the approaching chase. Simeoni stood in a small, grassy clearing a short distance from Lauri, both silent and motionless as statues. The bear came on at a dead run that made the earth thunder, its gaping mouth showing a dark red maw. Toward Simeoni sped the panting brute. The man fired and the honey-paw tumbled to the grass, but it rose again and rushed at the gunman. Then Lauri's gun flashed fire, a sharp report echoed around, and the bear lay still at Simeoni's feet, lay without moving a limb, blood flowing from his head and chest.

The brothers soon gathered around the fallen bear. It was a huge old male, its head pierced at the base of one ear, and a hole in its side. The first hole, they all knew, had been made by Lauri's bullet, for an animal whose brain has been punctured will drop in a flash, never to rise again. The hunters sat contentedly around the shaggy forest warrior preparing to drink to the kill. The dogs too sat contentedly near their fallen foe, looking on nobly. It was a beautiful evening. The wind had died down and the sun was sinking into the dark fringe of the forest. It was a pleasure for the brothers to rest awhile on such an evening after the hot and noisy struggle.

Juhani: Let Lauri have the first drink. He shot like a man, hit the rascal in a perfect spot, and the bear went down on his paws like hay before a scythe. Take a healthy snort my boy!

Lauri: Maybe I'll take a swallow, for once.

Juhani: You're new at drinking, as innocent as a lamb. You've never had a taste of it.

Lauri: I know what it tastes like — I can tell it from buttermilk, but how it feels to reel around full of joy-juice, that I don't know.

Aapo: Think a little, Lauri. I would rather forbid than invite you.

Lauri: We'll try it.

Aapo: And hope it's not the beginning of a bad habit.

Lauri: What are you babbling about? Take a drink. We've got reason to be a little jolly.

Juhani: There lies our Roaring-Boy like a big haystack, and we've saved the life of many a cow and horse.

Timo: I know for sure that the owner of Viertola will shove a free bottle of liquor into our pockets, at least a quart or two.

Juhani: I wouldn't consider that too much, seeing that we saved his herd of bulls from this monster.

Aapo: He does have a big herd: forty horned head. All summer long, they live day and night in the woods, but during the winter they haul all the manor's manure out to the fields. Their free summer life in the woods, though, makes them almost wild.

Juhani: God keep our dogs from getting mixed up with them — they would soon make mincemeat of men and dogs. Remember Nikkilä's plight with Honkamäki's bulls; he was in a real panic, even though there were fewer there than in this glowering herd from Viertola. He would have been killed because of his dogs, which always run to their master for protection in a scuffle, if he hadn't run into a sheltering wall, a strong pasture fence that finally stopped the bull's charge.

Aapo: Let's be on the lookout. I heard their hoarse bawling from that hill awhile ago. I don't think they're far away from us. But what's Eero doing by that tree?

Eero: There's an otter in the hollow under this rock.

Juhani: Can it be?

Eero: I'm sure of it. His tracks go into this hole but not out again. You can see them in the sand.

Aapo: Show the tracks to the dogs. The wagging of their tails will tell us if anyone is at home.

Juhani: Here, Killi and Kiiski.

Tuomas: They're gone off again, probably trailing a rabbit.

Eero: We can pry this rock up together.

Tuomas: People have tried sillier things. Give me your ax, Juhani, and I'll cut us each a strong pole to pry with, and we'll lift the rock up together now that the dogs have come back.

Thus they spoke, and Tuomas cut a stout pole for each of them, four of birch and three of mountain ash. But suddenly they heard a heavy pounding and thrashing in the woods, which seemed to be approaching with alarming speed. Poles in hand, the brothers listened and wondered, waiting for whatever would finally appear out of the woods. They could hear an ugly, confused bellowing, and the dogs whined miserably every now and then. Soon a horrifying sight burst into view. Ten angry bulls came charging at them, driving back the dogs who fled for their lives toward them. The men's hair stood on end and cold shivers ran through them. Without pausing, the bulls came on, bellowing deafeningly; staunchly the brothers stood their ground, and a ghastly struggle began. The brothers struck with their stout poles; horned heads cracked, and already two of the bulls lay on the field, pawing the air with their hoofs. But death now threatened the brothers.

Timo fell, and a bull was stooping to gore the fallen man's breast, but Tuomas's mountain ash pole came down heavily, breaking the beast's backbone. Bawling, the animal sank lifeless to the earth, and Timo was saved. The same destruction threatened Aapo, but Juhani and Eero saved him. Juhani clubbed the bull forcefully between the horns, while Eero tugged at its tail to pull it away. This animal too soon lay on the field, pawing the air with his hoofs. Timo lost his club of birch in the fray, but soon he spotted Juhani's ax lying on the ground; he snatched it up and began to flail away furiously. He struck to the right and he struck to the left; bulls' bellies were horribly gashed open, and blood, guts, and urine gushed out onto the field. Pale-faced, the men fought on in the jaws of death, and the dogs too did their best, their teeth gripping the bulls' throats like steel cutters. Great was the confusion as the fracas surged to and fro — poles rose and fell, broken horns flew through the air, and the cries of the brothers, the yelping of the dogs, and the bellowing of the bulls blended into one horrifying uproar.

But at last the conflict subsided. Seven bulls were lying dead on the ground and three of them had fled, the first with but a single horn, the second with none, and the third otherwise badly mauled. Pale and goggle-eyed, the brothers stood on the bloody field. Stained in red, Timo stood with the soiled and bloody ax in his hand, like a slash-and-burn woodchopper. The brothers could hardly understand what had happened. It seemed like an awful dream — the tumult that had overwhelmed them like a violent whirlwind, raged among them for a time, and then suddenly subsided. They gazed in horror at the large number of animals that lay before them on the bloody ground: the monstrously huge bear of the spruce woods and the seven fat bulls. They themselves had taken hard knocks in the battle — Aapo, Juhani and Timo especially — but all of them were still on their feet. There they stood, poles in hand, panting and sweating and silently staring at one another.

But they barely had time to catch their breath when another danger was upon them. The whirlwind was succeeded by a hurricane, and the end of the world seemed at hand. The ground shook as from an earthquake, the woods crashed, and a horrible bellowing filled the still evening air as thirty-three savage bulls galloped toward them. The brothers listened wide-eyed to the din without moving a muscle. As silently as a herd of pigs after a long chase listens with cocked ears in the brush by the fence corner to hear if their pursuers are still after them, so the brothers listened, until the herd of bulls burst out of the woods. Then they threw down their poles, took up their guns, and fled full tilt with the dogs, the bellowing bulls hot on their heels. Toward the boundary fence between the Jukola woods and Viertola Manor flew the brothers. In their path lay a shallow pond with a surface cover of vegetation, but there was no time to avoid it. Through it they ran, without hesitation. Water splashed, spray and scum hid them from sight, but they were soon in the open air again. Their flight was like the moon's course through the blue fields of the sky. She does not turn aside for a flimsy cloud that tries to block her path, but sails through it serenely and emerges on the other side brighter than before. Stately and steadfast she goes on her way. But the Jukola boys ran like rabbits or wild goats for danger was hot on their heels. They came to the strong, new fence and flew over it like a thunderbolt. Some twenty paces beyond it, they stopped in a broad meadow to see if the fence could save them. The raging, roaring herd of bulls reached it. There was a loud crash. The spruce fence lay shattered, and the bulls were closer to the brothers than before. Next they ran over an echoing meadow, men and dogs in the lead and the beasts after them, bellowing and kicking up sod and dusty sand, as a winter storm sends snow swirling high in the air. The brothers ran at a furious pace with the fear of death in their hearts, for they believed they were taking their last steps along life's path.

Then Aapo shouted, "Let's throw away our packs but hang on to our guns!" Thus he spoke, and six birchbark packs fell as one to the ground. The seventh still bobbed along on Lauri's back; he was not of a mind to let it go yet. The move was of small help, for the awful thumping and bellowing came closer and closer. But once more Aapo

shrieked out miserably, "To Hiisi Rock, to Hiisi Rock!" He was refer-
ring to a certain enormous boulder that stood in the dismal wilderness.
Toward it the brothers sped. Soon they were at its foot, and in a flash,
men and dogs were climbing to its top. Tufts of moss flew afar as their
paws gripped the jagged rock, their nails clinging tighter, surer, and
sharper than ever a lynx's hooked claws. Thus were they saved from a
ghastly death, but close had they come to its jaws. Barely had they
mounted the rock when they were surrounded by a milling herd of
beasts bellowing and pawing the ground. This rock, the men's refuge,
was a nearly square, six-foot-high craggy block that stood in the
woods some three hundred paces from the meadow. There the brothers
sat now, sweating and panting fearfully from their flight to escape angry death. For a long time they sat mute and wordless, but finally Juhani opened his mouth:

Juhani: Here we are, brothers, and thank our lucky stars. It's a jaunt
we'll remember as long as there are bulls on this earth.

Aapo: Here we are, but how will we leave here? A bull is a stubborn beast and the ones here are in a rage at their companions' death,
which they would like to avenge many times over on our dogs.

Juhani: And we would have to drink from the same dipper.

Aapo: Except for this rock's precious height.

Juhani: It was a welcome sight, it was. We climbed up it as fast as
squirrels.

Eero: "And then we took a drink."

Juhani: That's right. Thank God we have the liquor, if we have to
learn how to fast here.

Lauri: I didn't throw my pack away.

Juhani: And we owe you thanks, brother. But bring out the pewter
bottle, toss off a good swig, and start it going around. We could stand
a little bucking up.

Aapo: But we have to be careful with the stuff in such a tight spot.

Juhani: A healthy reminder. So take a middling snort.

Aapo: Moderation is always best. Remember that this will be our bed, maybe for more than one night.

Juhani: God spare us that? I hope hunger soon drives that forest of horns away from us. So here we sit on Hiisi Rock, like seven owls in the wilderness. But where did this rock get its name?

Aapo: From a strange story.

Juhani: Tell it to us to pass the time. This is just the place for tales and stories.

And Aapo told them the following tale.

Once there dwelt in his castle among the Lapland hills a powerful prince of Hiisi, the mightiest magician of the north. He was the owner of a noble and beautiful elk, incomparably swift of foot. One day in early spring the graceful animal went out to frolic on the crusted snow and wound up roving the length and breadth of Finland. Many an archer, seeing the golden pelt and the bright eyes of the animal, rushed in pursuit with his tempered arrows. But no one could keep up with the animal: a man on skis was soon left far behind. At length the elk arrived in Häme, where there lived a superb skier and accurate archer. He picked up the trail of Hiisi's handsome elk and set out in swift pursuits gliding on his smooth skis, a mighty bow on his shoulder. The elk ran over the smooth snow at blinding speeds but the archer followed even faster. For a long time they raced across open flatland and up and down steep hills. Finally weariness began to overcome the elk: it gasped as it ran, its pace slowed, and the man drew ever nearer. Then a strange thing happened which had often been seen to stop an archer's arrows in the past. The elk turned suddenly and approached his pursuer prayerfully shedding copious tears. But without hesitation, the cruel man let fly his shaft. It pierced the lovely animal's brow and Hiisi's elk fell, dying the white snow red with its blood.

At that moment Hiisi, who was journeying through the gloomy valleys of outer Lapland felt a sudden twinge in his heart and knew that his golden young elk was in danger. He rushed up the hill where his castle stood and began to focus his magic scope on the south. Far away in a dark spruce forest, he saw his elk bathed in blood and writhing in the pangs of death, and he saw the murderer standing near his victim with a look of triumph on his face. He flew into a terrible rage, tore a huge block of stone from the castle wall and sent it flying high in the air toward the bowman in the wilds of Häme. With a rush and a roar the enormous stone flew in a high arc to the dome of the sky and sank down toward the day again. Square on the archer's head fell the stupendous weight, burying the man beneath it forever.

Juhani: And the man's death was our good luck. Where would we be now without this stone? Lying there as bloody, gutted carcasses.

Tuomas: We'll get our fill of this yet, I warrant you.

Juhani: God help us before it's too late!

Timo: We'll have to snore the night away stacked up on one another like barn swallow chicks in a nest.

Aapo: That will never do. A sleep-befogged man would soon tumble off and fall prey to the bulls. That's why two of us will have to keep watch over our sleeping brothers at all times, one on either side.

Juhani: Wise advice, and we'll follow it closely. We'll have to spend at least a night here. We can tell that by what the bulls are doing. Three of the devils are sprawled out on their bellies grunting and chewing their cud, the fiends! But lie down boys, Aapo and I will watch till about midnight. Lie down, lie down! God bless us!

Aapo: Woe is us!

Simeoni: What bad luck we've run into.

Juhani: Misery, misery, nothing but misery. But lie down, boys, and ask blessings on your soul and body, in God's name, and go to sleep.

Thus they spent the night, with two of them staying awake at all times, while the others lay sleeping on the mossy rock. Long was the night but dawn came at last. The sun rose, but their fate remained unchanged: a circle of swaying, tossing horns ringed Hiisi Rock on all sides, and sharp pangs of hunger were already pinching their stomachs. But they hoped the same merciless visitor would do its work in the bulls' bellies, eventually forcing them to find pasturage. So they hoped, and waited for their foes to leave, but soon realized to their dismay that there was plenty of animal fodder in the wilderness sedge grass around Hiisi Rock. This the bulls began to nibble steadily, never moving out of sight of the rock.

Juhani: They have no intention of clearing out. They plan to make this their house and home till winter, devil take it.

Eero: The devil is in them.

Timo: They have no problems here. The woods give them food and drink, but we have nothing but dry moss.

Simeoni: But it's because of the dogs that we're sitting here. I'm afraid our only way out is to throw Killi and Kiiski to the angry bulls.

Juhani: That's cruel advice.

Aapo: Which we won't follow lightly.

Juhani: Not while Juho Jukola can stand up.

Tuomas: Will we, to save our hides, throw away the ones who saved us from the deadly claws of animals so many times? And would we gain anything by it? I doubt that.

Juhani: So do I. After ripping the dogs to shreds, the bulls would settle in nicely to wait for more stuff to gore with their horns. I'm sure of it.

Simeoni: Well, yes, but what will we do when our bellies really start growling with hunger?

Juhani: First hunger growls in the belly, but soon it pounces on the throbbing heart like a cat on a fat mouse's neck, and then a proud man crumbles. Hard, hard is our lot. What shall we do? — I'd like to know too.

Aapo: Let's yell out loudly all together. Maybe someone in the woods will hear it, or maybe it will be heard all the way to Viertola and set people to wondering.

Juhani: It's worth a try.

Timo: Let's give a good loud yell.

Juhani: Like the very devil. Let's bust out all together with a world-shaking yell, all at the same time for the greatest effect. Now then, get up and get set. The third time I clap my hands, we'll give a yell, we'll yell like seven men. One, two, three!

They bawled out in unison with all their might, so loudly that the rock and the ground under and around it trembled. Even the startled bulls retreated a few paces. Frightful was the initial burst of shouting, as well as the succeeding yowl with which the miserable howling of the dogs was blended. Five long shouts they shouted; the forest roared and the echoes ranged far afield. After the fifth and loudest, they sat down again to breathe a spell. Having rested, they took up the task again, shouting seven times, then waiting to see the effect of their action. Faces black, eyes bloodshot, and chests pumping hard, they sat there on the mossy rock.

Juhani: Wait, wait and see what that does. People are fools if they don't understand that a bunch of men wouldn't yell like this unless they were in great danger. Wait.

Eero: If this yelling doesn't bring help, then we're done for. The sun is setting in the west again, and my hunger is getting fierce.

Simeoni: God have mercy. It's been a whole night plus a day and a half since we last ate.

Timo: So it has. Listen to the grumbling in my belly; it's grumbling and rumbling and even peeping a little. This is hard to take.

Juhani: It's hard, it's hard, we know it, we believe it. Our own bellies tell us so.

Simeoni: Long is a hungry man's day!

Timo: It's long, all right.

Juhani: Long and sad! Has your brain run dry already, Aapo? Can't you remember even the crow's cawing or the barn-owl's chatter to tell us about while we sit on this horrible Isle of Hunger?

Aapo: I remember a story that hunger brings to mind, but it won't lead us to forget food. Instead, it will remind us more strongly of both food and drink.

Juhani: You mean the man in the mountain? I've heard that one.

Timo: But it's new to me. Tell it, brother Aapo.

Aapo: It's the story of a man, a noble hero of the faith who, like the Pale Maiden, spent some time imprisoned in a cave in Impivaara, but for a different reason.

And Aapo told the following story:

In earlier times, when Christianity and paganism were still battling each other in Häme, one of the converts was a fine man, pious and dedicated to spreading the new religion, which he practiced devoutly, protected by the arms of the Swedish state. But the knights had to leave suddenly for home, and the Christians of Häme were subjected to a most terrible persecution by their pagan brethren. Some were horribly murdered; others sought salvation by fleeing into the depths of the wandering woods, into mountain caves, or any place they could. The good man mentioned above hurried into the recesses of Impivaara, but his pursuers, following his trail and lusting for revenge, soon found where he had hidden himself. "Shut the wolf up in his own den!" they shouted in malicious glee. Sealing the cave entrance tightly with a stone wall, they left the man to succumb to hunger and darkness.

He would have come to a miserable end, but Heaven performed yet another miracle. Barely had the last glimmer of daylight died at the mouth of the cave when a beautiful silvery glow lighted the cavern, and the man knew a mild, heavenly day in the cold heart of the mountain. And further miracles occurred, for lo, a sparkling spring suddenly flowed in the floor of the cave, the water of which did not diminish with use, and so the man always had fresh drinking water in his stone cell. Beside the spring rose a lovely green tree bearing the most beautiful fruit, which never diminished with picking, and from it the man drew sweet sustenance. Here he spent his day, praising the Lord; here he passed his nights, dreaming of the land of the blessed. And his days were like a summer day, warm and bright, and his nights a lovely twilight. A year went by in this manner, as rivers of Christian blood flowed in Häme. But when the dreadful year of persecution had run its course and a bright September morning sun shone brightly on the world outside, there came to the hero's ears the sound of hammers and iron crow bars attacking the stone wall sealing the cave-mouth. Light finally filtered in through the mass of stones; in a twinkling, the marvelous glow vanished from the cave, along with the spring and the fruitful tree beside it.

But why the hammering and hubbub outside the cave? A large band of pagans stood there surrounding a few Christians bound with ropes and condemned to death by starvation in the dark womb of the mountain. They could only assume that the same kind of death had befallen the man shut up in the cave a year ago. But they were astounded when the cave was opened and the hero stepped out with a bright and radiant brow. And a voice, whose sacred timbre penetrated to the very core, rang from his mouth, "Welcome, friends and brothers, welcome golden sun and murmuring woods, welcome!" Then the band fell on their knees before him, praising the God in whom he believed and who had saved him from a terrible death. In a firm voice, he told them of the beautiful miracles he had experienced in the womb of the mountain and with one voice the people cried out to him: "Baptize us too, baptize us into belief in the same God!" Thus they shouted to the man's great joy and freed the condemned prisoners from their bonds. The devout hero stepped to the bank of a stream and the whole crowd followed after him. Renouncing their paganism, they accepted baptism into the Christian faith. The men so recently fated for sacrifice stood above them on the bank, singing a hymn of thanks to Him who had saved them from a painful death and led the pagan children from darkness into light. So they sang, looking up into the heights of heaven.

Aapo: This is the tale of a devout man.

Juhani: And the pagans' baptism took place right where our wolf pen is now.

Simeoni: Faith works miracles. I'm sure there was no spring or fruitful tree in the man's cave. It was no light that shines for earthly eyes that made his chamber bright, but a firm and unwavering faith that satisfied all his bodily needs. The strength of his spirit was to him a fresh spring, tasty fruit, and radiant light. What was it that my former reading companion, Tuomas Tervakoski once said? "If you have the sword of faith and the shield of spirit, you can even go and dance the polska with devils." That's what the devout old man said.

Juhani: But a grown man's stomach won't run for long on pure faith and thin air. It'll rot first. And I'll swear that the man fed his face on richer fare than fruit and water. A man's body demands it, a body grown and raised here on meat and rye bread. Yes sirree, and they tell another version of the story too. They say that five black bull horns suddenly appeared on the wall of the man's cave. When he turned on the first, the best, clearest, factory-distilled whiskey came gushing out, which would make a man smack his lips, all right. From the second, he drew out hot, fatty, puckered pork sausage by the yard. From the third, a stiff arc of porridge cooked from new rye oozed out, and from the fourth, clabbered milk as thick as tar to mix with the porridge. And when his belly was as full as a tick, he opened the fifth just like that and pulled out a quid of Pikanell tobacco that swelled out the boy's cheek like a sucking leech. What better fare could an idle man ask for?

Timo: He was in heaven, he was. But where are we?

Tuomas: It boggles the mind.

Timo: It makes the head spin.

Juhani: A thousand dollars for a meal like that! A million dollars!

Simeoni: Hot, fatty, puckered pork sausage! Here we sit in the middle of hell listening to stories about how they rejoice and eat in heaven. Oh what are we going to do, brothers, what are we going to do?

Eero: Have faith, brothers, have faith.

Simeoni: Are you still cracking jokes, you monster!

Eero: It's my last gasp, brothers, believe me, my last gasp. I'm about to cave in with a sigh like a leaky bladder, a leaky bull's bladder. Oh, if we only had a warm loaf and the butter to spread on it.

Timo: And the world's biggest sausage on top of the butter.

Juhani: If we only had seven fresh, warm loaves, seven pounds of butter and seven sausages roasted over an open fire — that would be a party.

Eero: Bright balls of fire!

Timo: A man should always be wise enough to carry a big enough pack of salt in his pocket. Salt binds the insides and keeps you alive for weeks without so much as a speck of food in your belly.

Juhani: Oh, my boy, even salt won't keep you kicking for long.

Timo: But Iisakki Koivisto, the laziest man in the world, lolls around on Karkkula's sauna benches for days on end without eating a scrap of food. And what trick keeps the poor breath of life wheezing in him? The sly dog sucks on a lump of salt like a child at a mother's nipple.

Juhani: He often sits like a bird in a rye field stripping the grain into his mouth. Look, it's already late in the evening. We'll get no help from the world of men, and thirty-three snorting devils are pacing, forever pacing around us. But two of the devils are locking horns there. Go to it, go to it. Hustle your horns right through each other's heads, hustle till your brains splatter on the ground so there'll be two less to torment us. That's it, that's it! We'll even have a little fun to pass the time away. That's it! Keep up the sport for a long time and turn over the earth with your eight bony plows.

Tuomas: Whiteback and Whitehead are fighting hard.

Juhani: But Whitehead will win.

Tuomas: Whiteback will win.

Juhani: Let's make a bet. Here's my hand on it.

Tuomas: It's OK with me. Timo, break the handshake.

Juhani: It's a bet.

Tuomas: A quart of liquor.

Juhani: Agreed. Look, look at the two boys battling. But now they're kind of resting head to head.

Timo: And sort of hooking easily at each other.

Juhani: But now, now they're at it full tilt. Come on, Whitehead, my Whitehead, dig your feet into the ground.

Tuomas: Dig yours in tighter, my brave Whiteback. That's the way.

Juhani: Whitehead, Whitehead!

Tuomas: My rugged Whiteback with the steel-plated forehead. Now then, stop that endless butting and push your man to hell out of the place.

Juhani: Whitehead! The devil lop your horns off. Are you running away, you devil!

Tuomas: Running is right up his alley.

Timo: And the other is puffing after him like the devil. Hee, hee, hee!

Tuomas: Well, Juhani?

Juhani: I lost a quart of liquor. You'll get it once we're out of this jam. But when will that day come? Ah, many years from now under the bailiffs command, they'll haul a big wagonload off from here, first to the village and then to the graveyard, a clanking, clunking load of seven men's bones.

Simeoni: And so ended our sinful life.

Timo: And so it did.

Juhani: It was a miserable end. But open your pack, Lauri, and let's drink a round.

Aapo: Let's have one now, but save the rest for when we need it more.

Juhani: As you wish. But let's take a drink we can feel, and then yell like a shepherd's horn.

When they had drunk, they once more shouted in unison, and the echo reached the ears of Viertola's overseer as he walked by the drying barn on the hill. Not understanding its meaning, he said to himself fearfully, "The border-spirit is crying out there." But the brothers, jaws straining toward the sky, mouths gaping wide open like a dragon's, or nestlings' when they hear the approaching swish of their mother's wings, kept yelling deafeningly, ten times they yelled. And then they sat down on their mossy seat again, hope fading in their hearts.

CHAPTER VIII

The third day of the brothers' stay on the rock has come, and they continue to sit there constantly ringed by the bulls. At times, the animals move further off, but they always keep the brothers in sight, roaring a signal to their mates whenever the men try to flee their prison. One crops the wilderness vegetation, encircling it with his tongue and snapping it off, while another rests on his bulging belly grunting heavily as he chews his cud. Two of them do battle, half in play and half in earnest, and the clash of their horns echoes far and wide. At the very base of Hiisi Rock, one of them paws the ground and bellows angrily, throwing dirt and sticks high in the air. Stubbornly they stay on, to the pale rage and torment of the brothers, for the stout sons of Jukola expect to die. A short time ago, Lauri has taken a healthy slug of liquor and now he takes another, to the astonishment of the rest, who begin to scold him harshly.

Juhani: What the devil's got into you?

Aapo: What can you be thinking? Remember that we're all in the same boat.

Tuomas: Remember that we're in close quarters and have to move carefully.

Lauri: It drives a man wild!

Aapo: You can't do that here.

Lauri: To hell with everything. Let our prison spin like a millstone and throw seven hard-luck boys to the bulls. Spin, stone, from east to west, and whirl woods from west to east! Yahoo!

Juhani: You're drunk already, aren't you?

Lauri: Do you have to ask? What price life and the world? Not a moldy penny. Let it all turn to dust and ashes and blow away in the wind. Kersplash. Here's a drink, brothers of my heart.

Aapo: He's drunk. Take the jug away from him!

Lauri: You won't find that easy. The jug is mine. I didn't let go of it to be trampled by the bulls in the meadow. But you — you dropped your packs nicely like poor gypsies at the bang of a sheriff's gun.

Juhani: Give me the jug!

Lauri: It's mine.

Juhani: But I want it.

Lauri: You want it? If you want it, you'll get it right in the head.

Juhani: Do you mean to fight?

Lauri: That too, if you want it. But, my loving brother, don't fight. Here's a drink on it.

Timo: Don't drink, Lauri.

Juhani: Give me the jug now!

Lauri: I'll give you a whipping. Who do you think you are?

Juhani: Only a sinful man, but still your oldest brother.

Lauri: Oldest? Then you've had time to sin all the more and deserve a whipping that much more. But skål! said the Swede.

Tuomas: Don't touch a drop.

Lauri: I like Tuomas and I like little Eero a lot. But what can I say about the rest of you?

Tuomas: Shut your mouth and give me the jug! Here, Juhani. Put on a pack and take charge of the liquor.

Lauri: You're the only one who can make me change my mind. I like you and little Eero.

Tuomas: Quiet!

Lauri: Some men you are! What is Jussi Jukola? A dim-witted rooster; a lame-brained bull.

Juhani: Shut your mouth right now. My ears won't take that again.

Lauri: "Hear this, all you who have ears," preaches Aapo, the St. Paul of Jukola.

Simeoni: Oh you... Can you be the steady, sober, and quiet Lauri of old? Can you be Lauri? A crazy blabbermouth like you?

Lauri: Are you Simeoni, a sweet-talking Judas like you?

Simeoni: I forgive you. You're heaping fiery coals on your head forever and forever.

Lauri: Go to hell. You'll find plenty of coals there.

Simeoni: Atheist!

Timo: This gives me goose bumps.

Lauri: What's Timo mumbling about, that blear-eyed Jukola billy-goat?

Timo: I'll let that pass. Goat's milk is good too.

Lauri: Wha?

Timo: Goat's milk is good too. Thanks for the compliment, thanks a lot. So that's what we get from you. But here's another kind of stuff, your favorites Tuomas and Eero.

Lauri: Wha?

Timo: Look at your favorites — Tuomas and Eero.

Lauri: Wha?

Timo: The preacher repeats everything three times, but he gets paid.

Lauri: "Another kind of stuff," you mumbled. But I know what to compare them with. Tuomas-Boy is a noble ax, steady, manly, and rough, and Eero, the little cub, is a small, sharp, and biting hatchet, chipping away neatly, tossing little barbs around, the rascal.

Juhani: Good! But you called me a dim-witted rooster.

Timo: And he called me a billy-goat. Thanks a lot!

Lauri: Eero chips away, but he has the heart of a man.

Juhani: Good, good! But did you call me a dim-witted rooster?

Lauri: I called you a lame-brained bull too.

Juhani: Good, brother, good!

Timo: Calm down, Juho. He called me a billy-goat too, and I thank him for the compliment. A goat is no animal to sneeze at. That pink-cheeked lassy at Viertola, that Miss Lydia, she drinks nothing but goat's milk, nothing at all, so there too.

Simeoni: Could we call ourselves men if we paid attention to the words of a drunk?

Lauri: You a man? You? Oh brother! You would cry like a baby if you saw something girls never show to a nerd like you.

Juhani: Simeoni, Simeoni! I'd rather be stabbed with a knife than stung like that.

Simeoni: Well, well, we'll see who gets stung on Judgment Day.

Timo: You've called us everything from a rooster to an old ax, but what are you yourself, if I get worked up and insist on an answer.

Lauri: I'm Lauri.

Timo: Come on now. Just plain Lauri — that's all?

Lauri: Just jim-dandy Lauri, though you've had your fun pinning all kinds of names on me: badger, the man with the hoe in Konni's clock, sourpuss, and a thousand others. Hmh! I've heard it from all your lips. But without saying a word, I stuffed them all into a hollow tooth for safekeeping, and now I feel like spreading the lot around. Damn it, I feel like giving you each a wallop on the head and throwing you all down to the bulls like a bag of straw.

Aapo: Is this really Lauri, quiet, decent, well-behaved Lauri? I can't believe it.

Juhani: Aih, brother Aapo, aih. There's many a thistle in that wheat. I guessed it all along, but now I know what's in the man's heart.

Lauri: Shut your mouth, you Jukola bull.

Juhani: For God's sake, don't push me any further. My blood is beginning to boil, it's beginning to boil. You damned calf, I'll throw you off to be mashed by the bulls, come hell or high water!

Simeoni: Oh misery, misery!

Aapo: Calm down! Calm down! A fight is the last thing we want.

Tuomas: Use your head.

Juhani: He put me down shamelessly. A dim-witted rooster!

Aapo: And what about St. Paul? Calm down!

Timo: And billy-goat? What about that? Thanks a lot, twin brother of mine.

Aapo: Remember how close we are to the jaws of death. And brothers, I've been thinking, and I have a little tip to give you that's crucial to us right now. Listen: this rock is a ship in a storm and the storm is that angry, bellowing herd of bulls around it. Or shall I choose another image? Then let this rock be a castle surrounded by an enemy armed with cruel spears. Without a leader to organize and defend the besieged castle, confusion and chaos will seize on its men and soon they and the castle will be lost. That's what will happen, unless we act differently and establish law and order among us. Let there be one man whose wise counsel the others will obey. Get a grip on yourself, now, Juhani, and take charge of your brothers. You know that most of us will fall in and support your command in this besieged fortress.

Juhani: What punishment do we give someone who won't listen to me, whose ill temper leads to disorder and danger?

Tuomas: Let him be thrown to the bulls.

Juhani: Right, Tuomas.

Aapo: A stiff sentence, but our situation demands it. I accept the decree.

Simeoni: "To be thrown to the bulls," like the martyrs of old. No use to be lenient here.

Timo: To be thrown to the bulls, let that be our rule and statute.

Juhani: Let that be our rule and statute. Write this awful phrase in your hearts and live by it. My first order now is that Lauri shut up and go nicely to sleep; my second is that every man take a little nip from this pewter jug to ease his heart. So, here it is.

Lauri: What about me? Don't I get any?

Juhani: You lie down.

Lauri: There's plenty of time for that in hell.

Juhani: God knows, Lauri dear, where we may yet lie down.

Lauri: *God knows, Jussi dear*
       Where your hide may yet be nailed.

I sing like a man, clang like a clarinet.

> *Just a little boy am I.*
> *Mama's own small Jussi.*
> *Just a little boy am I,*
> *Mama's own small Jussi.*

Juhani: Save your song for now.

Eero: Save your little-boy song for me.

Lauri: Let's save it for Jussi Jukola and start to sing another great big song. Let's sing and dance. Yahoo!

Juhani: Watch out or I'll sentence you to be thrown to the bulls.

Tuomas: Lauri, I'm warning you for the last time.

Lauri: For the last time? Then you'd better stop.

Juhani: To think we carry on like this at the very gates of hell, like complete pagans.

Simeoni: God has good reason to punish us. Oh punish us, whip us on this rock of torment.

Lauri: A rock of joy this is, Väinämöinen's rock of joy, the old man they used to call the god of Savo. I heard a very funny song about him once from a rascal of a chimney sweep. I remember a dizzy sermon from the same kid, one he spouted freely through his grinning teeth and red lips as he stood in Kuninkala's sooty chimney. This is how he preached.

Juhani: Shut up, you wild animal!

Lauri: Let us preach for we've had enough of this group singing that they do in church. I'm the preacher, this rock is my pulpit, you are the hymn leaders, and the bulls around us are the sober, pious congregation. But first a marching hymn to the pulpit. You heard me. The preacher is waiting.

Juhani: You wait. You just wait. You'll be marched and hymned soon enough.

Lauri: You're the hymn leader, the old boy himself, the others your pupils, your linsey-wolsey types who fill the choir benches on Sundays and holy days, as red and sweating as turkey cocks. Here they sit gawking with their padded lapels and hair slicked down with butter and tallow, their dry little beards wagging a bit. But sit quiet awhile and sing Preacher Matti to the pulpit. It's true he skipped from Keijula tavern to the church, but he's doused his head and combed his hair now, and creeps to the pulpit all wound up to milk tears from old crones like a good lad. Now Jutte, my hymn-leaders sound off when I give you a dirty look. "Let 'er rip," as the preacher once said to the hymn-leader.

Juhani: Button your lip, you louse.

Lauri: Not at all, but "Open every shepherd his mouth" is what you ought to sing. But that's enough now; shut up and listen. Purse your lips nicely into a church-mouth while I preach. Now, chimney-sweep, lend me your quick thought and ready tongue.

"I want to preach a sermon from this pulpit on St. Peter's old over-coat and the ten buttonholes. But first I want to look over my flock of sheep. To my great sorrow, I see only stinking ewes and rascally rams. Oh you trulls, tramps, and tarts of Kärkölä. You flaunt your silks and shawls, but spit in my face if you don't cry out for Preacher Matti to speak for you on Judgment Day. But that's only hot air! Good day, Grandpa Räihä! I want a word with you. Take a leaf from old Grandpa Kettula's book. But you, Paavo Peltola, you devil you! What did you do last winter at Tanu's house-raising? You clinked glasses and pinched the lasses. But I say to you, my young bucko, take a lesson from Jalli Jumppila, or Preacher Matti will damn you in the end, you pagan Greeks and freaks. Then with a hood on your head you'll be sent off to hell. Open your ear flaps in time and hear what I preach and prate for I've been broiled in many a broth and the heart in this breast is like a seal-skin tobacco pouch. This boy has seen it all. In Helsinki I worked under a potter and did time on bread and water, and sat in the stocks and in other blocks. But the best of the deal is I never did steal, never muddied a man's well or messed with his Nell.

"Once I had a little chick, a tiny trick, a real doozy, but she skipped out, the floozy. I took off to find her and searched Finland and sea, Estonia and Germany, but found no trace of my own sweetie-face. So back to Finn-Island I came and there I found my dame sitting on a sand-dune down by Tampere. 'Hey there Terttu,' I yelled so glad, but she only got mad and snapped at me, 'What are you, you lump of coal, you tar-baby?' and scooted off into the nearest shanty. But me, always happy-go-lucky, I didn't cry, just stuffed a chaw in my cheek and hit the town's best bar a week, where the barkeep's ploy was every woman's joy.

"A stein of beer and two quarts of rye are a fair-to-middling bit for a tired throat and wit. Now cans are tipping and beards are dripping. The boys are singing and girls split with laughing. But I left the fun behind and took off down the street. My song rang out, shattered the windows, and shook up every last Tampere reindeer baron. But happy-go-lucky me, I scooted down the beach kicking sand and gravel in their teeth. I came to Pori then where they put me in a pen and hauled me round the fair. So on to Newtown where everyone called me down. To Turku I did flit where a knife my throat did slit. Then at last to An-ingaisten Street, where five clever chicks I did meet. The first gave me a kick and the second said, 'Don't pick on the lad, he's not so bad. Not the kind to gyp you or lead you on and clip you.' The third said, 'Why is he so sad?' and the fourth, 'We should help him in good time.' With her fist the fifth one thumped me and barked, 'Go to Hel-sinki!' Off I went to Hell's sink, where they put me in the clink and gave me the third-degree. I was pasted and lambasted. So I went along my way, as always bright and gay. With a heart like a sealskin tobacco pouch, I traveled, tramped, and sang along the hilly highway, until I came to Häme, stepped up into the Kuninkala pulpit, and so Amen.

"I will now read the banns. The sexton and the town cupper are eager to wed. Tomorrow is the date, tomorrow evening late. May they bond and stick together like Tartar-Paul's tar and pitch. The following farms are hereby summoned to day-work at the parsonage: Yllilä, Al-lila, Yli-Seppälä, Pimppala, and Alavesi. A dozen boards and twenty pounds of nails, a man from every farm and two from the best to patch the smaller pig trough at the parsonage. An old gelding, bob-tailed and built low to the ground, has skipped from Kiiala's pasture, a great big dark-brown thing, with a bell round his neck on an iron ring.

"But that's all for now, except that the lamb is a mild beast; he doesn't kick or bite in the least. But beware when a bull gets out of hand. He takes on trees and tears up the land, breathes fiery muck and splatters the cowherd's face and belly. And so once more Amen and whoops-a-daisy, and all of you off to your own coops and me to my walls of brick." Now that was a sermon!

Simeoni: You spout that godless rant, but can you read, you block-head?

Lauri: What kind of question is that: Can a minister read? Ill read you to death and never stop for breath, sing as long a hymn as a cow-barn timber. A priest should be a chanter, but yet no cantor. I will read the mass, and Eero the response.

Eero: I will if I'm not too weak from hunger.

Juhani: Are you going to fool around with a lunatic? You scamp, always up to your tricks. I might have known. And you, Lauri, just go nicely to sleep. Stop your clowning and pranks, or you'll get a swift, rough sentence: ten hands will throw you to the bulls. Cut out the non-sense now!

Lauri: The fun is just beginning, brother, it's just beginning. So let's dance. We'll wrestle and dance the Jussi until the moss flies. Like this!

Timo: You damned kid! You almost fell off the rock. Stand still! Stand still!

Juhani: Lauri, shall I say the awful word that will send you to be crushed in a second? The fateful word: "Let him be thrown to the bulls?" Shall I say it?

Lauri: Don't say a thing, just sing while I dance the Jussi. Yahoo!

Juhani: Let him be thrown to the bulls, and God be with him. Amen! That's it now, down he goes.

Lauri: Let's all go hand in hand, away from life's hunger.

Tuomas: Let our law be upheld. Go to your death.

Juhani: No, Tuomas, Hell no!

Tuomas: Down from the rock, boy!

Juhani: No, for God's sake!

Aapo: Tuomas's face is all white! God help us! Tuomas's face is all white!

Juhani: Would you do such a horror, my brother, my brother?

Aapo: He's as pale as a dying man, and horror is at hand. Get hold of yourself, Tuomas, I beg you, get hold of yourself. All of you get up and help Lauri, help him!

Tuomas: Out of my way!

Juhani: No, Tuomas, no!

Tuomas: Out of my way!

Juhani: No, Tuomas, no!

Tuomas: Out of my way. You're the judge and I'm the hangman. Let the law be carried out. Down from this rock, man, without mercy!

Lauri: Like a charcoal log down the chute at Nukari Dam. Yahoo!

Simeoni: Mercy, Tuomas, mercy, mercy!

Tuomas: No mercy, none at all!

Juhani: God keep us from a brother's murder!

Timo: As Cain killed Abel.

Tuomas: He dies!

Aapo: Control yourself.

Tuomas: He dies!

Juhani: The power of Heaven protect us. No Tuomas, this won't do.

Timo: Not at all. Lauri is a brother to every one of us. Stop!

Juhani: This is murder! Let's save Lauri, let's save our poor brother!

A fierce struggle ensued. One of the brothers grabbed Tuomas by the collar, another by the waist, a third hung on to Lauri's legs, a fourth clutched at whatever he could reach to keep him from tumbling off. The whole group resembled a roaring, squirming, many-headed, many-legged monster. Grunting, panting, howling, and tearing at itself, the creature heaved and rolled back and forth from one end of the rock to the other, while the frightened dogs, tails tucked between their legs, often teetering on the verge of falling prey to the bulls, scuttled back and forth in an effort to save their lives. Meanwhile the bulls crowded closer than before, staring bug-eyed at the horrifying contest. But general exhaustion finally brought peace to Hiisi Rock, and the brothers lay panting on the pulverized moss. At last Simeoni spoke, rolling his eyes in horror at the heavens as he delivered his sermon.

Simeoni: We're Christians, but we've become animals, devils. So punish us God! Strike here with the hammer of your wrath, beat the seven sons of sinful Zion to a bloody pulp!

Aapo: Well, it's always a five-to-one split with us; you know that. So let there be peace now and let's keep Lauri quiet until he falls asleep, the poor thing.

Tuomas: Damn you! I'll throw every last one of you down, if I want to, and I will if I get riled up again. So easy does it, boys, nice and easy. My blood is boiling; any little thing means death and all its horrors. So easy, nice and easy.

Juhani: Tuomas is a dangerous man. Give me a partner who flies off the handle every hour of every day, not a man like you, who is hardly ever angry, but when he is, gets so carried away that my poor life is in danger. Oh, this was a bad game.

Simeoni: Whip us, punish us, you powers of heaven!

Timo: Shut up, Simeoni. I'm going to pray.

Simeoni: If I say nothing, this rock will speak out. Whip us, flog us!

Juhani: Stop calling down worse destruction on us. We've had enough of flogging.

Tuomas: Look at him preaching like a loony, with his hands clasped and eyes like a death-owl. Shut up now!

Timo: Shut up, Simeoni, I'm going to pray. Let's all live in peace. Look at Lauri; he's drooping and falling asleep, the poor thing. So for God's sake, let's live in peace and forbearance until we set out for home from here.

Juhani: Home! We can't even get to our burial home in a hallowed churchyard. We'll die here, to be pecked at by ravens and eagles. I'll die right now, in this very spot. There now, I'm dying. Was that life? What was it worth?

Timo: Well then, was that life? What was it worth? That's quite a question.

Juhani: You didn't know, dear Mother, the misery for which you bore seven little cubs.

Timo: You didn't know.

Juhani: What if we have one more drink, squeeze the last drop from the bottle? Here, Lauri, drink and pass it around.

Lauri: I don't want your liquor.

Juhani: Ahaa, haha! So you've already forgotten Jalli Jumppila and the Kuninkala pulpit. Oh, you were frisking and romping on a line between life and death. It's awful to think of you standing wall-eyed drunk before God. What a terrible thought!

Simeoni: You can say that again!

Juhani: It was a close call, but now he lies there his face pale. Oh, it brings tears to my eyes, my very soul pities him. I would like to hide my poor suffering brother in the deepest corner of my heart.

Aapo: But in his sleep, he is able to forget the killing worm of hunger.

Simeoni: The third day! Let's sink down and die now.

Eero: And die we must, even with live meat in front of us.

Simeoni: That meat will be our death, our death.

Juhani: Right now, this hour and minute! This very second!

Timo: Let's kill the meat. Shoot every horn-head and we'll have meat by the ton. We have five loaded rifles and plenty of ammunition in Lauri's pack.

Juhani: Now that's an idea!

Aapo: Which will save us!

Eero: Really save us!

Juhani: Oh, how can we repay Timo?

Simeoni: You're an angel of the Lord!

Timo: Fresh meat, fresh meat! Nothing but fresh meat! He-hey! There are scores of freshly molded bullets and even more charges of powder in Lauri's pack.

Juhani: Just as you say, you wonderful lad. We have more than enough powder and bullets. There are thirty-three bulls here. Huh! What lame-brained numbskulls we are! Why didn't we think of this before?

Aapo: I thought of it once, but I forgot about the stuff in Lauri's pack, so I didn't mention it to you. Five bullets would take care of only five bulls.

Juhani: I was sort of thinking along those lines, but I didn't get very far. Thirty-three bulls. Good! Listen, you feisty sons of Kaura-Matti, if we shoot like men, every shot through the head or heart of a bull, then the road to freedom is open, the road to freedom is open. Oh, my trusty Timo!

Timo: Hah, and I was the one to say it. There's nothing else we can do. You can see that. Should we starve here like rats? Not men like us. Ha ha, and I was the one to say it.

Juhani: And now we'll bang and blaze away to open a path to freedom.

Aapo: You're right, Juhani! The path will run over many a bloody carcass, but it can't be helped.

Juhani: It can't be helped, so let the dark red blood flow around Hiisi Rock. Lucky dogs! Soon we'll be eating meat like wolves.

Aapo: But how will we pay for the forty bulls?

Juhani: It's a matter of life and death, and we have the law on our side. We'll dress the meat; let the fat-bellied master of Viertola pick it up if he feels like it. It's none of our business.

Aapo: Well, we'll see what happens after we do what we have to. But when the killing is over, there's still another job left to do. When every last broomtail is stretched out on the ground, we have to skin them at once. And one of us should go to Viertola with the sad news.

Juhani: Good advice. Skin 'em by all means, skin 'em before the hide sticks to the meat. Let's do it — no matter who gets the meat, hide, and guts. Throw the brute on the buck and strip off his hide. Each of us has a tried-and-true knife at his belt. Here's one as sharp as an adder's fang. So, on to the bloody work. Let every man with an empty gun load it with a sure charge, and let the bloody, bloody work begin.

Aapo: But brothers, we can still put up with hunger for an hour or two, now that we know we'll be saved. Let's try once more what men's voices can do, and wait out the last moments of our siege and suffering, the very last moments.

Juhani: Hunger is really pinching my stomach, but we'll do as you wish. Let's yell, and maybe we'll get out of this tight spot without shedding a drop of blood. It's a vain hope anyway. Well, we can wait a little longer; the terrible means to freedom is in our hands. So let's scream at the top of our lungs. I ask you, I order you to do it. Tuomas, still as a stone, you roar with the rest of us. Do it. I ask you, I order you to do it.

Tuomas: Stop waggling your jaw. I'll follow the rules of the group.

Juhani: Ready, set. One, two, three!

They raised their voices, seven times they raised them, and their shouts and the howl of the dogs echoed round about. Then they settled back to wait. Though their hunger was fierce, the certain knowledge of salvation gave them renewed strength. But one of their number, Brother Lauri, knew neither the pain of hunger nor the joy of hope. He lay pale and snoring at the feet of the others. — The brothers waited a spell, then waited another, and the third day's sun was close to setting. Then Juhani, hearing a faint rumble of thunder in the northeast, shouted in a loud and deadly voice, "Now, boys! God help us, Amen!" And the bloody game began.

A cloud of smoke covered gray Hiisi Rock, and from it death roared and flashed everywhere into the herd of bulls. First one and then another horn-head pierced by a bullet reared up and fell, gasping the strong life out of his breast. An animal whose brain was punctured subsided quickly, scarcely kicked once, and stretched his legs out as stiff as staves. Thus he yielded his life, and the dark red blood arced up from the wound and back to earth again. But he whose breast was traversed, missing the heart, raged for a long time, bloodily lunging here and there among those still spared by the bullets, until at last he tumbled headlong to the turf and lay bellowing and tossing his hoofs in the air. Soon the others, moved to a frenzy by the reek of their comrades' blood, began a frightful milling, rushing helter-skelter in a raging mass. Tongues hanging out, eyes rolling, filling the air with a horrid bellowing, they tossed limbs, sod, and soil high over their backs.

But like pale goblins the brothers stood wreathed in smoke on the rock, firing, reloading, and firing as the bulls kept dropping to the earth. The guns flashed and roared, but on high where the clouds rolled over the hills, there was a sterner flashing and roaring. Smoke and the sky's dark clouds cast a gloomy twilight over Hiisi Rock.

The bawling and shrieking of bulls, the baying of dogs, the bang of guns, and the crash of thunder resounded in the twilight as the storm roared in the treetops. It was a horrible moment; the air seemed as warm as blood. Lauri half awoke and opened his eyes, but could see only dim figures standing around him in the fearful gloom. In the agitation of his blood, he felt as if everything were swiftly sinking downward. Despair seized his mind, and he said to himself "Now we're sinking down, down, into the fires of hell, but since there's no help, just let it go." Having spoken, he turned on one side, closed his eyes, and fell into a deep sleep once more.

Wrapped in a smoky pall, Hiisi Rock mimicked the voice of the thunder like a mighty castle. Blood flowed around it and hoofs by the hundred waved in the air. Thunder crashed in the clouds, which began to pour down a heavy rain into the roaring woods. But now the slaughter was over; not a single horn was upright in the air. The thirty-three bulls of Viertola Manor lay on the ground, some stone-dead, others still kicking, while here and there could be heard the gurgling breath of a dying brute. Down from the rock stepped the brothers with their dogs and rushed to the shelter of a dense spruce, for rain poured down from the thunderclouds and the wind roared in the mossy woods. There they stood, eyeing the copious harvest of death while rippling streams of bloody water ran in every direction from Hiisi Rock. When the rain ceased, they stepped out from their shelter and wandered among their victims, staring in horror, silently grimacing, and now and then shaking their heads.

Juhani: There is plenty of meat here.

Timo: And blood too.

Juhani: And blood too, that's true. The ground around this rock would grow pepper for years, it's been so well manured. But let's kindle a fire and roast some fresh meat. Ah, will roast beef taste good now. Get some wood and pitchy chips, brothers, and I'll strike a flame. Timo, run to the meadow and get my ax and the backpacks we dropped in our flight. After we've eaten, we'll all start in together to "peel off the hides" as old red-bearded Krööni used to say. He rests in the earth now, and better so. The poor old man suffered from hunger here like a stray dog; he had no friends, no kin, no place to lay his head, and even his name has been dropped from the records. He fell dead in Kolistin's grain barn and all is forgotten now under the sod. There now, Eero, those are pitchy chips. Simeoni is bringing dry poles, and we'll soon have a blazing fire. Cut off some thick slices from the haunch of that brindled bull, Tuomas. I could sink my teeth into that spot right now, like a cat with a fresh and bloody feast.

Tuomas: A little patience — the roast will taste even better.

Juhani: First-rate. But let's be thankful we belong to a kin and country that knows how to do battle with hunger. Otherwise we wouldn't be bustling around here now, I'll vouch for that.

Seven rich cuts of meat were quickly roasted in the flames. Then they remembered Lauri, but did not want to disturb his sleep. He still lay on the rock, not having awakened even when doused by the heavy downpour. Timo had gone on his errand, found the packs in the meadow and the ax on the bloody battleground where lay the bear and the seven bulls, and returned with the packs on his back and the ax under his arm. They brought out six ring loaves, took the meat from the fire, and crunched the dry bread and the salt-sprinkled meat between their teeth. Killi and Kiiski too enjoyed a bountiful meal. But when all were fed, the men felt a sudden numbing weariness in their limbs. An over- whelming urge to sleep weighed them down, and one after another, they fell prone on the earth, their eyes closed in sleep. Lauri lay snor- ing on the rock, and the others sprawled out by the fire, as the sun sank and the September day darkened into night. So they rested among their victims, the slaughtered herd of bulls, and fierce Killi and Kiiski stood watch over the camp.

But finally they awakened, well into the night, awakened and felt their former strength back in their limbs. They arose and began to carry black, resiny stumps to the fire so that they could see to skin their prey by the ruddy light of the flames. Eero they sent off quickly to bear the news to the manager of Viertola. The dark red flame leaped up, lighting the earth and the gloomy forest. Eero took off for the manor while the others furiously set about stripping the hides from the fallen beasts.

Then Lauri awoke from his deep sleep and stared wide-eyed around himself, unable to grasp what he saw. A burning pile of stumps lighted the calm, dark night; on all sides, cattle wallowed in their blood, tongues sticking out between their teeth and bellies hugely bloated. Two had already been converted to meat and a third was in process. One brother skinned a carcass, another held on to a leg, a third hacked a bull's stout bones apart with an ax, and a fourth stacked a huge pile of meat at the foot of a fir tree. Lauri took all this in with his hung- over eyes, but finally he understood what had happened. Looking down, he saw a loaf with a slice of roast meat on it resting on a mossy hummock by the fire. Then he felt a fierce pang of hunger, stepped down from the rock into the warmth of the fire and snatched up the bread and meat. Yet he first took off his cap, clasped his hands, briefly bowed his tousled head, blessed the food, and began his tasty supper. With angry eyes and a scowl on his brow, he sat there eating in silence and drying his clothes in the glow of the pine fire while the others sweated and toiled diligently a few steps away, for they had a bear and forty bulls to butcher.

Eero delivered the news to the manager of the Viertola estate, who immediately informed his master, whereupon a heated milling and shouting arose. Eero went hot-footing it back, while the master of Viertola, frothing and fuming, rounded up every available man and set out for Hiisi Rock accompanied by a hulking crew of ten. The broad-shouldered manager of Viertola strode by his side, a fearsome pine cudgel in his hand. They marched swiftly on and approached a place from which a reddish light gleamed out at them. In it they could see seven men, like seven mind-boggling phantoms of the night, engaged in a bloody work with bloody knives in their bloody hands. One was skinning a carcass, another held a leg, one chopped up the stout bones of a slaughtered bull, another spread the hides to dry on the yielding boughs of a fir tree. The dogs too romped around, enjoying the discarded tidbits tossed aside by the butchers. Killi and Kliski soon took note of the approaching strangers and rushed at them barking ferociously, but the brothers hastened to call them off sternly. The furious master of Viertola stepped forward and stood there, fat-bellied, pop-eyed, drenched in sweat, and backed by the strength of ten men.

Aapo: Good evening, sir.

Juhani: God help us! This was a terrible game.

Viertola: Has all hell broken loose? Forty bulls butchered! Hell and damnation!

Aapo: It was done to save the lives of seven men.

Viertola: I'll show you, you bush raiders and bandits of Jukola! At them men and beat them till they lie there in blood like my fine bulls. Sails to the wind, men!

Aapo: Easy sir!

Tuomas: Easy sir!

Juhani: Stop your men, sir, and remember what keeping the peace demands of you.

Aapo: Let's talk reasonably about a stroke of hard luck.

Juhani: We are all under one law and are equal in its eyes. You came into this world as naked as I did, and you're not an inch better a man. And what of your rank? Let our bleary-eyed old rooster do his trick on it. There is one law for every man! And in this case, the law is firmly on the side of the Jukolas.

Viertola: On your side? Do you have the right, damn you, to kill my own bulls on my own land?

Juhani: Do you have the right to let bulls run free and endanger the life of a man?

Viertola: They were on their own land in a fenced-in pasture.

Juhani: Let's weigh the case in a balance. The piece of fence the bulls trampled down to our grief sits neatly on Viertola's side. But now I ask you: Why does a rich manor put up such a flimsy fence that cattle topple it in one charge?

Manager: The fence was as strong as steel, you bum!

Juhani: The bulls brushed it aside like a straw.

Viertola: What were you doing in my pasture — in my pasture, you hoodlums?

Juhani: We were chasing a bear, a dangerous animal that could as soon crush you as a bull. We killed a prowling bear and did the whole country a great service. Isn't it a public service to rid the world of beasts of prey, boogeymen, and Beelzebubs?

Manager: Shut your mouth and stop that chatter, you worm!

Viertola: Do they mean to mock us, the vermin? Beat them up, charge them.

Aapo: Easy now, my masters and men, think how we suffered on this wretched rock. We're all ready to go mad.

Juhani: That's right. Ready to go mad, stark raving mad! Our heads spin, our hearts are hard as rock, then a flash and heaven and earth shriek. Hah, three days and nights we've been tortured here on the border between life and death.

Tuomas: But now we've eaten bloody meat, breathed in the fumes of bloody slaughter, and here we stand, bloody knives in our bloody hands, in blood up to our elbows. God grant you heed our words in time, otherwise we'll turn this night into a hellish horror. Take heed, take heed of our words.

Eero: And let the bulls be a warning.

Juhani: Oh God, grant them a balm to clear their eyes and the self-control to keep them from goading us further. Give them the sense to heed the warning of the luckless bulls or there may be still more slaughter. Give them wisdom, Lord, or we will be their priests and wed them as one flesh and blood to these luckless bulls, turning these dark woods into a screaming hell. Oh Lord, protect the big-bellied master of Viertola and his bold men. Have mercy, Almighty Son of God!

Tuomas: Here we stand. Come on if you dare!

Juhani: Here we stand. Come on if you dare!

Viertola: Good, good! You can strut now, but I think the law will tell a different story. Then your tail feathers will droop, yes, and your miserable house will be gone right down to its stinking foundations. Let's go men! You have a haul of forty bulls now, but I'll wring them out of you down to the very last hoof. Let's go!

Juhani: Take your meat and stuffing before they spoil. They're no concern of ours. We just hurried to skin them before the hides stuck fast.

Viertola: Good, good! Home, men, do as I say.

The master of Viertola left with his men, mouthing harsh threats and curses, and the brothers set to work again. By the next day, all forty bulls were butchered, and the brothers returned home, carrying the huge, grayish black bear on a pole. But the meats, hides, and other remains of the forty bulls they stowed in the woods, guarded by two brothers. So ended the excursion born of Tinder-Matti's tales, which was to have been a duck hunt in Kourusuo.

CHAPTER IX

It is a September morning. A few days have passed since the brothers' grueling journey ended. For two days they have waited and watched over the meat from a distance, but no one has come for it; it seems destined to be a total loss. Whereupon the brothers decide to benefit from the spectacular heaps of meat in the woods and to live high at the stewpot for awhile.

And so they did. They carried in the carcasses, filling the storehouse with meat and draping the hides over rafters. Now an enormous stewpot boiled and bubbled in the stumpy clearing, almost non-stop from morning till evening, and the brothers' full bellies labored hard. Carefree and happy were the days they spent. They would eat, then tell tales and stories, or rest sweetly with their heads pillowed on mounds, while the meadow echoed with the roar of their snoring.

It was a beautiful morning. The sky was a bright blue dome, and a brisk northeast wind rustled the adjacent woods. Around the stew pot lounged the brothers, one sitting on a stump, another on the dry ground eating a hearty breakfast. There too the dogs lay sprawled on their bellies, their jaws grinding the strong, sinewy meat of the bulls. A settled peace and good cheer shone on every face.

Timo: Thanks to the master of Viertola for this meal too.

Juhani: Thanks and honor to him.

Aapo: But this feast will cost us dear yet. Viertola won't just let it go at that.

Juhani: We have the law on our side. Master Viertola must see that and forget about taking us to court. Let's eat the meat, brothers, and let it melt happily in our bellies. We are in the clear. But we need exercise, boys, we need to march, for beef is a heavy food.

Eero: Let's join hands and dance. Let's stomp out a brotherly round, and I'll bet you our stomachs shrink.

Juhani: Let's not hop around here like silly fools; let's play another kind of game. Ah, whatever happened to those wild young days of ours? Brothers, let's bat the zinging puck once more as we did on the dusty roads of Toukola. Here's a smooth clearing; we'll pull out every stump by the roots and extend the field across that smooth heath. We'll split up into two teams, and each man on the losing side will have to eat ten pounds of beef for supper.

Tuomas: Agreed.

Juhani: Ten pounds, brothers?

Eero: Exactly! Ten pounds as punishment for those driven back by the birchwood puck.

Juhani: Three on a side would be fairest, but there are seven of us.

Lauri: I'll drop out. I'd rather look for carving wood in the forest than run and sweat here like a harebrained kid. Play your game — I'm off to the woods with my old ax under my arm.

So saying, they finally finished their meal and set out to prepare the playing field. A strip was cleared across the meadow and extended along a level heath to the east. After a couple of hours they stood ready to play, sturdy shafts of birch in their hands. They were divided into two teams: Juhani, Simeoni, and Timo on one side and Tuomas, Aapo, and Eero on the other. The puck began to fly back and forth between them and the place echoed with the sound of staffs hitting the birchwood disk as it sped humming to and fro. But Lauri walks through the woods with his ax under his arm. He walks slowly, looking carefully around, always stopping when his eye spots a burl, a fork in a tree, an oddity, or a witch's broom high in the top of a thick birch or pine tree.

Now he finds the high stub of a windfall spruce, which he studies for awhile, and finally begins chopping hollows in its side. Having done so, he ponders to himself whether a redstart or a small mottled woodpecker might build its nest there. So he ponders, carefully marks the place, and goes on his way. But a little further on, he spots a weeping birch from whose trunk a huge, convex burl the size of a Christmas cake juts out. He chops it off and takes it with him, planning to make a formidable tankard of it. Then off he wanders, but soon his sharp eye spots an oddly-twisted juniper on the side of a rocky outcrop. "What would that make?" he wonders, and fells the juniper with a few blows of his sharp ax. He lops off its branches, looks at it smilingly for a minute, and starts off again. He hears the neighborhood cowbells, and gives a loud shout to scare off any wolves in the area. An echo rings round about in friendly reply. On he goes, and at length he comes to the crest of a heath, where he sees a large witch's broom swaying in the top of a pine tree rocked by the northeast breeze. He fells the pine, cuts out the tangled growth, and sits down to study his find.

For a long time he sits there checking and pondering over the witch's broom, the burl, and the twisted juniper. "How had nature started them out? What had twisted the juniper into so many curves and angles?" Then he lay down, resting his head against a deserted anthill overgrown with grass. Gazing at the treetops and the fleecy clouds floating by, he reflected on the structure of earth and sky. From far away on Impivaara Meadow, the slap of stick on puck sounded in his ears. Finally, wanting to clear his mind of all thought, he decided to take a nap, but sleep would not come. And what stratagem did Lauri use whenever the god of sleep was slow in coming? He would imagine himself either a little mole plowing through his peaceful underground manor and falling asleep at last on his fine bed of sand, or a coarse-furred bear resting in his dark, mossy den under the roots of spruce trees, while winter blizzards roared overhead. That's what he would think, and almost always his eyelids would soon close in sleep. And so it was now, as he imagined himself a young mole poking around in the bosom of Mother Earth.

He fell asleep, but his imagination went on working in a dream. He felt his whole body suddenly shrink into that of a sleek-furred mole — his eyes became tiny, and his hands puffed out into paws. He was a complete mole, burrowing deep in the heath among the pine roots. There he tunneled and dug, and finally worked himself up through the rotting center of a tall pine tree until he reached its top, and found himself sitting in a fine, mossy den in the middle of a witch's broom. "It's good to be here; I want to live here forever," he thought, his little mole's eyes squinting out through the window of his house. Below he could see the melancholy world shrouded in the mournful gloom of an autumn evening. He saw the steep hill of Impivaara, but at an infinite, soul-searing distance, saw the gloomy cabin in the midst of the dark woods, and saw his dear brothers batting the puck with the church provost on the foggy, echoing meadow. He felt like weeping bitterly, yet the tears would not flow, but continued rolling restlessly around in their source. He looked toward Impivaara: a strip of meadow and the heath beyond were covered with long rows of fresh, bloody steer hides, over which the puck sped whizzing. With their curved sticks of birch, the brothers struck bravely, but more bravely still did the provost strike with the sword of the spirit, a sword carved of the strongest steel made from old horseshoes — so boasted the provost himself proudly waving his weapon in the air and clashing it against the oaken shield of faith that hung on the left side of his breast.

Brows streaming with sweat, they hammered the disk, which flew back and forth between them, and the din of their blows and rushes sounded far off. But at length the provost noticed that the disk was not an ordinary puck: it was an ABC book with a red cover which the brothers used in their game. The provost was furious — he ranted and cursed the brothers, calling down a thousand devils on their heads. Pointing east, west, north, and south with his flashing sword, he shouted, "Eeyah, eeyah!" and from every direction swirling black storm clouds rushed with tremendous speed upon gloomy Impivaara. A thousand whirlwinds swooped down and joined into one, which wrapped itself around the brothers. Soon a helter-skelter cluster made up of six men had soared high aloft on wings of wind. Enveloped in a cloud of dust and mist, the brothers whirled around like a distaff in the deft hands of a spinner. Lauri the mole watched in horror from his witch's-broom nest in the leaning pine tree. First he saw a man's hand protruding from the whirling mass, then what looked like Juhani's massive jaw, then a coarse mop of hair flitted by. And now the preacher clanged his sword of faith against his oaken shield, and the cloud column began to glide toward the pine grove where Lauri rocked in his high cradle. At this his mole's eyes popped wide open. But the fierce whirlwind rushed on by, with the brothers' woeful screeching and wailing quickly rising and fading. Past him it rushed at a fearful speed, and the woods boomed, roared, and thundered like a thousand rapids. The tree where Lauri lay in the witch's broom fell with a crash, frightening him so that he woke up. He shrieked, leaped up from his mound, and cried out almost in tears: "God help the son of man!" Then for a long time he stared around, almost forgetting where he was. Finally his thoughts resumed their former course, especially when he noticed his paraphernalia nearby: the twisted juniper, the huge burl, and the witch's nest, as puffy as the Turkish Sultan's turban.

At last he set off for Impivaara with his ax under his arm and his goods over his shoulder, vowing never again to imagine himself a wild animal since God had made him a thinking person. So meditating, he went on, and spotted a small birch that appealed to his eye beside the trail. "What would that make? — A good pole for a wagon shaft," he thought. He soon hacked it off and had on his shoulder a good pole for that purpose. With this extra load, he set off again and soon stood on the heath, silent and morose, watching his brothers at their fierce and happy game. They struck hard and ran hard; Tuomas, Aapo, and Eero were winning, having driven their opponents to the eastern end of the field. When they reached the end of the cleared space, the teams

switched positions and Juhani, Simeoni, and Timo began a retreat toward their home again, although they fought against it with all their
might. It was hard to return Tuomas's shots, for the puck left his stick
whizzing and humming. It was just as hard to send the puck past Eero
without having his stick hit it. So on they struggled, and sweated, and
yelled their loudest. His wilderness load on his shoulders, Lauri stood
watching the battle. Killi and Kiiski looked on too, always sticking
close to Juhani and letting out a short bark now and then. The September sky was a bright arch overhead, a brisk northeast wind rustled the
trees, and somewhere in the wilds, a red-headed, yellow-eyed woodpecker tapped on the trunk of a dry spruce tree, occasionally chiming
out a clear, tuneful cry.

Juhani: Send the puck here and I'll give it such a shot it'll know
who hit it.

Tuomas: There now! That shot will drive you all the way back to
Lake Ilves.

Juhani: No it won't. Here it sits, brother, nice and neat. By God's
lightning, watch out for your shins, boy. There!

Tuomas: Hit it back, Aapo! Hit it back!

Aapo: It zipped past like a swallow. But Eero will hit it. Just as I
said. Good shot, Eero, good shot!

Tuomas: Good work, Eero, that was great!

Juhani: If it wasn't for that damned titmouse behind you, you poor
devils would soon be in the woods.

Tuomas: Stop blabbering and hit the puck.

Eero: Hooray! You missed it again.

Aapo: Not one stick hit it, not a single one.

Tuomas: No more than you'd hit a shooting star. Now what do you
have to say?

Eero: How can they say anything when they're running around with
their tails between their legs looking for their lost sheep?

Tuomas: What fun! Sing Eero, sing while we're having fun. Sing about Rajamäki's Regiment. Sing a song to last out the game and even do for a victory march at the other end of the field. Sing about Mikko and Kaisa's trips through the parish.

Eero: We'll sing for joy, and my song will speed the puck on its way.

> *High on Rajamäki*
> *Lives a well-matched pair.*
> *At least five trades they practice,*
> *Occupations rare.*
>
> *Hat of felt upon his head*
> *Old Mikko plies his trade.*
> *He snips — a boar is now a gilt —*
> *Then plays a serenade.*
>
> *Balls of pitch he carries*
> *Mixing trade with banter,*
> *Dousing, stopping bleeding,*
> *A really nice enchanter.*
>
> *Wifey Kaisa, snuffy-faced,*
> *Sucks her cupping horn,*
> *Working in the sauna's heat,*
> *On crowds of wives outworn.*
>
> *Five boys trail along*
> *On their perilous course.*
> *Heikka, oldest of the lot*
> *Rides his hobby horse.*
>
> *Fuzzy-headed Matti*
> *Is the second son.*
> *People call him "Sourpuss."*
> *And he's a shifty one.*
>
> *The next two are a pair of twins,*
> *Bear cubs at a game.*
> *The last is little "Bootsie."*
> *Mikko coined the name.*
>
> *There you have our regiment*
> *Ready for the road.*

By the dungheap stands the cart
Waiting with its load.

Let's strip down for traveling
Over hill and dale.
Go gelding and a'cupping
Carrying pitch for sale.

Kaisa with her snuffy face
Likes to pull the shafts.
Mikko with his chaw in cheek
Pushes with his staff.

Piled into the cart
Are the three young bears,
Sacks of pitch and cupping horns,
All sorts of junky wares.

Heikka on his hobby horse
Leads them as they go.
"Sourpuss" brings up the rear
His bottle cart in tow.

Finally they reach a town.
Front doors squeak and slam.
Dogs yelp and bark; children scream
And take it on the lam.

Many a watchdog has good cause
To hate old Mikko's life.
Many a kid's been frightened stiff
Threatened by Mikko's knife.

Up there on the cart the kids
Let out a deafening yell.
Mikko shakes his fist
Kaisa damns them all to hell.
What a din the dogs set up!
What a fright the kids are in!
When Rajamäki's Regiment
Comes a'roaring in.

Galloping on his hobby horse,
Heikka tears the place apart.

"Sourpuss" stamps across the floor
Drags along his bottle cart.

Now the feisty hobby horse
Gives a lusty kick
Smashing Matti's cart to bits.
The poor kid throws a fit.

From the dungheap Kaisa brings
An awful stick at last.
Heikka gets a whipping then.
The blows fall thick and fast.

Then the twins go at it
Tear each other's hair.
Kaisa turns on them now
And drubs the tussling pair.

Heikka whimpers, "Sourpuss" bellows,
The twins shriek and stop their squabbling.
Kaisa hollers, stamps her foot:
"You gypsies, you hobgoblins!"

Cries like hers would drown out cranes
O'er northern marshes flying
Or drunken auctioneers
Their trade in horseflesh plying.

Juhani: What's Aapo trying to figure out now? I hope you haven't lost our tough, cross-grained puck.

Tuomas: It bounced off the path on the heath and I think it stopped near that little spruce. Well hello, Lauri! Why are you standing here so still and sour?

Eero: How are things in the woods, Lauri?

Juhani: Just ask him. He's standing there like Heikki Pajula, old Hessu from Myllymäki with a load of old shoes on his back. But Aapo, you old windbag, why so poky?

Timo: Hurry up, brother Aapo, hurry up!

Juhani: He's peering and searching like a cat for its kittens.. .."Oh the wind blows free and bows down the trees..." Get out of the way,

Kiiski my dog, watch out for your paws. Did you hear me? Out of the way... "Oh the wind blows free and bows the trees. / I hear my love's voice far away on the breeze..." Now now, Kiiski, poor Kiiski, no mercy here. You can sit in peace and watch the puck fly. But damn it all if we don't find it. Everyone look for it now!

Eero: Here's the sucker.

Tuomas: Put it here between my thumb and finger.

Aapo: And send it to them from a real man's hand.

Juhani: Right. And here's a real man's bat to meet it.

Tuomas: Stand back or you'll get a lump on your head.

Aapo: It went flying by.

Eero: Ah, poor Juhani. Why are you swatting the air?

Juhani: Hit it back, Simeoni, bat it down so hard the earth will ring. Oh, you slowpoke. Now, Timo, let me hear the crack of your bat. Damn your hide. You deserve a dozen lashes, you stick-in-the-mud!

Tuomas: Right on, men. They can't do a thing. But let's march the Rajamäki Regiment right out of town. Do you remember, Eero, how the smoke used to pour from Hemmo's sauna?

> *Good news travels swiftly,*
> *Not laggardly or poking.*
> *Cupper-Kaisa has arrived*
> *And Hemmo's sauna's smoking.*
>
> *A sauna full of hags,*
> *A hundred horns are sucking.*
> *Many a world they've laid in ruins,*
> *These gossips, sighing, clucking.*
>
> *On her cupping tool*
> *Kaisa smacks her lips.*
> *Greta talks through gritted teeth*
> *Squirming in her grip.*
>
> *But what's that other racket*
> *Out there in the yard?*
> *Sows and boars are wailing,*
> *Piglets squeal so hard.*

Why are sows all shrieking
And teeth of piglets gnashing?
Look, beneath the door,
Mikko's knife is flashing.

All that Mikko does is well.
Nary a job does Kaisa shirk.
Now both man and wife enjoy
The feast that follows work.

Off then to another town,
Time to move along.
Mikko, always gay,
Fiddles a parting song.

Along the border of a field
Runs the travelers' path
Dogs escort them on their way
Barking in their wrath.

The twin cubs whimper Kaisa cusses,
"Sourpuss" bawls out fit to bust.
Mikko stones the barking dogs.
The road is choked with dust.

At last there comes an end to
The awful hullabaloo.
Even the dogs head for home
And leave the traveling crew.

The children cry no more,
Their eyes are dry of tears.
The Rajamäki storm is spent
All quiet are their fears.

But over Korppimäki
There's tumult in the sky.
On the far horizon
Thunderclouds go by.

Of this awful regiment
I've sung the final note,
And now at last the time has come
To wet the singer's throat.

Eero's song ended, and so did the exhausting game. The sun sank deep into the mossy pines. The sweaty brothers marched toward home — the winners Tuomas, Eero and Aapo, along with the losers. Last came Lauri, with his heavy load on his shoulders. In the yard, they set a pot full of meat to cook over the fire. They began their meal at the same time, but Juhani, Simeoni, and Timo had an awesome quantity of meat to swallow — ten pounds, as they had all decided — and they had to finish the task without mercy, for Tuomas stood threateningly over them. Nobly they chewed and swallowed, although their stomachs often revolted and their eyes grew bloodshot. At last Timo and Simeoni reached the goal and rushed, grunting and wretchedly grimacing, into the house, where they fell asleep on the rushes. But Juhani had to stay on awhile at his grim meal, even though he bit and chewed diligently. Silent, staring stiffly at the woods, he sat on a stump and ate, angered most of all by Eero's outbursts of laughter. Finally he bolted down the last mouthful. By then his face was horribly red and puffy, but at last the half-chewed lump plopped down into his stomach. Grunting and holding his belly, his face twisted, he spun around, rushed inside, dropped on the bed of rushes, and fell asleep. The others followed to take their nightly rest.

When they awakened at last from their deep sleep, juryman Mäkelä and another man were standing in the room. They had been sent by the master of Viertola with a summons to court for slaughtering the bulls. The brothers stood silent listening to the juryman's summons, then got up and dressed as the fog of sleep gradually cleared. Juhani scratched his head angrily, then roared out:

Juhani: This is a serious matter. Seven lives were at stake. And what are a thousand animals compared to the life of one man?

Mäkelä: The animals were roaming peacefully in Viertola's own, fenced-in pasture.

Juhani: But the bear, who is an enemy of both man and bull, an enemy of all order — he was not roaming peacefully on Viertola land.

He was ready to make a peaceful meal of the master and me and Mäkelä too, all poor souls that have been dearly bought, I should hope. Keep that in mind. See here, Mäkelä, there's many a turn, twist, and trick up here in my noggin, and one of these days I'll peacefully cram them down Viertola's throat. I won't tell you now just exactly what they are, but before the judge I'll come up with something or other, whatever the case and its complications demand.

Timo: We're not exactly children as far as court cases go. We showed a real gift of gab, God save us, in that knotty suit for child support brought by Kaisa Koivula. I'll always remember how they yelled out: "Juhani, son of Juhani Jukola and his younger brother, Timotheus!"

Juhani: Shut up, Timo, shut your mouth like a mole right now. So, Mäkelä, the case is just like I said.

Mäkelä: So you won't even try to pay Viertola's damages?

Juhani: Not a cent, not one red cent! We stand on our rights, and we'll win come hell or high water.

Mäkelä: But I hear you're feasting on beef here. Whose meat are you wolfing down?

Juhani: It's beef, beef, the rich red beef of Viertola's bulls. And we don't wolf it down; we eat daintily, just enough to fill a hungry Christian's belly.

Mäkelä: By your own admission, you've laid your hands on meat that you have no right to.

Juhani: Otherwise the meat would have rotted and spread rashes and scabs and plagues and boils all over Finland. So we saved our country from great misery. And if you ask us why we didn't bury the meat to stay out of jail — which would be a really stupid question — but if you ask us why, then we would answer like this: we did not want to commit the great sin of denying our country and its rulers such hearty, juicy food as beef, especially when we think how many boys have had to gnaw on pine bark like a goat this year.

Mäkelä: Well, to tell the truth, you were right in taking what Viertola so proudly refused. That settles one issue, but the crux of the matter is the damages. I'm afraid they'll take that out of your hides before this is over.

Juhani: They won't find that easy. We'll lose our fields and house first, down to the very cornerstone.

Mäkelä: Well, I've done my duty and stated my opinion. Goodbye.

Juhani: Tell us one more thing. What is the provost planning for us?

Mäkelä: Everyone is talking about that, but you can't trust rumors. But I can say one thing for certain: the provost is in close conference with the bishop about you, and the bishop will soon bring fifty Cossacks into the parish.

Juhani: Fine!

Mäkelä: Fifty horses and men.

Juhani: Fine! Finnish boys have turned back Cossack pikes before this.

Mäkelä: Still, it's too bad. But it can't be as bad as they say. Does it make sense? "A company of Cossacks, a dusty company of pike-wielding Cossacks, and floggers to go with them." Who would believe such idle talk? Fifty men are coming, that's all.

Juhani: Let 'em come!

Mäkelä: Is that all you have to say, you devil? I'd give a million to be rid of them, to be rid of such a disgrace. It's so silly! Armed forces in our parish because of seven men? It's ridiculous, it's stupid! But that's what our bishop has arranged.

Juhani: It's all just fine with me!

Mäkelä: It's awful, it's terrible! But goodbye now.

Juhani: God keep you, Mäkelä. And you too, Taavetti Karela, go in God's name and keeping.

Tuomas: Can there be anything to it?

Juhani: So, my boys! Forty bulls and a company of Cossacks. Drown me deep in the waters of Lake Ilves.

Aapo: I doubt very much...

Juhani: Forty bulls and a battalion of Cossacks with pop-eyed flog-gers. Drown me deep in the clear waters of Lake Ilves.

Aapo: Calm down, man, and stop raving.

Juhani: You heard what he said.

Lauri: The old man was lying. I could tell by the look in his eyes. He tried his best to keep a straight face, but he was lying, I swear it.

Aapo: That Mäkelä is just a joker. They send Cossacks out after thieves from Karja and outlaws from Nurmijärvi, not after upstanding men without a black mark in the parson's book. Mäkelä is a real joker.

Tuomas: But he's always been a worthy man.

Aapo: As honest as the day is long, but a joker. He has the trickiest dodges to keep you in the dark until he has you flopping in his net. Oh, if he were mean and cold-hearted, he could outdo the devil himself in evil tricks, but he's only trying to do good here, even if he mangles the truth in spots. The rascal! That was some story he told us! I almost fell for it myself.

Juhani: Poor me, I was scared out of my wits by the rascal's tales, but now I see they were nothing but lies. Cossacks here? What next? Ha, Ha!

Aapo: But that's enough of tricks — bring on the food. Go and light a fire under the cooking-stone, Lauri. My belly tells me it's dinner time.

Lauri went out and built a blazing fire. Soon the others followed and settled themselves around the rock. Again they cooked a pot of fresh meat for their meal and began to eat, but Juhani, Simeoni, and Timo were in no mood for meat today.

Eero: Eat your meat, boys. Eat your beef, Juhani.

Juhani: Eat it yourself.

Timo: I don't like all the fat on this beef, not at all.

Simeoni: My sinful body shudders every time I look at that pot.

Timo: Will I ever be able to eat fresh meat again? Take it away!

Juhani: To have to cram ten pounds of beef into one's belly. Ten pounds! Like a wolf. It's too much. It's the end of me. Meat is what we live on here, and it no longer tastes good. That pot looks like it's full of black frogs. Oh, I could almost cry.

Timo: Cry? What's the use? Take my word for it, a tear hasn't blurred my eye since we laid my old mother in her grave. I did sniffle a little then. Otherwise, when things get tough, I always think, "Oh well, the worst that can happen is death." Why worry? Time always has new shifts to show us.

Juhani: Right! And I'll show you one now. I'll show you, damned if I don't. A little spark of an idea is glowing in my skull. Yessiree! This numbskull of mine is not the numbest of numbskulls. Uh-huh! The spark of an idea is glowing.

Timo: What kind of spark?

Juhani: That's not just an empty space between my ears. Uh-huh!

Timo: Have you thought of a way out?

Juhani: There are thousands of pine stumps around us, by God, pine stumps as black as trolls.

Timo: Of course there are! But what good will pine stumps do us now?

Juhani: Oh ye of little faith. We'll boil the sizzling tar from the stumps, make it into pitch, shiny black lumps of pitch to sell for money. If Mikko Rajamäki can do it, so can I. But we should give our thanks to Eero, whose ditty about the man made me think of using the pine stumps. It's our only way to make money. There is less and less game; selling it will buy us no more than bread and something to wet it with. As for meat, I'm off it forever. But pitch and tar will pay for everything. Let's take a lesson from Mikko.

Timo: Let's do it. And we should take up Mikko's other trade too, if we're to earn our bread in this new life. I know that to clip a cat and dog neatly, you put one in a leather sleeve, and the other in a keg, but there's more to the art than that. And it's kind of shameful too, which is something else to consider.

Juhani: Go to hell with your gelder's knife. I'm going to burn tar and cook pitch. You'll see how much money the balls of pitch will bring in. What do you think of my idea, Aapo?

Aapo: I've been mulling it over and it makes some sense, but the pitch alone won't be enough to keep us in bread, much less pay for a court case against a rich gentleman. And if we lose, we'll really be out of luck.

Juhani: That's true, but what's to be done? Both sides want justice here.

Aapo: Let's come to terms and forget about the courts.

Juhani: What can we use, my boy, to pay for the bulls and come to terms with that hothead Viertola?

Aapo: Even with pitch, tar, and wild game, which is shrinking at an alarming rate, there won't be enough. But look — one idea breeds another just as one word breeds another. While you were talking about the pine stumps, I thought of the endless wild woods of Jukola, where pine, birch, and spruce trees grow in thick groves. In a few days, seven men can easily fell twelve acres of trees. We'll burn the slash, plant and harvest grain, and take it to Viertola as payment for the bulls, leaving enough in store for our own needs. So there will be bread for those afraid of meat and blood. As for Viertola, if a first field doesn't meet his price, a second or perhaps a third will. But until the grain waves in our fields, we'll wring out whatever the woods will yield: at least three of you still like the taste of meat. Let two years pass by, and when the heading grain stands ready in our fields, we'll build stacking frames and hammer storage bins into shape just as on a proper farm. But look — if we decide to adopt this scheme, let one or two of us go quickly to Viertola to talk it over with the man. I think he'll cool down in the end and decide to accept the crop from our field. They say that all in all he's a decent sort.

Tuomas: That advice is worth considering.

Juhani: It's a man's advice, not some silly old woman's.

Aapo: We'll consider it and decide the issue tomorrow.

The day passed, night came, another day dawned, and the brothers decided to follow Aapo's advice. Two of them, Juhani and Aapo, set off to speak the language of compromise to the fiery master of Viertola. The man they feared was soon placated and agreed to await a bumper crop to pay his damages. Why shouldn't he? The rugged wilds of Jukola offered him great profits of many kinds. Highly satisfied, the brothers left the manor to carry home the happy news.

Two or three days passed and all the brothers set out for the woods, bright axes on their shoulders. Last marched Eero, carrying in his hand a brush-hook made from a broken old sickle. The brothers had picked out the broad south slope of a hill thick with pine trees as the site for their field. At its upper end stood a towering grove of pines. So the felling began: the axes rang, the woods echoed, and tree upon tree fell with a crash. In the van rushed Eero, cutting the tough and wiry undergrowth with his brush-hook. So several acres of dense woods were felled, and the tangy odor of green needles and fresh pine chips scented the air. And now a clearing lay exposed on a south slope of Impivaara, a huge open space, whose like had scarcely been seen before. The work had been finished in five September days. For three days and nights, the brothers rested from toil, sound asleep and snoring in the cabin. When their bodies had had enough rest, they went on hunting expeditions in the yellowing woods. Over thundering hills they trod, through gloomy woods; and their accurate shots laid low the herds of Tapiola as stores for the coming winter. But wild game was becoming very scarce near Impivaara, and it was time for the brothers to seek other means of livelihood.

Winter came. Snow covered the ground and a bitter wind swirled through the meadow, piling snowdrifts against the cabin wall. Inside, the brothers dwelt in the sweaty heat of the loft, resting from the many toils and troubles of the past summer. They bathed diligently, slapping themselves with soft switches and basking in the soothing steam which rose hissing from the heap of stones and spread quickly around the room, finally forcing its way out through cracks in the walls and vanishing into the bone-chilling air under a somber gray sky. Thus the drowsy men spent both day and night. And there on many a winter night, they watched through their small window-opening the pale flashing of the northern lights. Beyond a bearded spruce on the crest of the mountain glowed an expansive arch of light. Silent, flashing, the play of light kindled, dimmed, and kindled anew, flare after flare, reaching from the broad portals of the north to the high dome of heaven, while a dim and intermittent glow flickered about the surrounding sky. From the cabin loft, the brothers watched the display, marveling and making wild guesses at the cause and origin of the striking phenomenon. But they wondered and pondered in vain.

Now and then, however, when the brief day was dawning, they went out into the buffeting wind and sped through the frost-covered woods on their slippery skis. As luck would have it, they sometimes bagged a nimble heath grouse, sometimes a gray squirrel or other denizen of the woods. In the wilds, they came upon the rounded tracks of a lynx, running in a pretty pattern across the snow. The dogs were immediately in a frenzy, a sign that the beast was prowling close by. Soon Killi and Kiiski broke into a whining bark and set off quickly in pursuits with the brothers rushing after them. Through the woods went the chase, then up a rocky hill, sending snow and moss flying from the crags. In front fled the lynx, its eyes flashing as bright as two mirrors reflecting sunlight, pursued by the wrath of baying dogs and the rush of seven men on skis. Now the chase skimmed along the high ridge of Kamaja toward the southwest, where day's fading star shone dimly upon them. Right and left, north and south, the lowlands echoed the fiery zeal of Killi and Kiiski. But suddenly, the competing voices stopped, for at the moment of its greatest danger the hook-clawed lynx had climbed swiftly to the top of a spruce tree. The spruce received it gladly, but could not shield it from death. The dogs raged on, flashing eyes searching for their prey in the tree above, from which a low growl sounded, and the spruce shook its head threateningly at the pursuers. But with clatter and clamor, the brothers skied up, lungs and cheeks burning. Then Tuomas said: "Call off the dogs, brothers, from a risky fight, where their bellies would soon be ripped open." Thus he spoke, and the others took a firm grip on the dogs' coats while Tuomas took aim and fired. Down dropped the bleeding lynx, and the dogs yipped and lunged to get at their victim, but could not. The lynx lay on the bloody field, writhing and jerking, tearing at everything with its sharp claws. But another bullet pierced its brain, cutting short its agony, and it collapsed. Once more the spruce shook its locks threateningly, casting a glistening shroud of snow over its dying son, for the brisk spirit of life was leaving the heart of the lynx and vanishing into the air as a mist. So ended the mighty chase on spruce-clad Kamaja Ridge, from which Mount Impivaara and the meadow below could be seen off to the southwest. Toward it the joyful brothers now set off with their prey.

Thus did they ski uphill and down through frost-covered woods and over level fields, and the gleam of their bared brown chests shown from far away. And thus they passed away the time, most of it in the cabin's warmth, for the sleepy, rayless sun lingered in the tropical world of the south. It had moved far away, the fiery source of life; on some days it scarcely lifted its brow above the blue fringe of the woods. But then it turned and began its journey to the north again.

Summer had come, and the brothers trimmed the fallen trees. The huge heap of brush dried out on warm days, and the time for burning drew near. Without sending word to their neighbors, without letting a soul know, the brothers set off to burn the field. The slash was set afire, the fierce flames roared high in the air, and soon the dark smoke rose nearly to the clouds. On roared the fire, turning the slash to ashes in the bright sunshine. But not content with the slash and trees in the clearing, it surged at last with a roar into the pillared hall of the pines. Then the horrified brothers rushed to battle the overpowering force with all their might. They swept and beat the field of heather, their brooms of spruce flashing and whistling in the air and thudding into the earth so that the sandy heath boomed. But the raging fire was untamed; it rushed forward kindling all in its path. Finally Juhani shouted loudly: "Every man take his pants in his hands, dip them in the spring, and beat the dry grass with them." They ripped off their pants, dunked them in the cold, bubbling spring, and began to beat and pound the burning heath. The fiery ash and soot flew high, the earth resounded as if a cavalry troop were galloping over it at top speed, and the wild flames were baffled. Black as soot and bathed in sweat, the men collapsed feebly to the earth, puffing and panting from the hot game.

But the field was burned clear. It was plowed and planted, worked with a stick harrow drawn by the strength of seven men. Finally a stout fence was built around it and before the coming of winter, sprouts of rye were thriving in the field. But suitable holes and gaps were left in the fence and set with heavy deadfalls to be the death of many a rabbit.

CHAPTER X

So the days passed by, and with the second summer the time came to harvest a crop. In the field waved a luxuriously abundant harvest, the like of which had scarcely been seen before. The brothers mowed the field in the heat of the blazing sun. Soon the rippling grain was converted to shocks, which in turn disappeared into the cabin. There it was dried in the warm loft, then threshed below by beating against the wall. Finally the field stood bare, the grain was threshed, and the greater part transported to Viertola, although twenty barrels was left for the brothers' own needs. The grain paid one half of their debt, and the man from Viertola promised to consider it paid in full if they would let him plant the field once more with oats, give him logs from the Jukola woods to build an imposing new granary, and return the forty steer hides to him. The brothers agreed to the deal.

And so they emerged from a troublesome situation, which nevertheless had left their storehouse with more grain than was needed for the coming winter. But this would lead to more momentous events. Those plump kernels of grain soon turned Juhani's mind to thoughts of a distillery, and he was quickly seconded by Timo. At first, the others objected, but in the end, Juhani and Timo's will prevailed. Juhani preached that liquor, if enjoyed wisely and in moderation, was a joy and a blessing, especially for such as they, young ravens in the dark backwoods. So they set about the project, building a small hut in the wolf-pen trench and bringing in the old still from Jukola, for the tanner lacked the wherewithal for distilling. And now smoke rose into the air from the trench at Impivaara, and the still produced an abundance of clear liquid.

The brothers began to enjoy themselves, nipping from morn till eve, and time flowed by like a river. Within two or three days, a continuous music roared in their ears, like the sound of a distant bassoon, and the world spun merrily before their eyes. Clad only in shirts. they lolled about the cabin, from which was heard a constant roar and clamor, sometimes the thumping and bumping of a wrestling match, sometimes the crashes and blows of a brawl. Then the stout cabin door would fly open and a man come racing out with another hot on his heels. Around the cabin they ran, coarse shirts flapping and swarthy legs flashing. So they ran until the fight was renewed or the others rushed in to establish peace and harmony between them. Then together they marched into the cabin again, drank a toast to friendship, and sang a happy song, bellowing without restraint.

Lauri alone abstained from boozing. Remembering his wild drunkenness on the Rock of Hiisi, he had made a noble vow never to touch a drop of liquor, and he kept his oath. Now he roamed the woods in silence, looking at deformities in trees in search of wood for household utensils. He also busied himself in the field with deadfalls and often returned with a young rabbit in his bulging bag. Once when he was out checking his traps, he saw a certain brown animal in a deadfall. "The Lord be praised; I've caught a fox!" he exclaimed in satisfaction, only to follow with a harsh bellow, "It's Viertola's brown cat." So he shouted, hurled the cat angrily into the woods, re-set the deadfall, and set off again to visit his other traps and his snares for grouse. So he spent his days in the chilly woods, while the others drank themselves pop-eyed in the toasty cabin.

It was nearing Michaelmas, and the brothers were in the mood for a proper celebration. They prepared a rich load to take to town, the price of which would pay for food and drink in honor of the holiday: rum, a bottle of beer, eels, herring, and wheatbreads. Arduous was the hustle and bustle of men around the cart on that brisk September morning.

Sacks were hoisted and settled in place and ropes drawn taut with double half hitches. It was all done lightly and at top speed, for each of them, with the exception of Lauri, had poured a dizzying morning draft down his throat. Soon the load stood ready in the yard, and Simeoni and Eero set out for Hämeenlinna, a barrel of rye and ten cannisters of whisky on the cart and old Valko in the shafts. — But in the cabin, the uproariously happy life went on; liquor was drained from stoups, and day after day went by. A week passed and then another, but the travelers to town were not seen or heard from. The brothers began to suppose this, that, and the other. While they puzzled over it, the tenth day dawned, with Simeoni and Eero still lingering on the same unknown road.

The sun rose and boisterous joy was at its height in the cabin. Loud was the speech for each man was boasting of his strength. But Lauri sat silent in a corner, carving a gun-stock of cross-grained birch. — Loud was the speech.

"A lad built like a log wall!"

"Head over heels when a man hits!"

"Do you remember, brothers, what a sweet shot in the jaw Antti Kolistin took from this fist? He took it like a man, and the earth shook and the sky creaked when the tall lad fell."

So they vied in words, now and then gulping the sparkling liquor from the stoups. But suddenly a hot quarrel sprang up between Juhani and Timo, in which the oldest brother lost his temper completely. For Timo was in no mood to give in, but argued stubbornly using proverbs, biblical citations, and lame comparisons. Juhani's spleen rose, his eyes flashed fire, and at last he stopped speaking abruptly, reared up like a tormented bear, and charged at his headstrong brother. But Timo took flight. With nothing but a shirt on, the boy rushed out to the meadow, with Juhani, similarly clad, in pursuit. The pursuer, however, stopped a few paces from the threshold, while Timo, thinking his enraged brother was right on his heels, ran on and on, twisting and dodging through the stump-filled meadow. And now, fearing that his pursuer was about to seize him by the neck, he opened his mouth and bellowed hoarsely, looking awkwardly back over his shoulder. But his eyes opened wide as he saw Juhani standing far off by the cabin steps, scratching his neck and gazing at two wretched travelers who came dragging out of the woods toward the cabin. The others rushed out too, as red as men sitting in the sauna's heat, to make peace between the warring brothers. But soon all eyes turned toward Simeoni and Eero, who were finally returning from their trip. And a sorry state they were in.

Valko, now no more than skin and bones, walked with unutterable slowness. His head hung down between his legs, and his grievously sagging lower lip dragged along the ground. The men were in wretched condition too. Faces and clothing spattered with mud, they sat on the cart like two crows in the rain. Simeoni's hat had been stolen along with Eero's socks and boots. Of money, they had only six kopeks left, which unknown to Eero, were in his vest pocket along with a crumbled cookie. Where had they dispensed with the money for the load? They had spent it on wheat bread and whiskey in Hämeenlinna and were now arriving home empty-handed and badly hung over. Silent and completely dumfounded, the others watched the apparition from the cabin door, and Simeoni and Eero read their frightful doom in that gaze. Simeoni thought it best to take to his heels. Abandoning horse and brother, he leaped down from the cart and vanished into the wilds. Eero too thought of using the same tactics, but hoped soon to free himself of all blame and stand guiltless before his brothers. Thinking thus, he decided to keep going.

Arriving at length in the yard, he put on a most doleful expression and without a word or sign of greeting, stepped down and began to unhitch Valko. But now he faced a heated interrogation about how the trip had gone and how the price of the load had been lost. Eero told them everything, reminding them that the money had been in Simeoni's keeping, that Simeoni was giving the orders and that he, as a younger brother, had to obey, that Simeoni was older, wiser, and more experienced than he, a young, uncomprehending bull-calf. Thus he de-

fended himself, but the others knew well enough that he was not guiltless, as his hangover testified. Therefore they saw fit to punish him
immediately.

Tuomas grabbed him by the collar and laid him flat on the ground
as lightly as if he were a doll, and Juhani took a trimmed fir branch
from the manure pile and gave Eero's rump a heavy-handed dusting,
while the lad wailed loudly under the blows. Having done this, Juhani
tossed the switch aside angrily, saying, "God grant this be the last time
I punish you. May this basting cause a change of heart in you. I hope it
will, but I'm afraid it's a vain hope. A good child punishes himself,
but even whipping won't mend a bad." Thus he spoke and strode angrily into the cabin, heading toward his bed of straw. As he passed the
fireplace, he saw the cat sitting sleepily on the sauna stones. He put a
piece of bread into his own mouth, bit it into small pieces, and gave it
to old Matti, who relished the gift, slit-eyed and purring. Then glaring
around, Juhani climbed up to the loft, stroked his belly once, lay down
on the straw, and pulled the warm sheepskin robe over himself.

From the dark woods, a horrified Simeoni watched Eero's punishment and heard his cries. Knowing full well that he would have suffered an even worse punishment from his angry brothers, he thanked
his lucky stars for the sheltering woods and moved further from the
light of the clearing into their protecting embrace. His heart was as
gloomy and barren as the autumn woods around him. Long he wandered through the mossy trees, coming at length to rocky ground
where blueberry bushes grew and where a dismal breeze sighed
through yellowed birch trees. Whither should he wander in the bewil-
dering maze of woods? Where should a man flee, whose life was
cheerless and dark? Dark too was the night of death.

But in the yard near the cabin door, the brothers were busy feeding
the exhausted Valko a flour mash and rubbing him down. Eero, despite
his deplorable condition, sat on the threshold grinding his teeth with
rage, while Juhani lay in the loft under the sheepskin robe. But when
Valko was fed and let out to pasture and the cart was set in its place

against the cabin wall, the brothers went in, bitterly recalling the goods they had saved in vain for the festival. Finally Eero too entered without saying a word, but with a furious scowl on his face. Then Juhani, raising his head from under the cover, looked down from the rim of the loft and spoke the following words: "Are you still scowling, you bull-calf? Didn't you deserve the beating you got, you mule? Hang it all, if we had given you what you had coming, I doubt that you'd be stamping into the cabin on your own two feet. Believe me, you can thank your lucky stars that you got off so easily. But Simeoni can expect something different. Oh, he'd better rub his back well with bear grease before he dares to open our door. He has it coming to him, he really has it coming. To sell the whiskey when the tavern keeper had him soused to the gills, to buy it back at many times the price, to soak up the sacks of grain to the very last kernel for overpriced chicory and syrup water — in a word, to throw away the whole cartload, whiskey and all, for syrup-water, wheat bread, and cookies. Oh, who would have thought it of Simeoni? Is that his goodness? The fruits of many devout prayers? But it's no great wonder. Sad to say, devout men are strongly drawn to drink, especially to closet tippling. Stupid though I am, I've come to see that. Take for instance the master of Härkämäki, who has the name and fame of a pious man. This same windbag spends his day as drunk as a fiddler, with his face as red as a bed of coals. Watch him as he rises from his hymnal and book of homilies in his study. He makes straight for a cabinet, and does a little trick, a bit of sleight of hand. Now he steps outside and lurches toward the stable, and the poor hired boy knows he is in for a long lecture. But even the worst preacher's sermons must come to an end: the door finally creaks and the old man shuffles sidelong to the cowbarn. Then the poor maid is on the griddle as the old man, face as red as a rooster, catechizes her, quacking and squawking in his anger. Oh, you old clod! Well, even famine years have to end, so let's step from the cowbarn into the house. There a real ruckus begins. The stormiest of tirades falls on his wife and daughter, one that lasts for an hour or two. His wife even storms and snaps back at him from time to time, but his poor daughter is silent and lets fall a tear. Oh you lout! But finally the preacher's throat gets scratchy and he goes to his study cabinet to wet it. Now to pick up the hymnal and sing till the door posts tremble. So his days waste away until the week is over and on Sunday morning he goes lumbering off to church in his buggy, his daughter by his side, stocking cap on his head and his coat collar turned awry. Then he sits in the Lord's temple, lips pursed and eyebrows piously arched, clearing his throat in a righteous way, as solemn, sober, and serious as a freshly castrated bull. He sits plumped down there like a boundary marker in the woods, but what happens when he gets back to the yard at home? With lightning speed, he rushes for the cabinet in his study, and now the old man drains the bottle dry. So devoutly does he drink, this pillar of the world, such a raging thirst is his, this born-again soul. And the same would be true of Simeoni, if fate were to put him in Härkämäki's shoes. It is true that for some years a better spirit has been at work in Simeoni — one can't deny it — even if he's been preening his soul's wings a little too much. That's all well and good, but in many ways, he's as much a child of this world, as big a sack of sins as I and many others. And now he's pulled a real devil's trick that calls for a sound drubbing. Giving ear to the devil's whispers, he's drunk up a costly cart load of goods, not bringing back a single crumb as a treat for our feast. Grrr! It makes me grind my teeth. Well, he'll get his lumps yet — so hard the cabin will shake." So said Juhani, peering down from the edge of the loft; then he sank back on his bed and slept. The others too lay down to rest and slept soundly until the next morning.

But there was no sign of Simeoni, not for many days and nights. It was cause for apprehension, even sorrow, among the brothers, especially when they heard from Eero of his true condition. For after a few days, Eero's bad temper had softened a little, and he let them know how things had stood with Simeoni on their return trip from town. Often Simeoni had even spoken of some little old men an inch tall who, he said, swarmed around him by the thousands. So Eero told them in a soft mutter, and his story changed the brothers' attitude toward Simeoni. Sad at heart, Juhani set out to find his lost brother, traversing fields and woods, shouting out his name. At the foot of a hill, he met Tinder-Matti searching ax in hand for fungus growths and gnarls on trees, with which his shirt front was already stuffed. Matti told of hearing a wretched voice wailing far off in the woods the night before, a voice he thought resembled Simeoni's. This brought a sharp pang to Juhani's heart, and he hurried home shedding hot tears over his brother's unhappy fate. Now a general search through the whole woods was decided upon. Each brother was to go alone in a different direction, and the one who found the fugitive was to take him home, climb up Impivaara, and inform the others by blowing on a birch-bark horn. Eero brought out his horn from a shadowy thicket, a mighty birch-bark trumpet four feet long, the sound of which could be heard at great distances. He submerged it for the night in the rippling brook that ran through the wolf pen, for the bugle, made at the height of the spring sap season, was dry and leaky.

Early the next morning, they set off on their mission. Impivaara was the point from which six men set out on paths like spokes from the hub of a wheel. A clamor now arose, in which shout swallowed up shout and echo chased echo through the endless depths of the forest. The din receded ever further and the wheel expanded hugely. Had you been standing on the crest of Impivaara, you could have traced the rim of the wheel by drawing a line from shout to shout. So they journeyed, each on his own course. The air was calm and clear and the September sun shone mildly. Bellowing loudly, Juhani went crashing up hill and down. Soon it would be midday, yet his ears did not hear the voice he longed for. But at last, as he continued to sound his tireless throat like a brass horn, he heard a strange, hoarse, and feeble response. The voice seemed to come from a hollow between two mossy crags sheltered by a few tall fir trees. Juhani hurried to the spot where he found the lost man in a pitiful state. He was a dreadful figure: hands clasped, eyes staring like those of an owl, hair standing up in tufts, he sat at the foot of a dense spruce. There he sat, his body twitching, humming the tune of a hymn in a faint and quavering voice. Juhani started to ask how he was, but getting only a strange and confused response, he hurried quickly home with his precious find. When at last he had taken his brother into the cabin and barred the door on him, he marched up the ridge with the mighty horn in his hand. A broad, calm, forested world shading into blue in the distance surrounded him, and the setting sun in the west shed a glow of russet and gold on the old bearded spruce on the ridge top. Juhani set the horn to his lips, but it refused to sound, emitting only a few faint squeaks. He blew once more, but no clear sound came forth. Then he swelled his chest again, filling his lungs to bursting, and blew a third time. His cheeks bulged fearfully and the birch-bark horn blared forth a solemn blast. The echo sped afar in all directions, soon answered by happy voices from the east, west, north, and south, weak and fading voices from the eternal twilight of the distant blue woods. A short time later, the brothers began to appear one by one in the yard and cabin, and eventually they all stood around Simeoni, watching with pity in their eyes as he perched on a bench like an owl on a barn roof, staring soberly at them.

Juhani: Simeoni, our brother.

Tuomas: How are you doing?

Timo: Do you know who I am? — Not a word. — Do you know who I am?

Simeoni: Of course I know you.

Timo: Who am I?

Simeoni: Hmh — Timo Jukola. Why shouldn't I know you?

Timo: Right. I'm Timo Jukola, your own brother. Things could be worse, boys.

Simeoni: Huge and horrible is the day that approaches and its name is the terror of destruction.

Aapo: Why are you prophesying this?

Simeoni: *He* said it.

Juhani: Who?

Simeoni: *Him,* my partner on the trip.

Eero: Who, me?

Simeoni: No, the monster who led me. Oh, my brothers, I'm going to tell you things that will make your hair stand on end like the fur on a raging bear's neck. But first give me a little drink to strengthen my heart, and let it be the last I ever swallow.

Juhani: Take a drink, God's handiwork, here it is, my dear brother.

Simeoni: Now I'll tell you what I've seen and heard. it's a warning to us all. Listen, I saw *him.*

Juhani: Who in the world did you see?

Simeoni: The chief devil, Lucifer himself.

Aapo: You saw him in a dream or in delirium caused by too much drinking on the trip.

Simeoni: I really saw him.

Timo: What does he look like?

Simeoni: Like stupidity itself, but look, he had a fox tail wagging behind him.

Timo: Was he big too?

Simeoni: About my height, but he can take on any shape he chooses. When he first appeared, he came as a noisy gust of wind in the thicket where I sat. "Who is it I cried out." "A friend," he answered, then took me by the hand and told me to follow him. I did, not daring to resist and thinking it best to do what he wished. As we traveled a long, thorny, rocky road together, he kept constantly changing to all sorts of shapes. First he skipped along before me as a small, mewing kitten, turning back to give me a completely foolish look. Then he shot up into an enormously tall man whose head reached the clouds. From up there, he shouted to me: "Do you see my head?" Always saying whatever would please him, I marveled at his height, saying that my eyes could hardly make out his crotch. He laughed loud and joyfully at this, then looked at me sharply. He followed this with many other tricks and at last he led me to the top of a high mountain,

bowed down before me, and said: "Get up on my back." I was horrified but did not dare to object and climbed dutifully up to his neck. I
did ask him: "Where are we going?" and he answered, "We're going
up." Then he began to huff, sweat, and squirm, while I, poor man, was
continually tossed this way and that like the monkey on the dog's back
at Hämeenlinna Fair. But finally two motley wings popped out of his
shoulders. He shook them once or twice, and now we began to soar
upwards toward the moon, which shone down on us like the bottom of
a brass tub. Toward it we sped, leaving the earth below at a dizzying
depth. Finally we reached the moon, which is, as our blind uncle used
to say, a round, shiny rock island in the air, and there I saw marvels
and wonders, marvels and wonders. Oh, a sinful tongue cannot de-
scribe them!

Tuomas: Do the best you can.

Juhani: Do the best you can, even if it isn't equal to the gravity of
the matter.

Simeoni: I'll try. Well, we reached the moon and Satan took me to
its very rim, to a high hill, on which stood an even higher tower made
of leather, of boot leather. We climbed the tower, with him leading and
me following; for a long time we kept mounting the spiral stairs. Finally we stood on the tip-top of the boot leather tower from which I
saw many lands and seas, big cities and wonderful buildings below us.
I got up enough nerve to pluck at Satan's side and ask, "What is that
we can see way down below us?" He glared at me and snapped angrily: "Sacramento, boy! What have I got to do with you? But that is
the world we left behind. Look and consider." Thus he spoke, and with
a sigh, I began to look wisely and closely, and I could see the whole
sphere of the earth. I saw the British Empire, I saw Turkey, the city of
Paris and the country of America. I saw the Grand Turk rise and wreak
havoc and destruction everywhere, with huge horned Mammon on his
heels driving mankind over the whole world like a wolf going after
sheep. Thus he ravaged and rampaged until he held the whole world
and America in his grasp. I saw all this and again asked Satan, pluck-

ing at his side: "Is the whole world which is my home destroyed now?" Grimly he answered, "Sacramento, boy, what do I have to do with you? But this prophecy concerns an event which will soon take place. Look and consider." And sighing deeply, I did look and consider. Yet I dared to ask one more question: when would this happen? He replied with an angry outburst: "It will happen just as two leathern trumpets appear through this wall right in front of us." And now he gave a long whistle. Oh, if I could only explain it to you!

Juhani: Do it if you can. What marvels and wonders you have seen! It is an omen of something, maybe of our ruin, of God's punishment falling upon us, if not of the end of the world. What other sense does it make to roam around the moon with the devil?

Simeoni: And in a leather tower!

Juhani: In a leather tower. What sense does it make?

Timo: In a boot leather tower!

Juhani: That's right, in a boot leather tower. Oh, tell us everything, even if it does send chills down my spine. This sifting is likely to do my sinful heart good. It is so hard and stiff that only hell's mallet or heaven's fire-hammer can touch it. So let it roar and let it pour, brother, let it pour down even scorpions, for we need it. And then what happened?

Simeoni: Then listen, listen! Satan gave a shrill whistle, and just as he had said, two leather horns, two monstrous trumpets came bursting through the wall. They began to roar and howl horribly, like maddened lions, and to pour forth smoke, sulphur fumes and brimstone gas from their gullets. We were soon coughing hard, coughing and gasping and covering our ears against the braying of the two fearful horns. Their sound grew louder and louder, the great leather tower shook and finally collapsed with a crash and a roar and we fell along with it, covered by scraps of leather. What happened to Satan, I don't know, but I fell head over heels, lower and lower, from the peak, from the very rim of the moon and down toward the earth on a four-foot wide piece of leather. But the leather, which came from the moon, was drawn toward the moon, and I, who came from the earth, was drawn toward the earth, you might say, and since the weight of my body overcame the lift of the leather piece, I kept sinking down, but slowly, just as if I were sailing through the air on an old crow's back. I lucked out completely, for without this leather craft, this airship, I would have smashed into the earth like a bag of guts, for I no longer rested on Satan's wings. But slowly, slowly, I now sailed toward my beloved home on earth, and finally landed at the foot of the spruce tree near the place from which I had left on my voyage with Satan. I still held the leather sheet in my hands, on which I now noticed these words written in red letters: "This with many greetings to the Jukola brothers! When as a fiery sign, like to a glowing eagle's tail, is seen under the clouds above, behold, the end is near unto the day when this is to happen. Given at the boot-leather tower on almost the last day in what is truly most likely the very last year." This is what was written on the leather tablet which I let go of and which flew off toward the moon. That is the whole truth about my doleful journey.

Juhani: Wonderful, marvelous, and horrible all at the same time.

Timo: But at least you learned how to read on that wild goose chase.

Simeoni: Don't you believe it. I'm as stupid as I was before.

Timo: But you must have gotten the knack. Try it. Here's the ABC book.

Simeoni: What of it? It's like looking at Russian or Hebrew. At the time I knew by the soul's power much that is dark to me now; once more I'm a poor human being, the same awful, sinful soul as before. My head is in a whirl, for the day has come. My head is in a whirl, for I have seen Lucifer. Aiee, how hairy he was.

Juhani: Oh, us poor boys, oh?

Simeoni: A thousands oh's! My head is in a whirl, my head is in a whirl? I have seen Lucifer. My head is in a whirl?

Juhani: Pray to God, brothers, pray to God?

Simeoni: Let's all pray together. — I have seen the hairy strength of Lucifer. Let's all pray.

Timo: Well, since we have to, why not?

Juhani: How awful this is, aa-ooh!

Timo: Don't cry, Juhani.

Juhani: I'd cry tears of blood if I could. We've lived like Tartars, caroused like Mohammedan Turks. But now let sermon follow song, let a new life begin for us, otherwise the horrible wrath of heaven will come down on our heads like a mountain and sink us to hell. Yes yes, boys, we have been warned with omens and wonders, and we can expect the worst of devils if we don't heed the signs in time.

Lauri: We can expect the worse. I have something to tell you too. Listen, while you were batting the puck on the meadow, I was wandering in the forest looking for wood to carve into utensils. Lying on the heath, I had an amazing dream. I watched as if from the top of a tall pine tree while you were wildly batting the puck over fresh steer hides on the meadow. And guess who with. My brothers, you were banging away at it with our own fiery provost. And then what happened? The provost finally noticed that it wasn't an ordinary puck, but an ABC Book with a red cover. That made him so furious that he waved his sword and shouted out: "Eeyah, eeyah" and a fearful whirlwind came up quickly and tossed you into the air and drove you along like chaff. That's what I dreamed, and that dream has a meaning.

Juhani: It must have. It foretells a devil's polska for all of us, no doubt about it. We've been warned from two quarters now, and if we don't take heed, then fire, pitch, and pebbles will rain down on us, as they did once on the cities of Sodom and Gomorrah.

Aapo: But let's not be too terrified.

Tuomas: I'm not really sure of it, but maybe everything Simeoni saw came from a sotted brain.

Juhani: What are you saying, man? Are you taking God's mighty works in vain?

Timo: Don't speak against God's works and wonders.

Simeoni: Oh, I've been to the moon and seen Lucifer, and my soul is hugely fearful. Woe to me and woe to all of us.

Tuomas: What misery? But have another drink and go to bed.

Simeoni: What good will that do?

Timo: There's none left.

Tuomas: That changes things.

Simeoni: Thank God the poison ran out. And never will a drop of drink touch my lips again, I promise, I swear it.

Juhani: Curses on this potion from hell!

Timo: We went wrong when we started making the stuff.

Aapo: Whose idea was it? Answer me, Timo and Juhani.

Juhani: Well, you liked the taste of it too, didn't you? And besides, what's done is done and whining and sniveling won't undo it. Well, well, it's water under the bridge, and from now on a new rule applies. To the trench, and ax in hand, I'll hammer that wicked copper idol that cursed still into a shapeless mass and scatter the hut like a magpie's nest.

Simeoni: Do so, my brother, and heaven will rejoice.

Juhani: I'll do it.

Aapo: Why destroy gear that we can honestly sell?

Juhani: Look at it this way. The man we sell the still to — what kind of health tonic will he make with it? The same stuff, the very same stuff that drove us to the brink of ruin. This still will drive many more to the same misery. I want that sin to be far away from me when I come in the end to be judged by God. Now then, let's smash the still and level the hut.

Aapo: Let's sell it to the state to coin into money.

Juhani: It'll yield coins aplenty even when it's crushed. Here's my ax. Take yours too, Timo, and go with me to the wolf pen. And we'll go to church tomorrow because it's Sunday, we'll go to church and pray on our knees for that one poor deathless soul of ours. We're badly in need of prayer. To church, every man of us, otherwise we'll be basted by Satan. To the wolf pen, Timo.

Juhani and Timo now went down to the trench, smashed the still into a shapeless lump, and destroyed the hut. They spent the night in the soundest sleep, rose early the next morning, and began to get ready for church. Aapo had their father's old hymnal under his arm, Simeoni carried *The Voice Crying Out,* and Juhani and Timo their copies of the ABC Book. On the way, they spoke as follows:

Simeoni: Listen, the nearer we get to the Lord's temple, the more the storm in my soul calms down and the more my heart revives. Oh, a wise man walks the path of piety, but the stupid and blind wallow in the muck of sin. Alas? When I look back, that ill-fated trip to town appears in my mind like a horrible hell ringed by the blue flames of drink.

Timo: Therefore I beg you, my brother, don't ever do it again. Is that any way to act? To stuff your face with saloon booze day and night, and swill sweet syrups like a big shot? Now, now, this isn't meant as a scolding but as a brotherly warning.

Simeoni: I did wrong, and so did all of us when we took to making and drinking liquor. But let's all make a vow now to shun the drink that turns the son of man into a beast.

Juhani: Into a pig, into the lowest kind of grunting razorback. So boys, let's give old booze a firm farewell handshake and tell it in God's name to leave us forever. Now Aapo, tell us the story of the pig in the mud puddle that our blind uncle once told us. Tell it while we walk.

Aapo: I'll gladly tell it. Oh, may it make us despise that fiery water more than ever.

Aapo told them the following:

It was a Sunday morning. A pig was wallowing in a mud puddle in the bright summer sunshine, watching the people pass by on their way to church. Heart aching with envy, he gazed at the noble, beautiful form of the human beings, thinking of his own scruffy shape. Such a bright radiance beamed from the brow of a few passers-by that his own eyes were deflected, and he was furious with God for not making him a human being. When he had grumbled and complained his full, he stretched out his legs, closed his squinty little eyes, and fell asleep. But when he awoke after some time, a man lay near him, a drunk who had fallen into the mud puddle and was about to choke on the muck. Sensing his danger, the pig pitied him, gripped his collar with his sharp fangs, and dragged him to dry ground. Having done this merciful deed, he gazed at the man for a moment, gave an ugly sneer, and said: "You miserable man, you look so ugly that I can't stand to look at you any longer." Thus spoke the pig, walked grunting away, and began to root up the earth.

Juhani: An apt story. But that's Jukola Farm over there. And a good thing that it's far out of our way, for it would break our hearts to see our old home. And it's a good thing that Toukola and our enemies are far away too. You see, I'm afraid that if we met them and they mocked us the least bit, I would be at their throats like a cat. I still haven't forgotten the beating they gave me, or my promise of an awful revenge.

Tuomas: I haven't forgotten them either.

Simeoni: We should forgive and forget.

Juhani: Well, let it be. If they eat crow and come to me begging for pardon and admitting they did wrong, I'll willingly forget everything, even shake hands and shed tears. But if they won't stoop to this and still snap at me, then I'll grind my teeth until the sparks fly.

So speaking, they approached the Tammisto house. Many people, men and women, were standing about the yard, and a voice could be heard counting, "Once, twice, three times," then asking, "will anyone offer more?" It was a limited foreclosure auction, conducted by the sheriff himself, who sat by a small table on the porch writing the names of buyers and prices in his book. At the moment, the farm's lowing cattle were being sold. The brothers stared in amazement, wondering why such things were being done on a Sunday. But in their roaring drunkenness at Impivaara, they had confused the days of the week, which speed man's time on its course. Today was Monday, a plain, ordinary weekday. The brothers had taken it to be a Sunday, and so had set out book in hand for church.

They looked around for their trusted friend Kyösti, but he was not there. He was wandering far off in a field, staring at the ground and thinking to himself. Finally Juhani asked a few men standing nearby how they dared hold a public auction on Sunday, on the Lord's Sabbath. Laughter and tittering spread like wildfire from man to man through the whole assembly, and now the brothers surmised the true state of affairs. Dumfounded, they stood red-faced and silent for a long time, listening to the jeers and laughter of the people. A group of men from Toukola came up and inquired derisively about the new Impivaara religion, asking about its calendar, and what this eighth day of the week was called. The brothers listened, and suddenly their rage flared up and the storm broke. Like chained dogs let loose, they rushed screaming at the Toukola men and a fearful fight arose in the Tammisto yard.

Simeoni was unwilling to enter the melee, and all the books had been left in his keeping. He gripped them tightly and watched the fortunes of the fierce battle with miserable, shifting eyes and a tortured expression. But seeing Aapo hard pressed by three men of Toukola, seeing with a sick heart his poor brother's face turn pale, his eyes stare dully at the treetops while stunning blows rained on him from all sides, then Simeoni set the books down on a rock nearby, rushed to Aapo's rescue, and was soon lost in the wildly surging battle.

The official in charge tried at first to stem the raging flood, but realizing that he was helpless, stepped aside in time and looked in amazement at the brothers' boundless strength. Such violent force, such whirlwind speed, the brothers had never before demonstrated. The desire for revenge, long smoldering in secret, finally burst into flame and spread in a horrible fire storm. Prodigious was the tumult and uproar. Pale and trembling, women fled the battle zone, some carrying, some leading their little toddlers by the hand. The maddened cattle, both the superb bull and the staid cows, galloped to and fro, and shouting, bellowing, and clamor rang out as the Jukola brothers flailed away while the men of Toukola and their many allies struck back. Cheeks ashen pale and gnashing his teeth, Juhani swung right and left at the enemy troop, his jaw twisted in rage. Like a rugged crag, broad-shouldered Tuomas charged forward, and wherever his heavy fist struck, a man fell — sometimes two at a blow. It was seen to happen that when he struck one man, the victim fell with such force that he took down the man next to him. His rough, brown cheeks burning with rage, Timo struck like a woodsman swinging an ax deep in the forest. Even Eero played a man's part in the fray. He was often seen scrambling down at the others' feet, but he would always struggle up from the heap and rain blows around like a pinwheel rocket. Lauri raged more furiously than anyone; as pale as the angel of death, he grappled and struck, and everyone crumpled or fled before him.

People watched the struggle in horror. Everywhere they saw ghastly pale faces, hideously panting nostrils, muddy snouts here and bloody masks there. See the sullen flame of hate in their eyes as they lunge toward the target of their wrath, not caring if they are met with fire and brimstone. The people saw all this and heard a snarling and gasping as horrible as a wolfpack's in murderous battle in the dark forest on a September night.

Such was the onset in the yard at Tammisto, and ever more fiercely the battle raged. Here lay one man and there another, spilling their blood into the sandy soil. The dark red blood of the brothers was wetting the earth too, for the men of Toukola were now fighting with knives. But no knives hung at the brothers' belts, for they were on the way to the Holy Temple. When they saw their hot blood running, they snatched up poles from the ground for weapons, or broke off staves from the nearest fence and charged wildly forward. But soon they encountered the same weapons in enemy hands, and now poles and staves began to play about the heads of the men. It was still uncertain who would win and who would bow in defeat. Although the brothers fought nobly, they were opposed by a numerous foe, and blows rained hot and heavy upon them.

At that point, a man appeared on the field of battle, a man who quickly weighted the balance in favor of the brothers. From the field, running at top speed and roaring madly came brawny Kyösti of Tammisto. An ashy pale figure of horror, stout stave in hand and tufts of hair standing up like a goblin's, he fell upon the Toukola rear like a thunderbolt, throwing them into confusion and infusing new spirit into the brothers. Bellowing and rolling his eyes like a mindless lunatic, he struck out ferociously. The brothers redoubled their blows on the other side and at last the enemy fled wildly — those not felled by the staves.

Off toward home ran the brothers, shouting to Kyösti to come along. But Kyösti did not hear them call; he kept rampaging in the yard without pause, an image of horror screaming and raging. The brothers were already speeding along the dry, sandy lane. When they reached a small bridge between two fields, they heard Kyösti's voice behind them. They stopped to look back and saw a wild man with a stave on his shoulder running toward them, roaring and waving his hand in the air. Soon the dreadful Kyösti stood before them. He was sweaty and panting, his eyes askew with rage and defiance. There was no understanding his garbled speech, in which a long-drawn-out shout was often sounded: "Alamaloo oh alamaloo!" The brothers begged him to go with them to Impivaara, not to return to that den of wolves, but he stood where he was, staring and mumbling to himself. Suddenly he glared fiercely at the brothers and said, "Go home now!" and turned away. The brothers also turned away and went off in the opposite direction. In a short time, Kyösti's thick voice sounded again, and looking back, the brothers saw him standing in the lane, shaking his hand and head, and heard him shouting loudly, "Go home now!" Then he rushed back by the road along which he had come, while the brothers hurried to their wilderness cabin, many with huge lumps on their heads and bleeding wounds on their arms. Staring stiffly ahead, they marched quickly on, a deadly gloom chilling their thoughts. So ended the battle in the Tammisto yard, from which many were borne home senseless, and many were dealt wounds which marked them forever.

CHAPTER XI

It is the evening of the same day that the furious battle took place in the yard at Tammisto. The brothers are sitting in the cabin after having salved and dressed their wounds as best they could. There they sit, glowering at the floor with eternal dark night in their hearts. They reflect on what they have done and know what punishment threatens them. A frightened silence prevails as they consider their wretched, hopeless plight. At last Simeoni opens the following dialogue:

Simeoni: Tell me one thing, brothers. How can we escape the clutches of the Crown?

Aapo: Oh, there's no trick to get us out of this scrape, not one under the sun.

Juhani: We're in a hole, down in a really deep hole. All is lost, all hope and cheer!

Tuomas: We're in the devil's hands and he'll have no mercy. Let's just shut our eyes and take our medicine. We meddled with an officer of the Crown in the performance of his duty, a grave offense, and we beat up some men badly enough to cripple or even kill them — but in that case all is well. They'll put us away, and we'll lead a carefree life on the Crown's bread.

Simeoni: Oh, poor boys that we are!

Timo: Oh the poor sons of Jukola! All seven of us!

Lauri: I know what I'm going to do.

Juhani: So do I. We'll all cut our throats.

Timo: No, damn it!

Juhani: My knife, my bright-bladed knife! I'll set seas of blood flowing!

Aapo: Juhani!

Juhani: Let the blood of seven men flow into one pool and let seven men drown in that flood as the people of the Old Testament once drowned. Where is the birch-handled dagger to solve all our problems.

Aapo: Calm down, man.

Juhani: Out of my way, and out with this damned life. A knife!

Simeoni: Hold on to him!

Aapo: Here brothers!

Juhani: Out of my way!

Tuomas: Be reasonable, boy.

Juhani: Let go of your brother, Tuomas.

Tuomas: Sit down and be reasonable.

Juhani: What good is reason when all is lost. Do you feel like reasonably taking twice forty lashes on your back?

Tuomas: No I don't.

Juhani: Then what will you do?

Tuomas: I'll go to the gallows, but not before they force me to.

Juhani: Let's get it over with right now.

Tuomas: Let's think it over.

Juhani: Ha! Ha! All is lost.

Tuomas: Not quite yet.

Juhani: The arm of the law is reaching for us.

Simeoni: We'll leave Finland and go to Ingria as shepherds.

Timo: Or to St. Petersburg as gatekeepers.

Aapo: Those are silly schemes.

Eero: Let's go and sail the seas as our brave uncle did. Once we leave the shores of Finland, we'll be out of the Crown's reach. We should try for an English ship. They pay men well on its masts.

Aapo: The idea's worth considering.

Tuomas: There may be something in it, but remember that before we get to the coast of Finland, the Crown's bracelets will be on our wrists.

Timo: If we got out of Finland with whole hides, how long would it take to get to England? It's millions, even thousands of millions of miles away. Oh hoh!

Aapo: But listen. If we join the wolf pack, we won't have to fear their teeth. Let's enlist in the army for a couple of years. It's a tough decision, but the best one to make in this pinch. Let's march off and join the famous Heinola battalion that drills and skirmishes all summer long on Parola Heath. Keep in mind while you think about it that the army takes care of its own.

Juhani: I'm afraid, brother mine, that you've hit on the right scheme. The barracks have saved many a boy from a tight spot before this. That big lout, the Karila hired hand, for instance. He took a notion to beat on his master a little. Things would have gone badly for him, but presto, in a flash the lad had a gray coat on his back and it saved him. That settles it. On to the barracks! Our great-uncle died in the Kyrö War, where a thirty-foot log floated in blood; our own uncle died in a war on the shores of Bothnia. So have many other men, and we're likely to fall too, fall as hallowed heroes. Better to be dead and in heaven than here on earth among these human beasts of prey. It makes me weep. Yes, it's better there than here, oh yes, a lot better!

Tuomas: My brother, you'll wring tears from all of us.

Simeoni: God look down on us and let the sun of mercy shine.

Their discussion ended in tears, in a general storm of weeping. Not a single brother's eye was dry. But the evening grew darker, night came; all left off weeping and fell into a deep sleep. The next day they continued poring sweaty-browed over the best scheme to save themselves. Sharp was the watch they kept around the cabin to see if the forces of the Crown were approaching even from a distance. So they watched and pondered, and the barracks, appalling as the prospect was, still seemed the best refuge. They therefore decided to go as a group to Heinola and sign up for a six-year hitch. When the next day dawned, they began the long journey, sad of mind and sore of heart. Onward they marched, not thinking that passports and church permits were necessary for their enterprise — onward they marched with packs on their backs, heading first for Jukola to ask the tanner to take care of their livestock and keep an eye on their cabin.

When they reached the Viertola road, they met the sheriff and the marshal, who came jouncing toward them. The brothers were nonplussed, thinking his errand had to do with them. They were of a mind to run into the woods, but marched on ahead, believing that two men could never take them prisoner. But they were mistaken; the sheriff was riding about the parish on a completely different mission. He was a good man, brave, high-minded, and always cheerful. He would listen highly amused to stories about the Jukola brothers and their life in the woods and was their patron and defender rather than their enemy. And now, as he drew abreast of them, he began to speak out cheerfully:

Sheriff: Hello, hello! Where are the boys marching to so soberfaced? Answer me — don't just look at me like a pack of wild wolves. Where are you going with those packs?

Juhani: We've got a long way to go.

Sheriff: You mean you're going to hell?

Juhani: Did you want something from us?

Sheriff: What could you give me? But then I suppose a man can ask even if he can't afford to buy. You're scowling and glaring at me. If I wasn't used to looking even the devil in the eye, my heart would be pounding a little. Ha, ha, ha, is it the devil that's working in you?

Juhani: I have one question to ask. Is this going to be a matter for the Crown?

Sheriff: Is what going to be a matter for the Crown?

Juhani: Hmm. This, this.

Sheriff: What, you burr-headed lout? What?

Juhani: The fracas at Tammisto Farm.

Sheriff: Ahaa! That sport the other day. Mmhmm! I have something to tell you about that.

Juhani: Did anyone die?

Sheriff: No, thank your lucky stars. But fire and brimstone! You drove a Crown official from his duty and overturned his table to boot. Think about it.

Juhani: We have thought about it and understand what it will bring down on us. Yes, the devil has us now and we've chosen to cast our lot with him. Hear this! We're on the march now, up hill and down dale, making the dust fly as we tramp the road to the big battalion at Parola. We're fleeing to that last corner to get away from people, those angry devils who press in on us from all sides as if we were wolf-cubs in a trap. We're off to Parola and woe to the man who tries to stop us! The Crown needs men. A war is brewing, so we hear. Soon we'll be wearing the Crown's uniform, and then try to stop us, you devils. Ee-yah! I'd like to bite this world in two, bite it in two like an eel. I could cry for grief and rage at the same time, weep and shake my fist. We're off to Parola. Men are like ravens there, the men at Parola.

Sheriff: You dolts and blockheads! You'd leave your own peaceful cabin on your own land for the whistling whips of the barracks?

Juhani: Better that than breaking stones in a chain gang. And besides, a man from Häme has hide an inch thick, you'll see.

Sheriff: Breaking stones in a chain gang? Why?

Juhani: You yourself, sir, are planning to drag us there in clanking chains. And why? Because of that ill-fated prank in the Tammisto yard, because we beat on the Toukola boys a little, a beating God knows we were mightily egged on to. And now you want to make this the Crown's business, to "make a mountain out of a molehill," as the saying goes.

Sheriff: You're lying. To hell with you. I've got more important business in mind.

Juhani: If you grant us the mercy of sending us to hell, which I don't believe, we'll still have the men of Toukola on our necks with the law. We were unlucky enough to strike the first blow, which hurts our case, but they won't get off without paying the piper either. There are plenty of wounds here which haven't had time to scar over, and those wounds testify to something, they do. But if we escape the men of Toukola, we still have to face the day of judgment that comes every year: the reading day. I'll quote that fine boy Paavo Jaakola, who said: "Life would be all right with one less day in the year, that damned reading day." And he said too: "It's not the pain but the shame." That was after his scalp had been badly stretched at one of those hair-pulling parties. But what happened to him at the same frolic next year? Well, the teacher made him sit under the table like an owl, and his pretty young bride-to-be saw him there from the porch of the test-room. The poor girl fainted, just flopped over on the threshold like a poor little goose — it was a bad scene. Afterwards Paavo began to drink like a man, got the gate from his girl friend like a man, and finally died as a miserable horse skinner. That was the end of dashing Paavo, who wasn't dumb, truly not. He was one of the cleverest and wittiest of young men, but his stepmother thrust the book upside down into his hands the very first time, and so reading-day became a day of terror for him. And should it be that way? Mikko Kukkoinen, a man as big and strong as a pine log, with a face as broad as Granny Tuhkala's cat — but not one of your good readers — in a shed one reading-day he heard the chime of the preacher's sleighbells and it frightened him like a lamb. So awful it is — this hair-pulling, nerve-racking shindig. And some day, we know, the provost may force us to go there, and from there to the stocks, that block of shame. And from all this the Crown's coat will save us. To all this we say farewell forever.

Sheriff: You brainless billygoats, what lunacy are you cooking up? Well go on then, go, keep marching as far as the Crown's dusty road will take you. What the devil do I have to do with you? The Tammisto business is all settled, I assure you. I swear it, you louts. It's all over with, and the Toukola men's lips are sealed. Hoh, I did it the same day as the battle when I saw that no one was killed. The rascals threatened a lawsuit, but they brought it on themselves. When I threw my weight into the scales, they were as quiet as moles. I've got many hooks in them to jerk them up short if need be. So they'll keep quiet and feel they're well out of it. As to your standing with the provost, I ask you, has he been pressuring you lately?

Aapo: No he hasn't, and we wondered why.

Sheriff: And he never will again, you mark my word. And who brought all this about? Who but your old sheriff. And now you say he's trying to play the devil with you, you thankless scoundrels. Whatever the cause, like a fool I've taken a fancy to this wolf-cub life of yours. Ha, ha, ha! Well, fun has its place too, pure fun. But for the last time, I have no quarrel with you and neither has the provost, for he's come to understand that you can't make a silk coat from birchbark. So then, you're in no danger, boys, none at all, though you deserve a sound basting, you blockheads. But go home nicely now! Right now, I say! Well then, Impivaara Company, left turn, march! March straight home! Home you scamps, and go in God's name. — Giddyap, Whitey!

So saying, he twitched the reins and the sheriff's lightmaned gelding, known throughout the parish, broke into a trot again. Off they sped with a clatter, the old marshal's hat flopping up and down in back, and dust swirling after them. Like seven pillars of salt, the brothers stood by the roadside and watched them go. Wordless, wondering what to think of all this, they stood and stared at the departing men until the sheriffs buggy disappeared around a bend in the road.

Timo: How old the marshall's grown since we last saw him in the Kuokkala woods with mother and the villagers!

Juhani: What do you make of the sheriff's smooth talk, Aapo?

Aapo: I think he's an honest man and was telling the truth, but let's be on guard. You can't trust the upper crust.

Juhani: Let's be ready to head for the woods. He's got the devil in him and he's trying to lure us into a trap.

Tuomas: He wanted to trick us into going home where we would be easy prey for him on his way back from Viertola with a gang of men. He knows you can't take on the Jukola troop with a few men. He'll come and round us up neatly if we wait for him.

Juhani: Ha, that's what I think too. He's a hunter hot on the trail and we're the animals he's out to capture. Something awful must have happened, something even the barracks won't save us from. So let's turn bandit and light out for the woods. Off the road, boys!

Aapo: Oh, what shall we do?

Juhani: It's done already. Here stand seven outlaws of the woods. But let's try as far as possible to be decent and merciful bandits, always asking nicely for food to satisfy our hunger, and then if goodness doesn't work, we'll use force, but always avoiding bloodshed and murder. Let's go now.

Simeoni: Juhani, Juhani what are you saying?

Aapo: Oh where can the poor lot of us find safety?

Juhani: The outlaw trail? Let's go now?

Tuomas: Shut your mouth, you crazy fool! I'd sooner go to the everlasting cold of Siberia than to eat bandits' bread. You wild animal, are you serious or are you making stupid jokes? What am I supposed to think of you?

Juhani: Alas brother? My head is in a whirl now, and I don't know what I'm saying or doing. The sheriff was here, and disappeared into thin air, but that seems ages ago, ages! That's where he disappeared, where I'm pointing with my thumb like Tinder-Matti. He disappeared in a cloud of smoke there, and the white mane of his war horse flashed amid the smoke. But that was long ago, so long ago!

Tuomas: Look here now?

Aapo: Now what is it?

Tuomas: You won't always spot Juhani sitting on the same branch when you take aim at him.

Lauri: Why are you rolling your eyes and shaking your head and snorting through your nose like that. There now. Be thankful your brain is still sound.

Tuomas: All right, let him cover up his idiocy as best he can. But what in hell are we supposed to do? Tell us, Aapo.

Aapo: I don't know.

Eero: Listen, brothers. We don't know for sure if the sheriff is trying to pull the wool over our eyes.

Lauri: I don't think he is, because I watched his eyes closely, and there wasn't a sign of guilt in them. And consider this: Why should he come so far without men when there are cabins and villages all along the way? Why should he drive by Impivaara and go all the way to Viertola Manor, where he has less hope of getting help than from the big villages he passed by? That's strange! And then come all the way back from Viertola to our cabin with his men? Nonsense! It doesn't jibe at all with his usual sound and sensible way of thinking.

Aapo: I can see that too, but it's not enough to bank on. A man thinks he's figured a whole matter out carefully, but things often turn out the exact opposite of what even the wisest men suppose. We have good reason to be afraid. Our crime is great in the eyes of the law, very great, and think of how unusually friendly the sheriff was to us.

Tuomas: They were not the words of a friend, but seething gall coated with honey. But what shall we do?

Eero: Let's do this: Let's go home, but not stay in the cabin for one minute. We'll leave the door unlatched so that it looks as if everyone is nicely at home, but we'll hide in the caves and hollows of Impivaara for two or three days, always keeping a close watch on our cabin. If during that time the sheriff comes along with his troops, we'll always be ready to fly to the safety of the woods and hills. But if no one shows up during those three days and nights, then we're in the clear.

Tuomas: Now that is good advice.

Aapo: Let's do it.

Tuomas: Let's turn around. Come on, Juho. Stop looking so sour.

They started off again for Impivaara and were soon standing in the yard of their home. Following Eero's advice, they left the latch off the door, climbed up the mountain, and concealed themselves carefully, some in snug, clefted crags and others beneath spruce trees growing on ledges. There they lingered, sharp eyes scanning the cabin, the stump-strewn meadow, and the gloomy fringe of woods. They rested, taking turns on guard for three days and nights, eating from their birch-bark packs and quenching their thirst from a clear spring that bubbled up from the ground and flowed down a rocky course. Gaily the little brooklet rippled, rippled the whole day long and all through the night, sounding to the listening ears of the brother on watch.

But when the third day's sun was hastening to its rest, the brothers descended the mountain and entered the cabin with light hearts, for their fears seemed to have been groundless. They were still not sure, however, and kept glancing cautiously out the window. The next day they sent Aapo out as a spy to bring them more positive assurance. For a day and a night, he hovered around farms and villages, and when he returned, his face beamed a message of peace. Now they all sat around the pine table with Aapo at its head, and he began to tell his brothers what he had heard.

Aapo: Brothers, that sheriff of ours is one of a kind. He's done what he said, and this is how things stand with us. The men of Toukola, though many have badly bruised limbs, huge lumps or gaping wounds on their heads, aren't breathing a word about going to court or of taking revenge into their own hands. All this is the sheriffs doing, the results of his dire threats. And what do you think of the provost? Well, the old man has granted us a lasting peace, for at the sheriffs urging, he has concluded that harsh treatment would be our eternal damnation. And listen further. When Härkämäki, that good old man, was talking to the provost one day, he mentioned us and growled out: "Who knows but what the boys might still turn out to be real scholars?" At this, the preacher said that he would greatly rejoice in the Lord if the miracle should come to pass, if the Jukola brothers should some day stand before him, sight-read passably, and recite the ten commandments and the confession of faith from memory. Those were his conciliatory words. This and much more I heard from the mouths of many men, the most trustworthy being Kyösti Tammisto, who never laughs or lies.

Juhani: Sheriff, you honorable man, I would run through a blazing fire for you! Well, let me be carried off by a bellowing black bull! I can hardly believe it.

Aapo: It's exactly as I said. But you can see from this that all gentlemen aren't really the great scoundrels we thought. Think of Viertola too, who soon softened and agreed to all we asked. And the provost — if we regard him without any spite, with a cool head and a kind heart — will soon rise to the highest rank in our esteem. He has a temper, but he is a true laborer in the vineyards of the Lord and has done the greatest good in our congregation. He has flattened many a vile tavern, forced many a man and his former "live-in" to become legally married. He has ended many bloody feuds among neighbors in perfect harmony. And what was the goal of his efforts with us? He wanted us to be respectable Christian men. Now he leaves us alone, expressing such a beautiful hope for us that my heart aches to think of it.

Tuomas: But now, men, let's read. Let's take up the ABC Books and hammer the words into our heads if it takes a maul to do it.

Aapo: If we do as you say, a new fate is in store for us. If only we begin the task now, not to let up until the job is done!

Juhani: I understand. Let's have a go at the ABC Book tooth and nail, with no let-up until we come out at the rooster's tail. Right! Maybe we'll soon decide, and having decided, we'll do it too, do it even if we have to sweat blood. My head is solid, pretty solid, but not altogether empty; there are a few things up there, I've got some brains. With daily practice, couldn't I do as well as some five-year-old slip of a girl? Why not? Hard work wins out over even the worst luck.

Aapo: Oh Juhani! Your words are so full of wisdom and manliness they lift my heart.

Juhani: Hard work wins out over even the worst luck. Yes, we'll just put our shoulders to the wheel, grit our teeth, and keep on pushing. But this matter calls for wise and deep thought.

Aapo: We'll try our best, for this is an awesome step. Look, if we can't read, even a lawful wife is forbidden fruit to us.

Timo: Is that so? Well, damn me, then it's worth trying, for the trick will get me a good wife — if I ever go so crazy as to want one. But who knows what might pop into this boy's head? Only God knows.

Juhani: Let's think the matter over wisely. We have such hard heads.

A few days passed and one evening they took up the question once more. All agreed to begin a diligent practice of reading.

Juhani: In two years' time, the ABC Book will be in my head, that's certain. But I feel sorry for poor Timo. His head is even harder than mine — twice as hard.

Timo: Not to worry even if it is twice as hard. You'll just learn your ABC Book in two years and I'll learn mine in four. The only thing we need is patience.

Juhani: Now then, that quip cut a whole bunch of days off the number — a year at least. But alee, my boy, we're in the devil's clutches now. We'll heave many a sigh and thumb this ABC Book to pieces before it's in our heads from cover to cover. God help us!

Timo: I want to learn the ABC Book!

Juhani: So do I, even if it's like eating rocks and raw potatoes. I want to do it because the provost has been so good and kind to us that I feel sorry for him. But where can we get a good and gentle teacher?

Aapo: I have an idea about that too. I'm depending on you, Eero. Uh-huh, you have a sharp mind; there's no denying it. Just thank God for your gift. Leave us for a few weeks; go out into the world with a lunch pack on your back and an ABC Book in your bosom. Go to the marshal, that fine wolf-caller, for instruction. He's an able man and I know he won't refuse you, especially if we promise him a rich, burned-over field and a few cock woodgrouse to roast. And when you learn the main points of reading, you can come back and teach them to us.

Juhani: Is that it? Is Eero going to teach us? Hmm, Eero? But I'll tell you one thing, Eero. Don't you get cocky.

Eero: Not at all! A teacher should set a good example for his pupils, remembering the stern day of judgment when he must say: "Here I am, Lord, and those whom you gave to my keeping."

Juhani: Look here, are you needling us already? Now this is how it's going to be. You are to teach me whenever I want, be as still as a fish whenever I want, and listen to me read whenever I want, and that's that. We'll make you toe the line, you know that well enough. But I think the scheme is a good one.

Tuomas: It's the best Aapo has ever come up with.

Juhani: A thousand dollars for this scheme.

Aapo: Eero, what do you think?

Eero: I have to think it over.

Aapo: It will work, no doubt about it. But there's a more important idea I want to bring up; it's a plan that will stand the test of time. My brave boys and brothers: Let's create a fine new farm in the wilds of Impivaara; let the strength of seven men shape it. Well, you stare at me in amazement; you look like owls. I'm not surprised. But think it over. Making a living in the woods gets harder day by day. Seldom do we hear a bear whistle or see a wood grouse fly up in our path. And we know something else: "It's not good for a man to be alone." So let's think about it — every wild rover of the backwoods must stay far away from the bridal bed, for a rover can scarcely fill his own growling belly, much less that of a wife and children. But let's clear the wide woods for hay fields and hoe this golden, sloping meadow for planting and bit by bit we'll build a stable, cow-barn, grain-drying barn, storehouse, and other buildings as need arises. And so we'll have the grand farm of Impivaara, better than our birthplace Jukola. And before the day arrives when Jukola is our own once more, the meadows here will be a beautiful green, the fields will wave with grain, and the spotted cows will come lowing home from the woods as evening falls.

Juhani: That was beautiful, but look, brother, we already have a farm. True, it's rented out now, but it will be our own again in a few years.

Aapo: But till that time, we'd be the worst kind of idlers, scarce willing to lift a finger, and our farm will likely be as run-down as before. The tanner, I've heard, is worth very little — a hopeless bungler who hasn't done much of anything with the fields or meadows. And even if that isn't so, it's always better to have two farms than one: Jukola and Impivaara. People will look up to us more, much more, and many a plump, blushing Häme lass will be offered us as a bride. Up and at it, brothers! Let's work with all our strength, for life is worth the struggle, and people, we can see, are not all that bad. The world gives back as good as it gets, and let him who "always suffers wrong" look to the state of his own heart. It's true that we've often been treated harshly, but in fact only by the Toukola roughnecks and I think they had cause for it. Be that as it may, peace and accord are always better, and we can establish peace again if we really and truly want to. Look, we'll work here like men of good character in the meantime, and when at last we go back to the fields of Jukola, our former enemies will regard us with more respect than before, and if we give back milder looks, the bright sun of a general peace will soon shine. In truth, we will have paid a price for all this, in toil and teeth-grinding care. But without them no crop is ever sowed on this earth. And note well, set clearly before your eyes the goal we will reach in the end: we will be men, friends to every one, we will own two farms, our future will be a "Cape of Good Hope," and our graves on the dim verge of life will seem not an abode of horrors but a lovely chamber of rest, dim anterooms to the bright halls of bliss.

Tuomas: Your words are fine and true, and I second your wishes. Brothers! Let's listen to him, for this means the world to us. It will bring a new life to this fringe of woods. I'm for it!

Timo: Me too!

Simeoni: God has heard us and our life grows brighter. I favor Aapo's beautiful idea.

Eero: So do I, for it's a manly step we're taking.

Juhani: And won't your poor older brother do likewise? I'm in favor of it and will forever call this our lucky day. We were so close to chains, or to the Crown's gray coat and the rattle of drums, but now all that is far away, and our home woods murmur around us. In our darkest night, our sky suddenly brightened and this light, we hope, will drive away all clouds and "God's candle will shine," as the shepherd brightly sings. Ah, God and the sheriff have done their best for us and we too will do our best.

The following day they sent a well-provisioned Eero on his learning expedition. With a birch-bark pack on his back and a bag slung over his shoulders, with an ABC Book stuffed in his shirt, he set off for the marshall's house. The others took up hoes and shovels and began to turn over the meadow around the cabin for sowing. Day by day the area grew, becoming a lasting graveyard for lingonberry and cudweed. But when they had hoed up a piece of the meadow they thought sufficient to sow food for seven men, they moved down into the woods below the meadow and began clearing a hay field in a century-old spruce grove which stood drowsing in its mossy coat. The sound of an ax echoed round and a spruce fell crashing to the moist earth. They trimmed the spruce branches and piled them up, to be carried to the yard in the winter, but the logs they bore up to the stump-strewn meadow as timber for the new grain and cow barns. In a steady single file marched the six men, a stout log resting on six firm shoulders. When they came to a mound, they all dropped their burden at the same instant. The log fell with a crash that made the earth resound, and the woods echoed the roar. Thus their hay field advanced ever eastward from the edge of the woods, and thus they obtained material for the projected buildings.

Eero too worked diligently at learning to read, and his skill developed quickly. On Saturday evening he returned home with empty sacks, but next Monday he was off again, full pack on his back and sack bulging, off for school, ABC Book tucked in his bosom. So the autumn passed winter approached. the brothers left both tillage and hay fields to rest until spring, and hurried to provide food for themselves and their livestock. Criss-crossing the dismal autumn woods with their dogs, they reaped a bloody harvest, while down on the shore, a tall hay-stack for old Valko rose again.

Winter had come and on Christmas Eve, Eero returned home, having, in the marshall's opinion, learned enough to teach his brothers. He had indeed learned with astonishing speed. He could sight-read clearly, and he knew both the ABC Book and the small catechism by heart. And now, when Christmas was over, the toil and study began. There they sat, with Eero as teacher and his brothers as pupils, shouting in unison the names of the letters as Eero pronounced them. As one they shouted, and the broad cabin resounded. Toil and torment this work was to them, utter torment, especially at first: miserably they panted and sweated. Juhani struggled the hardest; his chin quivered with concentration, and sleepy Timo, who sat next to him, suffered many a sharp rap from his fist whenever the poor wretch's head nodded again.

The brothers were also angered whenever Eero was not fully serious about his work and made stinging comments to them. He had already been warned many times by his brothers, but he couldn't resist the fun.

One bitterly cold winter day when an almost rayless sun shone on the southern rim of the sky, the brothers sat fully absorbed with the ABC Books in their hands. Their earnest but monotonous reading could be heard far off. On this occasion, they were beginning the alphabet over again.

Eero: "A"
Others: "A"

Eero: "B"

Others: "B"

Eero: So, "A" is the first letter of the alphabet and "O" is the last. "A" and "O," the beginning and the end, the first and the last. It's in the Bible somewhere. But have you ever seen a time when the last was the first, the "O" was the "A"? Isn't it a joke when that once little, weak "last" is suddenly the cock of the walk, the one that the others must look up to with honor and respect, as to a father, even though their eyes gape a little. But why do I get off the subject to things we're not concerned with now? Start reading again.

Juhani: Do I follow you? I'm afraid I do. But teach us nicely now, or you're going to be in for it.

Eero: Well, read nicely again. "C"

Others: "C"

Eero: "D"

Others: "D," "E," "F," "G"....

Juhani: Hold on, hold on! I'm lost again, poor me. Let's start from the beginning once more.

Eero: "A"

Others: "B"

Eero: "A," "B," "C," nellamenopee. What does that mean, Juhani? Can you explain it?

Juhani: I'll try to work it out. The rest of you come outside with me for awhile. We have something important to talk about.

So he spoke, then stepped outside, and the others followed him. Eero, a little uneasy, began to guess what their departure might mean. Out in the yard, the others pondered over how best to blunt Eero's desire to taunt them, which led him, ABC Book in hand to sneer not only at them but at God's word as well. They decided he deserved a sound whipping and stepped back into the cabin again. The fresh birch rod in brother Juhani's hand terrified the very soul of Eero. Tuomas and Simeoni laid firm hands on him, and the whip in Juhani's hand did its best. Eero screamed, kicked and raged. When finally set free, he glared around fiercely with murder in his eyes.

Juhani: Now then, pick up your book and teach us nicely again, you rascal, and remember this whipping whenever your wicked tongue wants to mock us again. Ahaa — does it sting? Well, I've been predicting for a long time that this would happen to you. For "evil is the scoffer's reward in the end," you can be sure of that. Pick up your book, I say, and teach us in a sensible and decent way, you scamp.

Tuomas: Stop grinding your teeth, sit nicely at the head of the table, and do as we say. Do it now without any more grumbling; otherwise the whip will dance again in my hand, and the storm it raises will be hotter than the last.

The reading began again, but Eero spoke the letters in a harsh and bitter voice, his eyes smoldering. The tension around the school table at Impivaara was of some duration, but in a few days, time softened Eero's angry mind and demeanor. So the brothers drilled in their attempt to master the art of reading, and they did progress, although very slowly at first, especially where Timo and Juhani were concerned.

CHAPTER XII

Summer came, and work in the fields began. Sometimes the brothers plowed and harrowed, sometimes cleared woods for a hay field, and sometimes worked at building their new cowbarn in the echoing meadow. At first it was hard to buckle down to work, but they overcame their natural inclinations and were at length able to toil every weekday from dawn to dusk. So the barn was finished, the field converted to fine-grained soil, and the hay-field extended deeper and deeper into the woods. Before them now lay Luhta Meadow, uneven and stump-strewn but yielding hay. Now came sowing time. The brothers sold another patch of woods, bought rye seed with the money, and Tuomas sowed the Impivaara field, three barrels of rye he sowed into its dusty furrows. Soon broad shoots of grain sprang up and glowed a rich green in the brisk September breezes.

The birch turned yellow, the aspen stood in its robe of purple, and damp mists enfolded Luhta Meadow into their glistening bosom. It was autumn again; the brothers were not forgetful of their winter needs, and they had four heifers and a stiff-necked young bull for their barn. Work and toil outdoors were over, and everything was already resting under the snow, but a new labor began in the cabin: toil at the table with the ABC Book. Diligently the brothers practiced their reading, and their skills increased, albeit slowly. They could sight-read fairly well now and had moved on to the task of memorizing the pieces in the ABC Book. Yammering and muttering in every corner, they strove to reach the rooster on the back cover. One after another, they did it, first Lauri, then Aapo and Simeoni and finally Tuomas, but far behind them Juhani and Timo still labored on. At last Timo too reached the desired port while Juhani still sweated over the confession of faith, huffing and puffing angrily. It wrung his heart to be the last, but hard work and diligence were the only cure, not his brothers' pity. He could probably sight-read more clearly and speedily than Timo, but Timo was better at memorizing.

But those who knew their ABC Book by heart, looking back happily at the toil and trouble they had endured, decided to take a few days off. Guns in hand, they skied about the woods; the white-furred rabbit fell to their bullets under the snowy spruce, as did the male wood grouse who sat stiff with cold on the bearded branch of a spruce tree in the dismal woods at the edge of the sounding heath. But at the table in the cabin, clad only in a shirt, ABC Book in hand sat Juhani, with drops of sweat oozing from his brow. Tearing his hair in anger, he wore down the thick pages of the book. Often he would grind his teeth in rage, leap up from the bench almost in tears, snatch up a pine block from the corner, lift it high overhead, and slam it heavily to the floor. The cabin rang with the blow and his short shirt-tails flapped. Every now and then he was forced to snatch up the block, for it was only with great effort that he could fix the book in his brain. But then he would sit down at the table once more and repeat the difficult part. Finally, with the coming of spring he too knew the book from cover to cover. With a proud look on his face, he closed its pages.

The snow melted, flowed as water to the meadow, and thence to Sompio Swamp. Now the brothers went about building the grain barn, which they set some distance from the cabin on the smooth ground of the meadow. Again the ring of the ax and the thump of the maul echoed afar. And when the path of the sun across the sky was at its height, when the woods and meadow were green and the rye was forming heads, the drying barn stood ready at Impivaara. Nature now wore her most gorgeous summer garment, the field breathed pollen, and high were the hopes of the men at Impivaara. But then the wind veered suddenly to the north, blew harshly the whole long summery day, and the air turned cold and dismal. Tirelessly it blew until evening when it subsided and sank to rest. The night was as still and cold as the grave; a gray frost lay on the bosom of the field like a smothering incubus on the flowering breast of a young maiden. Next morning the sun looked down with grief-stricken eyes at the night's work — a frosty, frozen grain field. Early in the morning the brothers stepped out of their cabin, looked in horror at the work of destruction, and gloom possessed their minds. In a few days their once lush field lay pale and withered before their eyes.

Juhani: There goes our hope, our field of gold. The stalks are still standing but the grain heads hang limp from them without strength or substance. Well, boys, next year's food has been snatched away from us.

Tuomas: A heavy blow, especially when you think how scarce wild game is already. We scoured the woods like lynxes last fall and got barely enough food for the winter.

Juhani: What shall we do? We can't just give up on a field that we wrung from the meadow with our sweat and toil.

Tuomas: That we won't do. We'll plant it again this fall. We know that there are frost-free as well as frosty years, more of the first than of the cursed rime-bearded ones.

Aapo: I'm afraid the frost will come to greet us every year as long as Sompio Swamp down there is a home for frogs and cranberries. It's only too likely. So if we hope to save our field from frost in the future, we should drain the swamp and drain the water and dampness away from its depths. We'll be killing two birds with one stone — preventing frost and making a new meadow.

Tuomas: I think we all agree that it's the best thing to do. We have to, if we're ever to make a farm of this wilderness.

So with shovels and axes on their shoulders, they went down to the swamp one day to clear it and dig drainage ditches. First they dug a deep, straight main ditch and then smaller ditches leading from it on either side. Soon high banks of moss, mud, and clay rose alongside of the trenches. They felled the low, dry birches that grew in the swamp and piled them up for burning next summer, thus adding more meadow to Impivaara farm. For many days they worked hard from morning till late evening. At length most of Sompio Swamp was ditched and from day to day its surface grew drier and drier. Now it was time to sow again. Tuomas sowed the field and soon grain sprouted from the earth. The brothers spent the winter like the last, practicing their reading, and finally they had memorized the small catechism. Lauri, Eero, and Aapo did not stop there, but kept on till they had completed the whole catechism. Many days they went hungry at their books, for hunting had been poor last fall, and they had had less time for it. They did roam the woods on skis even now, but their efforts were scantily rewarded.

At last the greening spring arrived, and the rye grew richly in the field at Impivaara. But once again the wind veered suddenly to the north, blew harshly the whole summer day, until at evening it subsided and sank to rest. The night was as still and cold as the grave and the gray frost lay on the bosom of the field, breathing cold death. Early the next morning the brothers stepped out of their cabin and looked in horror at the work of destruction. And pale and withered shone the field so green a short time ago. The men mulled over what to do next, what measures to take, and judged it best to dry up Sompio Swamp completely by clearing and digging, for they knew that from it the frost rose to their field. So they decided, and they moiled and dug in the misty swamp during the course of the summer, often experiencing a depressing hunger. The work was heavy then, and wearily they made their way home at sundown, with dark lines of pain and care etched around their lips.

But come fall, the swamp was ditched from border to border and its surface a dry bed of grass. It was now a fine hay field for the brothers, broad Sompio Meadow. Again the field was sowed and even some new strips for summer planting were hoed from the meadow. But the supply of wild game had been further diminished by the previous cold spring, and the brothers were less able than ever to gather stores for the winter. They were hard pressed by hunger that winter when six feet of snow covered the ground and it was bitterly cold. Wall timbers popped, rocks and crags cracked in the freezing air, and small, dead birds fell like frozen snowflakes to the ground. A traveler could see the spit from his mouth freeze before it hit the ground and slide tinkling along the smooth track left by a sled runner. — On such a day when the north wind howled under a clear, pale sky that sparkled with cold, the brothers sat in the sweaty heat of the cabin discussing their plight and ways to satisfy their growling bellies.

Juhani: This won't do. It's more than twenty-four hours since I last ate. And what kind of goody was that and how much of it was there? One thousand flaming devils! Two dry and pitch-stained squirrel paws. Nothing to put a dent in a grown man's appetite. What do you say to that, Tuomas?

Tuomas: Tighten your belt.

Juhani: Look, my middle is as thin as the waist of any sweet young thing, as thin as a dried nettle, and that trick won't work forever. It won't work, and whatever we do, we have to do quickly. This dreary moping crushes a man's heart, brother, crushes his heart and makes his mind droop.

Simeoni: Is there anything left for us but the open road, the long hard trail of the beggar?

Juhani: That should be our last resort. But my belly is as hollow as a drum. Won't even brother Aapo's brain come up with a single trick or gimmick?

Aapo: What can be made from nothing?

Juhani: The whole world was made from nothing, so couldn't at least one bran cake be made from it?

Aapo: If we were the Almighty.

Juhani: If we were only his stable boys, we'd be skipping around those golden mansions eating manna, pure manna, and drinking honey like water from a stream. That's the way we'd lord it up there, and we'd spit as we listened to some poor earthly beggar tell us about seven miserable brothers starving like wolves down there by muddy Sompio Swamp, huddled together in a smoky cabin like bats in a hole in a pine tree.

Eero: What silly stuff your mind dredges up! Let's go and check out that place in Kuokkala's woods we passed over too lightly last fall.

Juhani: The bears are gone to hell from there, I'm almost sure of it.

Eero: Almost sure! How stupid to sit here on our hands and starve when we might be able to rustle up a good roast. There's not much hope, but let's at least try. We'll head for the woods and if we don't find a bear, maybe there'll be some other animal, and if that doesn't work out, we'll be near Kuokkala's farm, where we can at least borrow a loaf of bread for each of us and maybe a few bushels of peas too. If our own efforts fail, we have to ask help from others. But we'll only borrow, and pay back when we can.

So said Eero, and finally the others thought it best to follow his advice. Guns under their arms and dogs trailing them, they skied off toward the Kuokkala woods. Their skis glided easily over the snow, but the brothers' pace was slow and panting, for their once springy knees were limp. At last they reached the area that was their goal and began to ski here, there, and everywhere, searching for a bear but all in vain. Evening approached and the brothers were ready to abandon all hope but at Eero's urging they decided to search once more near a certain crag in the woods. When they reached it, the dogs began to bark fiercely and out of a spruce clump charged a bear, who ran off with the snow swirling in its wake. Twisting and dodging he ran and the brothers skimmed after him, shifting course time after time on their gleaming skis while the frost-angry air hoarsely repeated the hubbub of barking.

At last a shot rang out from Tuomas's gun and the bleeding bear lay thrashing in the snow. The dogs rushed upon him and the man approached with his sturdy bearspear. Almost without resistance, the animal met his death through the spear of the man and the teeth of the dogs. Down on his front paws he sank, panting out his life on the bloody field. Hardly had this happened and the brothers gathered around their prey when again a fierce barking and thrashing was heard from the woods, and two yearling cubs climbed up from their den a few hundred paces from the first one they had come upon. A furious fight ensued between the furry cubs and fierce Killi and Kiiski, a tooth-snapping, blood-letting fight that went on until the brothers rushed up to the dogs with their spears. Soon they felled the fiercely battling bear cubs and put an end to the cyclone of flying fur.

Evening had come. They carried the fat prey to the foot of a mossy, spruce-covered crag and lighted a fire. To its windward side, they built a shelter for the night of bearded spruce, a webbing of fir branches held up by stakes and poles, which kept the wind from fanning the flames and allowed the fire to burn gently. Then the brothers took up their tasty evening task. They scored and skinned a swelling haunch from the mother bear, cut tender slices from it, roasted them over the fire, and joyfully filled their hungry bellies, nor did they forget Killi and Kiiski. Soon they were asleep on their mossy beds, their tired bodies well nourished and the pangs of hunger put off for many days. The dogs too rested sweetly after their long, hard chase, rested with their muzzles lying on their paws, now and then opening their eyes to gaze with satisfaction at the bloody beasts on the snow. There in the glow of the fire and the twinkling of stars, they all rested, while around them the frost cracked in the dry spruce trees and the cold breeze sighed a dirge in the deep woods. In the light of morning, the brothers skied off for home with their prey, a heavy but pleasing burden.

Early and lovely was the following spring. The brothers fished eagerly on bright Lake Ilves, and many a humpbacked perch and many a golden carp was tangled in their nets or caught on their hooks. On many a clear summer morning, they sat on the shore in the shade of a fragrant cherry tree flipping up with their rods the shiny creatures of Ahti's realm. Ducks flew quacking over the oil-smooth surface of the lake and many were tumbled from their flight by the brothers' bullets. Lovely was the spring on the shore of Lake Ilves, on the meadow, and on the field near the Impivaara cabin, where the rich grain flourished in the glowing heat of day and the gentle cool of night. This summer too the north wind often raged, bringing still nights of bitter cold in its wake, but deep in Sompio Meadow lay the frost, listening with ears pricked up but helpless to lift its head above the grassy plain. Thus grew the grain in the field and the hay in the meadow during this bright summer at intervals the gentle rain watered the fragrant earth. In the sultry heat of summer, the brothers mowed the hay and reaped the full-headed rye in the field. High stood the stacks in Luhta and Sompio Meadows; high rose the grain-ricks around the cabin. This summer brought them an overflowing harvest, always triumphantly recalled by the brothers as the "golden summer."

But one Saturday morning when the grain was harvested and the fall planting complete, the brothers set off on a journey they had long prepared for, on their way to the parsonage and the provost's testing. The provost dealt with them in a gentle and fatherly way, and soon saw to his great joy that their skill in reading was good, and in a few cases, positively praiseworthy. He declared Lauri to be the best reader in the whole large community of Toukola. He further characterized their understanding of religion as clear and faultless. Thus when they returned from the communion service on the following Sunday, each had in his hand a leather-bound Bible, a reward from the provost for his diligence. With satisfied but sober faces, they entered the freshly swept and leaf-strewn cabin, the work of Kyösti Tammisto, who had tended the livestock for the past week. After they had eaten and Kyösti had left, each man sat studying Scripture by himself, and a profound silence held sway in the room.

So passed the lovely summer. A cool, brisk autumn came, then winter, and another blessed summer. The years that ensued brought good fortune and success to Impivaara Farm. Diligence is the fount of good fortune, and so diligently did the brothers work and toil that the fields kept expanding, grain kept accumulating in the storage bins, horses were added to the stable and cows beneath the rafters of the barn.

Old one-eyed Valko still stood in the stable, but on either side of him was a sleek and slender filly, one bought from Tammisto and the other from old Kuokkala. Eagerly the colts crunched the clean hay from the fields, gazing at the world with the carefree eyes of youth. Now and then they caused some small annoyance to the old horse between them when they tried to greet him over the intervening wall. Ill-tempered Valko stands there with his ears laid back and his pendulous lower lip resting on the hay as his worn teeth nibble at it dully. In the barn stand ten cattle. If you open the door, eight grave and innocent cows gaze back at you, and two bulls as stout as pine stumps. The older has already been condemned to lose his freedom next spring and bow to the fate of a draft ox, but the younger will still be allowed to roam the pastures at will. Such was the state of the cowbarn, where the conscientious hand of Simeoni worked the hardest.

Bit by bit, all the buildings a farmer needs rose in the Impivaara barnyard. A proper sauna was built on the border of yard and field, and the loft disappeared from the cabin along with the sauna stove. In its place, a regular farmhouse fireplace was built. A fine floor of split spruce logs now extended over the whole room from rear wall to threshold; formerly only a half had been covered. Three clear windows had been installed in the earlier holes in the walls. Looking east now you could see the fields of the farm, and another broader hay field beyond Luhta Meadow which had formerly been Sompio Swamp. Across fields and meadows a farm road ran toward the church village and their former home — from the fields it ran into a thick woods, then over a heath to Teerimäki Ridge, which stood beautifully outlined against a band of clouds that glowed in the south. Looking west you could see mossy crags beyond the fields and here and there a short but sturdy pine tree on whose swaying crown the summer evening sun often gleamed. But the north window of the cabin looked out on the steep, rugged slope of Impivaara. This was the view of the world as you looked out from the broad cabin. But if you opened the stout door and looked east and northeast, you would see a rocky meadow strewn with stumps, a heath at its edge, and a soughing pine grove, from whose lap the summer sun rose into the sky. Such was the face of nature around Impivaara, which was now becoming a mighty farm.

Word of the change wrought in them and consequently in the barnyard and fields of Impivaara soon traveled throughout the parish. At first people could scarcely credit it, but the report proved true and was related with wonder. Gradually increased honor and respect was accorded to the brothers. They themselves, however, seldom left their own lands: they did not want to see Jukola until it was their own again. They had made a vow, and avoided seeing the beloved fields of their home even from a distance.

It was the last year of the ten for which Jukola had been given to another man to till. Come fall, the brothers were entitled to move back to the home where they were born. It was a clear, warm Sunday in June. The bright sun was streaming through the open door of Impivaara, drawing a glistening pattern on the leaf-strewn floor. Tuomas and Simeoni sat in silence at the table reading their Bibles; Juhani, Timo, and Eero were strolling about the grain fields admiring the flourishing beauty of the summer. Lauri wandered the woods in silence and Aapo had gone to visit Kyösti Tammisto. The sky was a blue arch overhead, a soft west wind fanned the air, the birch on the hill shimmered in its leafy mantle, and the white froth of bloom on the mountain ash spread its fragrance abroad. In the field at Impivaara, wave after gentle wave rippled through the grain, which glowed in the burning heat of the sun now hastening up to its midday height. Back home came the brothers: the strollers from the fields, Aapo from Tammisto, and Lauri from deep in the heath. Inwardly smiling they approached their peerless home, which gazed back at them with the same smile of peace, while silvery heat waves danced on its scorching roof. With contented hearts and shining faces, they stepped into the broad, leaf-strewn cabin.

When they had eaten, they sat here and there each thinking of something or looking at the book open before him. Near the rear window, which looked west, sat Aapo, fussing with his pipe and apparently deep in serious thought. Finally he opened his mouth to begin the following discussion.

Aapo: I met the tanner at Tammisto and talked over our business with him. He is getting a job as a miller and will be ready to hand over Jukola at the start of September. I said we hoped so.

Tuomas: The sooner he's gone, the better. Jukola has gone badly downhill in his hands, and he hasn't paid us a grain of rent.

Aapo: The law might force him to, but what would he pay with?

Tuomas: He'll never be able to pay unless he pawns his miserable soul.

Aapo: A work sentence might finally pay it off, but the poor man has a sick wife and many whining children.

Juhani: Let the poor thing go with God and be quit with us. He's had hard luck these ten years, you can't deny it, but even if he were blessed with the best luck in the world, he was never born to run a farm. That takes a man of mettle, which he has about as much of as a mitten. So let him go crank up his mill and we'll go and show how to make Jukola the best farm in the parish.

Aapo: It's always best to have a farm whose tilled soil and cleared fields we know to be the work of our own hands. Three of us can stay to take care of this new place; the others can go to dig and hoe the land of Jukola. But let's work with the strength of seven men in both the fields here and at our former home. And soon we'll have two fine farms besides two of the best tenant farms ever rented out, which will be portion, plot, and place for every one of us when the time comes for a general settlement to decide our future. And let's hope that our best hopes will come true. So then, all is well at last, so long as wisdom and good sense remain our guiding star on the road of life.

Timo: Much depends on a wife and her running of the household if a husband's work in rain and shine is to make them rich or poor in the end.

Aapo: Listen to Timo. He talks like a man of experience. What you say is true! A wife either raises a house to strength and honor or tears it down to the ground. I'm not talking about a house where the husband is a wild man who will lose a year's income in a minute — no manor's riches or wife's thrift could save a house like that, even if she were as sharp as a weasel and as stingy as a Jewess. No, just take an ordinary house and a husband who is an ordinary spender, and look, if the woman of the house scrimps and saves, then the house will stand, but the house with a spendthrift mistress falls to pitiless ruin, though the husband strive with the strength of ten men. The man may swill down enough to get good and drunk, he may get into fights in the village, for which the law will punish him, but these collisions we can rate as little blood-lettings, bleeding wounds on a person's body, to which I am now comparing the house. But a wasteful wife is a deadly worm in the household's belly, a moth, a cancer that drains all fluids and finally rots and destroys the whole building. Now I remember a story I heard from our grandfather, that ever wise, prudent, and far-seeing man.

And he told this tale:

There were two brothers, equally temperate and hard-working; both had identical farms and both had a wife and children. One of them remained a man of means, but the other grew poorer day by day and many wondered about it without perceiving the reason for the difference between the two. But one Saturday evening, Grandfather went to both houses on some errand. First he went to the rich man's house where the wife, having just finished churning butter, was giving out bread and butter to her children. Then he went to the poor man's house where the wife was doing the same, but lo and behold, this woman spread the butter at least twice as thick as her neighbor. And now the

old man knew the cause of one brother's wealth and the other's poverty.
Just as the second wife used twice as much butter, so twice as much of
everything else slipped almost unnoticed through her fingers. To do as
well as her neighbor, she would have needed two such farms. This was
the story told by the old man who was known for his wisdom.

Juhani: He was right to think so. A no-account wasteful wife is a
rat that gnaws away all a household's goods — as sorry a sight as an
old rag footwrapping in a reindeers' water-hole.

Aapo: Let's consider getting married the most critical act of our
lives then, for a bad wife is a man's ruin while a good and loving wife
is the height of happiness and a man's best friend, his golden honor,
who makes his home a haven of joy and peace. Let him treat such a
wife as the apple of his eye and the dearest treasure of his soul. And I
also think that far fewer worthless wives would be found among us if a
man always corrected his young wife's errors with tender words and
loving looks, always avoiding nagging comparisons to that fine wife
next door and letting his dear honored mother lie at peace in her grave.
So my brothers, maybe all of us will soon have a wife by our side and
little kiddies around us. This is not just idle talk, but considered opinion, and I want these words to be set deep in your hearts.

Juhani: You've always done well and given us the best of advice.
It's true! You've led us through the dark night of the wilderness with a
father's mind and tongue. Brothers, let us thank Aapo for the great
work he has done.

Aapo: Get out of here with that! Don't talk rubbish. Well — uh —
well. It's just that we stand here now after battling all together. We've
strained, striven, and struggled to escape from the dark jungle of mis-
fortune and to reach this broad open plain. But look, the weather is
bright and clear, the sun is near setting, and the carp are swarming to
spawn in the reed beds of Lake Ilves. Let's go and set out our trap nets
for a tasty breakfast tomorrow.

Down to Lake Ilves they went to set out nets for the golden-flanked carp that were merrily spawning, flashing along the lake's reedy shoreline. Simeoni and Timo were left at home to tend to the cattle. Lowing, bells clanking, the crooked-horned cows made their way back over the heath from the pasture. While they stood chewing their cud in the stump-strewn meadow, they were milked and then driven into a pen, where one by one they sank to rest on their bed of fir branches. Out on the calm surface of Lake Ilves rowed the others in their blunt-nosed dugout, lowering nets into the lake's clear depths along the jagged reed bank, while a reddish dusk glowed in the tops of the pine trees to the southwest.

CHAPTER XIII

The date set for repossessing Jukola farm, which the brothers had not seen for nine years, was a clear day in September. On the road to the church village, which runs through Luhta and Sompio Meadows, seven men were traveling ever further from the new farm at Impivaara, where Kyösti Tammisto had been left in charge of the livestock for a day or two. Walking abreast in the lead were Juhani, Aapo, and Tuomas; their stride was eager and their faces wore a look of quiet exultation. Behind them came a loaded wagon drawn by two young mares and driven by Lauri sitting on a small beer barrel filled with home-brew for the celebration at Jukola. Simeoni and Timo followed, each leading a lowing cow as a start for the Jukola herd. Last came Eero with a small, broad-browed bull assigned the task of increasing the number of cattle in the Jukola barn. Willingly the young bull followed the cows, trotting along behind them and bellowing proudly. Joyful, though already graying, Killi and Kiiski romped about gaily, now ahead, now behind, and now to one side or other of the procession. They were the only animals born at Jukola to return to their old home. Valko had died and now rested sweetly in a deep grave beyond the fence around Luhta Meadow; dead and buried was the mewing cat, Juhani's beloved Matti. Last to die and be buried was the cocksure rooster. Another bird now crowed cheerfully on the roost at Impivaara, another cat squinted down from the fireplace, and two proud young horses drew the wagon toward Jukola at a brisk pace.

So on they journeyed, leaving broad Sompio and entering the depths of the forest. The air was clear and calm, and the sun shone

gently from a pale-blue, smiling sky. Matti Seunala's meadow lay before them; beyond was the Viertola road to the village, which they
crossed on an uphill stretch over a sandy, piney heath. At last they
stood on the crest of Teerimäki, from which a smooth road ran downhill. The brothers stopped to rest their horses at its top, from which
they could see far in all directions. They turned their eyes to the
southwest where Jukola, their childhood home, loomed in the distance.
A tear soon dimmed their eyes and an odd languor filled their breasts
like waters rippling into the breast of a drowning man. Once again
they looked southwest, where Jukola loomed on the slope of the ridge
like a dim ghost from the past. Then they looked back to the north
where their new home at Impivaara smiled cheerfully among the
green, sprouting grain fields beneath the steep hill. So they gazed,
north, south, east and west, and tears of joy misted their eyes. But Juhani drew beer from the tap, and the tankard went round from man to
man.

Juhani: We're shedding tears, but they're beads of joy and triumph.
So let's drink and rejoice.

Aapo: Thank God that we stand here again as happy men. Happy
are we who recognized at the critical moment where our peace lay and
so brought forth good fruits before a gloomy fate was written on the
wall for us. That fact and God's guiding hand have raised us to this
noble and happy height where we now stand as conquering heroes.
Ten dear years have passed since we fled to the dark woods with overpowering rage in our hearts. That's what we did, and I believe that if
we had stayed there in the south, in a bitter atmosphere of persecution
and spite, we would still be heirs to grief. Luckily we left the place and
its people, and we are now changed men. Here we stand looking toward Toukola in peace and good will, with solid possessions and worthy behavior to back us up.

Well, there they are: dear old Jukola, the village of Toukola, the
church tower, and rich Impivaara. Our life's journey for the past ten

years lies clear before my eyes. See how it went. At first we tried something altogether impossible — to break into Christian society by that ill-fated excursion to the stately tower there on the horizon. It was a cursed journey of torment, but a power was at work in it which drove us into the wilderness. So we moved to that steep gray hill and built ourselves a stout cabin. But a greedy fire burned it to ashes and like wolf cubs we crept back to Jukola again. That was rough sledding, but it didn't bother us too much. Back to the woods we went and built ourselves another cabin finer than the first.

Again we lived as we pleased. Dogs romped, guns roared, and the warm blood of wild game flowed freely. But then stern fate set up a grim ordeal for us on that terrible Rock of Hiisi. And over there I think it stands, the rock of hunger, care, and dear good fortune, there where the dim verge drops off and the tip of a sparse spruce tree rises above the rest. There is the rock which brought us grief and pain. Yet we can call it our rock of good fortune. You can see that this moment of joy and happiness here on the crest of Teerimäki issued from that source. That awful rock in the wilds gave rise to the hard work of clearing the land, which brought us abundance of grain. But the grain brought on a great evil, the drinking bout so sad to recall. Yet what came of that? Drunken madness stirred up all the devils of hell to serve as a dreadful warning to us, shunting us off on another road. We received threatening reminders from two directions: Simeoni's weird spirits and Lauri's striking dream. And to our great benefit, we heeded these crucial signs from the hidden world. Like men, we vowed forever to stop drinking that damned, befuddling brew, and I hope we will stand nobly by that decision.

But we still had a very rough caper to contend with, the result of too much drink and our own crude and vile tempers, not yet made pliant enough, but still burning with a lust for revenge. We experienced that rage-shrieking, wolf-panting, club-crashing, blood-spilling day, that hot day in the Tammisto farmyard. Thus were we punished for our day of drinking. Yet from that day of retribution flowed our good fortune. Behold, when we stood on the brink of black horror, then merciful God brightened our lot by means of the sheriff. But what did we ourselves do? Like men, we took the trail of self-denial, toil, and action. We still had many struggles and straits to confront, but we broke their backs, kept charging forward, and here we stand now. Thanks be to God who leads us, to ourselves, who chose wisdom while there was still time, and to our mother, who reminded us of God's will and law in our childhood days. Some word or two of hers always sank deep into our hearts, from which a warning voice constantly whispered in our ears through the wildest storms. It kept our lives from sinking in shipwreck.

Juhani: Oh, if Mother were alive now, strolling through the yard at Jukola, and could see her sons approaching, she would rush all the way out to the sloping meadow to greet us. But the old girl is in heaven's halls now waiting for her children. We're coming mother, coming some day, with God's help. So let's go now, brothers, down the rocky hill.

Down they went, coming first to the dark woods, then to the burned-over meadow, and next to high Kiljava Heath, where screaming hawks soared through the air under the bright sky. Now they were on the hilly road beyond broad Kuttila Meadow.

Juhani: Boys, boys! The scent of home is in my nostrils already, sweeter than Our Lady's bedstraw. Boys and brothers, borne and birthed by the same mother, hear this good word: let's invite every man and woman, every last Jack and Jill we meet along the way to our homecoming.

Aapo: We'll do it.

Tuomas: So be it.

Timo: We'll invite them all, from bailiff to beggarman, so long as we meet them on the way.

Juhani: Everyone from Governor to town bum, and what a shindig it'll be. We'll stomp with the Toukola girls till the floor rocks and bark falls from the roof. It's true that only Aapo can dance the quadrille and all we know is the polska, but we can dance it like men. But where can we find a top-flight fiddler and a handy miss to make the coffee?

Aapo: I'm sure we'll find a way to work it out.

Juhani: Somehow or other we'll find a way. We always have. Even when things were at their worst, we've turned, twisted, and bent everything to our will, made everything come out right, and ten years have passed by in the wink of an eye. Tra la la. I haven't had a cup of coffee since Karja-Matti's wedding, but let it flow today in honor of our celebration, all seven of us, seven handsome men, with Aapo, Tuomas and Juhani stepping out and leading Impivaara's Life Guard battalion. Strapping boys, all of us. Even Eero isn't the runt of Finland, not by any means, even if it took a damned long time before he started to stretch. And yet now he's up to snuff, both in body and soul. The years in the woods did it, with our help: a couple of thrashings and he was as mild as milk. Isn't that so? What do you have to say?

Eero: It's true of my body, but as for my soul, I'm afraid it's still got a good store of spite saved up for you, the kind that sets the whole world on its ear. Right now it's drawing my eye to you from here in back. Next to Aapo, you look like a gawky wall-eyed goat walking beside a steady gelding.

Juhani: Is that so, Eero my boy? But today the spirit of joy and gladness smiles through all the air. So why should I care? I just sing away.

> *Tralala tralala!*
> *How can I be so gay?*
> *How can I be so full of joy?*
> *Tralalalalala!*

Who's that man coming toward us through the field?

Aapo: It's the old man himself, I think.

Tuomas: That's right. Well, hello to him!

Juhani: The sexton? In the flesh!

Tuomas: The very man! Well, hello to him!

Juhani: Great son of Heaven? The rascal himself, with his knotty cane in hand and the old provost's broad-brimmed hat on his head. May the black bull carry him off! The rascal himself, the rascal himself!

Timo: Our schoolmaster.

Juhani: But how did he teach us? That is the question.

Simeoni: Let us pass by with due respect.

Tuomas: We have to invite him to our homecoming. We agreed to.

Juhani: The devil? So we do, but first I'd like to give him a little something for old time's sake. He still causes me a little bit of heartburn. Just one little reminder and then let him join us if he wants to. He was my teacher. Good! Maybe it's my turn to teach him. I'll pose him a tricky little question from my Testament.

Timo: So will I. I've got a sly riddle tucked away here and we'll see how he solves it. Not that I bear him a grudge. My hair has grown back as thick as it used to be, but let's see how he undoes the knot I'll tie for him.

Aapo: Hush, brothers. Treat him with respect and show him we're coming back to the village as different men from when we left it. Let's be wise.

Juhani: As to being wise, that's just what I want to be. I'll pose him some deep little Bible questions just for fun. I've read the Testament from cover to cover, and I should hope I understand it. But honestly, Eero, tell me what I should ask him.

Eero: Ask him how five men and two fish were fed with five thousand loaves of bread.

Juhani: Shut your mouth, you godless imp, you blabber-mouth, you ditch-water goblin. I'll show you. I can ask and answer questions that the archbishop himself doesn't understand. I know what to ask, all right. But here's the old man.

Tuomas: I warn you, treat him well.

Juhani: I know how to.

Sexton: Good day, boys, good day?

Brothers: Good day!

Sexton: Looks like you're moving.

Tuomas: We are, sort of.

Sexton: Is that so, is that so? Hmm. Well, well, it's starting to blow. Do you think it will rain?

Juhani: Maybe so.

Sexton: It's blowing very hard.

Juhani: It is, all right, it's blowing hard.

Sexton: So it is, mhmm. So that's how you're moving.

Juhani: Little by little. But does the sexton have any pupils at his table nowadays?

Sexton: No, I don't.

Juhani: Not a single one in the dunce's corner with his hair all tangled?

Sexton: Heh, heh! No, my boy, not one. Hmm. Well, well, so that's how you're moving. Well then, welcome back to the home you were born in.

Juhani: Thanks a million, Mr. Sexton. We've come from the wilderness, and you see the heavy load our colts have to pull, with seven Testaments to add to the weight, seven gifts from England. And I think the deepest, hardest parts weigh the most of all. But what if we tried to lighten the load, to loosen up a few knots, bundles, and bags on it? Could the sexton...

Tuomas: Juhani!

Juhani: Could the sexton answer one question for me, one that many men have racked their brains over? Tell me, what were Zebedee's sons' names?

Timo: You and I make one, Coachhouse Antti and Jussi make two, so how many of us are there? That's what the man from Loimaa asked me once, and now I'm asking the sexton.

Juhani: Timo, shut your bread flap. So, Mr. Sexton, what were Zebedee's sons' names? That's my question. Listen to this, boys!

Timo: You and I make one, Coachhouse Antti and Jussi make two, so how many of us are there? That's my riddle. Listen to this, boys! How many, sir?

Sexton: Two, my boy, certainly not four. Yes, my dear boy, two and no more. Heh, heh!

Timo: Ahaa! I got you there. That's what I said to the man from Loimaa, but it can't be. There are four of us in the bunch, learned sexton.

Juhani: Can't you keep your damn trap shut until your older brother is finished. One thousand devils!

Timo: For God's sake, don't shove me in the face a second or third time. You bugger! You think I'm just a calf, a baby bull? Well I'm not, and I really get mad once I lose my temper.

Juhani: Shut up and listen. What were Zebedee's sons' names?

Sexton: A simple question. But our former provost once asked me: What was Zebedee's sons' father's name? Guess what the correct answer I gave was. Well, may I ask: What was Zebedee's sons' father's name?

Juhani: Well, ah, umm, well. Is that name in my New Testament?

Sexton: Truly it is. It's even in the question.

Juhani: Is that so… well, well, hmm. So it's in my New Testament? But… that's what I meant to ask you, but I was in such a hurry it came out a little different. I've heard the riddle but couldn't dig up the answer from my Testament. I'm not a learned scholar or doctor, not one of the clergy like the sexton. Even if he's at the tail end, like the one involved with old Viksari.

Timo: It was the beadle or verger who called himself the clergy's tail and switched old Viksari a bit.

Eero: It was the sexton.

Juhani: Sexton or beadle, beadle or sexton, I only mean to say that I'm not a member of that class and have no right to crow in church like the morning cock on the roost or to yank young louts by the hair. And if you want to hear the truth from me, do you know what the old Estonian, Kokki, said to the public prosecutor at Hämeenlinna?

Sexton: Well, what did he say?

Juhani: "Go to 'ell, ye bloody divil." Hmh! Who do you think is cock of the walk here? Hell's bells, old man. You see how the world's changed in ten years' time.

Aapo: Juho, Juho!

Tuomas: Now, brother, I want to put in a word too, and you keep your mouth shut for your own good. Forgive them sexton; they don't understand. Pay no attention to them, and please come with us to a little homecoming party at Jukola, for this is our day of days.

Sexton: I thank you, but time won't permit me to accept your invitation now.

Simeoni: Come and make peace between us and the men of Toukola. Do it in God's name.

Aapo: We beg you to come and make peace. Isn't it your duty as a man of the church? Take care that both God and the provost don't take offense at you for not being a peacemaker in such an important case. Think about it.

Sexton: Have your way. I'll follow you and do my best to shake the hearts of the Toukola men through my words and the power of the Lord. But first let's clear the air. I see hatred for me smoldering in your eyes, although it is weaker now, and I know the cause. Well, I was a stern teacher, stern and harsh, I admit it, and bitterly have I regretted it. But I myself, God help me, was taught in the same stern, harsh manner. Yet what did I mean by my strictness toward you? I meant your own good, your own good, of that you can be sure. And you can also be sure that right now, although I was a bit upset at meeting you, my soul rejoices, for I look on you as men, and know all about your deeds and trials while the last four of the Lord's years have rolled by.

Aapo: Thank you for the compliment.

Tuomas: We know you as a man of honor, and Juhani and Timo will ask pardon for their spiteful words.

Timo: I admit he's a man of honor, but he's a harsh teacher.

Juhani: If the sexton will admit that he didn't exactly treat us right, then I'll admit the same toward him, and so we'll be even, especially since I confess that we were pigheaded pupils on whose thick skulls his armor of patience was bound to break. And I ask you, who can prove that this tugging and yanking at our hair didn't do us some good. Who can prove it?

Aapo: So all is forgotten. Forward now, all together. Sexton, be so good.

They proceeded along the narrow road, beautiful and dear to the brothers, for they were now coming to the meadows, rocks, and stumps known to their childhood. A brisk west wind was blowing against them. Suddenly a frightful clamor burst on their ears and the Rajamäki Regiment came marching up. They could see Kaisa's snuffy face and flashing eyes under her black cap, as the old woman walked between the shafts scolding and cursing. But Heikka had discarded his hobby-horse and Sourpuss his bottle cart, and now they walked to either side of their mother, each pulling a shaft to help her draw the wagon. Mikko himself, black felt hat on his head and a huge quid of tobacco in his cheek, pushed with his staff from behind as was his wont. After him came the twins, each riding a hobbyhorse, and last of all, Mikko's little 'Bootsie,' dragging his bottle cart along the dusty village road. On the cart, you could see the sack of pitch, the bag of cupping horns, and the calf-skin pack holding Mikko's, Heikka's, and Sourpuss's knives. The fiddle too was there, wrapped in Kaisa's old red woolen head-scarf.

So the two incredible processions advanced toward each other, raising a din and a ruckus. Shying back and snorting, the young horses of Impivaara approached the regiment; Killi and Kiiski, the fur on their backs bristling, barked and growled fiercely, at which the twins and little 'Bootsie' ran for the shelter of the wagon, where Kaisa stormed and cursed at them, while Mikko waved his staff at the dogs and roared angrily. Both parties stopped and gazed at each other for a long time in silence, Rajamäki's Regiment in wonder, but the brothers in total shock, for they were thinking of the promise made on the road. Finally Aapo stepped forward.

Aapo: Peace be with you!

Mikko: The same to you, but call off your dogs.

Aapo: Hush, Killi and Kiiski.

Juhani: Welcome, man, welcome Mikko Rajamäki. How are you and what's new in the world?

Mikko: So-so, good and bad mixed, but good, doggone it, has the upper hand, and this life's hassle is alright, it's alright. Yes, boys, God be thanked, there's work and jobs enough in village and farmyard. No, no panic for Mikko so long as there's work and jobs enough in the world, even if a man has to trudge from farm to farm and village to village looking for work and bread. No, no panic for Mikko.

Aapo: We can believe it, and wish you ever more success in your work. But we have an idea, Mikko, and would like you to stay with us for a longer time. Listen to a word or two.

Mikko: Ahaa! I can guess what it's about. You're still stewing over our little run-in down by Sonnimäki Heath. It's a good thing we're on a public road and have the sexton as a trusty witness. Step aside, good friends and neighbors, step aside.

Aapo: Listen to us!

Kaisa: Out of the way, you scoundrels! Out of the way or the devil will grab you!

Sexton: You're mistaken, honorable Rajamäki family, you're badly mistaken. Listen to what I most solemnly say and swear. Ah, the life of the Jukola brothers is not what it used to be. It has changed in both body and soul, God help us! You must know that they have borne the loveliest fruits of change and conversion and are returning to their beloved birthplace as honorable sons rejoicing and willing to embrace the whole world. So they are inviting you to a joyous homecoming and reconciliation feast at Jukola, their former home. This is their heart's intent toward you in this moment of jubilation. Believe what your sexton tells you.

Juhani: It's just as the sexton says!

Aapo: Mikko and Kaisa! We want to act like men and forget the past. And what were you saying about that run-in at Sonnimäki? My good friend, we brought it on ourselves and deserved what we got. That's how it was, and I remember something else about that evening at Sonnimäki. Didn't your wife predict hard times for us then? She did and she was right. Storms came and beat us badly, but storm and clouds are gone and a beautiful day is dawning. But prophesy for us again, a brighter future, we hope. I hear you read fortunes best in coffee cups, and there'll be no scarcity of coffee tonight at Jukola.

Juhani: Beer and coffee?

Aapo: Beer and coffee? So come along and predict happy days for us.

Mikko: Kaisa will tell fortunes and I'll play the fiddle to liven up the party. It'll all work out fine.

Aapo: It'll be great.

Juhani: You're a top-notch man, Mikko.

Mikko: I'll play a merry march as we come to Jukola.

Juhani: You're in a class by yourself, Mikko. Play, and fill the world with shrill echoes, you God's creation.

Aapo: Everything is working out fine.

Juhani: Everything fits like a lock clicking shut.

Mikko: Turn your wagons around, Heikka and Matti, my boys, and you Kaisa, stop scowling and swing around toward Jukola.

Kaisa: I'll give you a swing, I will. If I were crazy enough to start trudging back on my old legs, do you think I'd go ahead and be trampled by their balky jackasses along the way? Let them push on ahead and we'll trail along behind.

Mikko: Right you are, Kaisa. You brothers take off first like a streaking comet and we'll follow you like its smoking tail. That wife of ours has a little bit of a temper.

Juhani: But she's some woman?

Aapo: A fine woman?

Mikko: So she is, drat it? I dare say so, and she's my wife.

Juhani: She's a trump card.

Mikko: That she is. It's true she has a temper, she has a temper, but when the old man gets his dander up, then mama shuts her mouth good and tight, she does, and there's no help for it. But I'm a softie of a husband anyway, I am, and I let Kaisa rule the roost. Why should I care, as long as everything is going well? Hallelujah, boys! We'll follow you like the shoemaker trailing the tailor into heaven. "We'll stick to you even if we meet the devil," said the shoemaker, tugging his tarred thread and gritting his teeth. So then, march, and let's sound off.

As one they started forward. The wind rose to a stormy pitch and the birch trees roared and swayed. Now the sun shone gently and now it was masked by lovely cloud patches which scudded swiftly on high, driven by the northerly wind toward the distant curve of the horizon. Up hill and down they traveled, and sweet were journey and storm to the brothers as they neared their home hill to the southwest.

But an old man was approaching them, black-bearded, ill-tempered Grandpa Kolistin. His bushy gray brows, like wings of a great horned owl, nearly covered his fierce eyes. In his day, he had been a crack shot and had felled many a bear and wolf. At length he succumbed to a grave illness which weakened his hearing so that only words screamed directly into his ear were audible to him. This unfortunate occurrence ended his bear-hunting days forever, and he wound up snaring small game. Fall and winter he set large numbers of snares in the woods, which brought death to birds, rabbits, and squirrels. He was a blunt, rough, outspoken old man, quick to anger, and with his own view of life. It was he who came toward the brothers along the narrow road on this sunny September afternoon.

Juhani: Hello, old man!

Timo: Hello, grandpa, hello!

Juhani: Stop, you worthy old soul.

Old Kolistin: Huh?

Juhani: Greetings from the woods.

Old Kolistin: What do you want?

Tuomas: Shout loudly into his ear.

Juhani: Here we are now!

Old Kolistin: So you are, devil take you. And lord have mercy on us here.

Juhani: What?

Aapo: The old boy is in a bad mood.

Juhani: What do you mean?

Old Kolistin: You can guess. Well, well, yes, yes, we'll soon have new tricks here again. That's plain to see.

Juhani: Brothers, this is an insult.

Aapo: Pay no attention. Just ask him to come with us to Jukola.

Juhani: Anyway, old man, since you are such a good old boy, we're asking you to come to Jukola for a rip-roaring homecoming party.

Old Kolistin: Why did you come here, you goblin? Why didn't you stay in your mountain holes till your miserable death? Why did you come?

Juhani: So, is this the thanks I get for the invitation?

Old Kolistin: It burns and stings and rankles when I think of my snares. Damn it! There's many a fat grouse will go from my snares into another's bag from now on. You louts. You lifted enough from them already.

Juhani: Are you calling us thieves?

Old Kolistin: Did I say it? Did I? But you can take a hint, even if you are such a stupid cuckoo chick, such a chuckle-headed wood grouse.

Juhani: Are you calling us thieves for inviting you to a party?

Old Kolistin: What did you say? Shout louder, like a man, and stop whining and croaking. — What did you say, boy?

Juhani: I invited you to a party because we're all your god-Sons.

Old Kolistin: You my godson?

Juhani: Me and my six brothers here. So come to the party, godfather.

Old Kolistin: Shut your mouth! I'm not your godfather.

Juhani: That's just what you are.

Old Kolistin: I'm not your godfather, I am not!

Juhani: Certainly you are.

Old Kolistin: Shut up, I tell you!

Juhani: That's just what you are, if Granny Pine was telling the truth.

Old Kolistin: Who?

Juhani: Granny Pine, the village midwife.

Old Kolistin: I don't give a hoot about Granny Pine, and I'm not your nor anyone else's godfather. Me your godfather? Fiddlesticks!

Juhani: Fiddlesticks? Is that so? But even if I wasn't carried to the minister as a blind, milk-toothed puppy, yet I'm inviting you to a party.

Old Kolistin: But I'm not coming, and I command you not to invite me.

Juhani: I'm inviting you anyway.

Old Kolistin: But I'm not coming, you devil! Shut your mouth!

Juhani: I'm inviting you anyway.

Sexton: Boys, boys, leave the old man alone.

Mikko: Well, let him go with God. He's a rough, simpleminded old man and he's looking at us like a wild dog. Let him go. Forward march, old man.

Juhani: Yet I see a foxy little grin back in those simple, sour old gray eyes of his, and he's got my dander up. I'm inviting you to a party, a wild party. I'm inviting you to fill your face with beer because you're a good old grandpa.

Old Kolistin: What did you say? Yell louder.

Juhani: You're a good old grandpa, but a little nosy. That's always been the original sin of the deaf.

Old Kolistin: Huh?

Juhani: "A nosy snoopy rag of a man," said the Swede, but otherwise a fine old grandpa.

Old Kolistin: You lout, you shameless lout! But does a wood grouse have a brain in its head. Not an ounce. Pooh! There's a big flock of them flying up from my feet now, a flock of wood grouse.

Juhani: Maybe seven of them?

Old Kolistin: Whatever. There they sit gawking at me from a birch limb. One of them is looking at me like a bull at a new gate. The instant he takes flight, I'll bang away and bag him. Right now seven louts stand gaping at Grandpa Kolistin like seven wall-eyed wood grouse. You louts! What do you want from me — what, what, what?

Juhani: I want to tell you with a straight face and true tongue that I'm no thief or lout or wood grouse, and in the same breath, that a certain old grouch, an old scalawag who is standing on the road not many thousands of yards away is a shameless old grouch, a big bum and a hobo, and I say it with all due respect.

Old Kolistin: What man, what man? You sawed-off cuckoo chick sitting on a dry pine, am I a hobo, am I, am I? Tell me, who is, you cuckoo chick.

Juhani: What the devil shall I blow into his damned ear?

Aapo: Don't blow anything. Let's just go.

Juhani: Not quite yet. He's such an old rogue, that old man. What the devil shall I blow in his ear?

Eero: Let me try. Here, you hold this bull.

Juhani: Yes, let him have a juicy blast.

Old Kolistin: What man, huh?

Eero: "Cuckoo, cuckoo!" said the little bird in the dry pine. "Cuckoo!"

Old Kolistin: There's a cuckoo!

Eero: You devil!

Juhani: Look at the old devil! He banged him one!

Eero: He banged me and my ear is ringing.

Aapo: Well done, trusty old Kolistin, well done!

Eero: To hell with him. He hit me so hard I saw stars.

Juhani: You know what you've done, old man? You hit a respectable man in the face with your fist right out on a public road during the holy sabbath. Oh, oh, old man.

Aapo: Well done, old Kolistin, you old barn troll, well done.

Old Kolistin: What are you babbling about?

Eero: Well said, stout Kolistin, well said!

Old Kolistin: You shut your mouth too, you weasel. I'll teach you boys to skip around under my nose. Grandpa Kolistin doesn't dilly-dally long before he starts swinging.

Juhani: I'll lay my hands on his burly collar and drag him to the beer party without mercy. Hey old man, now we'll march.

Old Kolistin: You go to hell!

Juhani: You'll drink beer till your belly bursts.

Old Kolistin: Let go of my collar or you'll get one in the mouth. Let go, you damned jutlander, you, let go!

Juhani: A barrel of beer.

Tuomas: Are you up to your fool tricks again, Juho?

Aapo: Leave the old man alone.

Juhani: He's been barking at us like a dog, God help us. How should we treat him? He's just a rag of an old man. But let him come to the Jukola jubilee, and drown his anger in drink. No, old man, I won't give in, I won't.

Old Kolistin: Take your hands off me!

Tuomas: Will you set him free? There, that's nice. Let him go. Go on, old man!

Juhani: I could have carried him to the happy party like a little child, for even the hair on my chest is flashing sparks. Son of God, have I ever stolen a single bird from anyone's snare? Or a rabbit?

Tuomas: Shut your mouth!

Juhani: Am I a thief? Well, am I?

Sexton: He didn't say so, boy.

Juhani: He was beating around that bush, though. Son of God, if only twenty or thirty years of snow were gone from his head.

Tuomas: Go on, old man!

Old Kolistin: You louts. Am... am... am I your hobbyhorse, you forest-faded, club-bait wolf-cubs? But I know how to teach you a lesson, yes I do, I still know how to teach you a lesson, you louts.

At last angry old Kolistin left them, muttering furiously to himself for a long time and spitting as he marched down the narrow road. The brothers too started off again, with the sexton following and the Rajamäki Regiment bringing up the rear. After they had gone on awhile, two women came toward them, the former Mrs. Männistö and her plump and lively daughter, Venla. They were walking briskly on their way to the lingonberry woods, white birch-bark buckets in their hands. The brothers were in total confusion at the meeting. They watched the approaching women in silence, and stopped before them. Now the two parties stood face to face, staring wide-eyed at each other. Finally Aapo stepped forth, told them of the firm oath made on Teerimäki Ridge, and invited them to the homecoming. Wondering what to do, mother and daughter stood inwardly smiling but with lips tightly pursed. Urged by the sexton too to accept the brothers' invitation and to come and make the coffee at the affair, they finally decided to join the happy procession. And so the sons of Jukola had an imposing negotiator and conciliator for the men of Toukola, a gracious mother and daughter to make the coffee, and in Mikko a man to play the cheerful homecoming march and make music for the dance with the Toukola girls. Thinking of all these delights, they marched ever more proudly toward their goal and stood at last on the sandy rise of Jukola's north field. Before them they could see Oja Meadow, beyond it Koto field, and higher up, Jukola house itself, looking sweetly melancholy. Silent and misty eyed, the brothers gazed for a long time at their home on the green, echoing hill. Meanwhile the sun was setting in the west and the wind roared with increasing force in the pines on the rocky hill south of the house.

Tuomas: There stands Jukola.

Juhani: Is that you, Jukola?

Aapo: Your shoulders sag and moss clings to your brow, revered mother Jukola.

Juhani: Moss clings to your brow, revered mother Jukola.

Timo: Greetings, Jukola. You lie before us as lovely as Jerusalem of old.

Juhani: Is that you, Jukola? Is that you? Oh, I can't hold back the tears from my rough face. My heart throbs and swells. Every place I look at returns the warm gaze of a friend. See how lovingly the window hole of the black cow-barn smiles at me. Welcome, welcome, you star of hope, welcome!

Eero: Welcome, welcome, you black star of hope!

Juhani: Welcome you dear manure pile down there, you beautiful good-luck mound! Ah!

Timo: It's beautiful, all right, but why wasn't it hauled out to the fields a long time ago? Really, what that pile shows and proves, what it means, is that the tanner is shiftless and lazy, completely, hopelessly lazy. Is it right for a manure pile to be sitting at home in September? That tanner really gets my goat. Well, I can forgive him today, the day of the Jukola jubilee.

Juhani: Welcome old manure pile, welcome? It's all I can say. I don't care what it shows or means. Welcome Jukola, welcome your piles, your fields, your meadows, as beautiful as heaven itself.

Timo: But heaven is more beautiful.

Juhani: Shut your mouth! This is more beautiful than Paradise.

Simeoni: Don't say that. It's a sin.

Juhani: My tongue speaks out what my heart whispers.

Lauri: I'd like to say something too, but this high moment has tied my tongue completely.

Juhani: *Say your piece and speak your mind;*
let joy burst from your breast.
Mountains roar and forests echo,
and for the moment heaven is hushed,
for this short and sacred moment.

Now that's verse for you, made up by a happy Jussi Jukola.

Aapo: That's enough for now. Let's get on with things.

Juhani: Let's get right on with things, the way a spawning school of fish heads for the farthest corner of a net. Let's go on before our honored guests get tired of our joy. After all, Jukola isn't their home, and besides, they've seen it more recently than we have. You Sexton, and you Granny Pine and your daughter, and you, honored Rajamäki family, don't take offense at this.

Sexton: No need to say it. We can understand what this moment means to you. It's a high, solemn moment of greatest joy.

Juhani: Beautifully put, perfectly put! Let's go now.

Tuomas: Let the guns roar and Mikko's fiddle sound.

Juhani: Yes, let's have a little music. One volley, brothers, one sharp volley. All together?

Mikko's fiddle shrilled and Juhani's, Tuomas's, and Aapo's guns roared almost simultaneously. The spirited horses reared high in their traces, and the cattle dashed off, one this way and the other that. But neither Simeoni nor Timo, and least of all Eero, would let go of the ropes in their hands. Gritting their teeth, they were almost dragged along by their respective animals, and the dry sand swirled up in clouds over the field. Soon the broomtails were forced to stop and return to the right course with the men. The procession continued on down, losing sight for a time of Oja Meadow, which soon reappeared as they climbed a steep slope and stepped in through the gate of Koto field. Mikko played his fiddle mightily, and Killi and Kiiski romped in fierce joy. The tanner's skinny, weak-jawed cur answered their barking, a trembling wretch limping around the corner of the house. But

when the children saw the Rajamäki Regiment nearing the house
again, they scurried quickly back inside with terror in their hearts,
shrieking loudly and hiding themselves, some up on the fireplace and
some among the clattering pieces of wood-carving stock. Possessed by
the same fear, the cur fell silent, curled his tail between his legs, and
crawled to hide underneath a bench in the corner. The yard was now
all hustle and bustle. The shouting of men, the clamor of dogs, the bellowing of the chunky little bull, and the shrill sound of Mikko's fiddle
vied noisily with each other as the wandering troop approached Jukola,
while the roaring north wind shook the dense pines on Kivimäki. The
brothers, their hearts filled with a softening mildness, stepped forth to
greet the people in the beloved yard of their former home. After shaking hands and unloading the wagon, they stepped as one into the spacious main room.

But Aapo and the sexton soon departed for Toukola to invite to a
homecoming and peace-making celebration the men who had so long
lived on terms of hatred and persecution with the Jukola brothers. And
when the sexton's gracious words had carried the invitation to both
men and women, he and Aapo hurried back to help the others prepare
for the party. A broad floor space was prepared in the cheerful room at
Jukola, large mugs of foaming beer were carried to the table, and neat
Venla bustled about the fireplace with her mother. The smoke from the
coffee fire collected under the sooty rafters, the roasted coffee beans
were ground in the teeth of the mill with a soft crunching sound, and
the tanner's wife's pot steamed on the fire. One person swept the yard,
another carried blocks from the wood pile into the house, and another
cut fir boughs to deck the floor — everyone was busy at something.
On a wide bench near the window sat Mikko, stroking an occasional
squeak from his fiddle.

But why is Granny Pine whispering so earnestly to Juhani out on
the porch, and why is he standing as wide-eyed and solemn as a man
facing judgment? Granny is telling him in a roundabout way that there
is no longer any obstacle between his heart and Venla's. Now the boy

is confounded; he puffs, sighs, sweats, and tugs at the hair on his neck. Then he asks Granny for a minute to think it over. A beaming Granny leaves him and Juhani steps out into the yard like a homeless troll, not knowing where to go. There behind the walls of Jukola he paces back and forth, sweating, sighing, blushing, stewing, and tugging at the hair on the back of his neck. But at last he rushes back to the porch, opens the squeaky door to the room, and says in a gasping, almost tearful voice, "If the sexton would be so good as to come out back, and you too, Aapo, dear brother." They complied with his request and soon the three of them stood beside the stout walls of Jukola pondering the matter which Juhani had informed them of.

There they pondered and discussed, and decided that Juhani should have Venla, who was after all, a fine girl. Then with firm, hurried steps, Juhani walked in and caught Venla by the hand, saying, "It's settled then." Venla, a little shy, hides her eyes and smiles, but lets her hand rest in Juhani's thick fist. Delighted, the old woman gives them her blessing, and the sexton wishes them success and happiness, reminding them in a brief speech of the chief duties that go with the marriage vows.

Now Juhani was betrothed, his old love newly kindled in his breast. Perspiring and panting, the bridegroom stole a look at his bride from time to time. Suddenly he rushes out to look at the horses in Oja meadow, and sees, yet doesn't see, both of Impivaara's young mares there. He would as easily have mistaken two cranes on the meadow's edge for horses, so bewitched was he by his bride-to-be, whom he could scarcely believe his own. The day seems miraculous to him. Then he rushes back again, longing to catch sight of Venla. Striding briskly out in the field, he hears the sound of Mikko's fiddle playing a spirited Polish march. His face contorts and a tear wets his eye, which he dries with his stout fist, feeling as if he enjoyed heaven's bliss. Reaching the yard, he does not see Rajamäki's twins before him riding their hobbyhorses over the ground at a brisk trot, nor Mikko's 'Bootsie' on the porch with his bottle cart. He steps firmly in, on his face a look of secret contemplation and lasting solemnity.

Little by little the men of Toukola assembled on Jukola hill. A group of them were already standing between the woodshed and the stable, pipes between their teeth, looking over the sleds and wagons and the tanner's spring buggy which he had bought at the market in Hämeenlinna. They stood for awhile looking doubtful and finally crossed the yard to the house one at a time, where they took up positions, some standing by the wall on either side and some inside the porch, listening to the clamor and bustle within. At last the door opened and Aapo stepped out to invite the guests in.

The men from Toukola entered and grouped themselves between the fireplace and the window on the left side. They stood there soberly, each one holding his hat up over his mouth. Aapeli Kissala was among them, and he kept looking back over his shoulder at the door; Eero Kuninkala was there too, and kept boring a hole in the floor with his eyes. Near them by the window sat Mikko with his fiddle, rolling a quid of tobacco in his cheek and spitting. Little 'Bootsie,' the apple of his father's eye, stood leaning against his knee. In front of the table, knotty cane in hand, stood the sexton, ready to begin a speech which would make a man's innards tremble, and stern was the look on his face. Clearing his throat and stroking his jaw between thumb and forefinger, he glowered to the right at the men of Toukola and to the left where the Jukola brothers were standing between the north window and the table, silent and staring at the floor. Near the hearth were the tanner's family, Granny Pine with her daughter, and Kaisa Rajamäki, who with snuff box in hand and snuff stains on her face, sat on a bench swaying back and forth. By the chopping block and the water bucket in the corner between the fireplace and the door stood the Rajamäki boys, Heikka, Sourpuss, and the twins, gazing saucer-eyed at the silent congregation in the room at Jukola. At the table stood the sexton. Deadly serious, he strokes his jaw in silence, opens his mouth at last, but checks his words again, clearing his throat. He throws another ferocious glance to the right and the left, grimacing as if he were chewing wormwood. Finally he spoke the following words:

"The devil, who roams the world like a roaring lion, spewing poison abroad, has kindled the flame of hatred and persecution in these neighbors' hearts. At first it flickered gently, like a flame in a pile of brush, but then it rose and spread like a monstrous forest fire. No bigger than a fly at first, it swelled like a force-fed steer and soon shut out heaven's light with its pall of smoke. So with the black devil in control, they went at each other over and over with their fists upraised, to part after a ghastly fight, black and blue with bruises, with gaping wounds, and huge lumps on their brows. What misery! Heaven itself sighed, hills, valleys, and even unreasoning animals mourned, while darkness and hell rejoiced. Many nodded assent to the idea that some day chains would clank, whips would whistle, and these boys would be marched off from their dear homeland to the icy tundras of Siberia. Such were the predictions of many, but they proved false, for which honor and thanks to Sabaoth. — Now see an extraordinary sight: The brothers abandoned the confines of men, they left their community and all humankind, and rushed off into the woods' dark night. Again many thought: This will turn them into bandits, seven ferocious, bloodthirsty bandits in the woods of Finland. But glory and thanks to Sabaoth, their predictions proved wide of the mark.

"Was it the devil who led them into the woods as he once did the preacher of Tuusula, or did the power of heaven draw them into the wilderness as it once did John the Baptist? I won't try to decide the issue now. But the devil did his best to lead them to destruction. With the poison of liquor and sweet syrups he lured them on, led them, as they themselves testify, up into that strange edifice, the so-called Boot-Leather Tower, and showed them our hemisphere as one frightful wreck in order to scare them out of their wits. That was his plan, but it recoiled in his face with shame, and drove the boys onto the right path before it was too late. They took up the hard battle, proudly began the campaign against the deep-rooted laziness in their own hearts, against the harsh unyielding earth, against the cold bogs and swamps, and won the fight through the unshakable determination of their own will and the aid of Lord Sabaoth! Huzza! Now they are back among people, not as outlaws but as decent men. With a grandly ceremonious clatter of swift wheels drawn by two proud young mares they come, followed by lowing, sleek-ribbed cows and a bellowing, broad-browed bull. Huzza! Sabaoth has won glory through them and the horned devil of hell has been shamed.

"Here they stand, men worthy of praise, offering the hand of conciliation to their former enemies. And, esteemed men of Toukola, you need no longer count it shame to call the Jukola brothers your friends, for now they emit a bright glow of honor rather than oozing the muck of shame. So accept the brimming chalice of concord, and mind that you don't let them reach out a hand in vain if you would escape the wrath to come. See, the sun is setting, looking back faint with love at the rainbow which glows in the east. Behold, it is the sign of the Lord's Covenant of Mercy and a crucial signal to former enemies that they should make peace, that they should join in idyllic brotherhood and deal the devil and his evil angels the worst blow on the brow they have ever taken. This is God's will and my wish, and anyone who will not incline ear and heart to my words, let him be cursed and damned and finally roasted by devils in hell. Hear me Sabaoth, hear me O Lord on high, hosanna!"

So spoke the sexton, and his words moved the women's hearts mightily. Granny Pine, nimble Venla, and snuffyfaced Kaisa Rajamäki wept uncontrollably; their sniffling was like the sound of a stout new cloth being swished about in a lye-tub by the hands of a laundress. But the men of Toukola and of Jukola stepped up to each other and shook hands firmly as a sign of concord. Their reconciliation was sober, candid, and sincere, though the glances they exchanged were sullen. But the sexton looked on with a smile of triumph on his face where he sat at the head of the table with a tankard of beer and a steaming cup of spiked coffee before him. Beer in white tankards went around the room from man to man, and eventually from woman to woman, for a group of women from Toukola had already assembled in the room at Jukola. Granny Pine's nimble daughter Venla carried coffee to them as they stood whispering to each other near the fireplace and chopping block. At first they refused it, accepting only after the bearer had tenaciously repeated her offer two or three times. Nor was Mikko forgotten, but beer and liquor aplenty were borne to him to wet the musician's whistle, which prompted him to spit vigorously on his fiddle's tuning pegs and to tune that often glued-together instrument. Finally a truly beautiful Swedish quadrille rang out in the room, but since no one stepped out onto the floor, he stopped its notes and loosed a cheerful, high-spirited polska. Long and earnestly he played, but not one couple spun out onto the floor. Finally the old man was so offended that he let his bow fall idle and, rolling his quid in his cheek and spitting, he began to pluck at his fiddle strings.

The people sat in silence. Near the back wall sat Aapo, now and then looking closely at a certain sober, roundcheeked, brown-skinned, blue-eyed girl, her lips prettily pursed in shyness and innocence, who was engaged in a whispered conference with Venla. Aapo watched her curiously, searching hither and yon in his memory, but he could not remember the girl's name. Finally he nudged the sexton in the ribs and asked him. The sexton answered quickly: "It's Hinrikka Kuokkala." Aapo's brow cleared, and he said to Mikko after a minute: "Give us a quadrille." Mikko began to fiddle again, and Aapo went over to the shy Kuokkala girl and asked her to be his partner. The girl followed him and took her place smiling slightly and blushing furiously. Couples from the opposite side of the room gathered on the floor, and at last a Swedish quadrille was danced in the big room to the shrilling of Rajamäki's fiddle. The fire blazed cheerfully, the torch on the wall flared and the floor boards boomed as with grave, earnest faces they danced their solemn, wordless dance.

Behind the table sat the sexton, who had enjoyed two spiked coffees and three cold beers. A seemly flush on his cheeks, he smiled as he watched the young people reveling on the floor. But when at last the long-drawn-out quadrille had ended, the sexton rose and announced that he was leaving. Having downed a parting toast and given a short farewell speech, he left the Jukola house contented. He refused the offer of a horse which was pressed upon him and set off on foot with his knotty cane in hand. Juhani followed him across the big barnyard and deftly opened the ramshackle old gate of Jukola for him. The lofty old peacemaker stood there for a minute longer, gazing up at the star-bright sky and talking to Juhani about wind and weather. At last he took his leave, and Juhani bowed deeply, scraping one foot along the ground so that sand and small pebbles spattered against the cowbarn wall. Then he returned to the happy room, saying to himself: "He has accomplished a great work." And toward the village, knotty cane in hand and broad-brimmed black hat on his head, the sexton walked smiling, with cheeks tinted a pretty rose color.

The clamor of joy and revelry rose in volume minute by minute until it became a thunderous rapture. Now the dancers flung themselves about in a quadrille, now in a dizzying polska, going almost without a pause, and the floor boomed and its broad beams bent under the young men's heels. The cheerful fire burned on and Mikko's fiddle kept up its merry wailing, while the roof echoed shrilly and the sooty rafters shook. From man to man and woman to woman the foaming brew and the steaming coffee punch went round, and in the coffee grounds, Kaisa Rajamäki read good fortune for the brothers until the very grave.

Thus they celebrated the brothers' homecoming, drinking a toast to concord from foaming tankards and not parting until the dawn.

CHAPTER XIV

Thus almost ten years had passed from the time the brothers had moved to the Impivaara wilderness, now transformed into a splendid farm. But soon the old Jukola was equally grand, if not grander, raised to that state by seven sturdy men. In the end their dear birthplace was divided into two: Old Jukola, their eternal mother, was governed by Juhani, and the other Jukola, which stood near the first, and was a fine house in its own right, was ruled by Aapo.

By general consent, Impivaara too was divided equally between Tuomas and Lauri. Of the tenant farms, Kekkuri was given to Timo and Vuohenkalma to Eero, to enjoy in perpetuity without fees of any kind. They all married, except for Simeoni, who sought neither wife nor land, but chose to live as a bachelor at Juhani's Jukola. It can be said of the brothers that they lived and built like worthy men, each in his place, and wanderers praised the hospitality of the Jukola and Impivaara farms, as well as that of Kekkuri and Vuohenkalma. Timo and Simeoni excepted, the brothers had forever forsworn inflammatory drink. Simeoni, though a decent man, occasionally slid onto the dizzying path of intoxication, and Timo as well, although less often, perhaps once or twice a year.

When Juryman Mäkelä died, who stepped into his place? Aapo Jukola, a man always on the side of concord and justice. When the old bailiff passed away, who was elevated to that honor? Eero, Juhani's son, of Vuohenkalma, a clever man who could read and write, and who even had a newspaper come speeding his way from Turku once a week. Juhani took Venla as his wife and spent happy days with her, although in truth a bit of grumbling was heard in the house now and then. For Venla, though a good homemaker, was just the tiniest bit mouthy and quarrelsome. Often she railed and scolded at her husband by the hour, "that lout, that mophead, that owl" as she was in the habit of calling him.

But Juhani could lose his temper too, and then he roared out roughly, telling the "old bag" to shut up this minute because God had given her a weaker brain than a man's. Thus would he lay down the law, hammering his fist on the table and roaring like thunder. In the end, Venla pretended to be a little frightened and quieted down, but laughed secretly by the fireplace with her mischievous maid, while Juhani yammered away on the bench by the table, often grumbling at God for having firmly assigned and granted him such an impudent and quarrelsome wife. But once a real row broke out because of Aapeli Karkkula, who was sitting on the side bench at Jukola, a little tipsy, when she and Juhani were squabbling. The fool made the mistake of meddling in a quarrel between husband and wife, heatedly siding with Juhani, who in a fit of temper had called his wife a "bird-brain." Stupid Aapeli, thinking it the thing to do, topped him by calling her "bubble-headed idiot, town pauper, and shanty brat." Juhani's eyes popped wide open, he leaped up like a fearsome bear, and he rushed at the dumfounded Aapeli, who scooted out like a rabbit with Juhani hot on his heels.

The door slammed, footsteps thundered on the porch, and the dogs, tails between their legs and yelping wildly, fled to one side and watched furtively as the men dashed madly around the rocky yard. Aapeli, bellowing frantically, raced ahead, while the raging Juhani galloped after him. From the big room of the house, the happy laughter of Venla and the maid pealed forth. But Juhani could not catch Aapeli and reentered the house from the porch, berating himself and promising to teach that uppity Karkkula calf a lesson some day. Once inside, he slammed his fist on the table and said, "You can abuse me, but leave my wife alone. You won't find her match in the whole kingdom of Sweden." Thus he boasted, and in truth, he could find no fault with her housekeeping, although she did treat herself somewhat lavishly to coffee, at which Juhani was often heard to grumble, but his wife paid small heed and let the plump pot bubble away. And Juhani was always willing to take a steaming cup from his wife's chubby hand. Whenever he went to town, he always remembered to buy a package of coffee and a sizable chunk of sugar.

Venla presented her husband with fine, vigorous heirs, but in the beginning things did not go exactly as Juhani wished. The first fruit of his love was a girl with impish eyes, but Juhani was annoyed that he had not been granted a bouncing boy. Yet he hoped for a different result the next time. A little more than a year passed, and Venla gave birth, but to another girl. The mother-in-law, smiling sweetly, brought the infant wrapped in white swaddling clothes to show her to the sober-faced father. Believing his hopes already fulfilled, Juhani was delighted and asked; "Boy or girl?" "Look for yourself, my son-in-law," the old woman answered. He looked and shouted forthwith: "Take your brat to hell!" Left alone, he added after a time: "God bless my brat anyway."

Another year went by, then a second, and Venla gave birth to a boy, a real chunk like his father. There was joy and rejoicing in the Jukola house, and even Venla seemed dearer to Juhani than before. And now the women set about choosing a name for him. One wanted to call him Franz, another Florentine, a third Erik Translatus, but Venla's preference was Emmanuel. Then Juhani himself stepped forward to the side of Venla's bed, pointed a finger and said, "No, my Venla, no. His name is Juhannes." And so the child was christened with his father's name. The father was very fond of him, sometimes calling him "chick-a-dee" and sometimes "crow chick."

Juhani's home life was mostly warm sunshine with intervals of wind and storm. When the clouds did gather, they soon departed and sunny weather returned. But his fortunes were not as propitious with regard to his townsmen and neighbors. Quarrels often broke out between them, bitter disputes over one thing or another, boundary fences or fence-jumping horses, pigs running loose and so on. Juhani was all too eager to settle disputes with his fists, and so any opponent's face and hair were in constant peril. A heated court battle was often imminent, but then Aapo, the staid juryman, would always hasten to intervene and settle the case with his conciliatory tongue. Nor was Juhani slow to make peace, especially when he saw that he was wrong. He was also industrious when it came to the farm's outdoor work and chores. Hired hands could never complain about his work in the fields or when handling a thundering timber in the woods.

Once when the hay was drying in Vehkala meadow, which was deep in a gloomy spruce woods, Juhani showed his dreadful side to both man and God. The whole broad hayfield had been raked into windrows and the haying crew was gathered merrily around the hay-barn to enjoy their lunch. But the master looked in terror at the fiery red clouds that sailed menacingly across the sky. In back of the hay barn was the stump of a birch tree; at its root, unobserved by anyone, Juhani dropped to his knees and begged that God would spare his sweet and succulent hay from the rain. He prayed in silence, but hardly had the haying crew finished eating when a thunder-cloud rushed out from in back of the spruce tops. Flashing and roaring, it poured down a wild deluge of rain. The hay was soaked in an instant, before a single stack could be built. Rakes in hand, the workers hurried back from the field to the shelter of the barn, but Juhani stayed outside in the lightning and rain, his face black with rage, cursing horribly. He stood there as the heavens roared, beating his right fist into the palm of his left hand and cursing wildly. Each time the word "perkele" rattled through his gritted teeth, he would rock forward a foot. Looking upward, he howled at the top of his lungs, "What business does heaven have on my hayfields with its manure carts?" His wife Venla cried out reproachfully from the haybarn, "What awful things you're saying, you sack of sins!"

But the man paid no attention, and shouted still more vehemently at the dark, gloomy clouds, "I ask you, why is heaven hauling manure just when I'm making hay?" When they heard his wild talk, the women and girls in the barn clasped their hands tightly and prayed devoutly for the man. As the lightning flashed, they sobbed a devout blessing on deeply bended knee. Pretty, mild-eyed children hid their faces, one in a mother's bosom, another in her skirts. Many of the little ones thought Judgment Day had come, for earth and heaven were bathed in fire as lightning flashed and crackled and thunder roared far and wide, while rain poured down and the woods moaned sorrowfully. Noticing the women's actions, Juhani raised the volume of his curses, but the women too redoubled the sound of their prayers.

In the barn with the others was the Seunala girl, shy young Anna, whose eyes shone like twin stars under her pale, translucent brow. It was said she often saw strange visions; in a trance her spirit traveled to the bright realms of the blessed and the dark abysses of the doomed, and of these she spoke wonders. She had often foretold deadly destruction for the children of man: war, famine, plague, and finally the end of the world. Always a sober, silent, and gentle girl, she suddenly rushed out to the meadow where Juhani was cursing, dropped to her knees on the ground, heedless of the pouring rain and the jagged flashes of lightrung, and prayed in a voice almost loud enough to be a scream.

She prayed that God would pity the blind, wretched man and not strike him with the fiery hammer of His wrath. Thus she prayed, looking skyward, a wondrous fire in her eyes and heaven's flickering light on her brow. And lo! Juhani fell silent, although he glared angrily aside at the maiden. Finally, feeling that she had gone on for too long, he took the praying girl by the arm and led her back into the barn, saying: "Go in, you poor thing, go in and stop getting wet for nothing. I don't need anyone praying for me." The girl went in, but dropped down at once onto the hay, her clear voice still ringing out in prayer, while the women near her shed scalding tears. Juhani stood outside

302 Aleksis Kivi: Seven Brothers

leaning against the wall with a look of apparent repentance on his face, but his breast was still heaving with rage.

Soon the rain and thunder moved on, and in the following day's blazing sunshine, the hay was gathered in Vehkala meadow. But the master of the house was absent. Where was he? The voice of the Seunala girl had continued to echo in his ears, giving him no rest. Early in the morning he went, downcast and repentant, and confessed cursing God and heaven to the provost. At first the provost berated him sternly, but soon switched to words of consolation, and Juhani returned home with his mind at rest. After that incident on gloomy Vehkala meadow, a settled change could be noted in Juhani's disposition and behavior. A brimless round cap appeared on his head; he wore his coat with the collar turned up, and had its length altered, leaving only short tails like those worn by the "born again" folk to be found here and there in Finland. He went around dressed in that fashion and appeared in church more often than before. He always sat in his assigned place beside the sober master of Härkämäki with a dead serious look on his face, now and then clearing his throat like his companion. The storms both in the Jukola home and abroad in the fields became less and less frequent, and finally the day of brother Juhani's life drew toward its evening in almost total peace.

Simeoni lived unwed in Juhani's house, enjoying its food and drink and working ceaselessly at the household chores from early morning till late at night. He was sparing and tight-fisted by nature, increasingly so as the years went by. With a miserly eye, he watched over the activities of both men and women on the farm. It was his mouth that uttered the phrase which still lives in laughter on the lips of Jukola and Toukola folk.

One day when he was chipping out a breadboard for Venla with a small hatchet, as the people were eating from a heaping bowl of pork stew before them, he reminded the whole group: "When you put just a tiny bit of pork stew on the bread, it makes the whole thing taste so good." At the words, both men and women burst out laughing, and Juhani himself, after a short laugh, saw fit to scold his brother a bit for his excessive miserliness. But Simeoni replied: "I'm just urging moderation on you, warning you not to make a god of your belly, which is a sin, a deadly sin. And who is unnaturally tight-fisted? Not me, but that Kalle Kuninkala, who was consumptive. When he knew for sure that he was dying, he went to make the liquor for his own funeral. He knew that he was the best man at it in all Toukola; he used only the tiniest bit of grain but got plenty of the sparkling brew from it. And so it was. The poor wretch sat beside the still in the sauna dressing room glassy-eyed and needle-nosed, coughing and gagging. There he sat and they carried away drink from there by the kettleful. At last he too dragged himself away, dragged himself up the steps into the porch, from the porch into the house, laid his frame full-length on the bed, and in a few hours the lad was cold. That, my good man, was miserliness, miserliness that did not loose its grasp even on the brink of the grave. That we can call unnatural tight-fistedness." Thus Simeoni defended himself refusing to submit to being called a miser.

Simeoni was constantly in the good graces of master and mistress, for he was a faithful and dependable caretaker on the farm. They could stay away from home without a worry, knowing that Simeoni was in charge.

One dim evening during the Christmas season, Juhani and his wife went with their younger children to visit both Tuomas and Lauri at Impivaara, leaving Simeoni in charge of the house again. The sledding was good and the party went smoothly and swiftly through the woods beneath the bright sky. Plump, sober little "chick-a-dee" sat on Juhani's knee, while the youngest child, a pretty and spritely girl, lay in Venla's sturdy arms, wrapped in a fine woolen shawl. She was enjoying her mother's teat under the warm cover as the sleigh sped clattering over the snowy meadows on the way to Impivaara.

Night came, the male and female help at Jukola hurried off to the revels at Toukola, and Simeoni alone ruled the roost. Two of the children were forced to remain under his yoke, the two older daughters of the house, one of them nine and the other a child of seven. They had not been allowed to go visiting with their father, nor did Simeoni let them go to the revels with the others, which made them furious. But that did not matter to Simeoni, who had decided to use his power just as he pleased.

It was now completely dark, but the usual evening fire was not blazing on the hearth. The children began to complain and to nag at their uncle for light and a fire. But he ignored their demands and lay as usual on the hearthstone with his hair hanging down over its edge. He lay there reasoning with the girls. "Oh yes, there'd be plenty of fires if you had your way. Hey, this isn't the Vantaa foundry. You airheads, you have to learn that wood is costly stuff. Tell me what we'll burn after all the woods are cut down. Club moss? Well, that's how things will go here, if everyone doesn't look ahead in time. My sinful husk of a body can do with less, and so can you, you idle, rascally kids. Get under the covers; it's warm enough there. Indeed, if you had your way..."

Thus he spoke, but the children, who were clever little scamps, were not used to giving in to their uncle. They sassed and snapped at him, arguing vehemently, mocking, now and then showing rows of white teeth in their anger. When that was no help, they had the nerve to yank at his wretched hair, which hung down from the stone, and were able to give it a lusty pull before the poor man could get up from the stone. Managing to rise at last, he snatched up a sooty limb from the corner, banged it on the floor, and threatened to knock the feet out from under them. Then the scamps darted out of the house and the birch door slammed shut after the little fugitives as they dashed off.

But soon they were bold enough to come back in and demand their supper. Simeoni let them fuss and fume for a long time, and finally got up, took a splint from the rafters, split it in two, and lighted the splinter for a torch. By its light, he ladled out gruel from a pot for the girls, but by no means lavishly, a mere two or three scoops. Then he carried the bowl to a high chair and called the children to come and eat, but he covered the pot with the lid from kneading trough, weighting it down with the chopping block from the corner. The children were dissatisfied with their portions and demanded more, asking at least for bread. Clever little Venla's crying rang out clearly. Simeoni bit off a piece the size of a man's thumb from a loaf of bread and offered it to the girls, but in view of its size she would not take it. Instead, she struck out angrily, sending the piece of bread flying far out of Simeoni's hand. The man lost his temper, pursed his lips, and pinched the girl's neck hair between his thumb and finger, saying, "You slut! Are you mocking God's precious gift? Is that the way it is? Well, if you had your way..."

The girl began to cry more bitterly, but Simeoni paid no attention to her and went to light the evening fire in the fireplace. From a few wretched, charred pieces of wood, he nursed a pitiful flame, meanwhile scolding, "Just keep your mouth shut, or I'll get the switch from the corner and give you a good thrashing. The little devil knocked God's gift out of my hand and into the corner. Well then, go without bread and spoon the gruel nicely into your belly like your older sister there. It's plenty of supper for two girls. We can't afford to live and eat like the rich in our house. Just keep your mouth shut, you no-account. If you had your way..." So he spoke while he sat on the stone and built up his poorly burning fire, not noticing that the little scamp, spoon in hand was angrily showing her teeth at him and moving her little jaw in time with his words.

This time, however, the girl's tears and angry words were of no avail, and the children had to be content with the portion their uncle had given them. At last, an overpowering drowsiness sent the girls to bed, and they soon slept soundly beneath the warm sheepskin cover. But Simeoni's fire made the room more cold than warm, nor did he wait for the brands to burn out. Thinking it right to conserve put out the sad and dim evening fire, slamming the damper shut and ignoring the stinging smoke that drifted into the room from the open fireplace. He relighted the splinter of wood and ate his supper from an oaken bowl — a moldy piece of bread and the dried heads of six herring.

With eyes that burned intensely, the dogs watched him eat, following the path of his hand from bowl to mouth and mouth to bowl, but not one crumb from Simeoni's fist was left over for them. Having eaten, he clasped his hands, dropped to his knees before the fireplace, and shedding scalding tears, he thanked the Lord, son of David, who out of pure mercy had always fed him, who was but a sack of sins. After rising, he opened the door and began to shoo out the dogs "to guard the house from robbers." Those were his words, although no robbery had occurred at Jukola within the memory of man. A stormy winter wind was blowing, and the dogs, reluctant to leave the rustling straw of the room, raised a fuss which ended badly for them. Whining, their tails between their legs, they finally ran out to escape Simeoni's weapon, the sooty birch limb.

This done, he carefully bolted the heavy porch door, holding the flaring torch clenched between his teeth. Back in he went, and raising the torch to his left, he glanced at the girls sleeping cheek-to-cheek and sweetly dreaming beneath the soft covers on their bed, as pink as two fresh roses of summer. He looked at them with a smile on his face and tucked the fleecy edge of the cover more closely around Venla's neck. As he turned again toward the hearthstone, he said in simpering baby-talk: "Of course you can sleep in peace with your bellies so full of gruel." So he spoke, and decided to lie down himself to rest for the night. But once more he dropped to his knees, clasped his hands tightly, and shedding scalding tears, he thanked the Lord, son of David, for all the good he had enjoyed, and prayed that His hand would guard the house through the coming night. He prayed for himself, for the little ones in the bed, and for all people on earth. Then he lay down on his beloved hearthstone and fell asleep at last, with the coals on the hearth gently warming the soles of his feet.

But the house was cold, dreary and cold, for the maids and hired hands to sleep in when they returned at midnight from the games in Toukola. Next morning they grumbled sullenly at Simeoni, and when the master and mistress of the house returned from their visit, both maids and children accused him angrily. But it didn't bother Simeoni, who sat whittling by the chopping block — he merely remarked in an offhand tone of voice: "We just can't afford to live like the rich in this house."

Thus lived Simeoni in his former home, old Jukola, working diligently and always on guard, keeping a sharp eye on the management of the farm, both indoors and out in the fields. But there were times when he had not a care in the world. He would come back from the village completely drunk and happy, ranting loudly as he paced back and forth across the floor, an object of fun and a laughingstock to both young and old in the house. But the next day he would be deathly ill both in body and soul. Groaning, hands clasped, he would lie on the sooty hearthstone with a terrible feeling of remorse eating at his heart. But one occurrence did reduce the number of drunken spells and the long days of remorse. Juhani placed in his hands a costly gift from town: a huge, stiffly-bound Bible that weighed almost twenty pounds. Great was Simeoni's joy and delight, and he never stopped praising and thanking his brother for the good deed. From that time on, he left the tempting glass almost completely alone.

Now on Sunday and holiday afternoons, he was always to be seen sitting with the Bible and studying the Word, so he was not as much exposed to the mind-altering drink. But then it happened on a Halloween evening. In a cheerful drunken daze, the man bellowed, paced, and wheeled about, then finally fell into a sweet sleep on his stone, but next morning he again felt the pangs of bitter remorse in his heart. What did he do then? Standing at the head of the table, the Bible open before him, in a loud preacher's voice, he called everyone in the household, young and old together, placed two fingers on the Bible, and glaring up at the sky, he swore a sacred vow that he would never again touch a drop of drink, not one single drop, as long as he lived.

One year passed, then another, and yet a third, and Simeoni still stood firm in his vow. But once again he succumbed to his besetting sin, and his lapse was the cause of a terrible disturbance in the household. The poor man now viewed himself as a betrayer, a soulless worm who had broken a vow made with "two fingers on the Bible." For that reason, he sought to end his miserable days. Hastily, but with a firm tread and a mind as cold as ice, he left the house, climbed up on a beam in the stable, knotted the rope from the old dappled mare's blanket around his neck, and tied the other end of it to the highest rafter on the roof. Thus he made ready to hang peacefully, to sleep the sleep of death. Now his eyes stared stiffly, his cheeks puffed out suddenly, and his hands clenched tightly into fists. But the measure of his life was not yet full.

The old mother-in-law of the house went to check her hen's nest in the stable loft, saw the man on the rope, and let the house know it by her screaming and shrieking. Juhani rushed to the trouble spot and rescued his brother from the jaws of death. With a single stroke he cut the rope and weeping and wailing and wondering aloud, he carried his brother into the house. Around them flocked the women, weeping, crying out, and beating their hands together. Juhani carried his brother into the bedroom and laid him on Venla's high-piled ryijy rug. He soon came to and sat on the edge of the bed sighing mournfully and staring down at the floor without saying a word. Juhani, the stub of a pipe in his teeth belching smoke, hurried grieving to Aapo's side to tell his brother the strange thing that had happened and to ask his advice about Simeoni. His own opinion was that a moderate beating administered in secret by the brothers, followed by a sound cursing-out in God's name would be best for the man. Aapo considered the punishment useless and hurtful and decided to use only the power of words on Simeoni. After he too had lighted his stubby pipe, the two brothers set off across the field from Aapo-Jukola to Juhani-Jukola to talk sense to Simeoni, the son of sorrow.

Aapo greeted Simeoni with an affectionate handshake, and having filled his pipe, began with sober mien and voice to speak grave words of reprimand, soon followed by words of consolation. Simeoni listened mutely for a long time, staring in misery at the floor. But Aapo, perpetually relighting his pipe, gesturing with his hands, and gazing out the window at the horizon with melting eyes, kept waxing more and more eloquent. His words fell from his mouth like a gleaming cascade of gold. Now bitter-sweet puckers appeared around Simeoni's lips and tear-laden sobs burst from his throat. Juhani's chin now quivered and twisted, and soon he too whimpered and dissolved into tears. Even Aapo's eyes gleamed with moisture.

Thus was Simeoni's heart turned toward life and hope again. His face shining with that hope, he crushed his brother Aapo's hand in parting, thanked God for once more showing him mercy, and gradually took up his usual chores in the Jukola household. Thus virtuous Simeoni, — never touching another drop, spent his placid days, now whittling on the end of a log, now chopping fir branches in the fragrant yard, now sitting at the Bible studying the Word of God.

Aapo was the master of the other part of Jukola, now known as Aapo-Jukola. His house stood a few hundred paces from the mother-home. He took Hinrikka Kuokkala as his wife, a pretty woman, pleasing in every respect, a busy housewife and a gentle soul. Aapo too was pleased with her, but thought it best to keep giving her tips and reminders about how a household should be run. This he did in a proper schoolmasterly manner and tone of voice. His wife listened either without saying a word or laughing a guileless, happy laugh, her eyes crinkling at the corners. Master Aapo often saw fit to counsel the maids and little serving girls too whenever their performance of duties and chores failed to please him. Once the oldest maid was given a curt lesson in how to sweep the floor by the master. For Aapo, in whose opinion the girl did too slapdash a job of sweeping, leaving dust piled in the corners, suddenly lost his temper, snatched the broom from the girl and with a deft hand began anew to sweep the room from the rear wall toward the door. When he reached the center, he put the broom into the poor girl's fist again and said,"Now that's how a good girl sweeps a floor." Then the mistress, who had watched from near the fireplace as Aapo, broom in hand, fussed at the girl, laughed her guileless, melting laugh, her eyes crinkling at the corners as she leaned over with her palms on her knees. That caused Aapo, when he had left the maid, to turn a stern look of rebuke in her direction. But in any event, he always observed justice and moderation both with his maids and his hired hands, for which he received commendation from all sides. He also practiced the art of healing, which he had learned by diligent study from an old textbook on medicine. He often succeeded with his medications, many of which he concocted on his own from herbs; and his cures for erysipelas, diarrhea, fainting spells, the mumps and scabies were especially well known. As a masseur, he was without peer; many a man had found relief at his hands. He often cured stomach cramps and spasms by skillful massage alone, and since pain observes no regulations or taboos, more than once a woman found herself forced to lie down to be stroked by Aapo's palms when her stomachs churned and burned ceaselessly.

There was a woman, wife of the old rag-man Matti Tervakoski, who suffered from a recurrent nightmare. It plagued her in a most exhausting way for weeks on end. During spells when it stayed away, she believed herself free of the nightly affliction, but it would recur suddenly, and she was once more forced to live with her tormentor. She had gone to many a doctor and witch-healer, but always in vain. At last the fame of Aapo Jukola's great art and power of curing illness reached her ears, and once more she set off to seek help. A bundle on one arm and the sock she was knitting in her hands, she made the long and difficult journey to Jukola, and there she was cured forever by Aapo's ministrations.

Aapo was born to be a juryman. He would sit on the courtroom bench, often with a hand cupped behind one ear, listening closely to developments in a case. There he sat, manfully erect, and now and then a smile of self-satisfaction flickered across his lips. His verdicts were always wise, impartial, and just. Even the judge was aware of that fact, and always listened patiently to his rather long speeches as, with outspread hands, he explicated his opinions.

Thus he dwelt peacefully in his home, an able master and a good father to his frisky children.

The first part of Impivaara to be cleared was ruled by strong, broad-shouldered Tuomas as his domain. Who was man enough to swell his chest before the master of Impivaara? Great was his strength, and his whole being breathed an air of self-assurance and power. There was no fuss and ado in his work and in his management of the farm, yet he upheld discipline and the Lord's precepts both indoors and out in the fields. He was the most generous of all the brothers and treated suffering victims of ill fortune mildly and benevolently. He did not inquire and probe into the root and source of misery seeking help, nor did he censure the man who was himself to blame for the beggar's staff he held in his hand. He gave to all without distinction, considering them equally unfortunate. Above all, he was indulgent to little wandering beggar girls who trod the pauper's path shy-eyed and hearts quaking in fear. He had taken two such wanderers into his own care, and they were fostered and cherished as fondly in his home as his own little ones, of whom there was no lack, lively boys one and all.

He was married to the only daughter of Härkämäki, a noble and grave woman, worthy to have the hero of Impivaara as her spouse. The woman was stately in form and inner being, at once brisk, sober, and calm. Her bosom swelled proudly, and her thick flaxen braid swung prettily on her sturdy shoulders under a white and red checkered kerchief. Perpetual peace dwelt on her brow and a stern and sincere fear of God lived in her heart. Such was the mistress of Impivaara, a proper woman to rear the little ones of the house, both her own and the adopted ones. Often her eyes, sublime and tender, rested dreamily on the sweet girl, a shelterless orphan who had wound up in their home. Thus Tuomas's days moved on in peace toward the calm harbor of the grave. Man's life here is often compared to a stream, but I would compare Tuomas's life from his becoming master of Impivaara until his death to a broad river which flows calmly and majestically to the infinite and everlasting sea.

On a heath at a distance of two or three rifle shots to the east was Lauri's newly cleared farm, the other half of Impivaara, also known as Laurila. There the quiet man lived, busily tilling his land, working hard in the fields, but happier in the woods and swamps.

He had wedded a wife from Kuokkala farm, one of a pair of twin girls. Lauri married the one, and the other became Timo's wife and the mistress of the Kekkuri tenant farm. Lauri's wife was quite a woman, broad-bosomed and somewhat stocky. Her shrill voice rang far off like the sound of a sharp clarinet, especially when she stormed at her husband in a fit of rage, her dark brown eyes flashing fire.

But Lauri would sit whittling in silence, unconcerned, as his wife raged on like a whirlwind. And that was a torment that made her fume all the more. But from time to time the man reached the limit of his patience, and then it was best to back off. His wife would suddenly fall silent, run out as fast as she could, and hide in sheltering nooks and crannies of the cowbarn. There she would lurk for awhile, now and then peeking out to see what had become of the row she herself had instigated. She would linger there until the man's angry mind had settled down.

But placid Lauri was seldom angry, for often when his wife stormed and railed, her husband would leave for the woods, pipe in his teeth and worn ax under his arm to hunt for carving wood, birch bark for shoes, and buns on trees. Gladly he tarried on these expeditions seeking, studying, and calculating. And only when the sun had long since set and everything had gone to rest, would he walk home in the mild summer twilight, carrying a huge bunch of roots, warped pieces of wood, and birch bark on his shoulders. Often on the way home he would meet the powerful bull, thick-necked Hälli, coming toward him along the sandy road in the evening mist. The animal was hot on his way to the village with fire in his eyes.

Then force met force, and Lauri, bellowing harshly and shaking his ax handle, would finally force the stubborn animal to turn back. And so they marched toward Laurila, Hälli in the lead and the master following. Hälli would try to turn right and Lauri immediately waved the ax handle to the right; Hälli would turn left, and Lauri's ax handle threatened him from that direction. And so the bull found it best to travel toward home, yet he kept tossing his head angrily and blowing out hot blasts of rage through his nostrils. At length they went by Tuomas's house, where the maid heard the tramping, the thump and scraping of feet on the sandy road. "Who's out there so late at night?" she wondered, getting up in her nightshirt. Befuddled with sleep, she stepped to the window, peered out, and saw the neighbor's bull and its master in tandem walking gravely and soberly along the road. Ahead went the balky bull, with the master on its heels, now and then shaking the ax handle, and carrying a neat, round bundle of wood for carving and birchbark for shoes on his shoulder. At last they disappeared from the maid's view, but now the bull opened its snout and loosed an awful, shrieking song from its throat. The heath resounded and the sky echoed.

Then Lauri said: "I'm going to give it to you now. Are you acting up? Ahaa, you scoundrel, go home nicely now. None of your slippery tricks, none of Kaura-Matti's hooks and crooks will do you any good. You know that." Thus he spoke as he strode on after the bull, which snorted a proud and fearful march, the sound of which carried to distant villages through the still night.

But Lauri shut up Hälli securely inside a fence to keep company with his own farm's cattle and stepped into the house where a cold supper awaited him on the table. Everyone in the house was sweetly sleeping; only the mistress lay sleepless in bed angrily awaiting her husband. After Lauri had eaten, he finally entered the bedroom, to be met by an angry squall. It was his wife, ranting and jabbering furiously at him from her bed, crackling like fire in dry juniper, fuming about that "damned lout's tramping around in the wild woods."

Wordlessly her husband undressed, lighted his pipe, and at last lay down beside his wife, who continued to rail and scold. When his pipe had burned itself out, Lauri set it down carefully near the bed, tugged the covers up a little higher, and then said firmly: "Be quiet now, ask a blessing, and sleep in God's name while the good weather holds. Remember now, while the good weather holds." With that, his shrewish wife would hold her tongue, although her heart rebelled in her bosom. Angrily, she jerked the covers over to her side and finally slept, as did the man by her side.

So would Lauri linger well into the dark night on his happy trips to the woods. What he saw that was worthy of note, wonder, and contemplation, he seldom said a word about during the course of the week. Only on the following Sunday morning, usually while they ate, would he tell his hired hands about one thing or another.

Once when he returned from the woods, his mind was deeper than ever in meditation and thought, but no one could guess what he was mulling over so fixedly. Silent and more surly with each passing day, he moved about the yard, snapping sharply at his wife and men, something he had seldom done before. A cloud of profound and disturbing meditation constantly covered his brow, casting a deep shadow over his eyes. For one long week he remained in this state. At length Sunday came; Lauri and his men sat at the table in complete silence.

Finally the master opened his mouth and asked his companions: "Men, I want to ask you something; explain this to me. Five days ago, when I was crossing the smooth rise of Koivisto meadow over a fresh, light snow on the ground, like the thin cotton blanket we have now, I saw some marks that my brains can't figure out. Damn it! Night and day my mind has been threshing out the matter, this way and that, along a thousand byways. But listen. I saw some tracks in the field, a man's tracks, which I followed slowly.

"But suddenly the tracks ended, and fox tracks began, clear fox tracks, which continued up the rise and down into the woods. There hadn't been a one, not a single one, up to that point. Where had the man disappeared? He had gone neither left nor right, forward nor back — no, he had stepped straight up into the sky and the fox had stepped down from it to continue his tracks in the snow. Or had the man carried the fox in his arms, and there where his trail ended, mounted the bushy tail and ridden through the grove to the village road? Such tricks are impossible, but I can't think of anything more probable to figure the thing out. What do you think, men? Are there still wizards in our parish? Did the man change himself into a fox through the power of the devil?" So he spoke, and the people were greatly amazed, nor could any of them solve the puzzle, but all concluded that wizards had been at work on Koivisto Hill.

But Lauri's heart could not rest; after eating he set out for Koivisto meadow. Arriving at its smooth slope, he saw that the same phenomenon had been repeated: the change from man to fox tracks in the fresh snow. He flew into a rage and said angrily: "Is the devil himself frisking around here?" He screamed the words through gritted teeth and kicked at a mound of manure that showed under the snow. Bright metal flashed forth from it, particles of manure and chopped straw flew high in the air, and the stinging jaws of a fierce fox trap clamped the man's ankle in a crushing grip. Lauri's eyes flew open wide and he bent down quickly to loosen the stubborn device from his smarting, swelling ankle.

Shouting curses, he flung the trap far away on the ground. Now he had discovered what trap had been set in his field, but he still did not understand the strange transformation of the tracks in the snow. Angrily he started off for home, limping badly and gritting his teeth when he stepped on the foot caught by the trap. Soon recognizing that he needed support in walking, he began looking for a stick in the grove near the village road. He saw two birch poles in a thicket and when he pulled them out, he discovered that they were a pair of stilts, with a very natural looking fox paw whittled at the base of either one.

Then his face brightened up and everything became clear to him. Now he knew that the fox trapper, in order to hide all cause for suspicion from the fox's eyes had always approached his traps on this type of stilts when he checked them. With this trick, he left a fox's and not a man's tracks behind him, which the clever Reynard of the hills would certainly have avoided. So the matter was clear to Lauri, and he moved off with a lighter heart, although his shin was aching and as stiff as a cane.

It happened that crabby old Kolistin, checking the squirrel snares he used to set between stakes along the fences of fields and meadows noticed Lauri's tracks and was highly perplexed. "A man and a dog have been through — here, but what am I to think of this freak — a one-legged dog! What the devil! A one-legged dog has trotted along beside his master over this stump-filled meadow of God's. What the devil should I think of this trick? Are wizards and Laplanders running loose? Huh?" Thus he pondered as he stood in the meadow, clutching at his coarse black hair and nibbling at the wad of tobacco between his front teeth, his gray eyebrows drooping in a fierce frown. Finally he started off again without understanding the apparition in the meadow, a one-legged dog hopping along beside its master. He puzzled over the matter for a long time without saying a word to anyone, until on his deathbed he asked his loving daughter-in-law what she thought of the happening, which gave him no rest even in the jaws of death. With tears in her eyes, the woman spoke directly into his ear, begging him to clear his mind of all such thoughts and to remember only his immortal soul. The old man said not a word in reply but kept staring straight ahead and took the weird puzzle of the meadow unsolved to the grave with him.

Soon the bite of the trap's jaw on Lauri's foot was healed, and he worked as before on his farm, now in the woods and now in the big main room. Thus he lived with his spirited wife and his children, who never lacked shirt, sock, daily bread, nor whip, as long as they were in their mother's care.

Timo ruled the Kekkuri tenant farm, and his wife was the other Kuokkala twin. She was a match for her sister both in her outward form and inner character: a strongchested, pug-nosed, brown-skinned block of a woman. She was said, however, to have a softer heart than her sister, his brother Lauri's wife. She was very dear to Timo, although sometimes his hair suffered a sharp tugging in her hefty paw, for it was not a good idea to try to lord it over her. Timo always did his best to oblige her, and generally the household ran smoothly. But there was one thing that disturbed the domestic peace from time to time. It was a deeply-rooted habit of Timo's to drink himself groggy once a year, usually around Halloween, and to spend a day or two in cheerful company. But that brought on a ruckus when he finally thought it best to return home again.

One Sunday at the end of October, the man went a little astray and joined Kyösti Tammisto and Aapeli Karkkala in a merry binge. In the cool attic at Tammisto, they tilted a gleaming black bottle, sang, and hugged each other like dearest friends. Thus they passed two days and nights, whooping and singing and gazing carefree and bleary-eyed out through the window of the high and breezy room. They looked out over a yard splattered with manure and a cow-barn littered with straw, over a rocky hill, over fields and meadows all the way to far-off Lemmilä marsh, where swans soared circling here and there high up near the rim of the clouds on their migration to southern lands. Carefree, they looked out with dim goat's eyes, singing away and tossing their heads to and fro, heads which buzzed and popped merrily. Far away were the sorrows and griefs of ordinary, suffering mortals.

But the third day dawned at length and the friends woke up on their dismal bed with splitting headaches. Gone were both money and drink, and there was no trick left to get their wives to open a new bottle. Silent and sourfaced, Timo decided to head for home; down the lane he shuffled, sadly he climbed the hill, thinking of Kekkuri's hot-tempered mistress. His coarse broadcloth pants drooped miserably, his shirttails hung out loosely between pants and red-striped vest, and his bloodshot eyes stared through little slits in his face as he walked toward Kekkuri. His hair was tangled in a thousand knots and his bared breast shone like the scoured side of a copper kettle. On he strode, sad of heart; and woods, hills, and valleys looked on angrily. The yellowed birch voiced a strong accusation, and so did the gloomy spruce. A pine stump stood by the road like a nasty black troll. All nature, once so dear, now turned a cruel stepmother's face on him. But at the moment his eyes were not on trees, rocks, and stumps, for he was looking ahead, thinking of Kekkuri's hot-tempered mistress. Whenever he met anyone on the road — young or old, man or woman — he could barely bring himself to cast a sullen glance their way, and hardly would he have done more on this journey if the Grand Duke of Finland had met him on the rocky path. Silent, thinking foggily of his home and wife, his hired help and children, he walked on, and now and then a sudden but subdued sigh burst from his bosom.

Finally he reached the yard of his home and stopped to think whether he dared enter the house, whether there was any way under the sun to mollify his outraged wife to some small degree. For a long time he stood there rubbing his head, looking this way and that. At last he noticed a pile of wood in the woodshed, and a thought flashed into his mind: "Now I've found a way," he said to himself. He began loading blocks from the pile onto one arm, and when he had a gigantic load in his lap, he went stumbling toward the house, expecting to pacify his hard-hearted wife with this ruse. Dragging his feet noisily, he mounted the stairs, entered the porch, and shouted innocently, "Open the door, you kids in there, boy or girl, open the door." Finally a boy, little milk-mustached Jooseppi, came and opened the door, and in stepped Timo with his load, not saying a word and staring unblinkingly straight ahead. And when he had dropped the load of wood into the corner with a crash, he said: "Looks like the wood pile is almost down to nothing, but there are plenty of trees on Jukola." Having said this, he ventured a quick glance at his wife, and saw a thundercloud that threatened vengeance glaring back at him.

A tense moment was at hand. His wife had time only to scream, "Where have you been, you devil?" before landing two slaps on Timo's cheeks, two bitterly stinging slaps, one left and one right. The ringing sound was succeeded by an awful silence during which Timo's hair suffered violent abuse, and the world swam before his eyes. But he finally flared up, seized his wife's arms in his own thick paws, sat her down neatly on a bench, and held her there easily for a time. His hair a tousled mess and his face as red as fire, Timo scolded the raging woman in these terms: "Watch out now, or I might let you have it good and proper, you slut, you daughter of a jackass. You think you can go on abusing me like this? Ahaa, you're badly mistaken. There's mighty few can lay a hand on my hair, not just any old woman. And sorry to say, I've got the kind of temper you hear and see so much of nowadays."

Thus he threatened but without carrying out his threat. Nor could he bring himself to do it, for he really loved his wife. She, however, screamed furiously: "Let go of me, damn you, let go of me right now!" Timo was in a terrible quandary: Should he let go of his wife or hold on to her longer? She screamed again, louder this time. Timo freed her hands, but his hair was immediately caught in the mill again. By now, he was really angry and decided to let his wife go to the devil. He tried to march grandly out of the house, but his exit was slow and circuitous, for his wife was on his neck like a small brown cuckoo hawk harassing a ruddy male wood grouse, whose feathers are left floating in the air. But not too much hampered, Timo made his way out, nor did his wife let go of his hair until they reached the threshold, where she still threatened to teach him another lesson. Down the steps marched Timo gravely, saying as he went: "I know a way to teach these old women." Off he went, disappeared behind the hop garden, but with a sly grin, he doubled back to the stable and climbed up into the loft. There he shoved down a couple of bunches of hay to the horses in the stalls, lay down on a soft rustling bed, and having thought briefly of his wife's hot-headedness, he fell into a deep sleep.

Night came, a freezing cold night, but there was no sign of Timo in the house. Finally his wife went to bed, her mind occupied by morbid thoughts of her husband: "Maybe he's hanged himself in his frenzy, or thrown himself into the bottomless depths of Nummi meadow's wellspring, or else he's fallen asleep in the woods and is freezing off his nose, claws, and paws, the poor thing." So she thought, and promptly burst into a bitter fit of weeping, lying there in bed without her dear husband. She sighed and sobbed there for an hour, then another, her ear waiting uneasily for the sound of footsteps on the porch. More and more of the night passed without the sound of a man's approaching footsteps.

At last she got up, dressed, lighted the many-studded lantern, and went out, intending to look for the lost man. But she did not go out alone into the dark night; she was very much afraid of trolls, spirits, and ghosts of all kinds. She was also terrified of their own sauna, where an old pauper had just died, white-bearded Iisakki Honkamäki. So she woke up her maid Taava to go with her. Taava rose, dressed, and followed her, snappish and angry, into the cold, gloomy night. First they searched the sauna, then the drying barn, but in vain. They came back into the yard again. Weeping, the wife went to the edge of the field and feverishly, persistently, began shouting her husband's name. The woods and the drying barn on the grassy plain echoed the sound. Finally the women heard an answer from the stable loft, a hoarse grumbling, and they rushed toward it. Lantern in hand, the wife hurried to the loft and found Timo, who rose befuddled by sleep from his rustling bed, staring owl-eyed at his wife like a bewildered old ram torn loose from wolves in a meadow. It will not turn for refuge to the man who has rescued it from the wolves' jaws, but suddenly, to everyone's surprise, it goes trotting off after the wolves. Now and then the stupid fool stops, paws the ground, and gapes wildly about. So did Timo, not recognizing his own wife immediately. Perhaps his brain was still a little clouded by drink.

Wife: What are you sitting here for? Come into the house, I tell you. There's no need for a human being like you to be torn by the claws of the cold. Come on in, Timo.

Timo: So who are you?

Wife: God help us! Are you so far gone that you don't know me any more? You see, you see how sin and the devil distract a poor soul here. Oh, oh!

Timo: What are you blubbering about now? Who are you, anyway?

Wife: Oh, oh, oh! Timo, Timo!

Timo: Huh?

Wife: Don't you know me any more? I'm Ulla, your wife.

Timo: Oh, yeah, that's right.

Wife: Come on in. Don't hang around this cold loft. Oh, you poor thing!

Timo: So what if a gentleman sleeps in a hayloft? Keep still. Don't talk like a child. This is a great place for a man.

Wife: Come on now. Take my hand and come down nicely.

Maid: You devil, you won't even let a maid get a decent night's sleep, but she has to go poking around in every corner looking for you, you drunken pig.

Wife: Come on now. Take my hand and come down nicely.

Maid: Give him your hand yet. I would drag him out to the yard by the leg.

Timo: What's Taava so worked up about? Shut up, girl! There's not a pittance or peppercorn of worry for any of us here.

Maid: I'd peppercorn him if I was that black sheep with the loose bowels.

Wife: Shut up now and hold the lantern. Can't you get down yet?

Timo: Give me time and I'll get there. You just go ahead into the house.

They went into the house, wife and maid in the lead and Timo following. The maid went straight to bed, but the wife quickly made supper for her husband. On the table, she set a ring loaf, butter, beef-stew, and large potatoes cooked whole, and Timo sat down to eat with a will. But the wife sat watching him from the opposite end of the table, a look of sadness on her face and tears in her eyes.

Wife: I tell you, you ought to stay safely at home, since I'm such a hot-headed shrew of a gypsy. I tore at your hair again. What could have gotten into these old hands of mine? I tore at your hair again.

Timo: Oh well, so you tore your husband's hair. What are you moaning about, since there's no harm done? But it was quite a yanking — a real currying you gave me. Tee-hee! But hang it all! Go and get me some beer.

Wife: Why do you hang out in the towns and taverns day and night? Is that right?

Timo: It happens only once a year, isn't that so? You can't deny it.

Wife: Where have you been out carousing and who were you with? Tell me! What scoundrel were you with?

Timo: Well, I did have company, I did.

Wife: Where were you wallowing around and who were you with? Tell me right now.

Timo: Ha, with Kyösti Tammisto and Aapeli Karkkala in the attic at Tammisto.

Wife: What did you drink?

Timo: Just booze. Nothing that costs more. Where could we get rum, or whiskey and beer to mix?

Wife: You heathens! If you died this minute, you'd sink to the bottom of hell without mercy.

Timo: Seldom, seldom, God knows, is any man ready to die. But why should a man die here in the prime of life? Draw me a beer.

The wife drew a foaming brown brew from the barrel for her husband, who having eaten a huge meal, drained nearly a full tankard. Then they both went to bed for the night.

But another facet of this wifely temperament remains to be told. On Sunday and holiday mornings, when she was to go to a communion service with her husband, this wife would, shedding scalding tears, always beg her family to forgive any trespass she had done them. It was a moving moment in the life of the Kekkuri household.

It was such an occasion on a warm Sunday morning. With more melting words and more burning tears than ever before, she had begged forgiveness of everyone, from her husband on down to the cowherd. Timo, with a satisfied smirk on his face, went out to hurry the hitching of the horse to the wagon, his shirt collar high on his neck, adjusted by his own wife's deft hand. To the hired man who was hitching the horse, he said: "That wife of mine is a really good wife, you can't deny it. Where would the kids and I be without her, the best of women? No, devil take it, three hundred rubles wouldn't make up the loss if she died, no, not even four hundred, believe me, Kaape, my boy." So he spoke, and clever Kaape quickly agreed, with an innocent look on his face, although when he was on the other side of the gelding, a roguish pucker appeared on his cheeks.

Finally the wife stepped out in her rustling new skirt and gleaming linen, her cheeks puffy from weeping, approached the buggy, clambered sedately aboard and sat sighing on the seat. On her right, reins in hand, sat Timo, as ruddy as a full harvest moon, full of health, blood, and strength. He twitched the reins a little, chirruped once to the horse, and soon the fast gelding was trotting along the church road. They disappeared into a shady opening among birch trees, and for a short time, a dust cloud hung glimmering over the sunny road.

On the Vuohenkalma tenancy beside the village road, Eero, the youngest brother lived and built. He was the wise and industrious bailiff of the parish, in whose well-planned ambushes many a wolf, lynx, and bear lost its life. The sheriff often used him as an agent in the province, for the business Eero took care of usually turned out well. His skill at writing and keeping accounts brought him many jobs and chores, but also a good deal of money. Nevertheless he did not neglect his farming, but directed all its doings in an organized and keenly alert manner. No one could loaf on his lands. His eye was always roving sharply around like that of a hook-beaked hawk on the limb of a dried birch tree in the bright summer sunshine.

On Sundays and holidays, he either read the newspaper or himself wrote about parish news and affairs for some newspaper. The editors always welcomed the pieces he sent in. They were all highly pithy in content, and sharp and clear, sometimes even brilliant in style. This kind of activity broadened his view of life and the world. To him, his native land was no longer an indefinite part of a vague world, its kind and location completely unknown. He knew where it lay, that dear corner of the world where the people of Finland lived and built and struggle and in whose bosom lie our forefathers' bones. He knew its boundaries, its seas, its quietly smiling lakes, and the woody picket fences of its piney ridges. The complete picture of our homeland, with its kind, motherly face, was forever imprinted deep in his heart. And out of this arose a will always to strive for the best and greatest good fortune for our land. As a result of his valiant, tireless striving, a public school of sorts was built in the parish, the first of its kind in Finland. And he founded similarly beneficial institutions in his own congregation. — In all his household doings, his eye was always on his eldest son, whom he had decided to school in the arts and sciences.

His wife was the slender daughter of Seunala, shy-eyed Anna, who had seen strange visions in trances and predicted many wonders. She was the mistress of the free, rich farm of Vuohenkalma, but her sway was limited. Most of the household concerns and activities were in the hands of her husband. The keys to the flour-bin clinked in his pockets, and he decided on and meted out the necessities of life to both men and beasts. He was the one who paid the maids and hired help. His wife was often melancholy; she would stand by the pot on the fire in silent thought. But when she leaned over her little one's cradle, her eyes would beam with delight. She would rejoice when he squirmed and gurgled in her lap, and when she fed him the milk from her own breast, when she cared for and clothed him, and as she herself put it, "reared him as an heir to the sacred city of peace," then the shy woman's eyes would shine.

One summer Sunday evening as the sun dropped toward the northwest and the air and woods were still, she sat alone with her child on a bench by the table. Eero was out looking over his fields and clearings, and all the household help were off visiting.

An idyllic calm prevailed both outdoors and in the Sunday spaciousness of the main room, where the leaf-strewn floor seemed to smile. There was peace and quiet; only now and then could the distant clanking of cowbells be heard from the birch-covered hill. The young wife sat on the bench prattling at the child, who gazed up from her lap like the glow of morning. "Tell me little one," she asked, halfway between song and speech, "tell me, how did you find your way home? — I came along the Turku Trail; I tripped the oxen road of Häme — But how did you know your home, my little one? By the dove-gray dog beneath the steps. I knew the yard by the golden well, by the preachers' horses still in the haybarn, and the ale keg in the straw. — But how did you know your mother dear, and how did you know your father? — Mother dipped from the pot by the blazing fire, she dipped and she sang in a bell-like voice, a linen cloth around her neck, cloth white as the snow and blue as the sky. And how did I know my father? He was whittling the handle for an ax, whittling beside the golden window. — So that's how you found your way, and that's how you knew your home, and that's how you knew your mother and father at home. But where can your father be now, and does he remember us? Of course he does, and if he forgets you, I never will, not ever in my life and even in death, my morning glow and evening sunset, my joy and my lovely sorrow. And why are you my sorrow? Ah, this world is treacherous and stormy, and many a sailor on its seas has sunk into their eternal depths. Tell me my child, my summer's delight, tell me: Wouldn't you like to sail away into the harbor of everlasting peace with the white banner of childhood still gleaming pure? The dark manor of Tuonela stands on the shore of calm and misty lake. There in a dim grove, in the womb of a misty thicket, is a cradle prepared for a child, with white linens and blankets. So hear my song; it guides you to the lord of Tuonela's land. Oh hear the song of my heart!

Grove of Tuoni, darkling woodland!
Sands that form a golden cradle,
Lead my child there to lie sleeping.

There my child will find his pleasure
On the lord of Tuoni's manor
Guarding the cattle of Tuoni.

As the night lets fall its shadow,
There my child delights in leisure,
Rocked by the maiden of Tuoni.

There my darling bathes in pleasure
Rocking in his golden cradle,
Lulled by the song of a night bird.

Grove of Tuoni, peaceful woodland!
Far from hatred, far from struggle,
Far from the evils of mankind.

Thus she sang to her child, and never have the chords of the kantele chimed out as clearly as did her voice in that Sunday-spacious main room. But when she stopped singing, she stared silently through a window at the distant heights, up at the sacred, dizzying heavens. The sky was clear and bright, not a wisp of cloud to be seen under its dome; only a summer swallow, scarcely visible to the eye, darted here and there in flight, as light and swift as the thoughts of a happy child. There she sat, her sun-browned cheek pressed against the sleepy child's temple, her eyes looking up at the blue of space, with the glow of peace on her brow.

Her husband returned from the woods and heard his wife's song in the yard. It had never sounded so beautiful to him. He entered, walked to the rear of the room, and sat down beside her. It was a rare display of affection. His wife turned quickly toward him, set the child in his lap, pressed her brow to his breast, and burst into tears. The man put his arm around her neck and brushed a straying lock of flaxen hair back over one ear, and they sat there on that calm Sunday evening on the white bench by the white table.

So Eero lived and built on his farm, the youngest of the brothers; and now I've told you something of each brother's life from the oldest to the youngest. I still want to tell about a Christmas party at Juhani-Jukola, for the brothers had decided to get together once more on the Christmas straw at their former home. They had all gathered with their wives and children in the big main room at Jukola. The din was deafening, for a large flock of children was running and romping on the rustling straw. Near the fireplace a group of sisters-in-law sat conversing pleasantly, and the buxom mistress of Kekkuri, Timo's sturdy wife, was deftly stirring Venla's gruel pot, which boiled with a full white froth.

At the foot of the hearth sat Simeoni, hymnal on his knee, ready to begin the group singing of the Christmas hymn. Around the table at the rear sat all the other brothers, talking of earlier times, of days in the dark woods and the stump-strewn meadow of Impivaara under the chasmed, roaring mountain. The memories of past dangers, battles, and toils blended sweetly into one, just as woods, valleys, mountains, and upland heaths merge in the blue haze of the distance. Everything fused in a dim and lovely dream and a gentle languor filled their breasts.

So they looked back on the past, as does a cowherd on an autumn evening when nature has gone to rest and the gentle grove glows yellow; he looks back at the sweet meadow where he strove, suffered, and sweated during the summer. He recalls a warm, sunny day, when thunder roared in swarmed in clouds, driving the cattle into a frenzy.

Before evening he gathered the herd and marched happily homeward to the clanking of bells. He smiles as he recalls that day. Thus too, a sailor growing gray on shore calls to mind long-ago storms at sea. Clouds enveloped the ship in darkness, the foaming waves threatened death, but before nightfall, the wind subsided, the waves sank to rest, and the sun shone again from the brightening east, showing the way to port. Now the sailor remembers the storm with a calm joy. So the brothers recalled bygone days as they sat talking around the table at Jukola on a golden Christmas evening.

The pot was lifted from the fire and a real bonfire built of birch blocks. By its light, they began the festive song. The noisy flock of children soon fell silent, and the brothers stopped talking by the table as Simeoni began a lovely hymn and the women's voices joined in. The song echoed to the crackling of the brightly burning fire, and shy Anna's clear, sweet voice rang out more beautifully than any. When they finished the last song, they sat down to supper, and finally lay down on the straw for a night's rest. Early the next morning, they woke up to go to the resplendent church glowing like a starry sky with the light from thousands of candles. From it they returned in the full light of dawn, racing each other home, to spend a happy Christmas day at old Jukola.

But this is the end of my story. And so I have told you of seven brothers in the wilds of Finland. What more is there to tell of their days and deeds here on earth? Their life ran a peaceful course to its height at noon, and sank as peacefully down to its evening rest, during the circuit of many thousands of golden suns.

THE END